# Cut Flowers

Sean Boling

Published by Sean Boling, 2011.

This is a work of fiction. Similarities to real people, places, or events are entirely coincidental.

CUT FLOWERS

**First edition. June 9, 2011.**

Copyright © 2011 Sean Boling.

ISBN: 979-8224588435

Written by Sean Boling.

To Mom and Dad, who managed to put down roots in an environment that rarely allows for it.

# TUESDAY 9/23

Farmers around here don't care that they live next to the ocean. They are aware of it, naturally. Fog, winds full of salt air, lower temperatures—the coastal climate obviously influences what they can grow. But farmers don't speak of the sea in reverent tones as do some fishermen and the more Zen-influenced surfers along the coast, or even those who just like to pull over and admire it from the shore, like me, before I moved here. I used to drive out to the ocean and stare at it and figure that would make life better for a while. But on a farm, the Pacific Ocean is strictly business. Life is only made better by the ocean if the crops it allows for have grown well, and the season is a prosperous one. There's just not enough time to watch many sunsets. Between planting seeds and making money come a million different chores, some as obvious as watering the fields, others as elusive as checking for rust on the submerged pump in the well.

Then there are the unexpected chores, like the errand Dodge and I are running today for the farmer we work for, Joe Mirabelli. We're scouts, keeping an eye on Highway One for the INS. They've swept a few ranches to the south, in Watsonville and Salinas, shipped out busloads of illegals. Usually the INS will call first to let you know they're on their way, because they don't feel like going to the trouble of transporting anyone down to Mexico, but this is obviously one of those other times, one of those times they need to flex some muscle for Sacramento. That kind of grandstanding comes in bunches, so Joe has us parked ten miles south of his ranch in this rest stop town with a cell phone, an enormous older model complete with antennae that seems to get better reception in an area otherwise too remote for most signals, ready to give him a head start if we see la migra heading north. Then he can haul any of his men without papers to a campground way back in the woods, built as a Labor Day retreat for the land owners he leases from.

Come to think of it, this town we're sitting in is a pretty good example of the local mindset. The whole town is on one side of the highway. No regard for aesthetics. Leave that to mother nature. There isn't much space on the west side of the highway, true. What space there is erodes a little every year from the beating it takes at high tide, leaving a line of cypress trees atop the cliffs to hover precariously by their roots over the rugged beach below. But enough space for an overpriced restaurant. Thirty-five bucks for a tiny piece of swordfish and a lot of rice, but look at that view. No, not here. Not in this town. What do we need? A general store? Post office? A deli? Fine, build the damn things. Now get back to work. Back to the fields. Still, people love it, this town. They say it has a lot of charm. What it has is the ocean next to it. That's all that matters. Sun, fog, everything looks good. Except a person. A person can get better-looking by the sea, but only if it's sunset lighting with no wind. Gives you that glow, without squinting.

Now Dodge, he could look like a vice-president of something, a CEO, if he wasn't missing teeth. Two of them. Front and center. Top row. He'd have to shave his mustache, too, or at least the handlebars of it, and shower more often. Dodge gets a lot of sun, too, from being in the fields, so his skin's been tanned to the consistency of a wallet that's spent years in a back pocket—a corporate trait only if it's afflicting the skin of some VP's wife just back from a Sandals Resort, and Dodge wouldn't fool anyone in a pair of Coco Chanel sunglasses (even if he ditched his Rain Bird Sprinkling Systems baseball cap). He's got the cellular phone on the seat next to him, which helps, even if it does belong to our boss. The van, though, belongs to Dodge, and that doesn't help at all. The only reason a phone would be necessary in a vehicle like this is because it so clearly doubles as a place of residence. We're eating deli sandwiches, on Joe, on company time, and the smell from the back of the van is rough on an appetite. It's like sitting in a hamper. Dodge likes to drive it on errands whenever possible because Joe reimburses him for gas.

"Any idiot can grow brussel sprouts." Dodge is commenting on the conversation we can hear from across the quiet highway. Some of his old speed-freak drinking buddies are hanging out as usual in front of the town's facade, and one of them, a guy named Vic, is preening for the others about some work he did for a local sprout grower. Dodge continues with a chuckle. "Sprouts. You can ignore 'em for weeks, run 'em over with your tractor, and the shittier the weather gets, the better they grow."

"Your father grew sprouts," I remind him, trying to get a conversation of our own going.

Dodge blows some air through his nose, in what could be a laugh, since there is something like a smile on his face. "See what I mean?"

His father died a couple years back. According to Joe, if Dodge shed any tears, they were tears of joy. Dodge has always gone by his mother's last name, Hidalgo, and he never even knew her. At the reading of the will, Franky Demos left his son Dodge one dollar, one dollar exactly, which was a lot worse than nothing.

I kick myself for choosing that topic and hope it will disappear if I concentrate hard enough on my sandwich. But that makes me think about the hands that made it. We bought them at Playa Blanca Market on the other side of the highway. We're parked on the empty side, essentially just a dirt lot where people park to gawk at the view or negotiate their way down the cliffs to the beach. The guy who owns the market works there by himself, except some weekends. That's the only time the place gets busy, with all sorts of people taking Sunday drives. But all they ever want are chips and sodas, so if you ever lift up some essential item from the shelf, like flour or vegetable oil, it leaves a clear spot amongst the dust. Since it's a weekday, the guy ran out from behind the cash register to make our sandwiches without washing his hands. I used to have a friend who worked at a bank, you see, and she would show me her hands after work, and they would be pitch black with dirt from handling all that money. But it's Tuesday, thank God, and Playa Blanca will be lucky to gross twenty bucks in cash, not including our sandwiches. I got mine on a sourdough roll. Dodge gets wheat bread. Easier to chew.

Vic approaches from across the road, apparently finished with his turn in the spotlight of the downtrodden conference we've been eavesdropping on. I thank him under my breath for providing a more definitive distraction from the latest failed conversation between me and Dodge.

"Joey lets you eat on the clock?" he asks, draping his elbow over the open window.

"Sure," Dodge snaps. "But then he's a flower grower. Different breed."

Vic laughs a little too hard and Dodge tells him not to bother, that no matter how long he stands next to the truck kissing ass, it won't get him a job with Joe and he should go back across the highway in front of the Whale Watcher Bar & Grill and keep begging for change from the tourists stopped to stretch their legs.

"You're an asshole sober," Vic tells Dodge, and he trots across the highway in time to greet a tour bus pulling over en route from San Francisco to either Monterey or Carmel, or both, and maybe even a quick stop in Santa Cruz along the way. Squinting German-looking types intimidated by the sun file off and teeter along the shoulder like the undead. The first thing each of them see is Vic, all pathetic in the eyes, and a brave smile. It's his only chance. Once they see the ocean, Vic is forgotten, and the cameras are raised.

"I guess you're just like the old cast members of Saturday Night Live," I say to Dodge.

"What do you mean?" he looks at me. I already know I shouldn't have bothered.

"You know, Dan Aykroyd and all those guys? They weren't as funny when they got off drugs."

He takes a bite of his sandwich as if I never said anything in the first place.

"Could just be a coincidence," I mop up.

Unlike most of the friends I've had, TV references don't work with Dodge. But then Dodge isn't really my friend. He's a co-worker. And that's probably the way it will always be since he didn't spend all those hours in front of a TV set. Dodge was too busy running from truant officers, lighting things on fire, getting married too young, having kids too young, developing a taste for dope. We usually work separately, anyway. He drives the tractors and forklifts, does whatever needs to be done around the ranch—he can build anything and repair everything else. I drive the trucks, or whatever has to go out onto the highway, because Dodge isn't covered by Joe's company insurance policy. Too many tickets.

"Lucky for me I'm a drug snob," he says. "I grew up around so much money I just can't get into the low-grade shit those losers are willing to shell out for. I guess that's one thing I owe to Franky. One good thing."

I'm glad Dodge is talking. I always let him have the next word after we've failed to communicate. I'm never sure if I've pissed him off. I come close quite a bit, I figure, because I've heard him use "college boy" as a term for many of the fools we encounter at shipping companies and wholesale nurseries we deliver to, those boys with the world by the balls who stand there sipping coffee and talking to you while you're unloading three dozen buckets each filled with fifty pounds worth of water and cala lillies. I went to college. I wore a suit for several years. Sometimes I wonder if Dodge feels as insecure around me as I do around him. Not likely. Not here, in his territory.

He continues. "But then I may not've gotten hooked if he didn't spoil us all so rotten."

I'm a little surprised. I always hear about how hard he worked as a kid.

"I got bored easy," he explains. "Comes with money, city or country money. Boredom."

It never ceases to amaze me that Franky made so much money. I could understand if he grew artichokes, the other major vegetable of the coast, but I've never met anybody who likes brussel sprouts.

"A lotta military contracts," Dodge tells me. "One more reason not to join the army."

Dodge starts telling me about the four-wheel drive races they'd have up White Creek Canyon after it rained, so it would be nice and muddy and he and all the other spoiled farmer kids could run each other into the banks easier, new trucks and everything. "They can blame the imports and the overseas growers all they want," he says, "but the real reason all these businesses, all these growers are going under is because they all raised a bunch of worthless kids who got no sense. No sense whatsoever."

Life in the fast lane. A dirt fast lane. I'm about to tell him how we used to hide in alleys and throw lemons at passing cars. I don't. Working with Dodge is helping me talk less than I used to. Keeping my mouth shut is the best way I've found to fit in around here. Questions are okay. Questions turn people into a source, an expert. I ask Dodge what la migra looks like, because this is the first time I've had to do this for Joe.

"Like park rangers, sheriffs, any fuckin' dude in a uniform. But in bunches, like they're going to a funeral."

One of us probably could have done this errand easily enough, but Joe doesn't like to take any chances. He figured one of us could have our head tilted back, grabbing the last sip from a Pepsi can when the INS drives by, or be too busy fiddling with the radio.

But Highway One is only two lanes here, and there's plenty of it stretching out from each end of the town. You can hear and see a break in the traffic just fine, especially on a weekday like this, when there really is no traffic, just sporadic cars and trucks, and maybe a tractor. But that's Joe. No chances. He's worked too damn hard. He also knows I'm still in the habit of looking at the ocean quite a bit. Almost a year now, driving this highway almost every day, and I still can't take my eyes off it.

"Like I said, looks like a funeral," Dodge says.

I turn my attention back to the highway and see what he means: half a dozen vans roll by with sirens on top. I grab the phone and call Joe to give him the news. He says something back which I cannot hear because Dodge starts his engine at the same time. He's such a gifted mechanic, there's a good chance his van has a discarded Boeing 747 engine under its hood. I plug my exposed ear and Joe repeats his orders:

"Tell Dodge not to pull out yet," he hollers through the static of our poor connection. "La migra's gonna remember that piece of shit van if it turns up here too soon after they do."

The engine stalls before I can relay Joe's orders, so I just tell Dodge to hold off on re-starting it. The ignition blast has caught the attention of the tourists, however. A couple of them snap a picture of us colorful locals in our beach bum "piece of shit" van. They laugh and give us the "hang loose" sign. Dodge gives them the finger. They laugh and gesture for him to do it again, this time for the camera. When we finally take off, Dodge swerves his U-turn wide enough to send them sprinting for the curb.

Those tourists did choose their destination well, I must say. Fall is the most gorgeous time of year along this route. Green is just starting to challenge yellow for dominance of the hillsides and meadows, and most of the farmlands are lined with orange. Pumpkins are such a staple out here nowadays that a lot of farmers plant them before they really know what they're going to do with them, and Dodge's father knew this. Franky Demos would buy the fields for much less per acre than it cost the poor bastards to grow, as he had the means and connections to ship the pumpkins farther and wider than they ever could. Everyone knew they were getting screwed. But farming's rough on your credit, and in the eyes of most farmers, seeing a big wad of cash in your hand beats seeing all your hard work plowed under.

Joe plants his share of pumpkins, too, but in addition to orange cultivates some more specialized breeds—red, gray, white, and all different types of gourds and squash—which appeal to his floral design customers who buy from him at the San Francisco wholesale flower market. But even the orange breeds he grows for the grocery chains receive a lot more attention than on most farms. He and his son Aldo, who does all the actual growing now so Joe can focus on the customers, have a hard time watching their pumpkins tossed carelessly into bins by the hundreds when harvest time comes. "We're flower growers, godammit," Joe says, "We only toss something if it's dead." Son Aldo would probably say the same, if he said much of anything.

There is no getting around orange right here about now. Even the most half-assed farmer is contributing to something beautiful and large and natural, with a minimal amount of human guidance required to form the autumn landscape—intervention unseen, for the most part, by those marveling at 65 miles per hour on a Sunday. Orange randomness of the crop finally sprouting is followed by orange rows, as the yield is cut from its vine and placed single file to wait out its destiny. Greens and yellows keep the coast breathing, but orange keeps them coming back with their cameras raised.

Orange convinced me to stay here last fall when I wasn't so sure this was the place. It is one of those hot colors I remember being told to imagine flowing through my body from the top of my head to the bottom of my feet by some therapist trying to help me relax. Red, yellow, orange, my choice. Now imagine you're next to a body of water, on a beach, on a lake shore. The sun is shining. Someone is with you. Someone you love very much, but someone you have unfinished business with. You want to tell them something. What do you want to tell them? I honestly don't know, doctor. I could say I'm sorry. That would be a good start, I imagine.

Now that I actually find myself next to some real water and surrounded by hot colors you can actually touch I may be able to figure something out. What I imagine and what I end up seeing have often been irreconcilable. I imagined myself married to Janet as soon as I met her, practically, then eventually saw her as my wife. Actually saw her as my wife. But imaging myself as a husband and then seeing myself as one...imagining we could get away with the lifestyle I plotted and then seeing what happened. What I see. I see...

A straight away section of Highway One that splits an artichoke field in two, and Dodge floors his van. As if it would help in case the van flipped and launched itself into the fields, I grip the door handle and press my back into the seat without Dodge noticing, I hope. The car in front of us appears to be standing still in light of our speed. We overtake it. "I know it's a pretty view, folks," Dodge mutters as we pass, "but some of us work here."

A beat up old Cadillac parked on the ocean side of the highway up ahead grabs his attention. Dodge ogles the car and says with the quiet wonder of discovery: "a fucking Cadillac." We get closer and we see a few surfboards jutting out the back window from the back seat. In the distance to the west, two guys in wet suits are making their way back from the ocean across the artichoke fields, each toting a surfboard under their arm. The surfers in view, Dodge grows concerned about the future of the old Cadillac.

"That poor Caddy don't stand a chance," he says. "Goddamned surfers. They want you to call their lives pointless. They dare you."

I look to the other side of the road, at the fields inland through the passenger window. Two irrigation workers are shifting pipe from one parcel of artichokes to another. It's a sunny day and they're dressed in rain gear, each carrying a metal pipe on their shoulder long enough to use as a pole vault. Below them in my field of vision, the aisles of crops roll by in an optical illusion as a single pair of legs sprinting along side us, trying to keep up. But the field ends. We win. Symmetry gives way to the brush, unkempt and wild outside the border. Scraggly, green, and shiny, as if always breaking a sweat, some call it "coyote brush," its wiry deep roots always searching for water, making the most of the slightest opportunity for life.

Dodge eases up a bit as the straight away blends into a curve, a downward curve, the coyote brush disappearing above cliffs of sandy clay which rise from the plummeting highway. The cliffs part like drapes being pulled and we are hurdling directly past a beach, its sand leaking onto the shoulder of the road. A bridge carries us over a freshwater creek which runs from the swampy marshlands on the right, through the sand dunes, and into the ocean. The fresh and salt water meet between the dunes and swirl for position, the fresh always winning with its current so consistent and relentless, the salt always pulling back into its source. The vast majority of the earth's surface belonging to the ocean, and it still loses to a wispy creek. Perhaps the ocean has spread itself too thin, its watery empire impossible to keep tabs on, the creeks of the world thus seeping into its cracks. Sunlight bounces off the waves as they continue to make their break, forever falling short, and the strain on my eyes is worth it, worth a look at the kind of demonstration life on earth is capable of providing.

To the point where I cannot squint any longer, I turn from the waves to look over the other side of the bridge at the marsh as we fly by. A Great Blue Heron fishes amongst the reeds which line the creek bed knifing through the slough. Legs as high as the surrounding cattails, swan-like neck poised and curled, ready to spear a fish or frog. Waiting...watching. In a snap of your fingers the head jerks forward, the neck extends, the beak impales a fish—dangling for a moment at the tip of its life, then engulfed and swallowed. The great bird moves on, tip-toes silently to a new spot. Ruthless behavior if it wasn't necessary for sustenance. I used the same excuse for a while, it's all part of the job, but it was really just for fun. Until somebody got hurt. Then, just as our mothers used to predict, it wasn't fun anymore once somebody got hurt.

We start to climb, the highway now a ramp, out of the valley created by the once-mighty creek now serene, up to the peak of the cliffs on the valley's other side. At the top, we disappear into a fog bank. It creeps windblown from below the edge overlooking the ocean, sweeps across the highway and covers us. Visibility handicapped, Dodge does not let up. He does not slow down. There's enough sun, he says, to burn this off. This is just a patch of fog.

And yes, we do emerge back into the light. No weather can hold its pattern for long on this moody quilt. A single day can mean both rain and shine from one gas station to the next, the "next gas" being 36 miles away from now, according to a sign we pass along our current vista. From here, up ahead, we can see our destination, Point Año Nuevo ("New Year's" Point)—the land sticking its neck out, forming a section of the coast which appears to have been carved by a scythe, then filled in by the ocean. Crescent moon-shaped as seen from above by gulls and brown pelicans, the small bay is favored by scores of fishing boats as a safe place to anchor late at night, a respite in between the grueling chores necessary to make a living.

The point carries on its back a state marine wildlife reserve, a bird sanctuary, and Mirabelli Nurseries. From our vantage the protruding land appears as a double-layer cake, two-toned and a mile long, its cross-section marked on the lower half by cliffs the color and texture of sand castles, its face draped with crevices casting shadows from the shoreline clear up to the cake's top layer, which is marked by variations on green: scrub oak and Monterey pine dotting the swarthy brush of the state reserve, while further to the north a thick row of cypress towers along the fence line between the reserve and Joe's ranch, serving as a windbreak for his crop.

Off the tip of the point, just out of its reach, lies an island. A long sandbar fenced in by a rocky border, the surf constantly churns and swirls around it thanks to the bumpy shallowness surrounding it. The island's perpetual white water border gives it the illusion of motion, as if it is motorized and in the process of heading out to sea from its dock at the end of the point. But it never moves, of course. Everything around the island moves, but it stays in place. On the island stands a house once occupied by a lighthouse keeper. All that remains of the lighthouse is a rusted metal tower blown over on its side, while the house looks even more abandoned than its decades of emptiness should reveal thanks to its position—shoved off the coast and into the eye of every storm passing by.

When I decided to live on the coast, I thought perhaps that house would be just the place. Emptiness in the eye of the storm. If any of my old business professors or supervisors from my early resumé-building jobs had an ounce of poetry in them, they could have written a very eloquent evaluation of me with that one line. Emptiness in the eye of the storm. But of course it's illegal to live in that old house, and too big for just one person I suppose. Contrary to the old expression, I believe a man really can be an island. He just can't live on one. A small one, at least.

This part of the day is so spotless I can even see the surviving lighthouse several miles further up the coast. A gorgeous whitewashed tower apparently built to fulfill the aspirations of every amateur photographer driving along Highway One, from here it's just a blurry white line, a match stick with its flame flickering in the breeze. Its light is the only reason I spot the lighthouse from here, flashing our way every three seconds from atop the point a few miles north of the ranch—one, two, three, flash—marking the point beyond our own.

"Those vans drove right by," says Joe, swinging his arm to the north, the direction they were headed. "Right by."

He's standing outside the office, a corrugated metal shed in which most people would probably store tools and lawn mowers. But this one has a desk and a phone and a couple of file cabinets in it. Dodge added windows a while back, too.

"They're going after those big bastards in Half Moon Bay, I'll bet, the good folks at Bloom-Wells," Joe chuckles. He hates them, and anyone else who turns a blind eye to the legal status of their workers, mainly because he knows the main reason they'd rather not legalize them is so they have an excuse not to abide by American labor laws. Joe prides himself on working to get all his employees their citizenship, or at least the proper work visas if becoming an American does not appeal to some, and treating all of them as the laws dictate (if not better). But citizenship is a slow process, no less frustrating than any other task involving federal bureaucracies, to the point where you can understand why so many companies finally say "to hell with it" and take their chances. So it is, then, that despite Joe's best efforts and wishes, several of his men have been forced to hide out at a damp and deserted weekend retreat on a Tuesday, caught between the law and their jobs.

Joe loves to give the system hell, even if it is just within earshot of Dodge and me and no one else. "Shit, between the truck loading docks up there at Bloom-Wells and the greenhouses, they'll need a goddamn 747 to haul everyone down. Christ, they've even got a snack bar there, don't they? Next to the receiving area?"

"Yeah," I tell him. "They've got a lot of people up there. You want me to get the men?"

"That'd be super," Joe says, and claps his hands—one time, very loud. Then he asks us if we ate.

"Sure did," says Dodge. "Coupla sandwiches."

"That's good," says Joe, "'cause we're gonna be busy tonight. You need to fuel up so we can run you both ragged."

He laughs after he says this. We know when he's joking, but he likes to make sure. I have never worked for anyone as fair and honest as Joe Mirabelli. One look at him and you know he is incapable of any great cruelty. He looks like Pablo Picasso, but not the Picasso posing for photographers with his arms crossed defiantly in front of a warehouse full of his genius, or sitting at a café in his younger years in black and white, an intense frustration in his eyes. No, Joe is the picture of Picasso holding his baby boy at the beach, sitting on a towel lifting the baby up to make a funny face at him and say boogey-boogey-boogey. Joe's energy is overwhelming but pleasant, quintessential San Francisco North Beach Italian. Always talking with his hands. If you bound his hands together and restrained his arms he would be mute, unable to tell you exactly how fair and honest he really is, he and his family. Joe is not afraid to tell you.

He and Dodge walk over to check on the truck load going into the city tonight, to the wholesale flower market. Joe calls over in Spanish to his foreman, Javier, who resembles one of those faded tintype photographs of a gaucho from a Time-Life coffee table book on the Old West, but without the fierce look in his eye and wearing an Oakland A's baseball cap instead of a cowboy hat. Joe grills him for an update from the fields: how much product is still standing? Well, then how much of it needs to be cut and hauled to the packing shed?

Joe's Spanish is fluent but inaccurate. Everyone knows what he's saying, but he never bothers to conjugate his verbs properly and sprinkles in lots of English when it comes to small words like conjunctions and prepositions. With verbs, for instance, it's tu tengo instead of tu tienes, and a typical sentence goes something like, "if tu tengo no mas azul, then dame mas blanca instead." I've sampled just about every "Learn Spanish in However Many Days" CD on the market, thanks to all the hours I spend on the road. I'm in that smart ass phase of learning a new language where I know the rules well and have a decent vocabulary, but probably couldn't ask where to find a toilet if my dignity depended on it. No practical experience. Not the first time that's been a problem in life.

Joe discusses inventory with Javier and Dodge as they walk towards the truck—a ten-ton bobtail rig, the tractor permanently connected to the trailer, a refrigeration generator jutting out of the trailer just above the roof of the tractor, humming as it blows cool air over the flowers inside, the family name painted in a logo across the sides of the trailer and both doors of the tractor. Joe told me once that his son Aldo learned to drive it around the ranch when he was just nine years old. I was trying to catch fly balls and grounders at that age, so I asked Aldo if the story was true. He said yes. I asked him if it was hard to learn. He said no. I asked him if it was fun. He said yes. How much fun? I asked him. He said it was a lot of fun. "Lots," he said, to be exact. We're the same age. Generation gaps can apparently happen within the same generation.

I pry open the door of a dusty old pickup, one of a dozen or so lying in wait around the ranch yard amongst the tractor implements. Several of the trucks came from abandonment by the side of the road, restored by Aldo for random use around the ranch. The truck I use on my routes belongs to Joe, and he doesn't want it driven around the fields and the yard. Too dusty. Any truck taken on out on the road has to be clean, has to indicate fastidiousness, a trait for which most hard-working farmers do not have the time. Showing up in a clean truck is enough of a novelty, Joe figures, to make people remember you in this business. I fan the dust away that rises from the upholstered seat as I sit down behind the wheel. I can't remember if this is the truck that requires constant depression of the gas to start it up, or vigorous pumping. The window is down on my side, so I try to roll it up. It won't budge. Therefore, constant depression. Reminding myself by color is impossible, each truck being the color of dust.

The camp where the men are waiting is at the end of a narrow dirt road winding parallel to the creek which supplies water to the Mirabelli reservoir, through a redwood forest in the foothills to the east, on the opposite side of Highway One.

I wait for traffic to pass. Just a few cars, their passengers staring at me as they drive by. I'm waiting for the day someone wants to take my picture as a memento of their trip to the coast, but that could be a very long wait. I must disappoint them, don't fit their image of who should be behind the wheel of such a truck in such an area. Dried up muddy tire tracks are caked across the pavement, leading from the main entrance of the ranch over to a gate on the other side of the road.

Past the gate, which I leave open for my return trip, there are thirty acres of flowers being grown by Aldo in the flatlands stretching to where the hills begin their ascent. Gently I roll through the aisles of hybrid delphinium, several feet tall some of the stems, blooms exploding up their length—purple, dark blue, lavender—the colors making one last stand before winter comes and the main crop switches from their kind over to lilies and violets, which handle the winter rains better. Many of the field crops grown by the Mirabellis are perennials and bloom year-round, but for business purposes the family has established certain growing seasons for all but the daisies, the toughest crop, the backbone of the business. Even if they had greenhouses and could control the conditions, Joe says, he prefers the seasons.

"Some of these guys, the big shots, or guys trying to be big shots, they got too goddamn many balls in the air, trying to juggle them," he says. "We stick with a few at a time and do them better than anyone else. The best in the whole goddamn market."

Usually Joe completes this assertion with a fist to the table, or if there's no table around, a rat-a-tat-tat motion with his finger and thumb acting like a gun. Spend any time in their fields, and you can't argue with him. This field is on about its fourth bloom, they've been picking product off it all summer, and Aldo's still got the stuff yielding stems up to your neck. With the right kind of music drowning out the engine noise, you could feel as though you were floating through this land, the fragile tips of the flowers rolling past your windows, the hummingbirds and dragonflies circling you, as you fly right alongside them.

At the base of the hillside looming behind the delphinium, the entrance to the camp road meets up with the creek for their journey side-by-side through the gulch, between the hills that often reach high enough to be called mountains in the wild stretch of forest separating the Pacific Coast from the Bay Area, farmland from industry, serenity from opportunity and all other points east. This natural boundary is why the locals around here call people from the other side, the well-lit peninsula, as being "over the hill"—a purely geographical reference by those who make it. However, a glance at any relief map seems to prove that the coastal region is the older of the two. Lives on this side are lived in a flux of pine-scented back roads and beach fronts, Idaho-by-the-sea, the land walking a thin line between shore and mountain. Lives on the other side are lived in a sprawl, the hills sloping down and out well before reaching the bay, leaving a plane more ripe for development. At some point in the ancient geological past, water entering the bay through the Golden Gate must have been as close to the mountains as it is on this side before at last receding to unveil the future site of Silicon Valley. And all that time, as the peninsula by the bay was trying to establish its roots, the Pacific coast kept its head above water, daring anyone to try and settle along its rugged narrowness. The dare still stands. Population records maintain it. If the peninsula was unattached to the earth, if the water surrounding it flowed underneath it and the land mass floated like a barge, it would tip over thanks to all the weight loaded on its bay side, with the ocean side flipping straight into the air.

The camp road used to be a logging road around the turn of the century, so to call it a road may be less accurate than calling it a trail. The owners, the Wheeler family—owning most land around here not owned by the state—they only use the camp a few times during the summer and on Labor Day, and hire out some locals in the late spring to clear the way for their well-scrubbed sport utility vehicles (a rare opportunity for the Wheelers to actually shift into four-wheel drive). Very much from over the hill, the Wheelers only see the coast as an escape, an enchanted place where the living is easy, and figure seven bucks an hour ought to satisfy any of the residents of this Shangri-La who feel up to taking a chainsaw to any fallen trees, digging through any mud slides, and reinforcing any potential slide areas along the flanks of the old logging trail which have accumulated over the rainy season. Needless to say, then, this drive could be a lot more treacherous if the INS ever decides to pay a winter visit, or early spring.

The trail is often dark. Redwoods keep many stretches in perpetual shadow and dampness. I was once told by a docent at a state park up in Marin County that local Native American tribes consider redwoods unlucky, shady nesting areas for evil spirits. In the same breath, she told us how many weddings are held in the circular grove of redwood trees we happened to be standing in at the time, my wife and I. We asked her, then, what the divorce rate was for the marriages performed amongst the infamous trees, but she did not have that information. There was no reason to believe it was any higher than the already-alarming normal, but we thought it could offer certain couples a tangible excuse for their failed marriages when words could not come up with a satisfactory explanation, when a simple cause-and-effect reason was nowhere to be found. We were pretty clever then. Just ask us, we would have told you: ain't we clever? The docent laughed, even though she had probably heard the same joke in varied forms many times before, and we figured it was because we told it so well.

I only wish that we could have attributed our collapse to some redwood trees, me and Janet, could hang our problems on some hook besides the one we nailed into the wall, that awful creation of ours. Some resolution that did not involve anyone else, that would not pull them down with us. We would be kidding ourselves, of course, but we did that all along. And we were so good at it. We looked so happy, up to the point where I cannot look any longer, where I have to turn my head away...

The redwood trees. Ah. The redwoods look so beautiful—in the grove that day, along the camp road now. Thanks again for the distraction, Mother Earth.

Ferns love the conditions beneath the redwoods. Dotting the shady landscape along the creek bed, they give the illusion of thousands of fish bones turned green with mold lining the shore; caught, eaten, and tossed aside with their heads missing. Only the ribs left over. Green ribs sprung from the ground, bowing at the slightest breeze. I follow the creek.

The men are making the best of their stay. Four of them are playing two-on-two volleyball with a soccer ball, which would hurt like hell, I imagine, if it weren't for the fact they're all using a closed fist, punching it as hard as they can across the net strung between two young redwoods. A couple of other guys play horse shoes, the equipment always left by the Wheelers with no fear of theft, as what good is an old horse shoe except to see who can throw it closest to a metal stake driven into the ground? All of their hats are in place on their heads: white straw cowboy hats and baseball caps emblazoned with logos of popular sports franchises—Bulls, Packers, Forty-Niners, Lakers, Cowboys—the names and mascots smeared with dust. Sports the men do not follow or even understand, many of them, but which have inspired fashionable baseball caps. One guy, Gerardo, a friendly but mean-looking stocky type, whose good side is a much better place to be than his bad, even wears a University of North Carolina hat—the same colors as the flag of El Salvador, powder blue, his very reason for wearing it, I'm sure. It is spotless, looks brand new, and has so for months.

On a picnic table close to the creek, Manuel sits with his wife and two-year-old son, Daniel. They watch the games and point things out for Daniel's sake. Manuel is a legal resident. His wife and child just got here, legally, but there is a chance the paperwork may be hung up or in transit, a chance not worth taking. He waited two years, Daniel's entire life, to get his family up here. I wave to him as I stop the truck in the middle of the camp, by the campfire pit, and motion him and his family to join me in the cab as I open the passenger side door.

"Ola, Manny," I call out. He comes with us to the wholesale market when Joe knows it's going to be busy, and on those occasions I have a chance to practice some Spanish. Any situation where you are forced to make an idiot of yourself, like speaking a foreign tongue, is of course much less humiliating at the person-to-person level than before a group.

"Venga," I say, and run the next phrase in my head a few times—"Tu y la familia, venga aqui conmigo"—before saying it out loud. He smiles and the three of them approach with a "gracias" from Manuel, and I'll be damned if I can't remember how to say "you're welcome." I panic and just wave my hand as if to say "no problema," which I don't actually say because I've said it too often, and it's such a rookie expression.

Daniel crawls in next to me, his legs sticking straight out ahead of him like a couple of sandwich rolls with shoes stuck on them. The shoes are tiny work boots, still so smooth, the leather still fuzzy and tan. I run through the old "mucho gusto," "igualmente," "commo estas" routine with Daniel, the standard disc A of any set of instructional CDs. Then Manny says something rapidly to me, unpredictable, and I am struck dumb. Something about his wife. Have I met his wife? No, I guess, and I am correct. And relieved. Now I am allowed to repeat the introductory stuff again from my CDs to his wife, and in the process set a personal record for longest sustained human interaction in Spanish. Manny senses my accomplishment and resulting mental fatigue, and gives me an English break.

His English is slightly better than my Spanish, and he also wants to learn more, so we kind of feed off each other. I tell him what happened in as clear a manner as I can imagine in English—avoiding contractions, prefixes, suffixes, staying in the present tense, slowing the pace. In a few years, Daniel will put us both to shame once he starts school here. Bilingual before age ten. I envy him, look at him, and smile. Manny and I are the same age. His son sits between us. His wife focuses all her attention on the little boy.

I look through the back window at the truck bed. Most of the men have piled in, but they are all hooting in the direction of the volleyball court. Gerardo has dropped his hat, the University of North Carolina baseball cap, powder blue, like the El Salvadorian flag. He swats it across his thigh repeatedly, holds it up to check its shape after such a thrashing, then dusts it gently with his hand. The men holler at him, teasing. Manuel chuckles and explains the situation.

"It is only a hat, they tell him."

Gerardo is fixated on his hat, only looking our way, very intense, once it is safely back on his head. Clearly, anyone who decides to even playfully swat it off again will be risking their life. Gerardo is the only Salvadorian in the whole crew. The rest are Mexican. They continue to ride him all the way back to the ranch, but no one dares knock the hat off his head, the North Carolina hat, powder blue.

As we pile out of the truck back at the ranch, Joe makes eye contact with me from across the yard and holds his hand up to his ear like a telephone and shakes it, thumb and pinky extended and wiggling. I walk into the office and sit at the desk, responsible for the phone should it ring. The men do not have to go back out to the fields. It's late and the slack has already been picked up earlier in the afternoon, by those whose papers were fool-proof. The men walk to the little stucco houses which line the front of the ranch, facing Highway One. Manuel turns to give me a wave, and with a nudge of the boy's shoulder, so does Daniel.

Calls to the ranch are sporadic after about eleven in the morning, after the regional grocery chains and larger wholesalers have phoned in their orders. Still, Joe likes to have someone standing by just in case, thanks to an old-fashioned aversion to answering machines and a love of conversation. So I wait by the phone on afternoons during those days in which we have not spent all morning at the market. I wait in a swivel chair and Formica desk built with the needs of an office building in mind, a skyscraper in a city somewhere stacked with large rooms filled with cubicles, bathed in white noise and fluorescent light with static electricity jumping out at you from everything you touch—desk lamps, keyboards, people's hands.

I wait for a call from the farm service reminding us that they need a soil and leaf sample, from an investment firm wondering if the president of our company would be interested in tripling his money, from a charity organization trying to land some free pumpkins for its fall festival, from a flower shop owner recently open for business, new to the market, calling to make sure we'll have her five bunches of royal blue bella donna ready and waiting for her on Wednesday when she arrives at our stall around four a.m.—which is about the time we've already moved about two-hundred bunches and still have three-hundred or so remaining. I wait for friends to call and Mirabelli family members, and for middle-aged ladies from over the hill to call who have seen the fields rolling by on a recent weekend outing and wonder if it is possible to take a tour of the ranch some time when things around the house become "just too much."

There is so much waiting I mostly watch. I stare out the open door at the flight paths of the barn swallows, blurring feats of blue and orange, looping, misdirection, brief dive-bombings as they bob and weave in mid-air, back and forth from nests they have wedged in between the right angles of the beams holding up the rooftops of the old barns. The barns are reinforced with corrugated metal siding now, and serve as packing sheds, refrigerated rooms, and garages. Together they form a sort of town square, with the central area of the yard serving as the motor pool. I stare at the blackbirds, a dark swarm of yellow eyes quivering from the telephone lines down to the arid ground between the sheds, pecking what they can from the dust in a nebulous procession across the ranch, rapid steps resembling a rumba, a conga line no longer following one another.

Some of the men are getting ready for a night out, walking from the houses to the shower shed, a change of clothes in hand, a white cowboy hat topping each neatly-folded pile. Tomorrow, Wednesday, is a day off for them. Calendars on a farm function non-traditionally, keep time at a different pace than those bought in book stores or gift shops. Work Sunday, but not Wednesday—for now, at least. And said schedule can change depending on the time of year, the weather, and how many men are needed and how many men are home visiting family in Mexico. There are no holidays, only days off. Fourth of July, Memorial Day, New Year's Day, those days mean nothing on a ranch. Not even Christmas to many, to those whose family is not waiting for them after work.

Changed now into clean clothes, hair wet and combed, any men with cars, the designated drivers, unveil their rides from beneath dust covers—shiny new paint jobs, not a streak on any window, even the hubcaps spotless. Never missed a payment, any of them, sure bets for a loan office. Money spent tonight will have its limits: always leave enough to send home, to the family. And all these slices come from an hourly wage comparable to my first job at age sixteen in the food court at the mall. Pups on a Pole. We sold corn dogs and looked at the clock every minute and a half. I managed to save enough money to buy a leather jacket at the end of the summer. When my income was at its zenith years later, well over six digits, an expense account, benefits, I often wondered if I was earning enough to support having a kid, one kid.

Through the front gate a man comes jogging, dressed in khaki pants and a crew neck sweater. Right past the men beginning to gather around their cars he chugs along, a vacant look in his eyes, not seeing them, or anything, it appears. Clearly not one of the bearded vagabonds loaded with ragged bundles and dirt who occasionally loom along the side of the highway, he may have been in an accident, may still be in a daze, traumatized. That's my first thought, at least, and Dodge's too, apparently.

"What's up, man?" Dodge calls from the door of the packing shed.

The stranger does not hear. He maintains the same lumbering gait—which doesn't quite fit his slight, wiry build—shoulders bouncing, suede shoes brushing the ground.

"What's up?" Dodge walks towards him, past the open door of the office. I stand up and hover at the threshold, tracking their course, Dodge and the jogging stranger. The man does not break stride. He is heading down the main drive separating the yard from the southern fields, back towards the Mirabelli's house.

"Hey..." Dodge moves faster to cut him off. The stranger responds to the sudden movement in the corner of his eye, turns to see Dodge, and alters his course in that direction.

Their paths are about to cross.

Dodge asks "Are you okay?"

The stranger flattens Dodge with a blazing right hand to the chin, lays him out completely horizontal. I hear the snap, and sprint from the office as he pounces on Dodge. I hear Joe holler something and see the men start to run at the scene as well. The man is on top of Dodge now, breathlessly beating on him with a flurry of roundhouse punches, left, right, left, right, left, right. I lunge with a few feet remaining, catching him as low as possible with my right shoulder. We are both airborne for a moment, before I land on top of him, his back scraping the ground. He isn't stunned at all. He's incredibly powerful. I can only get one shot in before he has thrown me off. Everyone else has arrived and it takes that many of us to restrain him. His strength is not even that of a bigger man, rather, it is not human. His body writhes and strains against our efforts.

"E equals m-c squared!" he shrieks in a near-falsetto, "E equals m-c squared!"

We all breathe heavily and clench our jaws trying to keep him down, all of us covered with dust, looking like a bunch of ghosts. Joe attends to Dodge, sitting up now testing his jaw with his hand, Joe cursing the stranger out, calling him all sorts of names which all begin with "fucking"... "fucking this," "fucking that," you "fucking bastard."

"I am Jesus Christ!" the stranger yells, and I can't help but laugh. It's such a cliché, the standard cry of the overdosed, it seems, assuming he's on drugs—a pretty fair assumption by now. The men laugh, too, looking at me and each other and singing "Vaya con Dios." Must be the same thing wherever drugs and Christianity are sold.

"I am Jesus Christ! I am the Son of Man!"

A county sheriff's car pulls into the yard, pulling a cloud of dust.

"Where the hell did they come from?" Joe wonders.

"I hope they got an extra billy club," says Dodge, eyes fixed on the writhing stranger.

Two sheriff's deputies get out from the front of the car, both a couple of younger bad-ass types out to save America. A middle-aged couple emerges from the back of the car, as though the deputies keep them along for the ride as a captive audience, and a constant reminder of who they are supposed to protect. The deputies sprint towards us with clubs raised.

"I am Jesus Chr—"

They club him across the face.

"Gets his eyes watering," explains the panting deputy. "You all can let go now."

We oblige, and the pounding starts. The two deputies work him over like they're hammering in a railroad spike or pitching a circus tent, one blow after another in near-perfect cadence. Occasionally, one has to suspend his club over his head for an extra couple seconds and wait for a better shot to present itself as the stranger rolls around in the dust. Once as the man curls over onto his stomach, a deputy pins his knee into the man's spine and handcuffs him.

"Scum of the earth," says the male half of the couple who got out of the sheriff's car. "Why stop now? Keep it going." A good look at them now reveals that the woman is holding a bloodied white handkerchief against her ear.

"Did you call the sheriff?" Joe asks him.

"That lunatic attacked my wife, ripped her earring off," he says.

"What the hell was he doing in your car?" Joe says, speaking for all of us.

"He was at the side of the highway a mile back or so, standing by his car, waving his arms. We pull over to ask if we can send for help once we hit a service station. We're from Texas, Corpus Christi area, and that's just the way we do things back home. Well, the guy jumps into the back seat, says he needs help, seems normal enough, so we pull out to drive him to the next town. That's just the way we do things. As soon as we're back on the road, he leans forward and pulls my wife's earring off, right out her ear lobe. We pull over to tell him to get the hell out, but he's already got the door open, looking at the blood on his hands and screaming about Jesus Christ. He jumps out and runs down the road. We stop at a call box and phone the sheriff."

The two young deputies lead the stranger towards the car. He seems subdued now, covered in dirt and blood. The moment they open the door, he goes crazy again, screaming and thrashing. They shove him in and slam the door quickly behind, as though capturing a wild animal. One of the deputies opens the front door and begins calling in the episode. The other one walks towards us. The stranger bangs his head repeatedly against the cage separating the front seat from the back.

"Knock it off," warns the deputy with the radio in hand. The stranger screams. The deputy smacks the cage with his fist. The stranger quiets down and just sits there.

"He won't feel anything until tomorrow," says the approaching deputy, acting as our ambassador. "They just keep coming atcha, won't stop. That's why we gotta beat 'em so damn hard."

"Fine with me," says Dodge, still moving his jaw around, finding out where it hurts most.

"Had one pick me up and throw me into a tractor implement last year," the deputy tells us, bragging perhaps just a bit. "Last year up at Phillips Ranch. Lifted me right up over his head."

"What are we talking about here, drugs?" Joe asks.

"You bet," says the deputy. "Probably some new mixture they're cooking up in a garage somewhere. So don't be surprised if you can't press any charges." He looks over at the married couple, then at Dodge. "He'll beat the rap," he says. "Not responsible for his actions, that sorta thing."

"All right, then," says Dodge. "Just have him come over here sober some time, and we'll settle this fair and square." He finally gives up inspecting his jaw, as though realizing his pride hurts a lot worse.

Joe looks over at Dodge with stern eyes, then tells him they'll talk later on. Joe knows Dodge is capable of actually following up on such threats, unlike most people, who say the same kinds of things just to blow off steam. The stranger lets out a random scream from the back seat, then continues to stare straight head, despondent.

The deputies divide up their time in taking statements. One listens to the couple, while the other one, having already established a relationship with us, takes our statements, which are all brief and like-minded. We saw a man run through the gate and attack Dodge when he approached.

The men who had just cleaned up for a night out wander off to perform the routine all over again. The couple from Texas says things like this don't happen in Texas. Another sheriff's department vehicle shows up to escort them back to their rental car.

The stranger screams. The deputies both tell him to shut up. They start the engine and head for the county jail.

Joe, Dodge, and myself, we figure it's about time to turn in and catch some sleep, since the market is later that night.

But one of the men comes running from the housing area. Seems the Second Coming ran through some of the rooms and trashed them before reaching the gate. Busted in a door, tossed around some furniture, ripped out an air conditioner, jumped through a window. None of the men noticed until they went back to rearrange themselves for the night upcoming.

Joe thanks him for the information. The man rushes back to the line of houses by the highway. Joe watches him, but doesn't really see him. He's just staring, seething, trying to estimate damage costs before even seeing the damage. We're waiting for the onslaught of cusses and curses, but all he does is remind us that we'd better get some sleep. Quietly, he heads back to the house to tell his wife and son what happened, and try in vain to take his own advice, to get some sleep. For the moment, he is a beaten man. Unnerving to see on a man like Joe. Even if it is only for the time being. Even though we know he'll bounce back.

Dodge walks to his van, and I walk over to my pickup truck.

"Hey, Stanford," says Dodge. I hold still. Dodge has never called me by name before. It's a nickname, granted—short for "Stanford Boy," because that's where I received my education—but it's all they call me around here. Everyone, that is, except Dodge. He's called me everything from "hey you" to "hey man." Until now.

"My fuckin' tire's flat," he says, catching up to me by my truck. "Gimme a lift to my place?"

I shrug and nod, still surprised he called me by my name.

"Don't worry," he continues. "You don't have to pick me up tonight. I got a patch kit I'll run down here with later."

"I wasn't worried," I tell him.

"Tough to tell," he grins. "You always look like you are."

We get into my truck. "You did good back there," he tells me. "You really hit that fucker hard. Got him before he did any more damage."

"Well..." I stall. "I guess it was just instinct."

"Yeah, but I didn't think you had any," Dodge says. "You're always up in your head. But you showed me somethin' today." Then he smiles and says "fuckin' awesome."

I finally get around to saying "thank you" as I start the engine.

Joe gave me the name "Stanford" as soon as he found out where I went to school. I didn't tell him for a while, afraid it would render me overqualified for the job. Once I realized that the only qualifications which really mattered were my clean driving record and the fact I rent a house nearby, I figured it was a safe peculiarity to admit, and Joe loved it. He clapped his hands and said he never imagined he'd have a Stanford boy working for him. He likes to introduce me to people as the first M.B.A. to work for the family business in its four generations of existence. "Moving up in the world," he says, referring to both me and the company. He doesn't question my motives for being out here, so he can have as much fun as he wants with my résumé. Not that I actually turned in a résumé. I may be from over the hill, but I didn't go that far.

"You're renting my family's old house, aren't you?" he says.

"Yes, I am."

"You know where I live?" he asks, and I realize that I don't.

"That's okay," he laughs. "I gotta remind myself sometimes, it's one place after another. And this one's temporary, too, believe me. I'm at the new house for now, the Franky Demos Memorial monstrosity, back in the guest house, until my brother and his wife need it again."

"What would they need it for?" I ask as we wait to turn onto the highway.

"They'll think of somethin'," he says, and we turn left into the northbound lane.

Dodge has been a personal project of Joe's for a couple years now. Franky Demos had finally severed his son from the family money. As a result, Dodge's wife left him and took their two kids along with her.

Dodge was desperate for work. Joe admits that he initially hired him as an opportunity to show everyone what a jerk Demos was. Most people in the community already had it out for Demos, anyway, but giving Franky's son a second chance when his own father would not was the most conclusive example ever presented to anyone, and Joe seized it. It was hardly a second chance for Dodge, however. He had blown several previous chances already, and Joe discovered why almost immediately upon his hiring.

"Christ, I couldn't believe it," Joe told me. "He'd unload the truck lickity-split, fast as hell. An incredible worker. Incredible. But then he'd finish, and he wouldn't know what to do with himself. He'd start climbing all over the goddamn truck like a monkey, climb up on the roof and dance around like he scored a touchdown, then he'd wrap his wrist inside the strap to pull the door down, and jump from the goddamn roof with the door rolling down behind him. I couldn't believe my eyes."

Joe realized that large amounts of speed had just as much to do with such exhibitions as gymnastic talent, and that Dodge was far from kicking his habits. Figuring Franky Demos had already been up in his son's face plenty of times, Joe tried a different approach. He sat him down and confided in Dodge how much he, too, hated Franky Demos, and proceeded to lay out all the back-handed schemes his father had pulled along the coast over the years—stealing irrigation pipe laid out in other fields, promising competitors a share of his water and then backing out just in time to ruin their harvest, ignoring farm labor laws—Joe spun them all in great detail, produced documented proof, and even admitted to Dodge his primary reason for taking him on as an employee: to spite the man they both despised.

Though his reasons for loathing his father were different than Joe's, Dodge warmed to the idea of cleaning up his life while simultaneously flipping his father a constant middle finger.

Motivation was no longer a problem. He and Joe were allies. Joe's core philosophy is keeping Dodge as busy as possible, working him hard, separating him from any temptation. No rehab centers or halfway houses necessary. When Franky died, Joe had his doubts. He worried that Dodge may have lost his inspiration, if not a father.

Joe never even considered Dodge's wife and kids. They had never seemed important enough to shake him up before. But now things were different. Dodge had confidence. He could see his life changing. And though the situation with his wife was beyond repair, Dodge thought that maybe he had a chance with his kids. They are teenagers now, a boy and a girl, and perhaps ready to forgive him for things which happened while they were so young. So Dodge hopes.

"I never did anything in front of them," he reminds Joe once in a while. "So why not? Unless my ex-fucking-wife brainwashed 'em already. Why can't I be their Dad?"

Ahead of us, a row of mailboxes is perched just high enough above some weeds on the left side of the highway. They each belong to households hidden from view, including mine. I have instructed my few visitors to turn right at these mailboxes, onto the gravel road facing them from across the pavement. I tell my visitors to turn their signal on when they pass the front gate of Mirabelli Nurseries to the south, or when they pass the entrance to Todos Verde Christmas tree farm to the north. No left on Main, right at the stop sign, and another right on Cedar, third house on the left, none of that. Around here, it's directions by landmarks, and it's up to you to decide which ones work best.

Gravel crunches beneath the tires as we ease off the highway. A contorted line of scrub oak trees, leafless and dripping with lichen, flares out along the banks of a thin muddy creek on each side of our path, forming a natural fence and moat parallel to the highway, but with no gate to impede our progress. Passing through the twisted bastion, farmland now stretches from either side, narrow fields which quickly give way to the hillside emerging just ahead of us. Their acres were filled with six-foot high sunflowers through spring and summer which were never harvested. The stalks now stand dead on their feet. Dried brown, heads drooping, picked on by gangs of wobbly crows, the once-golden crop looks like an army of emaciated men trying valiantly to stand at attention. Wild mustard has begun to spring from the cracks in the ground around their feet, offering the only glimpse of color in the drawn-out columns. Plowing them under does not seem to be in anyone's plans, either, as the men who planted the crop several months ago seemed to have disappeared behind the walls of the ranch houses looming diagonally to our left.

Nestled in an incline which holds its ground as the road begins to rise up the hill, every building strewn across the ranch yard is standing to a drum roll, it seems, moments away from collapsing into a heap of splintered wood. As my truck starts to climb along with the road, our vantage of the decaying spread improves. It must have been a beautiful place once, a nominee for a state landmark. It could have been filmed at dusk and tabbed for the month of June in a calendar called "American Ranches," or "Barns of America."

But by now any past glory or hope for the future is beyond the point of repair. In addition to the weathered structures, the ranch is surrounded by aged vehicles. Packs of dying breeds—tractors, trucks, and cars included—seem to have migrated here to live out their final days. The stunted machines surround the place, as if they are trying to prevent one of the buildings from escaping.

The only sign of life is an elderly Mexican man and his dog. The man stands next to an empty oil drum, keeping his eye on a fire burning inside it. He slowly turns and waves. He always waves and smiles. His teeth are long gone. His face seems to have fallen off an apple tree months ago, shriveling up to its current maze of lines, gouges, and grooves. His dog, a black and white mutt cross-bred through several generations of hound dog descendants, fixes his wild blue eyes on my truck and sprints our way. As the ranch starts to fade from view behind a line of eucalyptus trees along the side of the road, the dog catches up to us. He barks and bites at the tires, doing one or the other with each stride.

"I don't know how that dog has lived this long," mutters Dodge. "Every time. Every fucking time."

"What do you know about that ranch?" I ask him.

"Santo's place?" he says.

"That's his name, Santo?"

"Not the old guy we just saw," Dodge says. "That's his brother. But Santo, he runs things down there." He moistens his fingers, then squeezes out the burning end of his cigarette with a hiss. He throws it out the window. "I know he used to be Joe's foreman."

"Really?"

"Long time ago. I haven't seen Santo since I was a teenager. I don't know if something happened or what, but I don't think Joe likes him very much. Ask him about Santo, and he'll probably start his answer with 'that son of a bitch.'"

The dog finally gives up as we emerge from the tunnel of eucalyptus and plane out into the valley where my house lies. I see him in the rear view mirror, standing at the dim opening with his light blue eyes blazing from his black face and his pink tongue scooping up the air. Satisfied that he has chased us out of his territory, he pivots and trots home.

"Just seems weird," I say, "growing all those flowers and letting them die."

"It ain't normal, but I'm sure they got their reasons." Dodge is clearly not as intrigued as I am. "Could be just growin' em just for seed, could have some contract with a seed company."

"Yeah, could be." I let it pass.

Since I'm dropping off Dodge, I veer right at the tip of the meadow which rolls for several acres up to the house I'm renting.

The road rises again. We levitate above the meadow. Thick waves of grass unmask the wind, giving away its position. Two dozen head of brown cattle graze in a disjointed clique near the fence line of the old Demos residence. They are beef stock, passing through on their way to slaughter. Gretchen Demos, Franky's widow, leases the land for grazing while renting me the house. Just as well. I wasn't the only diluted expatriate from over the hill to file an application with the revered Mrs. Demos, all of us bent on fulfilling some "getting away from it all" fantasy. And none of us had any use for one hundred acres, except to stare at it and mentally pontificate to ourselves. Gretchen saw what she was getting into by renting the house. Nobody from this side of the hill could afford it. Cows make a nice accessory. More set pieces on which to meditate, and Gretchen makes some extra money in the process. Everybody wins.

We reach the pinnacle of the road, where it turns to the right for a quarter-mile straight-away to the new Demos residence. With the old house in full view now below us, a brand new Lincoln Town Car, off white, can be seen parked around the back. It belongs to Gretchen.

"Late on the rent?" asks Dodge.

"Nope," I say.

"Must be visiting then. Letting Ziggy piss on all his old spots. That means she's already been over the new house, thank God. I missed her." Dodge takes out the pack of cigarettes from his breast pocket, gets what he needs, then puts it back.

Gretchen lives over the hill now, in a condominium with a view of the bay through her living room window. She says if you press your right cheek against the glass you can see the San Francisco skyline to the north. I never thought Dodge had much of a problem with her, stepson to stepmother. Guilt by association, I suppose. She stayed married to the man who had a kid by one of his workers, so screw her if she can't even respect herself enough to leave that asshole Franky.

I understand she raised Dodge as her own, though, or tried to. I'd ask Dodge to expand, but I'd hate to make too much of him finally calling me by name. A few more open-field tackles of drug-addled trespassers, then maybe I can risk being more presumptuous.

The old house fades out behind us. The new one starts to emerge from the trees ahead. The houses are an architectural growth chart of the late Franky's ego. The old house looks like a house should look in this area: simple design, straight lines, whitewashed exterior with green trim, weathered shake roof sloping down from the top story windows, a front porch, a screen door, a swinging love seat. The new house is a sedentary version of a Porsche bought by an aging man in the heat of a post-mid-life crisis. Built high on a hill overlooking all he owns, for all to see, it seems to have been airlifted out of a gated community in the East Bay and dropped amongst the Monterey pines marching downward to the Pacific. Terra cotta roof, stucco arches, about as homey as an airport hotel, when parking in front you half expect some fellow in a majorette jacket and cap to open the car door and ask if you have any luggage.

Such a layout suits its current owner just fine: Roman Demos, Franky's legitimate son—his only pride and joy which had no value on the real estate market, the only human feather in his cap—Dodge's older brother. Half-brother (Dodge will correct you every time).

"Now if I can only manage to avoid Ranger Roman," Dodge says, "it'll be a great day."

Roman is head ranger for all the state parks in his jurisdiction, which includes the marine wildlife and bird sanctuary next to Mirabelli Nurseries, behind the tree line. Any problem Dodge has with Roman is perfectly understandable. I need no explanations, need not construct any theories. Roman could have been a real prodigy in the business world if he had been willing to sacrifice his status as a big enchilada here on the coast. The park service was the best way he could contrive to stay put without having to farm.

One side of the garage is open. The space is empty. Dodge clenches a victorious fist. His brother is out.

"Come to the front door with me, will ya?" he asks me. "I wanna see if Marcie invites me in this time if you're with me." He winks. "A little experiment."

We walk to the front doors, which are French-style. French doors on a faux Spanish colonial. Franky must have bought a stack of Architectural Digests and told his contractor to fit everything in that he circled in the pictures, everything that struck his fancy, everything that looked like money.

We tap on the glass and Roman's wife appears on the other side. She is attractive in the way I used to think the female mice were cute in some of those older Disney animated movies like The Rescuers or The Rats of NIMH. Dodge motions for her to open the doors.

"What is it Dodge?" she asks.

"Have you met Stanford?" he says.

"Briefly," she smiles dutifully.

I try to smile back, but fall a little short. Dodge looks at me, trying not to laugh at the results of his experiment.

"Hey, I was wondering," Dodge clears his throat. "My kids are set to visit me this weekend upcoming. Is it okay if they stay with me in the guest house?"

Marcie grimaces, sucks in some air through clenched teeth. "Better ask Roman," she decides, letting the air out. "Have you been keeping it clean?" she continues. "We're going to need it in a couple weeks."

"Yes," Dodge sneers. "I go out to my van if I want to make a mess."

"Roman should be home soon. I told him Mom was stopping by today."

"Gretchen? I guess he missed her."

"Oh, so you saw your mom on the road?"

"No. We saw Gretchen parked over at Stanford's."

I wonder how long before they simply start volleying one-word arguments at each other—Gretchen! Mom! Gretchen! Mom!

"You mean her old house?" she says.

"Yes," I cut in, stopping the next contest before it begins. "Her old house."

She looks at us both and decides the conversation is finished.

"I'll tell Roman you were here," she says to Dodge.

"Nice to see you again," she says to me.

Dodge nods. I wave. We leave.

Before we can go our separate ways, Roman's Ford Bronco pulls into the driveway. Brand new, white paint, with the "Great Seal of the State of California" stuck on its doors, the logo with a Grizzly Bear on it, all of whom were hunted to extinction along the coast years ago. A man in Roman's position even has a block of siren lights across the top of his vehicle. His surfboard is wedged underneath the siren rack.

Roman gives us a big wave and smile. He's wearing his ranger hat. He gets out and approaches jaunty-jolly. From the neck down he's wearing a wetsuit unzipped and pulled down to his waist, a neon beach towel wrapped and tied at his hip, and a Batman t-shirt. He is barefoot.

"What's up, hombres?" he greets us warmly, as if he wants our vote.

"Hello, Roman," I say, and accept his hand shake.

"So what's happenin', Stanford. Just chillin'?"

"Yeah," I say, trying to remember at what age I stopped talking like that.

"Cool," says Roman.

Dodge keeps quiet. Roman doesn't shake his hand.

"Hey, Dodge," he says. "We need the guest house in a couple weeks."

"Yeah, I heard," says Dodge.

"You been keeping it clean?"

"Sure," Dodge snaps. "Ask Marcie."

Roman reacts to Dodge's barb by not reacting. He turns his attention to me.

"Know anyone in a Lincoln Town Car?" Roman asks.

"You mean the one back at the house?" I ask back.

"Yeah, that one."

I hesitate, give him a chance to recant. He just grins, nice and wide, a mouth full of bright teeth contrasted against his surfer's sunburn.

"It's your Mom's car," says Dodge, jumping in ahead of me.

"Oh, yeah," says Roman, thinking nothing of it. "I forgot. It's so new."

"She's had it a year," Dodge reminds him.

Roman keeps on smiling, but his eyes are a tad more steely than before.

"I guess I'm just used to seeing her in the old blue truck," he says, a little too calmly. He keeps concentrating on me. "You got a minute to come in for a beer?" he invites me inside. "I've got some wheelin' and dealin' I wanted to pick your brain on."

I look at Dodge. An unexpected turn of events in his experiment. He tries not to laugh again, as with Marcie earlier, but this time it's a different kind of laugh.

"Why me?" I ask Roman.

"Dude..." he laughs. "Why do you think? Stanford M.B.A.'s don't retire to this side of the hill at age thirty unless they're hot shit. White hot."

"If I was so hot," I ask him, "why would I have to take a job with Mirabelli to make rent?"

Roman smiles. He knew I would say that eventually, it seems. He pauses, setting me up for his best shot. "'Cause you're just like everyone else who comes out here to live," he oozes. "You got bored."

Roman is not the kind of man you ever want to admit is right. But aside from being a couple years short on my age and my reasons for coming here, he is right. I did get bored. I had stared at the cows and the landscape and scanned the fields for bobcats and coyotes quite enough, thank you. It's all so beautiful, and I curse the day I was set in front of the TV to keep me occupied while Mom washed her hair.

The gravel crackles in a din beneath my tires as I drive home, to the old Demos house. The first time I drove this road, the sound reminded me of a radio in between stations. Nothing but static and crackle. Or a TV full of snow. White noise.

All I did was run when I first got here. It's all I could think of doing. I would run and my feet landing on the gravel established some sort of rhythm to the static. Instead of tires rolling over it steadily, there was a one-two-one-two beat. Left shoe, right shoe. Left shoe, right shoe. I jogged every trail within a ten-mile radius. Up into the hills, down across the fields, along the rocky beaches. Five miles in my new territory were not half as exhausting as two miles on a treadmill in a health club on my lunch break. I would startle deer, splash through creeks, feel myself stalked by vigilant red-tailed hawks, screeching out a warning, their voice straight out of the sound loop of some Western flick as they cut to a shot of a lone cowboy whose interests waver in the gray area between lawman and outlaw, rifle slung across his back, hat tilted low over his eyes, leading his horse to the tumbleweed town that so badly needs his courage. I tried to imitate the hawk, get it to screech at me again.

I ran over every trail the area had to offer. My head started to stay forward, fixed on the next mile. I listened to my breathing. I noted what time I left the house, what time I returned, timing myself.

I introduced myself to the Mirabellis one day, Joe and Aldo, as I jogged through their fields. When I bought a digital watch to see if I could break a six-minute mile, I hit up Joe for a job. It was time to see a different side of the coast.

And the money was running out. Roman was wrong about that. If I was hot, I wasn't hot long enough. Not by choice, either.

Gretchen and her dog Ziggy are taking advantage of the last few minutes of sunlight as I pull in next to her "city car." I drove a Benz when I first arrived here, but quickly sold it in favor of my pickup. It's impossible to keep a vehicle clean around here unless you're willing to wash it every morning (like Joe). A dirty truck looks like it's been working hard. A dirty car looks like it hasn't been washed.

She leans on her cane in the miniature orchard which fans out from one corner of the front porch. One type of tree for each fruit able to grow in this region—a lemon, lime, tangerine, pear, plum, a few different kinds of apples. She turns and waves, a bit sheepish. I've told her several times to stop by whenever she wants, but she still gets embarrassed when I happen upon her. Ziggy races towards my truck and pisses on every tire the instant they stop moving. He does it every time, which never helps Gretchen's peace of mind. "Ziggy!" she scolds him during the entire ritual. "Ziggy!"

"I'm so sorry, Paul," she calls out to me, limping her way out of the orchard. Gretchen is the only one around here who uses my real name. Paul. The name on the rental agreement. Paul Pryor. I was so happy when a nickname presented itself. God bless Joe Mirabelli.

"Don't worry about it, Mrs. Demos."

"Gretchen."

"Right. Gretchen." I smile at her and take a knee in order to pet Ziggy, a Boston terrier, quite low to the ground. Until she stops acting self-conscious over visiting her old home, I'll continue to call her Mrs. Demos and let her correct me, and I've told her so. I baby talk Ziggy as he desperately tries to lick my face. Gretchen finally reaches the driveway and I ask her to what do I owe the pleasure.

"I stopped by Roman and Marcie's just to double-check that the guest house is still available for the weekend of the sixteenth," she tells me. She always refers to her old homes by the names of the new occupants. "The professor from Santa Barbara who interviewed me for that history book is working on another project and was looking for a place to stay," she says.

"What is it this time?" I ask. "Anything he'll need your help on?"

"Oh, I think so," she says, in all sincere modesty. "It's a book about some of the big families from California's early days...so he tells me."

"Yeah, I guess you may be of some assistance," I tease her.

Her maiden name is Bacon. The Bacons were not quite Huntington or Hearst, but they came close for a while. Unfortunately, their pioneering spirit never made the transition to business savvy, and their central coast empire was unceremoniously deconstructed over time. If it wasn't a moron cousin who enjoyed going to Reno and playing cards very badly, then it was a loggers' revolt upending one of their lumber mills. If it wasn't a divisive family argument, then it was rampant anthrax destroying a large strip of dairy herd. And there was always a Franky Demos lurking around their edges, waiting to charm and marry a Bacon, his safety net and eventual ticket out of the farming industry. So much land to sell, so little business sense. I initially thought Gretchen leased this land because it was all that remained of the Bacon spread, but she told me that her plan had been to sell it. Problem was, people were so used to Franky's fire sales that she was mercilessly low-balled with every offer. Her retaliation was a "For Rent" sign.

She can afford it. Franky left her all of what he had left over. "Back pay," she calls it. "Hardship pay." Roman got the house—which he had been living in, anyway—she kept the condo on the peninsula, and Dodge got his one dollar.

"So is the guest house available?" I ask her, conducting a little experiment of my own.

"That's what Roman told me over the phone, and Marcie said so today," she shrugs. "I thought Dodge would probably be using it, but no. She said he's been staying at the ranch."

I debate telling her the truth, but decide she doesn't need it. Not now. Not at this point in her life.

"How's living on the other side?" I ask her.

"Just wonderful," she says. "I can order Chinese food now. There's a new place."

"So what's left?" I ask.

"Greek," she answers. "I still can't find a good Greek restaurant, much less one that delivers. Franky's mother spoiled me, I guess. A marvelous cook, she was."

"Have you tried the one on University, downtown Palo Alto?"

Gretchen makes a face. I tell her I guess I don't know Greek. Ziggy spots something in the fields and takes off after it.

"Probably a cow," says Gretchen. "His eyesight is failing."

She grows suddenly pensive and asks how Dodge is doing.

"Okay," I tell her. "He's working hard, trying to make things right, from what I can tell. But I only see him at work."

"Does he ever see his children?" she wants to know.

"This weekend," I say. "I don't know about any other times."

"That's good," she says, looking out at Ziggy's progress. He's found the spot, but sniffs around, perplexed. Nothing there.

"Do you think," Gretchen continues, "do you think he needs money?"

"Dodge?" I stall. I wasn't expecting any of this. Usually we just gab about city life versus country life. "I really don't know,

Gretchen," I tell her. "I know that Joe takes good care of him, pays him pretty well. Maybe you should ask him."

"Who, Joe?" she says.

"No. Dodge."

"Oh," she trails off.

Convinced Ziggy won't find anything, she calls to him. "Ziggy," she hollers. "That's enough."

The little dog comes sprinting. Gretchen looks up at the purple sky. Leftover light is all that remains. The sun has already set.

"It's garbage night," she says. "I've got to get home and separate it. I think that's my favorite part of living in a city. They take your garbage."

"Only so much of it," I say, a joke to myself which I don't expect her to get. She's not listening, anyway. She's looking across the meadow. Even as Ziggy comes nipping at her pants leg, she stands transfixed.

"You're so lucky, Paul," she sighs. "If I wasn't so scared about being far away from a hospital, I would have stayed. I'm just not strong enough for the coast anymore."

And some of us may never be. I would tell her so, but I don't want to interrupt her.

# WEDNESDAY 9/24

There is no getting used to starting work at midnight. My face in the mirror reminds me of this, but I notice how much less it shows nowadays when I am tired. The old indicators are there—lines and circles—but there more often. Betrayers of fatigue have the beginnings of permanence. Sure I look tired. It's midnight. But there just isn't much difference anymore than when I'm not. If I was famous, magazines would find a way to describe my features as something more than just pretty-boyish in decline. I would instead have "probing eyes" or "inquisitive lips" and a "troubled brow." My skin stretching and lines deepening would indicate a wealth of experience and mark me as distinguished. The word "tired" would never make it into print. But I am not well-known. I have to go to work at midnight.

From the front porch, I admire the quiet that is draped across the night. Fog clings to the meadow floor, which somehow lends an even greater silence to the landscape. Sips from my coffee mug echo through the darkness, a lone variation in tone against the sustained note of the crickets. The stars are so many that I have yet to spot any of the constellations I learned in my well-lighted past. All familiar patterns are lost in the flood of stars allowed to shine in this unimpeded view of the heavens.

I throw the rest of my coffee over the side and leave the cup on the railing.

The walk to my truck inspires a couple of Great Horned Owls to exchange hoots from one side of the meadow to the other. My footsteps, the owls, the crickets. The racket only gets more clamorous the longer your ear presses against the night—the ocean, you realize, that's the surf I hear, and the creek...I can hear the creek trotting out towards the ocean. Sea lions bark at each other, faintly audible from the marine life reserve next to the ranch.

I duck into the front seat and start the engine, contributing a new noise to the night. A pack of coyotes probably stops in their tracks a few hundred yards from here, a red fox runs without considering where to, and some deer have swung their ears in my direction. I half expect to see some of them in my headlights as I crawl along the gravel to the highway. But tonight only a skunk gets caught in the glare, scurrying ahead of me for a while before I realize he won't stop running until I stop following. I tap the breaks, shut my lights, and his shadow immediately darts off the road into the brush.

The hush in which such small movements are considered "action" is broken once I enter the ranch. Market nights are charged with a different dynamic than the standard pace of ranch life. Suddenly, at this ungodly hour, somewhere between too late and too early, you are reminded that this is a business. Out of the fields, into the profit margin. Time to subsidize the pristine photo opportunities for the passing weekend motorists.

The yard buzzes with idling engines and a certain battle-ready charge. Fog and dust mingle in the beams of headlights. Silhouettes go about their preparations, occasionally crossing the beams to be revealed for a moment...Joe, Dodge, Manuel. We'll be taking two trucks tonight. The big bobtail and Joe's two-ton pickup with the insulated metal shelter rising from its bed. Wednesdays are the busiest in the market, generating twice the business of Mondays and Fridays combined. Wholesalers from the further regions of Northern California come on Wednesdays, buying product for sale to their clients whose shops are too far away from the city to come in on their own time—Eureka, Fresno, Sacramento, Lake Tahoe. These outlets to areas otherwise inaccessible combined with the usual Bay Area merchants generate enough of a throng that we need Manuel and an extra truck.

"Stanford," Joe shouts above the engines, "You and me in the big rig. Manny's gonna drive the small one with Dodge."

I give him an acknowledging wave, and walk towards the bobtail. Joe shows no sign of the defeated pallor from early this evening, and his resiliency is worth a second wind. You look for second winds even before the race starts when it's run at this hour. The big truck grumbles with the weight of flowers fresh cut earlier from the fields now invisible in the darkness. The refrigerator noise competes with the engine's. I climb the passenger side. Joe's wife, Lorraine, is already sitting inside.

"Good morning, Stanford," she smiles.

"Good morning, Lorraine."

She is already shuffling papers on top of the combination-lock briefcase in which she and Joe keep their records.

"I have to start pushing papers now," she says, "the drive puts me to sleep otherwise."

Lorraine keeps the books for the family business. She resisted for a while, preferring to offer her services to various companies in the Bay Area. Finally, however, keeping it in the family, or at least not working for someone else, softened the potential blows of a graveyard shift three days a week. Mrs. Mirabelli still likes to maintain a certain urbanity about her appearance, often looking slightly out of place. Hair sprayed to a sturdy hold, makeup applied to a fine line, while the rest of us wander around glassy-eyed with coffee breath and cowlicks. She hums while she works, in lilting tones. If she played the piano she would be sure and fill in any spaces between notes with a tickling of the keys on the far end of the keyboard.

Joe climbs in, and we launch. Our two-vehicle convoy is led by the bobtail, with the smaller rig right behind. We pause outside the gate so that Dodge can jump out of the two-ton and close the gate. A horn sounds, a car pulls into the entrance. One of the foursomes of

Mirabelli employees is just now returning from their night out. Four white cowboy hats are the only things visible through the windows. Dodge gives them a wave and lets them pass before swinging the gate shut, wrapping it with the chain, and fastening the padlock

The drive along the coast at night is tiring, just as Lorraine said. The sights are now hidden. Only the crests of the waves catch the moonlight, only the trees at the tops of the mountains can be seen, shadows against the sky. The yellow line dividing the highway becomes hypnotic, pulling focus, reflector after reflector, weighing down eyelids already heavy. Headlights from the opposite direction are rare at this hour. An occasional truck out to beat traffic, fifty-foot trailer strung with orange lights around its edges, more lights across the roof of the tractor, provides a quick shot of adrenaline. Fleeting images of what it would be like to slam head-on into one of those big bastards make you throw back your shoulders, shake your head, sharpen your senses. Gripping the wheel tighter, the dragon passes. A gust of wind, blown off course for moment, but you saw it coming.

Joe likes to stay alert by talking—49ers, Giants, old stories, family history—which doesn't compliment Lorraine's choice of stimulant, bookkeeping. They bicker steadily, which still serves the purpose of exhilaration, of killing the first half hour of darkness between farm and city. The last half hour is for the most part suburban: shopping centers closed for the night, all-night gas stations servicing a random customer, empty parking lots, neon messages occasionally reaching out from their windows.

Ten minutes into tonight, however, during the darkened first half of the countryside, some unexpected lights appear off to the passenger side.

"Look at that, would ya?" says Joe, pointing out the site, as if there was anything else which may divert our attention from the spot in question. "They're working around the clock, now, godammit."

"Maybe they're running out of money, Joe," says Lorraine, "and they're up against the clock."

"You think they'd spend all those years getting the permits and then run out of money?" Joe waves her off, then rubs his forehead. "Shit," he sighs. "They're dumb but they're not stupid."

The lights shine a hundred yards or so off the highway, illuminating a construction area at the back end of a meadow, beneath a line of eucalyptus trees. The tree line is thinning out, unveiling the dark hillsides rolling eastward behind it. Light hitting the remaining trees from below give them a sort of gothic glow, similar to the effect of holding a flashlight under your chin in the dark, intensifying the contours of your face, scaring your friends. A few bulldozers are in the process of landscaping the site, which will one day host the confines of a resort they're calling a "health retreat."

My Mom went to one when I was quite young, a health retreat, but she called it a "fat farm." Only she wasn't fat. That's not what her mirror told her, though. That's how Dad described her predicament to me.

"They're comin' after my water, I just know it," says Joe.

"Can't they dig a well?" I ask.

"Sure, they can dig a well, if there's only one bathroom in the blueprints," he says. "Nobody's ever found more than eight gallons per minute around here, and that was on a four-hundred foot dig. Believe me, there'd be a lot more development around here if anyone tapped into a bigger source."

He focuses on the road for a few moments, then gives the steering wheel a hard spank. "Dammit," he snaps. "They're gonna dam that sonofabitch up, divert the stream, and leave me dick."

"We don't know that, Joey," Lorraine consoles him.

"We don't know that yet," Joe sighs. "But we will."

The lights pass, and we settle back into darkness for a minute before driving by the lighthouse. Its beam spots us, swings across us every five seconds. Momentary daylight. An orange triangle the size of a street sign reflects in our headlights, hovering along the right shoulder of the road. An old red tractor materializes behind it, the hooded driver huddled over the steering wheel, on his way to a nearby field. He looks over his shoulder at us, and the thick ray of light from the beacon sweeps across his cracked face for a split second.

"I guess we're in for some hot weather," Joe says. "A man's gotta be pretty willing to beat the heat to get up on his tractor at this hour. But that's fall. This time of year, things can get hot."

We crawl out of the truck. The stars are all but gone. The trees are no longer the tallest fixtures. Buildings rise above the motor pool of the market, buildings with billboards and lighted signs atop them. Individual noises are no longer discernible. The city overwhelms them. It's all just noise.

I jump out of the truck to guide Joe into the warehouse. The reverse lights flare up, the staccato beeps warn everyone that a large vehicle is going backwards. Joe keeps an eye on me in the side mirror. I wave my hands accordingly, then hold them up flat. The brake lights shine, the engine stops. Joe gives me a winking nod in the mirror. Lorraine walks over to unlock and open the gate of the "Mirabelli Nurseries" stall. Dodge and Manuel appear. They lower the hydraulic lift at the back of the bobtail, beginning the slow motion up-and-down rhythm of unloading. Joe comes around with an edgy little customer already at his elbow.

"He's parked at the end of the lot," Joe tells me. "His order's in the smaller truck. The whole load."

I drive the pickup down the center of the lot. The left side is dominated by two other warehouses like the one in which Mirabelli Nurseries sets up business, each structure the size of a high school gymnasium, each one housing several dozen growers. The right side resembles an aquarium—glass-front stores willing to accommodate the general public later in the morning as well as the wholesalers and merchants. The vibrating customer, a nervous wholesaler from Sacramento, beckons me over by his truck, which appears to be an old UPS delivery type re-painted with some flowers and a logo created by a fourth-grader. We make the switch, he signs the receipt, and I park the truck out on the street. Tenants are required to get their vehicles out of the market by three a.m. to leave plenty of space for the customers.

On the sidewalk outside the perimeter of the market, a mother and daughter team is collecting the discarded cardboard boxes from the back doors of the window-fronted wholesalers. They've got a pickup already stacked several feet high with their bargaining chips. I cut through one of the back doors, Yashida Wholesale. Business is already starting to heat up. Some of the customers have long drives ahead of them, traffic to beat. The local crowd will show up later. I weave through the mix of buyers and sellers. Yashida's men wear gray coats, cut like a doctor's. They shout the orders as they pack them. Another man shouts them back, double-checking, as he writes out a receipt—"two bunches purple iris...five bunches white narcissus..."

In the parking lot, wagons and carts rumble and squeak by, pushed by workers who were probably sleeping on park benches yesterday afternoon. The misbegotten temps follow roaring gay shop owners and ersatz Martha Stewarts to their vans, pile heaps of product on top of each other, all of it wrapped in newspaper, all of it doomed to a brief life of exhibitionism. Gladiolas, stems long and rubbery, bounce along in bunches slung over shoulders, as if freshly stalked and killed, the florist-as-hunter. Sunflowers lay across carts, heads hung over the side face-down, looking for their place of birth, finding only pavement. Delphinium are cradled in their adoptive owners' arms, napping, it seems, blossomed heads peeking out from the tops of their paper pods.

It would all be scored so perfectly by a waltz of some sort. I plug my ears and imagine just that. Now it's a dance precisely choreographed, full of symbolism, of something besides money, but of something I can't place. I only remember the chorus of the waltz I'm imagining, and move on when I don't know the rest.

I enter the hangar-like mouth of the warehouse. Passing by the neighboring stalls on my way to Mirabelli Nurseries, each human face seems to be staring back from a public bathroom mirror— the unforgiving light bulbs, every pore exposed, and the time of day not helping one bit. The stalls are separated by chain-link. Some of the stalls are inhabited by merchants specializing in floral accessories, wicker baskets and wire trellises stacked precariously, spilling out of their boundaries, reminiscent of an ancient bazaar. Grab the wrong one and they could all come crashing down. Voices and noises echo through the rafters. The same tired jokes about coffee, about needing it, about wanting it, lots of analysis borrowed from the sports page concerning the Forty-Niners and Giants, and always the standard complaints about business being slow, business being slow, business being slow—nobody in the history of the market ever saying (very loudly) "My God but I'm making a shitload of money. Business is booming, and I couldn't be happier."

"Is he all set, then?" asks Joe as I arrive at our stall.

"All set, patrón."

Manuel laughs at my Spanish, but I got it right. Pronunciation and everything. Just like the guys at the ranch. That's what they call Joe, and that's why Manny laughs. I learned by example, finally. Got my nose out of the books and the discs. Lorraine is making coffee, Dodge is wrapping daisies with Manuel, and Joe is wrapping some of the pre-orders.

"Hand me four bunches of Bella Donna, would ya Stanford?"

And so it goes most of the early morning. Non-stop. Buckets empty quickly. We bring the empties over to the drainage ditch running along the base of the wall and dump the excess water. Still, water covers the cement floor. Bunches are pulled and brought over to the table for wrapping, dripping all the way. We squeegee the floor whenever time allows, preventing slippage and law suits. We sweep the floor of disembodied blossoms and leaves, trying to maintain some semblance of order and diligence until things slow down around sunrise. Brief opportunities to sip coffee are interrupted by an incoming customer or by instructions from Joe.

"Stanford, you and Dodge find me forty-five good-looking bunches of white delphinium and wheel 'em over to Post Wholesale."

Dodge steers the wagon while I walk alongside draping a protective arm over the teetering layers of long-stem delphinium. We enter the adjoining warehouse and weave our way to the entrance of Post Wholesale. Immediately we are berated by a woman in the constant grip of tension. I have never seen her eyebrows anything but furled. She grabs a stem of delphinium and shakes it at her assistant as she talks, a pear-shaped older gay man whose job description must read "punching bag and calming influence."

"Is this open?" she snaps.

"Yes," he says. "Perfectly so."

"Exactly," she grinds her teeth. "Which is why I am completely fucked right now."

"You want it tight?" he says.

"I want it tighter than your ass," she tells him. He smiles at us. We try not to laugh. She realizes what she said.

"Okay," she corrects herself. "Tighter than his ass."

She points directly at me with the delphinium. Dodge loses it. The old punching bag covers his mouth and turns red. The boss and I stare at each other. I can see she's embarrassed, so I force a smile, lips sealed. I tell her we'll be right back with some flowers that are a bit more closed. I grab the delphinium. She surrenders it apologetically, but without an apology.

Dodge can't wait to get back to the stall and tell everyone what happened. I practically have to jog next to the wagon to keep up. "You see that old queen when the subject of your ass came up?" he says. "I thought his shoelaces were gonna come untied."

We pass a stall that I have seen many times, but only now does the name register: "Santo Farms." There are a couple of young Mexican guys working there. One is in a chair, fast asleep, with his head tilted back and his mouth wide open. The other has his elbows on the table, fighting sleep, waiting for customers.

"Is that the same Santo?" I ask Dodge under my breath. "From that crappy ranch by my place?"

"Sure is," Dodge says.

"Are either of those guys Santo?"

Dodge scoffs. "Santo's an old man by now. Like I said, I haven't seen him for years, but I know he's gettin' old."

The flowers at Santo's stall are obviously imported. Not a wilted petal or leaf, not a spot or hint of brown along the edges, and definitely not grown on their ranch. Each bunch is wrapped in a clear plastic sleeve, making the flowers appear to shine even brighter—roses, tulips, carnations. Definitely out of a box, off a plane, not a local field or greenhouse. Definitely grown in an equatorial climate. Hothouse flowers grown so far south they can be field crops. Low overhead. Non-existent, practically. Workers earning pocket change by the hour, in conditions not dictated by any laws, only the will of the patrón. Impeccable-looking finished products, dirt cheap. Something for Santo to sell while his fields dry out, dormant, without even a cover crop in place to offer fertile ground for the future.

Imports are the bane of local growers. Dozens of farms per year have been going under since laws were passed making it easier for imports to enter the country. Implemented ostensibly to encourage South American countries to export something besides drugs, the fertilizer hit the fan once drugs were discovered in the petals of a shipment from Colombia. Antsy farmers now had a case.

But the importers had deeply entrenched themselves by that point, a relentless team of lobbyists on call outside their doors. Money rolls through their operations at a volume equivalent to the decibel level at which it "talks" to lawmakers on all levels. The topic would be a lot hotter in the market if wholesalers did not outnumber growers these days so significantly. Keeping things the way they are, giving thinly-veiled cartels a free ride and laundry service simply makes too much sense to the buy-low, sell-high philosophy of a middle man. Too much business sense.

And so the struggle continues for the growers, from behind metal desks with simulated wood tops, rotary dial phones, and an eye on the skies. I have acquired my bias on the subject from Joe, naturally. I question very little of it thanks to my years in the Goliath corner of the mythological fight card. I was considered a threat, to those above as well as below me, and I adored the reputation. Nothing surprises me, least of all when there's a dollar at stake.

Joe looks exasperated at our return. I figure maybe Post called ahead to get in their version of the story before us. But that's not it.

"Your son called, Dodge."

Joe gives him the message knowing already what a call to the market this early means. Someone in that household, the ex-wife household, needs a ride later on. Dodge will have to take a two-hour break, head down the 101, south on the bay side stretch of the peninsula, out from the city and into San Carlos. He'll park outside the rented house, which looks so much like a rented house. Who the hell would buy it? That's what Dodge says. He'll sit outside so he and his wife won't see each other, won't argue. His son Oscar will come out and get in the car and deliver a message from Mom. "Don't drive like an asshole."

Dodge will have to borrow Phil's car, since Dodge is not allowed to drive any Mirabelli vehicle on the road. Phil is one of the perpetually down-on-his-luck employees over at Yashida's. Dodge trades Phil use of the car for a tank of gas. Tanks of gas are gold to those living hand-to-mouth, always in cash, with drinking or drug problems in their budget. Any chance to take care of the basics for free leaves more money for the vices. Borrowing Phil's car usually means Dodge borrowing money from Joe.

As much as Joe wants to help Dodge make amends for the past, Dodge's kids—the very object of his mission—those kids drive Joe nuts. Can't stand them. Dodge calls his son back, and all of Joe's expectations are lived up to.

"Oscar needs a ride to work," Dodge tells Joe.

"Work?" Joe says. "What happened to school?"

Dodge shrugs. "Says they've got him in some kinda work-study program."

Joe rolls his eyes. "Well, he oughta be well-rested. What time is it, for chrissakes?"

"He starts at seven. He's working at Wheel Deals in San Mateo, changin' tires, pluggin' holes and stuff."

"I mean now," says Joe. "It's damn near two in the morning."

"He had to pick up his Mom at work. She had a late shift."

Joe rubs his eyeballs with the base of his hands. "Then why the hell doesn't she drive him to work," he asks Dodge.

"She's too tired."

"Then what about your daughter? She can drive him."

"She needs the car."

Joe waves his arms in surrender. "Do what you gotta do," he says, and then Dodge asks him for gas money.

"Stanford," Joe turns to me, trying not to bark, "get me five bunches of lavender delphinium. Tall."

I hoist some out of a bucket, let the water flow from the hollow stems and drip back into the bucket, lay them across the stack of newspaper for Joe to wrap.

"Work study," Joe grumbles as he folds some newspaper over the flowers. "More like work furlough."

Dodge leaves to fulfill his obligation once the market slows down around dawn. Joe's frustration surfaces again.

"That family's been running him ragged," he sighs. "They know what he's trying to do, and all they do is take advantage of him. You ever met his wife?"

"No," I tell him.

"One fucking bitch, I'll tell ya." He looks over at his wife. "Sorry, Lorraine. I don't like you to hear me talk like that, but I mean it. Dodge is certainly no angel, we all know that, but that woman..."

"It's okay, Joe," Lorraine says. "She is a bitch."

Manuel laughs. As with anyone learning a language on the fly, he is most proficient at cuss words. Lorraine is pleased with herself. She doesn't get many laughs at the market. Too many male egos around to get a word in, much less a zinger. But she immediately feels guilty.

"Just remember, though," she announces. "Dodge gave her everything she needed to be one. It's been in the works a long time."

A trench-coated customer wanders in, a regular, easily mistaken for a homeless lunatic if not for the market badge dangling from her lapel. She chooses her path carefully around the buckets, studying the product. She plucks a bunch and sticks it up her nose, asking if it's fresh, asking every time. She's not going to help Joe much. She annoys the hell out of him even when he isn't pre-agitated. I lure him over to the Mr. Coffee machine on the back desk with a question:

"So what's the story on Santo?"

"Santo," Joe says, and clearly I have not helped ease his mind, either. He does make it over to the coffee machine. I at least accomplish that much.

"Yeah," I say, too late to take it back. "We walked by his stand earlier."

"He used to be my foreman, years ago. Christ. About twenty years ago, I think."

"That's what Dodge told me when we drove by Santo's ranch yesterday."

"Ranch?" Joe says. "That's not a ranch. It's a disaster area."

"That's why I'm surprised he has a stand. With flowers, no less."

"All imports," Joe swats at the air. "He's probably jamming drugs in the stems, that crazy son of a bitch."

Lorraine even gets into it from the front desk. "Tell Stanford what he did to us."

"That bastard," Joe says. "We fired him because he was taking money from the workers, telling 'em they owed him for their passage to America. He'd go down to Mexico and recruit these guys, then pull that bullshit once they got here."

"But the other thing, Joe," Lorraine reminds him. "When he left. Tell him about when Santo left."

"Oh, yeah," Joe says, holding up his hands, fingers spread, as if to brace me for what I'm about to hear, and perhaps to calm himself down. "So we fire that bastard, and he steals two thousand dollars worth of seed from us to start up that shitty ranch of his. We couldn't prove it, he stuck 'em right in the ground, and he's been shaking seeds and cuttings from the same damn crop ever since. Never bought a bag of seed in his life. And for what? He over-plants and then doesn't pick any of it anyway. Except for more seed, maybe. I don't know what that fucking guy's up to over there."

Joe finally pours himself a cup of coffee.

Lorraine gets the last shot in at Santo. "Nice guy, short word," she says.

I don't know what she means, exactly. An old phrase that failed to cross generations, perhaps. I would ask, but the intention is clear, and I have said enough this morning.

"Is this fresh?" creeks the lady, still creeping through the delphinium.

"Yes," says Lorraine, imploring. "Everything is fresh. We grow everything at the ranch."

Joe nods with a mouthful of coffee. He swallows it and exhales loudly, as if to say that's right, that's what we do.


Joe heads back to the ranch earlier than usual with Lorraine and Manuel. The fields are scheduled for spraying by helicopter, and Joe wants to be there when the crew arrives.

"These farm service guys think they can push my son around, he's so quiet. Aldo's the best grower in the family history, but he wouldn't tell you."

I'm supposed to keep an eye on things, handle the last few stragglers, make sure they have market badge numbers before making a sale, and close up when Dodge returns. Dodge should have been back an hour ago.

"Don't say a word," Joe told me. "Let me surprise him with how goddamned angry I am. Let it build."

But he still gives us money for breakfast.

Dodge arrives later and looks even more panicked when he sees that Joe has already left. "Shit," he says. "Went to meet the helicopter, huh?"

"Yeah."

"Shit."

He ponders the ass-chewing he'll receive later, then looks around the stall to see if there's anything he can jump on me about with regard to cleaning up. Nothing.

"You ready for Gino?" he asks.

Damn. No. I'm not ready. Joe always takes care of him, so I forgot. Dodge is pleased, though. He got me on something, as trite as it may be. He's not the only one to screw up this morning, and he needed to know that. Dodge pulls a wagon and begins sifting through the leftover product, pulling any bunch which appears to have been dropped on the floor, accidentally snapped or stripped of so many buds. Then he retrieves a couple of buckets left in the refrigerator at the north end of the warehouse, buckets left over from last week's market. If it wasn't for Gino, Joe likes to say, we wouldn't need refrigerator space.

Gino is a market legend, late-arriving to scoop up the crap nobody wants for twenty bucks per transaction, leaving himself with a hatchback coup full of unloved flowers for the price of a single Mother's Day arrangement in some boutiques. He runs a stand on the wharf in the middle of tourist traffic, specializing in flashy bouquets which die practically right before your eyes, created from what his designers can salvage from the landfill he brings them. He's never had any complaints, because by the time anyone realizes they've been had, the self-aware sucker is on a plane back to Cincinnati or a bus bound for the wine country, the next stop on the itinerary. He also makes a fortune, which he tries to disguise with a cheap raincoat, moth-eaten sweater, and badly-tailored pants—the same outfit every time, regardless of the weather.

Gino bobs towards us like a crow on a picnic area scavenger hunt. "Where's Joe and Lorraine?" he rasps.

"Ranch business," I tell him. "Had to leave early."

"Oh..." He is clearly afraid of not getting his usual deal.

"But don't worry, Gino," I assure him. "We'll take care of you."

He is not at ease, however, until I accept the twenty he gives me without a dirty look. Then he beams and begins to circle the stall, pointing at everything he wants for his twenty bucks. It's all part of the routine.

"Sure, Gino," says Dodge. "Where you parked?"

He tells us and bobs away. Dodge continues to pile the discards on the wagon.

"Joe left us money for breakfast," I tell him.

"All right, then. Gimme a hand with Gino's shit, then we can close up and get the fuck outta here after breakfast."

Gino's car has flowers sticking out of the windows it's so full. Nothing is wrapped, just piled in by the armload. Dodge and I make our contribution and head to the Flower Market Café by the entrance to the parking lot. The sun now up, exhaustion is setting in, and everyone can see how terrible each other looks after so much time in the dark. Similar, I recall, to when the lights were turned on in the gym at the conclusion of a high school dance.

Most of the customers in the café are the business owners of the market. Few of the hired help frequents it, this morning being no exception, except a couple guys at the counter drinking coffee. It's too expensive for most cart-pushers, but we've got Joe for a boss, the only grower offering a per diem. We grab a booth. Dodge turns sideways and straightens his legs across the seat, feet into the aisle.

"I don't know why Joe doesn't just let me drive my van up here so I wouldn't have to borrow fucking Phil's car every time. I know it looks like shit, but it ain't like I'm gonna park it right next to the stall."

"Maybe that's not the problem," I decide to test our wobbly bond. "Maybe Joe doesn't want you to shuttle your kids around."

"Oh, no?" says Dodge, surprised but still interested.

"No. Because that's not going to get you anywhere with them. Nobody gets respect by kissing ass."

If I hadn't made such a valid point, he'd punch me, and he tells me so. Things quiet down, we order, and Dodge goes outside to smoke a cigarette—in deference to the posted signs, he claims, but really just a good excuse to get away and consider the issue. I can see him through the window, out on the sidewalk. He could probably pay for breakfast if he started to ask for spare change from the passing neckties on their way to work. He sees our breakfast arrive and stamps out his smoke. We start in without saying a word to each other for a while.

"I don't know how much you've heard about me," says Dodge between mouthfuls of scrambled eggs. "But I'd like to know."

"The basics," I answer. "Joe doesn't want to embarrass you."

"What's 'the basics?'"

"Oh, you know. Nothing you haven't told me yourself. Nothing we don't hear everyday from a million others. You had a problem, kept getting wasted, it cost you your family. Hell, if you were a has-been actor you could use it to jump start your career, make the rounds, get your mug on television. Doesn't quite play as well for the non-famous, though, does it?"

"So Joe didn't tell you about me dropping out of high school?" Dodge asks.

"No," I answer.

"Several high schools?"

"No."

"Private ones, even. Is Crystal Springs private?"

"Yes."

"I thought so. Looked like it. An old house. Classrooms had fireplaces."

"I know. I went to a dance there once."

Damn. I really wish I hadn't told him that. Dodge smirks at me.

"And he didn't tell you about my jail time?" he continues.

"No."

"The trafficking charges?"

"No."

"Busted me right at the airport."

"Really?"

"Mmm-hmm. And what about the time I tried to kill my father, did he tell you about that?"

"No," I say, the tone similar to a job interview. "He hasn't said a thing about that."

"With my bare hands, lucky for him. Gave Roman a chance to stop me, step in between us, which was great because I got a few shots in on Roman, too. Franky was an old fart by then, but I didn't care. I had good reason."

"Really?"

"Sure did."

Dodge stabs his breakfast with his fork. I wait. He eats. No more information is divulged.

Good reason, he said. Good reason to kill someone. I would like to know what he meant by that. Maybe my past was more justified than I realized. Perhaps certain key events were motivated by something perfectly reasonable. I wasn't dealing with anyone as vile as Franky Demos, of course, and I didn't kill anyone, not by myself, not directly. But still...

"Like I said, Joe didn't tell me much."

"Well, he's a good man," says Dodge. "I'd be pissed and kinda humiliated if you knew any of that. Especially the high school dropout part."

He smiles, throws back the last sip of coffee, then bangs his mug down on the table. Breakfast over.

There's not much left in the stall, a few buckets of bella donna, so we cart them into the fridge for Gino on Friday, and leave with a truck full of empty buckets and daisy boxes.

As with most collections of warehouses and loading docks, the market is on the outskirts of the city to prevent any big rigs from having to maneuver through downtown traffic. Upon leaving, then, we are immediately idling in a line of cars waiting to get on the freeway. Two times the light changes, green arrow to solid red, by the time we roll to the front of the left turn lane and wait through one more red. A front row seat, watching the cars exit the freeway, passing in front of us en route downtown.

Through the windows of cars newly-leased, men full of hair gel and exasperation; coffee in one hand, phone in the other. No time to steer, just keep an eye on the wheel, give it a nudge every so often. My former contemporaries. I may know some of them, undoubtedly hunted or was hunted by others—indirectly, of course. Never face to face. Through channels cellular, digital, electric. By the time it ever reached a handshake somebody had won, someone had lost, but neither forgot those early lessons concerning a firm handshake. You could damn near hear the bones cracking. The loser just trying to inflict some last-ditch pain, the winner beating his chest, each imitating each other like a couple of apes.

The women through the windows slightly tinted: all lips, puffy and painted, a splash of color amongst the pale foundations and dark glasses. Like the men, coffee, phone, and exasperation all in place. Mousse, not gel. One of three hairstyles, each option designed for the "woman on the go." Each style currently perpetuated by some lovable sitcom actress who plays a career-minded single girl. Each style worn with clothes to match. "Practical, yet sexy." Unique. They were told that, too, no doubt. "It's you." Another unique individual drives by, and another, and another. Unique, unique, unique. All unique. Maybe on the inside. Maybe if you got to know them. But who's got time?

Green light. I accelerate out of the left turn and pick up speed as we climb onto the freeway. Dodge is slumped down, cap over his eyes, asleep already. All traffic is headed in the other direction, towards the city, where the ocean side and the bay side of the peninsula come to a head. Our side of the median is lightly-traveled. I check the side mirror to see if it's okay to switch lanes. The city skyline vibrates in the mirror. Financial district skyscrapers tremble, all of them quiver in the morning sun. At the bottom of the reflection: "objects may be closer than they appear." The further away we get, the more objects appear. The skyline shrinks, the Bay Bridge crosses into the mirror, more and more of the white-capped water underneath the bridge seeps into frame, the port, the cargo ships, and then houses, clinging to the hills outside the city. The hills finally obstruct the city, and it's all houses and other freeways. Front, back, side.

A few connector ramps, slight grades up and down, billboards and more houses, the Highway One interchange, and then the final hill before the ocean. Up and over, suddenly at the edge of the continent. The water green, blue, bluest. From shallow to deep. Jagged coastline, rocks jutting up from the breakers just off the shore, like rocky fins connected to some tremendous large body just out of sight beneath the surface. Such sights must be taken in while trying to disregard the random remnants of civilization still vying for attention along the highway: aging cement office buildings and storefronts, some looking like they could be funky and hip, others just worn out.

A steep climb, above and away from the cheap-leases-by-the-sea, up and over a rugged cluster of hilltops and down towards the next stretch of civilization where the traces of it grow even more sparse, and consequently more expensive-looking. One notch down the convenience scale, one notch up on rustic charm. Restaurants and Bed & Breakfasts called either the "Pelican" something or the "Ocean" so-and-so, the "Beach" the "Shore" the "Anchor." An occasional wharf points out to sea. Horse ranches appear amongst the modern housing developments built with an old-fashioned facade in mind. Then there are the farms, some of Mirabelli's friends and competitors, interspersed further apart than they used to be thanks to either selling out or cashing in on the land (depending on whose version you're listening to).

At the south end of Half Moon Bay, a decision. Turn left at Highway 92 and wind your way fifteen minutes through the hills and into the mid-peninsula, the northern gateway to Silicon Valley, or...continue south, straight out of town and into the lonesome allure held by land undeveloped, or land at least closer to the way it looked hundreds of years ago. I consider this the official beginning of my drive home.

Drive home.

The two words have never sounded better. I love the drive. I love my home. I could never say the same for Interstate 580 or 680 and a house that was more of a staging area than a home.

The land, the land...such an overused mantra by now, approaching cliché, failing to resonate in the information age...the land is often breathtaking. A novelty to so many on the other side, the destination of a weekend pilgrimage, I now see it as I would a favorite movie: over and over again, but noticing something new every time.

The hills, for instance. They may appear as amber green still life imitations of the waves rolling towards them. But the hills, too, are animate. This morning, as gray sky is giving way to blue, the dark hillsides are revealing their trees, a few at a time, from the top branches down. A growing sea of green, only the dead ones sticking out, catching your eye. The sick ones, burned ones, only those trees stand out. The rest simply contribute to the spectacle. The rest are just doing their job. Eventually some topple, and I see the aftermath within hours of it happening.

I see lacerations of erosion cracking across the hills, getting wider, deeper, as though blood could begin to flow from them any minute now. A foundation so solid beneath our feet, still capable of buckling. Every farm perched on the edge of a cliff is scarred with areas where the ground seems to have simply dropped into the sea, where even the earth finally said "I can't take it anymore."

Cows, the throw pillows of any rural area, I see them in action now. They no longer appear stuffed and placed there like props to dress up the landscape. They sprint, heads nodding, udders swinging. They chomp on meadows so steep you'd swear their legs must be shorter on one side. They can even jump fences. Maybe one of them jumping over the moon isn't so far-fetched.

Red-tailed hawks stake a claim every quarter mile or so. Before, when the coast struck me as a painting on a porcelain urn, I may have noticed a hawk every five miles, if I noticed them at all. They stand squinting into the windswept fields, perched atop telephone poles, suspension cables, weathered fence posts, feathers tousling so slightly from the ocean breeze. The raptors stare into the landscape, bore into the land with their sharp eyes. They see the tall grass as scurrying with life. Bottom feeders of the food chain scamper across open ground for the sake of a crumb, wondering if the shadow will come. Wondering if today's the day. The shadow does come, spreads its chilly canopy. Wider, darker, until its prey cannot escape the deep end.

The hawk has to flap its wings a bit harder, a fresh kill dangling from its talons. Over the highway, over the truck. Hell of a way to make a living. I give a honk as it flies above our path.

"What's going on?" Dodge asks, stirring from his sleep, clutching his back.

"Oh, sorry," I tell him, thinking of an excuse. "Hitchhiker had a sign back there: 'Honk If You're Happy.'"

Dodge snorts. "Probably gave you the finger then, once you didn't pick him up."

"Yeah."

"Hippie motherfuckers," Dodge grumbles. "Peace and Love, but We Hate Society. So which is it, assholes?" He slouches back down, cap lowered.

The land is mine again, to admire in peace and solitude. No amateur photographers by the roadside this early in the morning. No double-decker tour buses with a microphoned driver telling everyone that the ocean is on their right. It's hard not to feel possessive over something so gorgeous. The feminine curve of the hills, impossible not to follow every contour despite the road ahead. Waves of distraction. There's work to be done, I know, I know, but the autumn colors look so good on her.

A truck approaches from the opposite direction, the opposing lane. A brown truck. Walter, the UPS driver. We pass each other, each of us lifting our hand off the steering wheel in a gesture of rural courtesy. Nonchalant. Every third vehicle may be someone you know, the highway so lightly traveled around here. You know me, I know you. No big deal. That's the way it's done. But I am so glad to know the UPS driver. I am so glad to know who's passing me. I only hope my wave came across as unconcerned as Walter's.

The construction site which intimidated Joe so thoroughly last night seems harmless in the daylight. The thinning line of eucalyptus trees actually allows for a less obstructed view of the mountainous horizon to the east. To the west is all that the resort guests will see someday—the ever-cresting ocean still waiting for an answer from the shore. What those future guests will see makes the project itself seem so small, so insignificant. An ocean view increases the value while pitying any attempts to match its splendor. Irony or justice? All we can do is watch. A plush carpet, hardwood floors, dirt, it doesn't matter what you stand on. The eyes are all that matter. There must be a business formula which can account for this law. Maybe I learned it in college and have since forgotten.

I pass a car abandoned on the right side of the road with its driver's side window bashed in.

"Stop," Dodge shouts.

"Jesus," I shiver. "I thought you went back to sleep."

"So what. Stop!"

I pull over as Dodge rolls down his window and sticks his head out to look back at the car. "That must be that fucker's ride," he says. "The dude who jumped me."

"It's in the right spot," I agree.

"Back up."

I put the truck in reverse and roll back towards the front of the car. Dodge gets out before I've even come to a complete stop and jogs towards it. I set the brake and join him by the car, which is parked by the entrance to a trail that divides an artichoke field from some uncultivated grasslands to its north. It's a Toyota Tercel, maybe ten years old with enough miles to dull the green paint job. The rear window and bumper are plastered with political sound byte stickers...

"Kill Your Television"

"Practice Random Acts of Kindness"

"Love Your Mother" (accompanied by a picture of the earth)

"Visualize Peace"

"Eracism"

And a picture of a cow with a red slash through it, an indictment of red meat. I figure then that the guy was acting out some drugs n' nature fantasy yesterday afternoon, and something went very wrong. The stuff was too strong, he took too much of it, and the fields were no consolation after all.

"You think the artichokes started talking to him?" I ask Dodge.

"I don't know," he says, as though I was serious. "I never took anything that strong." He starts to look the car over like an interested buyer. "Just the basics for me…booze, speed, pot."

I fear I may have touched a nerve. "Look, I didn't mean anything…"

"Hmm?" he didn't hear my apology. He's too busy staring at the bashed-in window.

"Nothing. I just didn't want you to think I considered you the resident expert on chemical reactions. I was just making fun of the guy."

He's still not listening to me. "Look at this," he says, opening the door and waving me over. The seats are slashed open. Foam stuffing is everywhere. The carpet on the floor is ripped up. "Even the rocker panels," Dodge says, pointing along the base of the door frame. The plastic panels have been pulled out and left on the ground. The outer and inner walls of the metal frame are scratched up, as if they've been scraped. Not just around the top, where the panels were popped off, but deep within the empty space between the outer shell of the body and the inner.

"I used to vandalize cars when I was a kid," he says, "But I sure as hell never went to the trouble of unscrewing the rocker panels." He stands up straight and takes out a cigarette.

"So what's your point," I ask him.

"This car ain't been vandalized," he says as he lights up. "It's been searched."

"For what, more drugs?"

"You got it, Stanford boy."

"By the sheriff?"

"Nah," he says, exhaling a stream of smoke. "They'd impound it first, do a more thorough job. This is pretty rushed. But whoever did it really wanted their drugs back. And whoever did it is no doubt pissed as hell at our little psycho Jesus impersonator."

I remember the man's appearance, the wiry build draped with preppy clothing. "You really think he was running drugs?"

"Let's call it an educated guess," Dodge grins.

"Interesting," I nod, not quite buying it.

"Could be," Dodge says, staring out at the fields, at the untamed stretch beside it. "Could be." He continues to look at the horizon for a while, with a purpose it seems, until with a final drag on his cigarette, he suggests we get back to the ranch.

The last couple miles to the ranch pass in silence, Dodge still deep in thought. The route veers inland as Point Año Nuevo starts to extend itself out to sea, and the ocean disappears from view. Past the Christmas tree farm, past my mailbox, the Mirabelli pumpkins start to wink through the cypress trees by the side of the road. The row of houses suddenly appears, and then the front gate.

I slow down onto the right shoulder and turn into the yard. Off to the side, at the edge of the yard where it gives way to the fields, Joe is in discussion with Roman. They are in their own space for a reason. Joe is bound to lose his temper during any conversation with Roman.

Easing closer, avoiding pot holes, we can see the explosion is yet again inevitable. Joe's gestures are choppier than usual, perhaps relating to a subconscious violent fantasy regarding his enemy. Roman is dressed in full park ranger regalia. He wears his uniform to its full capacity, reveling in its authority.

"Oh, great," Dodge sighs. "Let me guess, a duck got caught in the helicopter blades?"

I wonder if he's ever managed to catch sight of his brother without convulsing in some way. This time, I play along.

"Well, Dodge, they are his ducks."

I play along because I can relate to Dodge's disdain for Roman when it comes to the head ranger's own brand of environmentalism.

He likes nature well enough. His coyote call could fake out a whole den of pups listening for their mother. But he only seems to bother with nature if a particular issue will serve him and piss somebody off. Namely Joe, who considers himself blessed but for the fact he runs a farm next to a state reserve operated by a despotic chameleon. Ranger Roman refers to the birds as his birds. The trees are his trees. Almost touching if not for the house he built up in Mendocino County. He built it on some shoreline property previously classified as "untouchable" by the coastal commission of that area. Classified as such until Roman started pulling some strings. Apparently the surfing is fantastic.

I park in the center of the barns, the "town square" of the ranch. The combatants need their space. We get out and walk towards the office.

"I hope Joe remembers the house up in Mendocino," Dodge says. "May come in handy if he's trailing on points."

We reach the metal shed and find Veronica behind the desk answering the phone. She is Javier's daughter, born soon after her father became foreman, raised on the ranch ever since. She attends the University of California down in Santa Cruz. A thick textbook is open on the desk in front of her. Two more are stacked to the side. All of them familiar. The same business administration texts I used, slightly newer editions. Marketing, Management, Finance. None of it all that helpful once you start your job. They just want to know how badly you want it.

"Read any good books lately?" Dodge teases her. He and I lean on each side of the doorway.

"I will once I graduate this spring," says Veronica.

"So what's up with the home boys over there?" he asks her.

She sighs. "What else? If it's spray day, Roman's gonna be here. When I used to work as a docent over there and give tours, he used to pass around a petition to all the tourists and the other docents and have them sign it whenever the helicopters were out. All it said was something like, sign here to stop poisoning our environment."

"Sounds like something he read off a bumper sticker," I say, which gets a snicker out of Dodge.

Veronica looks over at me, an action I always appreciate. Her eyes are so open, as though she is always doing an impersonation of a deer. Not in the headlights, mind you. Not that overused expression. She is a deer striding through the woods with confidence. Receptive to all sights and sounds. Composed. Not a predator in sight.

"How's it going, Stanford?" she says, a little too sweet. She can be a hard read, disguised as she is by her lips. Tell a child to draw a pair of lips, and you'll end up with a rendering of Veronica's. Whether she's talking or listening, they're hard not to stare at. She may look like she's in a constant pout, but she's right inside your head, one step ahead of you more than likely.

"Fine," I answer. "And no. I am not going to answer phones for you. It's nap time, you know that."

"You're still young," she chides me.

"Age doesn't matter for these kinds of hours," I say.

"Whatever," Veronica says. "Worth a shot."

She'll graduate someday. She'll start imitating something else instead of a deer. A lioness, or a hawk. A hair-moussed hysteric. She's so much like I was in college. So much like Janet. It's understandable, then, how she thinks I'm insane for abandoning everything for which she is striving. She doesn't even ask me why anymore, why I came to the place she wants to leave so badly. Her dreams are still abstractions. Nothing concrete can stop them.

At least she seems to have a genuine interest in what she's studying. I went to college because that's what you were supposed to do after high school. The 13th grade. I programmed my career objectives based on money and how I would sound at a party in response to the question "what do you do for a living?"

But Veronica, she really seems to enjoy the work. I only hope she doesn't forget where she came from. Then again, I've learned lately just how difficult it is to forget such things.

"Hey, Stanford," she says. "I was wondering. Have you had like even one date since you've been out here?"

Dodge becomes interested. The ends of his mustache are turned up, a close-mouthed smile. It wasn't my intention to be coy. I just wanted the question to go away.

"No," I admit.

They both offer silent, teasing condolences.

"I'm still getting over someone," I say.

"What, were you married?" she asks.

"Yes," I tell her, which seems to take her somewhat by surprise.

Dodge, on the other hand, cries "Ha! And you're bummed it's over? I partied for a week straight when we pulled the plug. And my ex, hell, she may have had a fuckin' parade."

"We were a different situation, I guess."

I could tell them I'm still married. But this is hardly the time. I don't have any lies prepared in answer to the questions they'd have. And to be quite honest, I'd hate for Veronica to know. She'd think less of me, and think me unavailable all at the same time.

"Any kids?" she wants to know.

"Have you heard me talk about kids?" I ask her. "Ever seen me with any kids?"

"No," she says.

"So do I strike you as someone who'd abandon their kids?" I say, and realize that I'm snapping at her. I apologize. She apologizes for prying. I tell her she wasn't. I tell her and Dodge that I don't think the world owes me anything, but a "thank you" for not inflicting kids upon it from my marriage may be in order.

And as I'm telling them this, I see that Dodge has gotten very quiet. Jesus, and here I am apologizing to Veronica.

Mercifully, Joe walks over muttering to himself while Roman gets into his vehicle and curls around by the office, tipping his ranger hat to us through his open window.

"Dude," he calls out to me. "You and me over a couple of beers. Real soon."

I smile strenuously and almost wave. He speeds up and leaves us in a cloud of dust.

"If he wasn't so thoughtless I'd say he did that on purpose," Joe says, waving his cap in front of his face.

The helicopter suddenly rises from behind the tree line on the opposite side of the field, jumping above the top branches as if to say "boo!" It screams towards us and accelerates over the trees behind us. The noise quickly evaporates, leaving us all in silence, but none as conspicuous to me as the quiet coming from Dodge.

Joe tells us to go home and get some sleep. As we head to our vehicles I apologize to Dodge.

"For what?" he asks.

"That crack about abandoning kids. I can't believe I said it."

He shrugs, but also doesn't acknowledge my apology. "I gotta cut the grass up at the golf club in Half Moon Bay," he says. "Make a few bucks on the side. Me and the greens keeper go way back. Why don't you meet me there this evening, we'll have some grub."

"Don't you need a nap?" I ask him.

"Took one on the way home, remember?" He gets into his van and rolls down the window. "Be there before sundown," he tells me. "And wear tennis shoes."

Then he fires up his engine, which is louder than the helicopter's.

"Must be a pricey restaurant," I shout. "Should I bring some extra cash?"

"Ain't talkin' bout the food," he grins. "We got somethin' to do first, you and me."

Sounds like a challenge, but it's not as if I have any other plans. I nod and get into my truck as he peels out in a stream of dust and gravel. By the time I reach the highway and make my left, he has disappeared. The road is empty ahead of me.

Santo's ranch is void of activity. The old man, Santo's brother, he's not even there. Only his fire. The bonfire in the rusted oil drum continues to burn. Like the Olympic torch, it never seems to go out. I don't see the dog, either. But as I drive down the dark section of the road kept perpetually damp from the eucalyptus lining its sides, I hear him. His bark comes from the driver's side. I can see his ears bouncing in my side mirror. He barks stride for stride. At the edge of the eucalyptus tunnel, he stops as usual. I continue into the clear for a few moments and decide to stop, too.

I get out of the truck and stare at him. He stares back. He can't stand the silence, so he barks at me. I make a move towards him. A quick move, like a running back giving a head fake. He jerks backwards a few paces, recovers, and resents being made a fool of. Again with the barking.

A noise from the ranch and the dog runs back towards it. Voices. I walk a few paces likewise and look through the trees. A large group of the ranch hands are coming out to play soccer in a large patch of fallow ground which stretches beyond the oil drum, running below and parallel to the road. I count them as they fan out and begin to kick the ball around...almost two dozen. Enough to field two complete teams, and certainly far more than necessary to work that worn out ranch. The dog joins them and wants the ball. He barks and runs after it as the ball rolls from one man to another. And another and another. All those men, and all those dead flowers. It doesn't add up, but then neither does the fact that it's noon and I still have yet to sleep. I walk back to the idling truck and continue on to bed.

I reach the golf club with an hour of daylight remaining. Unsure how to negotiate the "Members Only" sign posted by the parking lot, I park my truck behind one of the overpriced motels in Half Moon Bay, which are usually referred to as "lodges," and then walk to the clubhouse. I played the course a few times before, and the inviting member had always provided me with a guest permit. I had always dressed appropriately. Khakis, spikes, collared shirt. I had my own clubs with poofy knitted club head covers. The grounds crew and caddies who were always in the background are now my hosts. Now I'm their guest. Dressed in jeans and a sweatshirt, I try to be inconspicuous as cliques of aging duffers come clacking in their spikes off the grass and onto the pavement, on their way to the clubhouse for a post-game gimlet or a rusty nail—one of those drinks on the brink of extinction. Their conversations so familiar. I could join in and dazzle them, give them some sound answers to the questions they have about retirement portfolios. But I'm not dressed appropriately for them to listen to me.

"Stanford," someone says. Temporary panic at being recognized. But nobody here would call me "Stanford."

Dodge is standing at the edge of the grass, by the entrance to the front nine. "Over here," he beckons, and disappears behind the hedge enclosing the first tee.

I cross through the opening and find Dodge with two other guys who look like they just crawled out from inside the hedge. Eyes red-rimmed, lips cracked, skin mapped out with blue and red capillaries—either from sun damage or alcohol. They could be anywhere from age thirty-five to sixty-five. Heavy around the middle.

"This here's Golf Ball Eddie and Champ," says Dodge, introducing them with a wave of his hand, an afterthought. "They're caddies. I already told 'em about you."

They nod. Whatever he told them, it didn't have much effect.

"Ever play speed golf, Stanford?" Dodge asks me.

"I've played golf."

"That's not what I asked."

"No. I haven't played speed golf."

Dodge smiles. Open-mouthed, even. He allows his missing teeth to show.

"First one in the hole wins," he says. "One point per hole. Tee off at the same time each hole."

He nods towards a line of loner golf bags, unclaimed equipment kept in the back of the pro shop, available to anyone without sticks of their own, or to any senile member who forgot theirs.

"Choose your weapons," Dodge says.

I hoist one of the bags over my shoulder. Golf Ball Eddie and Champ wheeze into a laugh.

"Speed golf," Dodge reminds me. "I recommend a driver, a five-iron, and a putter."

I take the prescribed clubs out of the bag. My playmates all go for a single club, each one grabbing a three-iron.

"You're a rookie," Dodge explains. "Rookies can't hack just one."

I toss the driver and the putter aside. "This one can."

"Suit yourself," Dodge says, not as impressed as I had hoped.

We all tee up in a row. Dodge turns to me before we start.

"First one in the hole. Just the way it should be, huh?"

Then he swings and lines his ball down the fairway.

"You asshole," Champ shouts. "You forgot to say 'go.'"

"Go," Dodge yells back at us while he sprints towards his ball.

"I'm aimin' for his head," says Golf Ball Eddie, swinging hard and slicing it into the trees. I hear him yell "fuck" as I start my back swing and focus on the ball.

"Played right into his hands, Eddie," says Champ, whose ball takes off on a line just ahead of mine.

As always, I slice the son of a bitch off the fairway into the rough. Some things never change. Chasing after my ball, however, I realize that I'm already an odds-on favorite to win this thing. Golf Ball and Champ don't run very well. Golf Ball sort of gallops thanks to a limp, and Champ can only trot as fast as the rhythm of his bouncing belly will let him.

Dodge, on the other hand, is already on his second shot. He smacks the ball another fifty yards on the ground and darts after it like a jack rabbit. This is definitely between me and him.

He's all over the place with his shots, but he's so damn fast. I check his position before setting up my approach to the green. He's putting. Back and forth across the hole, unable to get it in, his putts at least getting shorter each attempt. I nail a gorgeous shot onto the green, a few yards from the hole. But it's too late. Dodge finally sinks it.

"Pick it up, Stanford Boy," he says, lobbing my ball at me as I reach the hole. "Ain't no points for second place."

We wait for the also-rans to stagger ahead and join us.

"Good lookin' shot, though," Dodge tells me. "Too bad we're not playin' with your old cronies."

I know he's taunting me. I know damn well. I also know it shouldn't matter. But I was raised an American male. Fear of losing at anything has shaped my existence from the first kickball game at recess. So I'll be damned if I'm gonna get beat at something called "speed golf."

"Tee it up, boys," Dodge says as we walk over to the second hole. Golf Ball Eddie and Champ just may die on the front nine. Cardiac arrest, most likely. But Dodge has a saunter to his walk, a mosey. His ass is up between his shoulders.

"Ready?" he coos, and I slug one down the fairway before he can jump us again. I hear Dodge laughing. A golf ball whistles past my ear and I hear Champ yelling "Shit I missed him."

Competition was the last thing I came to the coast for. I figured there would be no fate to tempt. Then Dodge lures me out on the course. Well, hell. You asked for it, Dodge.

We're on the back nine within a half hour. A single hole used to take that long during one of my old palm-greasing schmooze festivals disguised as a friendly round of golf. As I anticipated, Dodge's energy was short-lived. No stamina, no sense of pacing. He doesn't know how to play for the long haul.

I have a commanding lead by the twelfth hole. I've clinched victory. Realizing this, the other members of my foursome change their strategy. I begin chasing down my tee shot when I feel my legs go out from under me. It's Dodge, hook-sliding me from behind, cheered on by Golf Ball and Champ.

Dodge pounces on top of me, pinning a knee into my chest. "First one in the hole," he says. "That's all I ever said."

I see Golf Ball and Champ racing ahead for position. Each has gained a spring in their step. I wonder if I've been hustled, or if the prospect of cross-checking me excites them that much. I push Dodge off me, sending him sprawling onto his back. He's laughing too hard to get up. I sprint towards my ball. Golf Ball Eddie tries to cut me off. I lead into his sternum with a forearm and spin around him, reaching my ball a few paces later. Champ is up ahead, anticipating the location of my next shot. I aim for the other side of the fairway, forcing him to switch direction as the ball sails over his head. I run up behind him before he has a chance to stop and turn around. He hears me coming and looks back over his right shoulder in mid-stride. I pass on his left. He turns to grab me and loses his balance, falling over with a loud grunt and something about my mother.

I reach the ball and look around. Dodge is coming hard, twenty yards and closing, looking to take another crack at me. Golf Ball and Champ have had their chance. They're out of it. I launch the ball towards the green and run. Dodge alters his course to get parallel with me. We stay like that for a few paces, as though running a race, heading for a tie. I make the fist move, go on the offensive. A sharp turn, I lunge behind him and drag my club through his feet, tripping him up. He takes flight. Arms extended, legs outstretched, he digs out two long streaks of grass with the base of his hands as he lands in a headfirst slide.

"Replace your divots, motherfucker," I yell at him as I pass.

Flat on his stomach, he props up his forearm on his elbow and gives me the finger. But he's smiling. That mustache is up at the corners.

I increase my stride and start grunting like an animal. Two shots later I'm in the hole. That's four shots. Par for the hole. I made par with a five-iron, and three guys trying to tackle me. I raise the club over my head and howl. I could be caked in mud, wearing a loincloth. The survivor of an ancient tribal initiation. The rites of passage, all mine.

"Golf Ball and Champ weren't so sure," Dodge tells me over dinner at a tacqueria in Half Moon Bay. "I had to convince 'em to let you in. Pretty select group, y'know."

"They are a selection. That's for sure."

One of the local Spanish radio stations is being piped through the treble-dominated speakers of the tacqueria. The current song is a Mexican cover version of "Please Mr. Postman." It's a ranchera, with new lyrics. Apparently the translation of "Please Mr. Postman, check and see, if there's a letter in your bag for me" has too many syllables for the melody. I can't quite get the gist of the new version.

"I was really gettin' tired of beatin' the crap out of 'em every time," Dodge says, giving his tamale a rest. "See enough of those guys walkin' around, their type, that'll scare you straight. You wonder when it's gonna be you."

He looks at me for approval, it seems. I'm just nodding, eating my burrito.

"Or maybe," he continues. "Maybe you start to wonder how you got there. You're already there and you wonder how you can get out, go back."

I feel like I'm supposed to say something.

"Well," I say. "That's the real trick."

"What is?" Dodge asks.

"The real trick?"

"Yeah. What do you mean by that?"

It just sounded good. I don't know what the trick is. It just sounded right. I've heard the phrase so many times that it seems applicable to any situation. Even this one. "How to regain your self-respect," I tell him. "Just what we're talking about, right? You do that, and then others will respect you. At least that's what I've heard."

"Like my kids?" he asks.

"Yeah," I say, a wave of tension shooting up my back. Nobody's ever asked me for personal advice before. All previous requests were strictly business.

"But how do you do it?" he presses on. "How do you get it back?"

"Well, that's the real trick, then."

He lowers his eyebrows at me. "No wonder your marriage broke up," he says.

"Before I had kids," I remind him, trying to get myself off the hook.

"All I know is what I'm doin' ain't workin'," he practically shouts in frustration.

"What the hell are you talking about?" I ask, lowering my voice as a cue for him to do likewise. "You've been clean for damn close to a year."

Dodge sighs and scoops a forkful of rice and beans from his plate, one of the few times he's touched his food. "What's keepin' me sober ain't a big thrill to my kids," he says. "They don't seem to take much pride in a workin' man. Especially when they know I coulda been part of the Demos family fortune if not for my fuck-ups. Their Mom makes sure they know that."

"Ah, hell Dodge," I assure him. "They'll come around."

"I ain't got much time," he says. "They're teenagers. Bored teenagers. They'll have families of their own pretty soon..."

"Wait a second," I interrupt. "You said they're teenagers. Families of their own soon?"

"They ain't like the teenagers you probably hung out with in high school, Stanny. And their Mom, she takes what you'd call a relaxed approach to raisin' them. Christ, she'd probably dig the idea of a grandkid by age forty. Got nothin' else goin' for her."

"Maybe they'll learn from experience. From what you and your wife went through, getting married too young and all."

Dodge sighs again. He looks at his food but doesn't make a move on it. "They just think I was stupid, that it was my fault, and that they're smarter than that."

He pulls out his pack of cigarettes, remembers there's no smoking allowed, and says "shit" before continuing. "They need a hero," he tells me. "Not some junkie markin' the days since his last fix. Just once they gotta be able to say 'that's my Dad' without them bein' humiliated by the fact. Then maybe they'd listen to me."

"Maybe," I say. "But trying to get a couple teenagers to listen to you is a pretty tall order for anyone."

And as if to illustrate my point, he acts like he didn't even hear me. He stares at an airbrushed mural painted on the wall of the tacqueria—palm trees, a deserted beach at sunset—wishing himself into the picture, away from here.

"I wish I could be more help," I say. He turns away from the mural and into the present once more, as though he appreciates my admission. "People make millions selling bullshit answers to other people," I tell him. "And I don't want to do that. How about I just spring for dinner instead?"

"It's a tacqueria. We already paid at the counter," he says.

"I already paid at the counter," I remind him. "And now you don't have to pay me back."

"Oh yeah," he grins. "Thanks."

I hurry through my last few bites so we can get outside and he can have his cigarette. He lights it up as soon as our feet touch the pavement.

"I didn't mean to get all heavy on you in there, Stanford boy," he says.

"No problem," I assure him.

"Sure it ain't," he chuckles into an exhale. "The second I started talkin' personal stuff you looked like you were gonna shit twice then die."

I can't help but smile along with him. "There's a reason Roman wants to talk finance with me and not marital problems."

"Gee," Dodge makes his eyes cynically wide. "You don't think he and Marcie are happy?"

And now we're really enjoying ourselves. We reach our vehicles with several drags left in his cigarette, so he pops the back of my truck open and sits down to enjoy them. "Don't think nothin' of it, though, Stanford boy," he says as we settle down. "I may just have a plan to get my teenage rug rats' attention after all."

"Oh great. Then what was the purpose of making me play shrink over tacos in there?"

"Just wanted to see if you had a better idea."

"A better idea than what?"

"Well," he stalls, "I been thinkin' a lot about that preppy junk runner who slugged me."

"And you're gonna kill him."

"Very funny, Joe College. Nope..." he tilts his head back and exhales a long, slow stream of smoke. "I'm gonna be the hero this time. Not the bad guy."

Rather than bothering to ask him how, I just keep looking at him expectantly.

"If I can find his source," he continues. "I can break it up and make a name for myself. Win back my kids and show the world a thing or two about me."

"Assuming there really was a shipment of drugs in that car," I remind him.

"Oh there was," he says. "And I got plenty of friends around here who can lead me right to the sweet spot."

"The stuff could have come from anywhere. He may have driven across country."

Dodge shakes his head at my contribution. "No need. There's plenty of pots on the stove out here. And I've already got a hunch about this batch."

He's authoritative enough on the subject to intrigue me, and my expression must be telling him so.

"Santo Farms," he announces. "Nothin' in the fields and a market full of imported flowers. The more I think about it, the more I'm sure it ain't no coincidence the dude's car was parked within pissin' distance of that old dump."

I try to think of another rational counterpoint, but instead remember the Santo Farms intramural soccer tournament earlier this evening. So many men on so sparse a ranch. And once I tell Dodge about all those men with nothing to do but play soccer, he's even more hooked.

"See?" he jumps up off the back of my truck. "You're open to the possibility. Admit it."

"Hey," I wave him off with both hands. "This is your mission, not mine."

"But what a team. The brains and the experience."

"Which one am I?" I kid.

"Come on, frat boy," he gets a little angry. "You ain't foolin' me. I know when someone else can see the bottom of the barrel just as clear as I can. You could use a little pick-me-up."

As preposterous as his idea may be, I certainly can't deny his point about my life. But I already know about what can happen when you try to make a splash instead of just lowering yourself into the pool and doing the necessary laps. I'm just getting used to the routine, to the rhythm, and I wonder if Dodge is the type who ever will. The story behind his name becomes so clear to me—ditching, avoiding, dodging.

"How long have you had the name Dodge?" I ask him.

His cheeks sink into his face a bit. "Why?"

"Just curious."

He takes a quick deep breath, agitated. "I don't know," he says. "My mother never got a chance to name me, and I sure as hell wasn't gonna keep no name given to me by Gretchen and Franky. It's their fault she's gone, for chrissakes. So it's just been Dodge for a long time now."

Having been put in my place, and Dodge now forced to reapply the bandages over his past, we stand silently watching the traffic pass by on Highway One. It's lightly traveled, but still manages to overwhelm the sound of the ocean. Even when the road is empty for a while, the white noise humming from the neon sign above us keeps the din up to our ear. And although changing the subject a few moments ago blew up in my face, it's my only option now in the aftermath. I certainly can't ask him what he meant by saying Gretchen and Franky are responsible for his mother's disappearance. Not now.

"So this is pretty important to you," I say.

"It's all I've got," he says, and finishes his cigarette.

On the way home I barely manage to keep up with Dodge, his foot heavy on the gas. As we put more miles between ourselves and the lighted signs, the stars seem to breed, multiplying by the thousands and no longer twinkling. They simply shine.

Dodge slows down when he passes the abandoned car, giving it another once-over on the fly, as though it's a woman walking down the street whom he may lean out the window and whistle at. The promise of a new relationship, the excitement of the unknown. Maybe this time the chase will be worthwhile.

# THURSDAY 9/25

A market-free morning. Morning in the traditional sense. Up with the sun, not the alarm clock. No blows to the head from a clock-radio alarm, those staccato screeches right between the eyes. I'm always forced to set it for alarm because no radio stations reach my room. No signals from over the hill.

Veronica is at school, so it's my day at the ranch. Answering phones, perhaps. Or a drive, delivering product or picking up supplies.

A good morning to drive the road to the highway with the windows down. Take in the smells. No prevailing waft of paved and piped civilization, its smoggy evidence hovering above it all. Drive by a eucalyptus, that's what you smell. Drive by the cows, you got it. You can even smell the sun, once you realize you can really smell the sun. You can smell it in the ground. The dusted heat in the afternoon. The chilled rays of morning. Of this morning.

An additional visual along the route: a bobcat scanning the meadow floor for breakfast. The fall tint on his coat, a sandier shade of auburn, he drops to his stomach as I pass, thinking he's hidden just below the grass. I stop and we have a stare down. Realizing there's so much separating us—a barbed wire fence, a car door, and ten yards—he relaxes. It's all in the eyes. He blinks. Tense before, at ease after. He gallops off on his own terms, bobbed tail waving good-bye.

A middle-aged sheriff's deputy talks to Joe in his office, taking up the extra chair. Older than the young deputies I've seen around here, he seems more like how an officer of the law should be cast. Destined to play the part. A Stay-Comb and Aqua Velva user who spends his free time coaching a Little League team, pushing the kids too hard and yelling at umpires until he's red in the face.

But his uniform is frayed. The Sheriff's Department patch on his jacket sleeve is illegible. Threads spring out from the various dark blue stripes sewn along his sides. The breast pocket is missing its button. It's as though he failed the law enforcement exam and bought a second-hand uniform at the Salvation Army out of frustration, dangerously wondering what could have been.

He and Joe are in mid-conversation. Joe's just been given some disheartening information, apparently. The Halloween sheriff fills the space with further explanation.

"Even if there was a chance to prosecute, it'd be a pain in the ass," he tells Joe, maybe even consoles him. "Cost, time, effort. Not worth it."

Joe runs his hands over his face, as if washing it. "Christ," he says. "Put some drugs in your system, you can do whatever the hell you want and not have to own up to it. Jesus."

"I know," says the sheriff. "I know."

"I just hope that son of a bitch doesn't come around here. If he knows what's good for him." Joe swipes his hands together. "For Dodge, too. Shit. I've worked too hard to get Dodge where he is, back up on his feet. That's all he needs now is a grudge, for chrissakes."

"Dodge just has to take his knocks, then. Forget about revenge," says the sheriff. "Be good for him. Can't lead a decent life if you think every little wrong deserves another one in return. Besides, that guy who attacked him ain't goin' anywhere. Didn't make parole on the other count."

The other count?

Joe finally acknowledges me.

"Stanford," he says, snapping himself out of his minor funk. "This is Bert Bodner, Deputy Sheriff. But you can call him Deputy Bert."

Bert chuckles politely as we shake hands.

"Bert just reminded me that he worked for us when he was in high school. Over the summer vacations," Joe says. "That musta been up at the greenhouses, eh Bert? Back when we were indoors?"

"Yep," says Bert. "Up on the hill off that road going out to the dump."

"Thank God we're outta that business," says Joe. "I'll never set foot in another frigging greenhouse. Worked out okay for you, though. Huh, Bert?"

Bert nods. Very modest.

Joe includes me again. "Bert's the county sheriff now. Runs the whole goddamn operation."

Bert's modesty turns fidgety. He scratches at the withered patch on his sleeve.

"Well, not exactly," he says. "I'm still a deputy. But since I'm from around here, the sheriff's office sorta consults with me about this part of the county. Lets me in on the strategy."

"Grow a few more white hairs," says Joe. "They'll vote you in."

Dodge arrives as they soak up the latest joke.

"And get a real uniform," Dodge says. "For chrissakes, Bert, who's dressin' you?

"Hello, Dodge," says Bert.

"Officer Bert," Dodge nods. "How the hell are ya?"

They smirk at each other. I have to know.

"So you guys know each other?" I ask.

"Used to meet quite a bit," Dodge says, picking up the jocular mood where it left off.

"No shift was complete without a call about Dodge up to some no good," says Bert. He doesn't seem quite as ready to joke about the past.

"We gonna start every sentence with 'remember when' or do you got some news for me, Bert?" Dodge asks.

"I've got good news and bad news," he tells him. "Which do you want first?"

"When have you ever had good news for me, Deputy?" Dodge grins. "Make some history and gimme that first."

Bert looks as though he might not tell him now, but then gives in. "We found a dealer's share of crystal methamphetamine strapped to the guy who slugged you."

Dodge looks as though he just heard one of his kids say they love him. "Really?"

Bert relaxes, seeing how the news brightens Dodge up. "That's right. So while we can't get him for trashing the houses and kicking your ass..."

Dodge laughs. "Wasn't responsible for his actions, was he?"

"That's what they'll say in court."

"Used that line myself a few times," Dodge says.

"At least we'll get the bastard on trafficking," Bert postures, now confident that the past is behind them.

But Dodge isn't thinking about the drug-dealing would-be Jesus. His mind is on that abandoned Tercel.

"Did you search his car?" Dodge asks.

"Once we impound it," Bert says. "Tomorrow, probably."

"Tomorrow?" Dodge double checks.

"We're backed up," Bert explains.

Dodge looks at me and would love to say I-told-you-so. Instead he turns back towards Joe and asks him if he needs him for anything.

"Aldo's out in field nine," Joe tells him. "Grab the open-air tractor and meet him there. He's got something for you to do."

Dodge salutes and asks Bert why he's never around much anymore.

"They keep the deputies on a pretty steady rotation out here," Bert says. "Keeps 'em from getting too close to the locals, from trying to work any angles. Easy to do in a small town."

"And how'd they figure that?" asks Dodge.

"I told them," Bert answers. "My recommendation."

"I just thought they used you as evidence," Dodge grins.

Bert simmers for a moment.

"I still live around here, Hidalgo," he says.

"Keep your uniform pressed if you're gonna make threats, Bert," says Dodge, and he winks at me and Joe before leaving.

Bert stares at the spot where Dodge was standing.

"Yeah, Joe," he says. "You sure have done a good job on him."

"Ah, you know Dodge," says Joe. But Bert doesn't respond. He hesitates and says he has to get back to headquarters, shivering himself back into a state of "official business." The reunion ends with some firm handshakes and some antsy pleased-to-meet-yous and good-to-see-you-agains.

I get orders to drive some boxes of daisies out to Tracy, a series of tract houses in the far reaches of the East Bay, teetering on the threshold of the Central Valley. One of our customers, a large grocery chain, owns an enormous central warehouse on its outskirts, on some windswept plains that have yet to be developed. Labor problems, the threat of a strike, all of it seems to be a semi-annual event amongst the truck drivers and the grocery heads. So none of the big rigs are heading our way today. It's up to me and the covered pickup truck. Joe figures it'll make a good impression on them, that they'll remember this gesture once their situation settles. I go ahead and let him think that. A company so big, the kind of corporation which takes on a life of its own, they'll remember? But that's Joe. The whole world is one big small town.

"Can you fuckin' believe that?" Dodge says.

He pins me against the hood of Joe's truck before I can get in. He smiles so uncontrollably he looks like a kid who just lost his front teeth naturally.

"Somebody searched that car," he beams. "Somebody wanted their drugs back."

"You were right," I tell him.

"I was right," he says, enjoying the way that sounds. "Godammit, I was right."

He lets go of me and basks in his correctness. At the risk of bursting his bubble I ask him "so what now?"

"Start makin' connections," he says, not the least bit fazed. "Start askin' why."

"Why Santo?"

"That's right. Nothin' on the ranch, a shitload in the market. Imported shitloads, no less. Let's ride that horse til it breaks down," he starts to pace. "I mean we got two options now. My first guess was they were smugglin', but now I figure they could be makin' it right there, if it's crystal meth like Bert said. Run some cookers up from Mexico, have some import group foot the bill. Brew up gallons in their own little lab. Wouldn't be the first time some chicken coop around here didn't have no chickens in it."

"I don't suppose going to the proper authorities ever crossed your mind," I ask him.

I already know the one-word answer ("No"). What I want is the information he'll use to justify it.

"They can shove Bert behind a desk pushin' papers," he tells me. "But they can't take away the angles out here. This jurisdiction is the edge of the world, Stanford boy."

"There are other avenues besides the sheriff," I remind him.

Dodge looks at me as if I'm a child who just asked when a dead relative was coming back for a visit.

"With no proof?" he asks. "Just a dealer and a creepy ranch? They're still our neighbors. We've gotta be a lot more solid if we're gonna narc."

I'm relieved that he's still allowing for the possibility it may be bullshit, all of it. But what about this 'we' stuff?

"You and me," he answers. "Two can cover a lot more ground than one. Didn't they teach you that in school?"

Before I can say anything he gives me a patronizing pat on the cheek. "Now's your chance to be helpful," he says, and bolts over to the tractor idling in front of the garage.

"Think about it," he calls to me as he climbs into the driver's seat. "Think about all of it. Make connections. Use that million dollar head of yours."

And he picks up the little kid imitation again, gleefully putting the tractor in gear and bouncing away as though seated in someone's lap. His father's, maybe. If his father wasn't Franky Demos.


Using my head. All along the highway, over the hill, across the bridge, over the bay. Using my head. All I can come up with is a thousand reasons not to bother. Reasons why all of it is highly unlikely. Besides, it takes more than a single action to redeem yourself, Dodge. Believe me, I've thought about it quite a bit. Ever since I learned that a single action can, on the other hand, ruin your life or someone else's.

Plunging into the valley I can see the warehouse stretching across the vacant grasslands beyond the housing developments which stick to the side of the freeway. Flattening out past the fast food restaurants marking the freeway exit and through the emptiness which takes me closer to the warehouse, it begins to look like it should have an airstrip next to it, and jumbo jets inside. The truck trailers surrounding it come across as metal parasites. Lampreys or leeches. Sucking their cargo from the open bays of the loading docks.

Getting past the front gate is a feat of patience and determination.

No, I wasn't given an access number. I'm from Mirabelli Nurseries. Not on the list? Can you call someone? I don't know, is there some sort of front desk inside? Of course there's a lot of desks. I have a phone right here in the truck. I can call them. I'll dial the number we use at the ranch. Oh, so the buyers aren't here? They're back in Oakland. In the head office. This is the produce center. I see. Are you sure it's produce? Me? Daisies. I have daisies.

Two drawn out phone conversations later I'm in. Dock 51, they tell me.

Sorry about that, they say. Never know how far union tensions will stretch. Sabotage becomes an issue.

No problem, I say. I understand. I've only been here ten minutes and I'm ready to go on strike, too.

The truck trailers loom so much larger than our pickup. Dock 51 is the only free space in a long line of big rigs. Most of them seem to be dormant. Sitting empty, waiting for one side of the dispute to cave in. I must look like a tug boat in a harbor full of cruise ships.

I back into the spot. The dock comes halfway up the opening of our truck's metal shell. Up to my waist as I stand in the back and begin to unload. I crawl up onto the dock afterwards and search for a wooden pallet on which to put the boxes.

Ceilings as high as a basketball arena. Red digital thermometer readings hang on the walls instead of clocks. 35° Fahrenheit. Shelves of produce, canned, crated, boxed, reach up just short of the rafters. Deluxe forklifts are necessary to slide items from shelves so high. Forklifts the length of luxury automobiles. Men stand on the rear platform of the yellow vehicles and navigate them around the refrigerated complex. Men dressed for winter, in down jackets, scarves, and gloves. They float around on their spotless rides, upright, feet never touching the floor. Silently drifting, a hydraulic hush the only sound made.

One of them sees me searching. He flows in my direction and asks what I'm looking for. I tell him and he points towards a far wall, so far and cold and gray. Then he swivels and glides away, as though standing on a high-speed moving sidewalk.

When it's time to file the paperwork I spot a glass cubicle in the refrigerated distance. Several people work inside it, each with their own desk. The effect is that of a human zoo on another planet ruled by another species. I actually feel like another species compared to my days behind a desk. I study them for quite a while, trace my roots, hold up my progress against my past. None of the subjects look in my direction. They just keep working. I have to knock on the glass and they glare at me, reluctant to open the little slot at the base of the glass on top of the counter. The cold air will come in. I press my bill of lading against the window. As though called from the lobby to the dentist's office, a woman with a strong resemblance to Big Bird approaches. We don't speak. She won't open the speak hole. Cold air. Heavens. We go about the business of passing papers and pen back and forth through the slot without a word.

Once the exchange is complete, she says something. I cannot decipher the muffled words through the glass. I cup my hand behind my ear. She raises her voice, exaggerates her mouth, and I can hear her.

"Is the sun still shining?" she asks.

# FRIDAY 9/26

On our way to the market in the early morning darkness we see that the Tercel has been turned onto its side. By local kids, most likely. Prove to the city bastard who left his car within their reach that it's just as dangerous in the boonies as it is in the projects.

But Dodge sees it as a sign. The car's turned upside-down. Get it? He implores me. Something's gonna happen. There's the car, and all those imported flowers, and a field full of dead ones. He's taking this seriously. That meth, he says. Bad stuff. Cheap and powerful. Dodge says he may not have lived this long if meth was popular when he was at his worst, his most addicted.

And so we lurk around the fringes of Santo's stand, one at a time, each of us eavesdropping and then one giving the other a full report.

Santo is once again absent. So we listen to his employees. None of it is the least bit incriminating. Customers ask the price, Santo's young assistants tell them the price. Any other question beyond "how much" is answered with a shrug and a bashful grin, or sometimes "I don' know."

Both men are awfully convincing liars if in fact they're in on any of the schemes Dodge is trying them for. They really look like they don't know. Don't know a thing. Sleep-deprived and deflated from living on a sagging ranch, no running water, horrendous sanitary conditions. I left Mexico for this? Language really has nothing to do with it. They just don't know anymore, and they don't care.

But Dodge is hooked. Attached himself to a new addiction. Distractions accomplished. So I can't deny him anything which may help. So I have to tell him about the bundle I notice at Santo's. A wrapped bundle for Gino is too odd to ignore. Perfectly wrapped. A beautifully arranged bouquet, no less. A bouquet for Gino? Reserved in his name? It sits in a plastic vase atop an overturned bucket against the back wall, beneath the banner reading "Santo Farms." A lovely apparition, combining with the bucket that hoists it up to form the shape of a holy grail with "Gino" scrawled in black Magic Marker across the newspaper funneled around it. Dozens of varieties of the freshest-looking cut flowers soar above newsprint clinging to the stems. Every possible color represented, it seems.

"A wrapped bouquet for Gino?" says Dodge, echoing my sentiments. And as soon as he spots it, his theories come in rapid succession. After one trip by the stand he figures there are small bags of pure meth attached to the stems, hidden by the paper. Then he offers up the possibility of uncut cocaine crossing the border inside some of the tighter blooms, which he speculates are fake. I suggest that it may simply be a bunch of flowers.

"The kids," he scolds me. "Think of the kids."

"Yours?" I ask him.

"Kids in general," he says. "You know. The kids. The future."

Which sounds awfully dramatic and slightly comic from a man with no front teeth. And in a way kind of shallow, like just about anything drug-related these days. "I'm a recovering addict" is no more startling than "I'm a tax attorney" as far as confessions go.

But then Dodge spells out just how we're going to offer Gino help. Make sure he's been to Santo Farms, he tells me, then we'll be passing by and ready to help. Dodge delights in the language of plotting, imparts information with the urgency and heightened hushed tones that suck a listener in. Like a general or a quarterback, a motivational speaker whose bloated fees are well-earned. Help him unravel the mystery bouquet? I'd sell Amway products for him at this point.

As if playing along without even hearing us, Joe asks us to start pulling bunches for Gino.

"And see if he needs any help with the rest of his haul," Joe adds.

"You bet," says Dodge, and he winks at me.

Gino and Joe go through the prescribed motions. An entertaining way to close out the morning shift for Joe, a sympathetic ear for Gino to reveal all his business dealings. So proud of them—the art collection, the second home, return trips to the homeland to bring back an Armenian bride half his age—he's got to tell someone. But the sweater, the pants, that car? Joe understands the act, plays along because it's fun. And Gino knows this. Actually, everyone in the market knows, and plays along for the same reason. This Gino does not know. But everyone enjoys his performance too much to tell him.

We load his wilting booty in the hatchback, and then we separate to ensure that one of us catches Gino on the way back from Santo's. Dodge's idea, of course. "Head him off at the pass," he says. He really does. John Wayne couldn't have said it better himself.

Dodge re-enters the warehouse through the opening closest to Mirabelli Nurseries. I take the long way back, entering through the rear of the warehouse.

Gino rolls a cart my way, the top shelf stacked so high with flowers he can't see me. The bottom shelf has only one thing on it: the pristine package from Santo Farms.

"Gino," I shout, nearly inducing him to seizure. He turns to me, eyes wide.

"Oh, uh...yeah?"

He has no idea who I am. Joe says it takes about four years of regular interaction before Gino starts remembering your name, much less where he knows you from.

"Need a hand?" I ask him.

"Oh, sure," he mumbles. He always mumbles. "Parking Space 43," he announces as he surrenders control of the cart over to me. Then he bends down and grabs the bouquet.

"Space 43," I confirm, and swing the cart down the aisle towards the exit.

I throw the flowers in a heap in the back of his car. I return to find him in mid-con job with one of the wholesalers, the two of them standing in front of the stall trying to decide which bunches of flowers are the most worthless. Gino clutches the bundle at his hip. I return his cart and ask him if he wants me to take that bunch he's holding.

"No," he snaps with surprising forcefulness.

"Wow," says the wholesaler. "When was the last time you refused some volunteer labor, G-man?"

Gino just laughs and pats me on the arm. He holds up the bundle. "Very important," he says, and shakes it like a wrapped Christmas present he's hoping will make a revealing sound. I smile and give him the a-okay sign.

When I hook up with Dodge back at Joe's stall, he's very excited to hear how Gino reacted to my offer. Dodge tells me the same thing happened to him. He offered to take the bundle and Gino said no. But not with the conviction as he did with me, since Dodge asked first. None of which clears up the question of the bouquet, however. He says we have to tail it out of the market, to Gino's stand.

"Tail the bouquet?" I confirm, just so he can hear how goofy it sounds.

"That's no ordinary bunch," he says. "It's evidence."

And so I go ahead and offer to follow the flowers before he even asks, being the only logical choice. I know the city. I used to work here all day, downtown, not just at night amongst the cut flowers. I can find my way to Gino's stand on the wharf. That's what I tell Dodge, and he concurs. He says that besides the market, the only other times he was ever in the city he was so wasted he can't remember anything. Besides, Joe would never let him out of his sight for that long, much less in the city. So Dodge agrees to meet me at a bar I know right across the street from the train station in Burlingame, a fashion-conscious suburb half an hour south of San

Francisco on the peninsula. I'll take the train, Dodge's commute to pick me up will thus be shortened, and we'll meet at four o'clock to beat the rush back over the hill into Half Moon Bay.

Our scheme in place, I tell Joe that I ran into an old friend outside the Flower Market Café on his way to work, and I'm meeting him for lunch. My alibi.

"But you look like hell," Joe says.

"It's not the kind of friend who would care," I tell him, though I can't recall ever really having such a friend.

"Aren't you going to get any sleep?" he asks.

I hadn't thought of that, and wouldn't have if he hadn't said anything. But now I start to feel tired.

"One of those mornings," I say. "You know how sometimes you just don't need it?"

And it's true. Maybe not now, but sometimes. Sleep deprivation has struck me in so many different ways I have given up trying to trace a pattern. I had a head start, too. I wasn't sleeping much before I started working for Joe, before moving to the coast. I would lie awake thinking of what we had done, Janet and myself. Then I would think about how it wasn't so much us, the two of us. It was me. My idea. I pointed us down that disastrous road. She may have been eager and receptive, but she didn't start it. And that's what the principal always asked in elementary school: who started it?

So I'd get up and wander around the house like some Lady Macbeth impersonator, fretting about imaginary stains on her hands. Blood she never spilled herself, but for which she was accountable. And then I moved to the coast and still kept pacing. Outside, even. Walking barefoot in the night-wet grass. Stark naked sometimes, because I could. Because no one else was around, and I thought that maybe all the space around me would swallow my nightmares whole. Or on a less metaphysical level, that a pack of coyotes would corner me and put it all to rest in a kaleidoscope of teeth and torn flesh.

Jungle law. But I found that the animals on the coast aren't as used to people as the random coyote or raccoon in the suburbs. Animals in my new home are still frightened of human beings. They know what's good for them. And I was grateful to them on my spontaneous night hikes. They were telling me I wasn't the only vicious bastard walking upright.

I wake up on a bench at a bus stop around the corner from the market. So much for not needing any sleep. My watch tells me I've been sleeping for about half an hour. No telling how many buses I've missed. Head reared back, mouth slack-jawed and probably drooling, and I'm wearing dirty sweats at a bus stop on a bench plastered with posters advertising all-nude reviews on Broadway. If they could see me now. The investment firm, my folks, Janet. How proud they'd be. I always did have an inkling in the back of my mind while at Stanford that the only thing an MBA would ensure is that I'd always be a disappointment in some way. I just didn't figure it would be in such a big way. I smell myself, Old Spice overtaken by body odor, realize my first meal of the day may end up coming from a hot dog vendor on the wharf, and almost retch.

I ask a couple of bus drivers if they go to the wharf and they tell me the next one does. Truth is I never set foot on a bus in the city before. I was in high finance. You drive to impress. Riding a bus does not impress a client, even if you pick up the fare for them. The city was always through a window. My car window, my office window. The inside looking out.

Finally "the next one" arrives. The bus is half-full. I offer up my fare and find a seat of my own. My first time, and I get to fly solo. I glance around at the passengers and feel very relieved that they don't drive cars.

After surveying the contents of the bus, I succumb to the heat and rhythm of the bus, nothing left to engage me. The vinyl seat vibrates along my thighs and up my back, like one of those "magic fingers" beds in a Las Vegas honeymoon trap. I doze off between stops, wake up with the driver's announcements, and admonish myself. Narcoleptic for a day. I force myself to stay awake by imagining what the people in the bus look like naked, and I start laughing. This only augments my appearance as an unwashed lunatic of no fixed address, so I laugh harder and can't stop, until a deadly look from the guy in front of me makes it clear my life may depend on it.

Sea lions bark, seagulls holler, and fish smell as I step off the bus at Fisherman's Wharf. In my heavy-eyelid stupor I imagine the wharf clamor is made just for me, directed at my emergence from the bus. "Thank you," I say. "Thank you. It's great to be here."

Gangs of tourists soaked in sunscreen stroll by, heads swiveling, not sure what to photograph first. Coit Tower, overlooking it all from its hilltop perch? The familiar facades of the seafood restaurants papering the wharf? The forest of masts rising from the boards docked in the pier, each one swaying in time to the wake rippling beneath? All of it so familiar, reproduced on so many postcards and picture-centered books that the tourists cannot resist aiming at the very same things, proving to their friends back home that it all really does exist.

I find Gino's stand easily. It's the only stand which doesn't sell little plastic mementos or preheated snack foods. Gino's in the process of unloading his wholesale bargains, hobbling back and forth from his hatchback to the employee entrance in back of the wooden kiosk. I'm kind of surprised that he didn't arrive earlier, but then he spends so much time bullshitting in the market. I position myself at an angle across the promenade from the kiosk, away from their direct line of sight. Gino bear hugs as many flowers as he can from the back of his car and drops them on the sidewalk at the feet of his designers, two young women both chalk white and partial to floral print dresses with cardigan sweaters. Gino rambles in his customary mumble while he works. The girls nod dutifully, long past trying to figure out what he has to say. At last he presents them with the mystery bouquet, complete with a finger-wagging set of verbal instructions. They both heave deep sighs of relief when he finally leaves.

The sun is blinding, so I buy a pair of cheap sunglasses from a knick knack stand nearby to continue my surveillance in a more surreptitious manner. Standing agape with my arm draped across my eyebrows in full squint, lips curled, just didn't strike me as appropriately sly. Not that his young employees would suspect their place of work to be the object of a stakeout.

I find a bench facing the stand from across the promenade and sit. The lenses of my new shades are so dark I may as well be wearing a blind fold. My eyes relax and I feel sleep coming on again. I get back up and buy a large Coke and a big soft pretzel to serve as a substitute for the standard coffee-and-bagel version of my morning caffeine-and-bread fix. The hot and cold items reversed. Once my brain gets over it, my body is grateful for the usual ingredients. My detective work begins.

Detective work. A phrase so laden with cinema-fattened romance. A task so dull I spend the whole time thinking that someday I'll be on my deathbed, reflecting on my life, and how desperately I'll want these hours back. These hours watching tired children whine to their parents just like I would whine if I had somebody to hear me. These hours noticing that if you stare at a flock of pigeons rooting along the cement long enough, you can eventually tell them apart. Hours watching the mystery bouquet stand pat, while Gino's young employees move hundreds of dollars worth of bouquets per hour. The buyer hands them to the recipient. The recipient beams. Mission accomplished. There are worse ways a man could rip people off, I suppose.

I ask a man with a large family what time it is. He tells me it's two o'clock. Very quick, as though he expects me to then ask him for spare change. I decide to force the issue. I get up off my bench, my muscles stiff with inactivity. I limp over to the stand and ask the two ladies how much for the bouquet in the back?

"That's not for sale," one of them tells me.

"Not for sale?" I ask. "What, you guys do special orders? Weddings, maybe?"

"No," the same one glares at me. "The owner just told us to hold it for someone."

"Sorry," I say, no longer responsible for my actions until I get eight hours of sleep. "I didn't mean to be rude. It's just so beautiful."

The other one speaks up. "Yeah," she squints at the bouquet. "I guess so."

"Not one of your creations?" I ask, trying to turn on the charm in spite of my appearance.

"Nope," she says.

"Well then why don't I take it off your hands. Clear the way for your work."

The charm may be working, or the young ladies may simply be acting polite in the way people do who are forced to be polite on the job.

"Sorry," the first one says. "Gino's orders."

"So how are you going to know it's the right person?" I ask, surprised at how quickly I thought of that, proud of my mind's ability to stay sharp when drowsy.

"Because he'll be driving a Lexus, white with gold trim, and he'll be wearing an Armani suit and have dark wavy hair and tan skin," says the second one. She really enjoys saying it, too.

I nod and slink away. In the midst of licking my wounds, I realize that such a description plays into the hunches Dodge has about Santo's operation. The mystery man they're waiting for sounds like he wants people to think he's a drug dealer, even if he isn't. Either that, or he has my old job. I decide to hang around until the mystery man shows up for his mystery bouquet, away from the flower girls' field of vision, just to see if they were jerking me around.

They weren't. The man shows up as advertised. The car, the suit, the hair. I drift more towards the front of the kiosk to catch the reaction of Gino's designers as they pass the bouquet to him with careful hands. All smiles and furtive glances at his various physical attributes. He offers them a tip. I can tell by the color and design of the bills that it's ten a piece. Nearly a year into my new life, and I can still differentiate currency from forty paces. They refuse. He insists. They humbly accept, their faces saying "isn't that sweet." He jumps back into his car, bundle in hand, and drives away. I watch the Lexus weave in and out of the traffic and say to myself "what an asshole." I realize that I forgot to get the license plate number and say it again about myself. Glancing back at the kiosk, I see the flower girls are looking at me and smirking. I can hear Dodge already. Don't send a college boy to do a man's job.

I have a hell of a time hailing a cab, looking as penniless as I do. Finally I pull out some cash and wave it. The next available is all mine. I tell the driver to take me to the Cal Train station at China Basin.

On the train ride I'm surrounded by a few suits who managed to skip out of work early, watching the urban scenery pass by the window. The rail yards give way to industrial warehouses, the bay flat and gray beyond it all, looking more like a vast parking lot than a body of water, as the sweaty underside of the city in turn gives way to the housing projects outside Candlestick Park. The airport and all its by-products glide past, and finally trees camouflage the suburbs lying a safe distance from the metropolitan epicenter, the bay disappearing behind the manicured forest.

My stop is coming soon. I turn my attention away from the window. The man sitting across from me is reading a newspaper. It strikes me as a comforting throwback to the pre-laptop and handheld device days. The comfort is sucked from the moment as I see on the back page, facing me, the bi-line for the reporter who pestered me when things went so absolutely wrong, when Janet and I paid for our arrogance. I had been questioned about my "relationship to the murder victim," the lurid nature of which made my story prime material for leakage to the press. The reporter's face lunges at me with each opening and closing of the section, each turn of the page. Smiling in the photograph above his column, the same Cheshire cat smile he used to try to gain my trust. The same leer plastered above the story which announced and admonished our lifestyle to his readership. "Catalysts of a tragedy," he called us in print, and then the rest of them came and milled about our front lawn. Photographers and cameramen and reporters with microphones and notepads, all of them waiting to pounce until the next big thing happened. Fortunately the next big thing happened within a few days, and when it did they were gone. Garbage and dead grass left in their wake.

All I want to do is apologize, I told him, and his smile turned to a concerned pucker and sincerely furrowed eyebrows. Then that's what we'll run with, he said. He just wanted some background information on Janet and me to fill out the story. And with that he smiled. With that he ran. And while I consider myself lucky to work for a man who rarely watches television and only reads the Sports section of the morning Chronicle, I also don't think Joe's lack of media attentiveness mattered the first time I met him. Janet and I were front page news for a day, and plummeted towards the back pages in the few days that followed. And by the time I introduced myself to Joe Mirabelli, plenty of fresh names had taken our place on the lips of the population. So many stories worthy of a sad shake of the head and an exasperated "what is wrong with people?" to some friends. Too many fifteen minute blocks of infamy to keep track of.

The bar across from the Burlingame station is no longer just a bar. It's a bar & grill, the kind of place written up every few months in magazines dedicated to "the good life"—pizzas and pastas photographed with all the airbrushed sensuality of a high fashion model spread, the interior complete with all the art deco that any downtown revitalization project has come to expect. I should have known. None of the old places are safe once a suburban downtown area proclaims itself "revitalized." Espresso and smoothies for everyone! White lights will appear in the trees along the sidewalk. Terribly thin women with long-brimmed baseball caps, stretch pants, and an ear piece will prowl the streets and brag about how busy they are, their chest-thumping poorly disguised as a series of complaints. Gray-bearded men will jog pushing an elongated baby stroller with one hand, holding a leash connected to a pure bred pooch in the other, proving to the world that they can have their cake and eat it too. At a dead sprint, no less.

I find a spot at the bar, overlooking the grill, and order a beer, "the lightest you got." Both sections are already filling up. The good old Friday work schedule is getting shorter than ever, I see. Fire spews from a brick oven looming in back of the tables scattered about the restaurant. The tables are mostly occupied by an older crowd, while the bar is rife with young comers high on invincibility. Three men for every one woman. The older couples in the restaurant appear to be regarding the bar as a stage, treating the scene as a floor show before dinner concerning youthful rites of passage and how embarrassing they can seem from a distance of several generations. They watch the young performers jockey for position, their sadder but wiser faces taking it in with a subtle blend of amusement tinged with envy. The happy hour crowd is completely unaware they're being watched, of course, and far too self-involved to care.

A hand comes crashing down onto my shoulder. I have a brief spasm and turn around. A GQ-savvy dresser, who looks a lot less like Tom Cruise than he thinks he does, points a finger at me.

"Pryor," he says, as if he just figured it out.

"Bergen," I point back.

Todd Bergen. Former drinking acquaintance and a distant second to me in job performance at the same firm. He used to try and make up for it with misinformed back stabbings inevitably followed by shameless apologies when confronted.

"Damn, man," says Bergen, trying to sound street-wise in his polo shirt and twill pants. "You drop outta society and still know where the new hot spots are."

"Well, you know," I shrug. "Some are born great, some have greatness thrust upon them."

"Yeah," says Bergen, now sizing me up, my dirty sweats and greasy hair.

"Shakespeare," I tell him, deliberately breaking his concentration.

"Huh?" he snaps out of his scrutiny.

"Shakespeare said that."

"Oh," says Bergen. "You remember Keith Alonzo?"

"Why, is he here?"

Bergen answers me by belting out Keith's name. Bergen always liked to hang around Keith, in the way people do who need the constant presence of a second fiddle. To call Keith Alonzo a useless employee wouldn't be fair. He's useless in all phases of life. Great hair, though.

"Hello, Keith," I extend my hand.

"Pryor," he says, unpleasantly surprised to see me.

"So what are you up to these days, player?" Bergen asks me.

"I'm working out on the coast."

Alonzo cuts in. "They've got jobs out there?"

"Farming jobs," I tell him.

"So what, you're like a migrant worker?" Keith asks. He and Bergen think that's pretty funny.

"Never thought of it that way," I say. "But I guess I am. On the move, y' know? Migrating."

"You live out there, or do you commute?" Bergen asks.

"I live out there."

"Where?"

"In a house, Bergen. They've got those, too."

"You get TV out there?" Keith weighs in.

"If you buy a dish, I suppose. But I don't have the time."

Bergen grins pure venom. "So you're a regular hermit," he says. "Writing any manifestos? Planning on dropping a letter bomb or two in the mail?"

"No," I smile, trying to keep it light. But Bergen's after me now.

"But you're, like, railing against society probably, huh? Feeling pretty above it all, I imagine."

"No," I say. Dead serious this time.

"You ever see Janet?" Keith asks. Still subtle as sandpaper, but thankfully giving me some space with Bergen. Albeit unintentionally.

"Not often," I say. "Not for a while. How's the firm?" I ask in a desperate plea to change the subject.

"Same as ever," says Bergen. "Like you never left."

"Welcome to the machine, eh Todd?" I wink at him.

"I knew it," Bergen shakes his head. "Got it all wired, now. Way ahead of the rest of us. So where's your beard and tie-dye, anyway?"

"Bergen," I pause, calming down before going on. "What's up your ass? You should be happy I'm gone. Now you can finally make a decent living."

"And that I am," he says. "I'm even thinking of getting married. Now that it's safe. Now that you and your switch-hitting wife aren't around to fuck it up."

I take a sip of beer. "Me and my wife," I ooze, "set our sights far too high to mess with you or anybody desperate enough to fuck you."

He takes a step towards me, but Alonzo holds him back, just as I expected.

"Must be nice to have a purpose in life, Keith" I tell him. "So clear and well-defined."

"Fuck you, Pryor," is Keith's predictable comeback, which makes me smile.

"Go walk Bergen down to the end of the bar, would you?" I ask him. "I wanna finish my beer."

They oblige, but once they're far enough away I can see them planning some kind of frat boy ambush on the sidewalk. Alonzo's talking up Bergen, getting him all red in the face about taking shit from a down and out smart-ass like me.

Another hand on my shoulder. Christ, who now?

Dodge.

"Got some good news for me?" he asks.

"Later," I tell him, recalling what a failure my stakeout was. "First come with me. There's some guys I want you to meet."

Dodge follows me to where Todd and Keith are hanging out. They take one look at Dodge, a man clearly with nothing to lose, and unanimously call off the attack without a word between them.

"Todd. Keith," I acknowledge them. "I'd like you to meet a good friend of mine. This is Dodge Hidalgo." And I put my arm around him.

The two of them look at me funny. But then so does Dodge. He's the first to gain his composure, though, immediately warming to the idea of messing with the khaki crowd.

"Nice to meet you boys," he extends a hand. Alonzo shakes it. Bergen stares at me.

"You're a real piece of work, Pryor," he says. "When you choose a lifestyle, you really go all out."

Dodge doesn't like the sound of that. He draws his hand back to his side, clenching it into a fist. Bergen's eyes bulge as a single bead of sweat trickles from the part in his hair and flows along his temple. Dodge notices it, then relaxes.

"Hell," he says. "I'd be ashamed of myself for wasting a punch on you. Be like hittin' a mannequin."

"Good man," I tell him, and put my arm back on his shoulder. I turn to Todd and Keith. "You might ask yourselves the same thing, kids," I say to them. "Is it worth it? Any of it?"

Bergen sneers. "Go hump a redwood."

And as we walk back to his van, Dodge sneers at me too.

"Buy a pit bull if you wanna scare people, Stanford boy."

"What do you mean?" I ask, a reflex action.

"I mean I was thinkin' of taking a shot at you more than your old school bullies back there."

"What for?"

"My good friend Dodge?" he repeats my introduction at the bar.

"So?" yet another juvenile defense on my part.

"Yeah, so?" he mocks me, then settles down a bit. "It was a good play, I'll give you that. So what the hell? Might come in handy later on in our little adventure if you don't wuss out on me first. Good guy, bad guy. Like a couple cops."

"You're reading way too much into this," I tell him.

"Am I?"

"Yes, you are," I stay after him. "And all the wrong things, too. You are my friend, godammit. I just thought we were a couple buddies watching each other's back in there. That's all."

Dodge gets quiet. We walk a few paces without a word.

"My friend, huh?" he says.

"Of course," I assure him.

He pauses again, but for only a moment. "Now that you mention it," he says. "You are startin' to smell like most of my friends."

I catch a nap on our way over the hill into Half Moon Bay, waking at the first stop light. Once we pass the light, the golf course, and a few scattered houses, the view planes out towards the ocean. The sun half-sunk into the watery horizon needs no commentary on how beautiful it is, but I decide to offer one up anyway to break the silence. I come up with:

"That's quite a sunset."

Dodge doesn't look at it, and immediately asks "how'd it go today at Gino's?"

"You really ought to look at this sunset."

"Come on, Stanford boy. How bad did you fuck it up?"

"Pretty bad."

"Did you miss who picked up that bouquet?"

"No. It was some guy in an Armani suit with a nice tan and wavy hair driving a Lexus."

"Really?" Dodge is quite pleased. And now so am I.

"Yup. Looked like Pat Riley after a trip to Bora Bora."

"Who's Pat Riley?"

"A pro basketball coach."

"Oh. You get a license plate number?"

I stare straight ahead. Looking out the corner of my eye, I see him staring at me.

"You didn't, did you?"

"That's the fuck-up part."

Dodge pauses, then says "Ah, hell. What would we do with it anyway?"

I can think of a whole lot of things, but there's no sense in stepping back in front of a bullet you've just dodged. And he's so excited, like when his suspicions were validated about the car being searched for drugs. Which reminds me...

"Is the car still there?" I ask him.

"Nope. Hauled it away. And now we've got Rico Suave pickin' up free bouquets from Gino. When's the last time Gino gave anything away?"

"I wouldn't know."

"Try never. Unless, of course, he was gettin' somethin' in return. Scratchin' someone's back so they'd do likewise. Gino..." Dodge grins and considers the name for a moment. "Who'd a thunk it?"

He quiets down. Making more connections, I assume. I turn just at the right time to notice a house I've never seen before. Through a break in the cypress trees on the ocean side of the highway, a modernist sore thumb perched out on the cliffs. Every so often I can spot one, these houses built on a foundation of relaxation and a New Age version of respect for the land. Any work surrounding these houses—gardening, landscaping—is done in the name of therapy. Peace of mind. Not for a living. Leave that to the splintered shacks propped right by the side of the road, those withered relics built strictly to store a rusted stew of implements, keep livestock, and provide shelter for a few hours of sleep every night. It takes more than a few trips up and down this coast to see between the views.

But then we pass the construction site—orange cones around its rim, men with chainsaws milling about their next cut, bulldozers dozing—and it occurs to me that the soothing effects of a room on the coast is emerging out from the trees and hidden valleys lining the ocean. The gloves are off once that resort opens. Subtlety has run out of space. Members only no more.

From around the curve of the highway brushing by the lighthouse, we can see smoke in the distance to the south. Smoke around where the ranch is. Dodge accelerates and soon we can see the fire. An orange pulsation with a steady procession of flames lashing out towards the sky. The fire is on the wrong side of the highway to be Mirabelli Nurseries. We take turns speculating briefly—I worry it's my rental, Dodge hopes it's Roman's house—before we see how close the blaze is to the highway and realize the fire is in Santo Farms.

"Somebody musta knocked over a Bunson burner," Dodge says. "But then a long day of cookin' up meth will make you drowsy and careless, I imagine."

We turn onto to gravel road and drive slowly. It's one of the old barns, the big one closest the fork in the gravel road where the trucks take and make their deliveries. The fire trucks are not there yet, and it won't matter by the time they are. The wood frame is already visible, the walls in charred pieces collapsing in bunches to the ground. The intersections of the beams spanning the sides look like dozens of burning crosses in a row, one after another falling into the growing heap of cinder forming a line around the foundation. Flaming shingles from the roof levitate and flutter like paper airplanes, crashing and burning on the surrounding dry ground. Some of Santo's men are stomping out the crash sites where the shingles land, making sure the projectiles don't start another fire. About a dozen other men are sprinting away from the scene, running through the dead sunflower stalks towards the forest along the base of the hill, disappearing into the dense brush thriving at the base of the trees, into the thickening darkness.

"Why are they running?" I ask. "No papers?"

"That and whatever else they have to be guilty about," Dodge answers with a wink.

Dodge stops the van and we get out. The old man stands with his dog on the outskirts of the blaze. He turns and gives me his customary wave and toothless smile. Another old man stands next to him, white hair reflecting the fire. He turns in our direction, too, once he sees his brother wave. His face is much more regal, his chiseled features enhanced by the light of the fire. Dapper, with an air of refinement, he has not seen hard labor in years. He sees us and narrows his eyes as though trying to read the bottom line of an eye chart.

"Is that Santo?" I ask Dodge out the corner of my mouth.

"That's him," he says. "Hasn't changed much. White hair, that's about it."

Santo seems to finally make us out. His eyes relax and he smiles. Mouth full of teeth, not a gap in them. Dodge and I tense up like a couple of school kids caught passing notes.

"You still a handyman?" he calls out to Dodge over the commotion, a strain on his raspy voice.

"I'm the handiest," Dodge shouts back.

Santo gestures back to the dissolving barn. "I may need you," he says.

"Don't call us, we'll call you," says Dodge.

Santo laughs. "The rolling stone," he almost coughs. "Still a rolling stone."

Sirens begin to wail in the distance, closing fast. Santo's smile disappears. He pulls aside one of the shingle stompers and says something directly into his ear. The man nods and then shouts the names of several others, attached to a "vamanos." They all run into the woods as the others before them. Only a half-dozen men remain.

Along with a couple of sheriff's cars, three different fire departments converge on the scene within a few minutes of each other—the Forest Service, the fire department from a small town north of here, and the volunteer department from the little town to the south where Dodge and I conducted our INS stakeout—all three of them just in time to watch the frame collapse. A few of them pick up where the shingle stompers left off, while the others pull a hose from each truck and spray the remnants of the barn, now a heap of burning wood resembling a huge camp fire. Along with the sheriff's deputies, the older and more important-looking firemen start asking questions about possible causes and any injuries.

One of the firemen approaches us. Dodge does all the talking. I figure he must know him, just like he knew Deputy Bert. But apparently not. No, Dodge tells him, we only came by once the fire was in full force. No, we don't know the people on this ranch very well.

"I thought all you folks around here knew each other," says the fireman.

"We wave at each other a lot," Dodge answers. "Does that count?"

"You don't live around here?" I ask the fireman.

"Would if I could, but housing's scarce. We're just stationed here. We all commute."

Another fireman taps our guy on the back, so he thanks us and turns to his partner.

"Find out anything?" his partner asks.

"No," our guy tells him.

"Me neither. The old fox over there owns the place. Says he doesn't know how it could happen. It's just him and his brother and a couple employees, and they were all having dinner together in the main house when it started."

Dodge and I look at each other as the two firemen drift further out of earshot. Before either of us makes a comment, though, we both take a precautionary glance towards Santo. The blaze now behind him from where we stand, he is for the most part a silhouette, only his eyes catching some of the light wrapped around him. He's looking in our direction.

"My truck's still at the ranch," I say, trying to disregard Santo's gaze.

"Yeah," Dodge answers, also uncomfortable. "I remember."

We get back into the van. Dodge starts it up and swings into a U-turn. Santo turns towards the fire as he follows our path, making it clear that he is really only staring at Dodge. Dodge waves at him. Santo waves back, lifting his hand as if imitating the gesture without realizing he's doing it, almost like a fan watching their hero drive by.

"You think he knows we heard those firemen?" Dodge asks.

"He doesn't look very angry," I say.

"Then how did he look?" says Dodge, slightly condescending.

"He looked like he wanted to hang out with you some more."

"Up yours," he snaps.

His reaction takes me by surprise. I'm about to ask what that was about, but on the shoulder of the highway, Joe and Lorraine are packed together in the passenger side of an old ranch truck, Aldo at the wheel. We pull over, facing them head on. Joe beckons us over, hanging out the window.

"So what happened?" he asks as soon as we get out of the van.

"Who knows?" Dodge says as we reach him. "The place was torched, and Santo ain't offerin' up any theories."

"Crooked bastard," Joe mutters. "Why do you think I'm sitting out here? Who knows what I'd do if I saw that son of a bitch."

I imagine Joe and Santo going at it. Santo's in better shape, but doesn't look real good with his hands. Of course, he used to be. But Joe has rage on his side. Motivation. Slight edge to Joe. Even money on the betting line.

"And you know what's gonna happen to old Santo on this deal?" says Joe. "Nothing," he swipes his hands together, answering his own question. "Not a goddamn thing."

"It's that Housing Inspector," Lorraine says from her tight squeeze between son and husband. "That pencil pusher and his double standard."

Joe slaps the dashboard. "That bastard. He goes around through every house where we put up our men, even checking to see that the batteries are fresh in all the smoke alarms, for chrissakes. And meanwhile Santo's guys are over there shitting in the creek, living like they're in a fucking dog house. I tell the guy, the housing guy, I tell him 'hey, good for you getting out the white glove with us, but you've gotta put it on for all the other ranches around here. Only fair.'"

"And they don't do it," Lorraine says.

"They don't budge," Joe keeps up his assault on the dashboard. "And that creek they shit in?" he points at us, a spot check to see if we're paying attention. "That creek runs into our reservoir, and those turds are the least of what comes floating in. All kinds of run-off, chemicals the farm service never even heard of. And I take the blame," Joe's eyes bug out to emphasize the ludicrousness.

"And that's where Fish and Game comes in," says Lorraine.

"That's right," Joe agrees. "The one and only Department of Fish and Game. I got the Feds after me thanks to that shit guy. 'Talk to the owner of that ghost town over there,' I tell those sons-o-bitches. 'There's your source.'"

"But they don't," Lorraine says.

"Never," Joe slaps his knee. "And I gotta come up with some fuckin' filtration system on the inlet. Costs me an arm and a leg. Christ, our pond's cleaner than the county water supply by now."

We all stand quietly shaking our heads for a moment. Aldo, of all people, breaks the silence.

"Hey Stanford," he says.

"Yes?" I answer, trying not to look too shocked.

"Is United Farm Supply open on Saturdays?" he asks.

"I don't think so," I say.

"No," Joe confirms.

Aldo sighs. "I need some urea and some bell beans. I need to plant a cover crop next week."

"We'll send him down Monday afternoon, son," Joe says.

"That'll be fine," says Aldo, and he leans back in his seat, out of sight.

"Farming on the brain," Joe taps his own head. "That's why he's so damn good. Eh, Aldo?"

"Yeah, Dad," Aldo says from the far end of the seat, only his hands visible on the steering wheel.

We follow the Mirabellis on our way back to the ranch. Dodge stays quiet as I watch the old ranch truck ahead of us. The three of them on their way to the dinner table. Another day of hard work behind them, to take pride in. Once in the yard, the Mirabellis keep driving back towards their house as we stop next to my truck. I wonder about their dinner conversation. Like so many families—those who still sit together at a table—the foibles of others will be a big topic, I imagine. But most of all they will discuss their own business: personal success serving more as proof of their good fortune than the misfortunes of anyone else. I watch them go, a hint of affectionate jealousy regarding how they made it this far.

"Roman!" Dodge blurts out, distracting me from the Mirabelli's shrinking tail lights.

"Where?" I ask.

"Everywhere, I'm sure of it." He slaps his hands together in true Joe Mirabelli fashion. "Ha! I'm gonna bust this coast wide open."

"What are you talking about?"

"Santo couldn't ditch those inspections on his own. He needs an insider."

"Roman?"

He points at me as if we're playing charades and I just guessed what word he was acting out. "Santo's land is state-owned. Who the hell else could it be?"

"How do you know the state owns it?"

"Franky sold it to 'em years ago, needed some quick cash for some shitty investment."

"And Roman has that much pull?"

Laughter sputters through Dodge's lips. "Greasin' palms and scratchin' backs is all he spends his time on, if the surf ain't up."

I'm not sure how willing I am to bite on this latest theory, but the idea of busting Roman over some dirty hush money is certainly intriguing. As was Dodge's reaction to my remark about the way Santo looked at him, which I suddenly remember now.

Dodge bristles when I ask him about it. "I don't like him," he snaps. "So what?"

"He seems to like you. So maybe you could get close to him, get some information."

"No thanks."

"Because of what happened between him and Joe?"

"I got my own reasons."

"Guilty until proven innocent, huh?" I kind of admonish him. "You of all people should be willing to give someone the benefit of the doubt."

"I worked for him once," he barks. "All right? Real brief. One week, tops. Hell, I've worked for everyone around here at some point."

"Really?"

"I was a kid. Thirteen, fourteen. I dunno. He had a bunch of Christmas trees, some firs he bought from some dude up in Oregon, and he wanted them flocked. I heard it from a buddy of mine, and I'd done some flocking before when I worked for a tree lot up in Half Moon Bay. Franky hated Santo as much as Joe does. I dunno the reasons why. Father Franky and I didn't talk much, as you know. But he hated the man's guts. So I figured pullin' a job for Santo would piss the old man off real good."

"And what happened?"

"He couldn't take his eyes off me. I was always catchin' him staring at me. Creeped me out. He put his arm around me once and I bailed. Told him to fuck off and walked."

"So you think he's gay, is that what you're saying?"

"Hell, you saw him. He's still got a hard-on for me."

"And so now you want to close him down because he may have put a move on you twenty-something years ago?"

"No," Dodge snaps. "I wanna shut him down if he's up to no good. I wanna do something right. But still...don't tell no one."

"About what?"

"You know. Santo makin' eyes at me."

I collapse backwards into the seat. "Oh, for chrissakes, Dodge. Who would I tell?

"I dunno."

"And what would it matter?"

"I've heard about those kind bein' able to spot their own."

"Dodge..."

"I know it's bullshit," he defends himself. "But other people might be stupid enough to believe it."

"Fine," I throw up my hands. "We'll just keep sneaking around and connecting dots."

I get out of the van and hang into the open window. "Have you ever thought about what we're actually going to do about it if we ever figure out what's going on over there?" I ask him.

"No," he says, completely matter-of-fact.

I give the door a couple of pats before stepping away. "Have fun with your kids," I say.

He nods and gives me an exaggerated look of exasperation. "Good luck is more like it," he says, then peels out in a cloud of dust, fishtailing around, drag racing through the yard and out the gate.

# SATURDAY 9/27

On the porch with a cup of coffee, sun high in the sky already drying the meadow. I slept a little later this morning, making up for the missed opportunities of the past few days. Dozing a few minutes at a time as the sun rose, images on the verge of being dreams joining me in and out of consciousness. The man jogging into the ranch screaming that he's Jesus Christ, his abandoned car ransacked and searched for drugs, the bundle from Santo to Gino to Lexus man, Santo's ranch sagging and paralyzed, not a crop in the fields but the operation somehow supporting three dozen men. And Santo. Such obvious pride in his appearance, living sequestered in that hive. Less one barn now. Not enough decent wood in the old barn to feed that fire more than a few minutes.

Several families of quail peck at the ground in front of the house as a single tribe, advancing across the matted ground between me and the meadow. Mothers and babies in the middle of the herd, the babies like little brown cotton balls on wheels, males on the perimeter, their black topknots bouncing in time to their hurried footsteps. One large male is the lookout. He jumps up on a fencepost and checks the upcoming territory for danger, head swiveling, topknot swaying, a pompadour doubling as an antenna. The group continues to roll forward and peck, roll and peck, and the male flutters ahead to make sure everything is all right. At the sound of his voice they keep moving. A born leader.

A muffled rumble cuts through the green-tinted tawny grass. The quail take off, a unified mass of flapping wing feathers and concerned calls. The rumble comes from the mouth of the eucalyptus tunnel leading to Santo Farms. An old green Pontiac Firebird emerges, with the dog chasing it. The car growls upward along the road leading to the new Demos estate. The dog stops and barks as if to say "and stay out!"

The car also stops. A teenage boy, pants baggy and baseball cap swung askew, jumps out and hurls a half quart milk carton at the dog. The carton is still half-full, milk spraying during its trajectory. A teenage girl is in the driver's seat. Lots of hair, smoking a cigarette, and laughing.

"Fuck you, dog," the boy yells, and eases himself back into the car as if somehow triumphant in whatever it was he was trying to accomplish.

Dodge's kids, I presume.

The car kicks up dirt and gravel as it starts back up the hill. The dog nuzzles the milk carton and begins lapping up its contents. I watch the kids bounce up the road. As the Firebird reaches the pinnacle of the hill, it stops.

"What are you lookin' at, dickweed?" yells the daughter. She give me the finger and makes the turn to Roman's house. So that's what Dodge is trying to reconcile with? I wish him good luck under my breath and wonder why it's so important to him. I assume it must be something I could only understand if I had kids of my own. I've heard that one before. But any comparison of Dodge to other parents I've known ends right about there.

But he's trying. He's tired of dodging so he's trying. I go inside and pick up the phone, dialing from memory.

"Hello, Janet?" I question the voice answering on the other end.

"Correct," she says.

"It's me Stan...uh, Paul."

"Who is Stan Paul?"

I'm at ease now. The first acknowledged screw-up still the greatest ice-breaker. "How are you?" I ask.

"Okay," she says with a trace of suspicion in her voice. "I've been thinking of filing for divorce just to flush you out of the woods. You have a phone now?"

"No. Just the land line in the house I'm renting. But it's funny because I was thinking this morning that I don't have an answering machine and maybe you've been trying to call me."

She pauses. "Not home much, are you?"

"I've been working down at the ranch quite a bit."

"No," she jumps on the very end of my sentence. "I haven't been trying to call you. Far be it from me to get in the way of your healing. Or healing process. I believe that's the proper term."

I resist the temptation to start trading punches. "I'm not sure what to call it," I clear my throat. "But there's a lot we have to talk about."

"Oh, yes," she says, as though what she really wanted to say was "no shit."

"So how about meeting me for lunch today?" I ask, and tension grips my chest during the ensuing pause. The kind of silent hyperventilation I remember from first dates—dinner and a movie, the prom, drinks after work. My first date with Janet.

"Sure." She drags the word out a little too long for comfort. Shhhhhhure.

"Previous commitment?" I ask.

"Not until dinner," she says.

"A date, then?" which I find encouraging. I didn't expect her to wait for me. I didn't want her to.

"Yes," she enjoys admitting. "Not very promising, though."

"Maybe some other time then," I say.

"You could say good-bye and hang up the phone just like that?"

"Well, if this isn't a good time..."

"No, no. You're not getting off so easy this time."

"You call any of this easy?" I push my voice to the edge and immediately regret it.

Silence again, hollow-sounding like the inside of a sea shell.

"I'd rather not talk about this over the phone," she says finally.

"So meet me today. I've gotten pretty good at this sort of thing lately."

"Talking?" she asks.

"Yes."

"On a personal level?"

"Not a client or a computer for miles," I remind her.

"So who have you been talking to, dearest, the silverware?"

"The trees," I say. "But they don't listen to me," I sing in my best Broadway musical baritone.

"Okay," she says. "Stop singing and I'll meet you."

"Your choice, my treat," I tell her. "Is there someplace new I simply must see?"

"How about an old haunt instead," she says. "Our favorite burger in Palo Alto. I haven't had one since you left. I need a healthy dose of red meat."

Five minutes from our old house. Our classic three-bedroom Georgian with the ivy running up its brick walls.

"Anyplace in a more neutral site?" I ask. "You live in San Jose now. How about we meet in Santa Cruz?"

""What are you afraid of?"

"Miles per gallon?"

"Come on, Pauly."

"Sweets, it's a full lap around the mountains in either direction to get there."

"Take Highway 84."

"I hate that road."

"But it's so you, Paul. So rugged."

"I damn near get car sick on that road, it's got so many curves."

"Well I want a burger."

"Isn't there anything near where you live?"

"I live in San Jose now, dearest, you said it yourself."

"Don't be a snob."

"I want to see some trees, Paul. I want to eat someplace with a patio, a restaurant with its own space, not just a glass storefront between a yogurt shop and a pedicure salon."

"Oh, listen to you. Why didn't you just move out here with me?"

A pause. I'm too busy clutching my forehead wondering why I said that to bother anticipating her response.

"I don't want that many trees," she says, and I laugh too suddenly to catch myself.

"Fine," I say. "See you there."

"I won, then, didn't I?" she asks.

"You won," I assure her.

Then she takes a deep breath, the kind often leading to a sob. I don't want to handle anything more over the phone.

"What time?" I ask.

"Twelve," she says, a bit too loud. Affirmation that she is now "composed."

"I'll see you then."

"I'll see you, too."


Highway 84 is the least traveled of the options winding through the hills, the most rustic path between the ocean and the bay. Its two lanes go along with the trees and contours of the hills rather than against them, making for a longer ride than necessary by practical engineering standards. A bizarre combination of YMCA camps and biker bars line its shoulders, and some of California's most famous drug addicts have holed up along some of its side roads and hamlets. Some drugs would actually come in handy about now. A sedative, naturally. Something that will make everything either all right or funny, make my head feel detached, hovering above my shoulders telling my body to relax. Something that will do all that and still allow me to drive safely. But I imagine nothing that advanced can be found on this trail. Strictly the old standards along 84. Many of its miles still seem to be trapped in the bumper sticker slogans of those days gone by. When people shake their heads and mutter about "California" under their breath, they are essentially referring to the time-frozen shores of Highway 84, whether they've driven it or not.

I'm late. 12:15. But no matter how late I am, I know Janet will arrive later. She'll stake out the place and wait for me before she'd ever go ahead and sit down alone. Our old burger fix is the kind of place where you order inside at the counter, so I take a seat on the patio and keep a lookout. My stakeout theory may be right. Her timing is just a bit too perfect. Within thirty seconds she makes her appearance. Crossing the street waving both hands at me, stepping onto the sidewalk looking as though she's ready to sign autographs, if for some reason she was approached. Dressed "casual" in the way catalogues interpret the phrase—subtle blends of earth tones and pale colors preceded by adjectives like "mint," "dusty," and "bisque." All of it costing much more than the highest figure you would think of for a pair of shorts and cotton sweater-type ensemble.

A pair of shorts. Just enough skin showing to make me think of every time she walked in the nude from the bed to the bathroom late at night. I'd watch her from behind, my eyes just able to make her out, the moonlit wings of her back split by the shadow of her spine reaching down between her cheeks swaying back and forth away from me into the next room. Then the light clicks on, and I see all of her. She can't see me, I'm still in the dark, but she knows I've been watching, so she smiles.

We hug without a word, hug for quite a while. As good as she feels and how sweet she smells, I have this vision of us as heavyweight boxers locked up for a rest during the final round, waiting for the referee to separate us so we can continue beating the shit out of each other.

"So," she says, our cue to unlock. "Did you get carsick on 84?"

"No," I answer, ambushed by some tension as I look into her eyes for the first time in months. "I do all right as long as I'm not in the passenger seat, I guess."

"Have you eaten?"

An absurd question, proving that she's also tense. "Not yet. I managed to wait."

"How nice of you," she says, acknowledging the laughable tone of our small talk.

"I'll go in and order for us," I say. "Assuming you want what I think you want."

"You assume right, I'm sure."

And so I walk across the patio, self-conscious, her eyes following me I'm positive, looking for signs of weight gain or loss. Particularly around my ass, of course. I order us a couple of Cokes to play with while we wait for our burgers. Ice to chew, straws to fondle, liquid to draw on during unbearable pauses.

I return and sit and think how I must be the envy of the men scattered around the patio, and those walking along the sidewalk who happen to look our way. If they only knew. Like the photographers and sketch pad artists along Highway One. If they could only see the underside of all the beauty. Not that this is anything new on my part. I always get the feeling during our time together that there's a lot of "what's he got that I haven't got?" telepathically aimed at Janet, who remarkably enough has decided to sit at my table so often.

I certainly can't blame them. She is striking but not intimidating, perhaps because even the most gorgeous person of mixed blood seems to be fair game for anyone to come up and ask "What are you? My buddy says Japanese-Mexican, I say Filipino." Her chin actually a bit weak, it's all in the eyes. Her eyes would have assured her a career in silent films if she had been born that much earlier. She'd play the exotic mystery woman held captive by a whip-wielding Chinatown pimp dressed like Genghis Kahn, her skin tone and heritage pasteurized just enough so that the Nebraskans at the nickelodeon could root for her and her pasty savior to reunite and live out their remaining days bearing children who pose no threat to the cold-climate gene pool.

"What did you order me?" she asks. The test I knew would come. Much more fun than actually telling me what she wanted, particularly if I get it wrong and have to go back inside and plead my case with the dour teenage girl behind the counter.

"Single no cheese, well done. 'Grill the fat clean out of it' I told them."

"You're a good man, Mr. Pryor."

"Is there a reason why you were so determined to meet me in this area?" I ask, then immediately retreat into my large Coke.

"Single, no cheese, well done," she answers.

I nod slowly, not quite buying it.

"Actually, I come here quite a bit," she continues. "Not here-here, but the old neighborhood."

"The old neighborhood," I say, the phrase sounding foreign to me. "Is there such a thing anymore, do you suppose? For instance, does anyone recognize you and say 'where have you been? The neighborhood's not the same without you.'"

I'm surprised she considers my question, but she seems grateful for the distraction.

"Our old next-door neighbors," she speculates. "I think they would ask how I am. If I ever got out of the car when I pass by."

"You stalk the house?"

She covers her face. Playful embarrassment.

I keep on teasing her. "I hope the new owners don't get the wrong idea."

"It's still on the market," she says.

"You're kidding."

"I had a deal in the bank, and it caved in. The guy filed Chapter Eleven or something. I was too pissed to commit the reason to memory. I'd already moved out and I couldn't bear having to do it all over again someday."

She breathes a bit heavy at the recollection. I keep quiet. I didn't expect her to have missed our old life so much. Still such the dense male. She tells me she wants to go to get a burger, and I honestly believe it's because she wants a burger.

"So is it empty?" I finally ask.

"I rented it to a visiting professor," she composes herself. "I got his name through our old friends on the alumni association. He's a former U.N. ambassador to Ghana."

"Wasn't that Shirley Temple's job for a while?"

"She was a U.S. ambassador."

"Oh. Of course."

"Anyway," Janet moves on. "My real estate agent says the boom is over for now. It's a bad time to sell. We may come down on the price. I mean, I can afford to hold out. My apartment's reasonable, work is good. But I want out of that goddamn place so bad."

"Where do you want to live?"

"I'm not sure," she says, and looks at me as if I'm part of the decision.

I stick to the surface. "So work's profitable?"

She nods. "That's why I can't believe the house isn't selling. I'm making a lot of people a lot of money."

"Maybe you're the only one," I say. "I ran into Todd Bergen and Keith Alonzo yesterday, and if they're any indication..."

"Where did you run into those guys?" she interrupts.

"I was in Burlingame."

"What for?"

"Business," I say, damned if I'm going to tell her that I was there to unwind after a day of trailing a bouquet of flowers. "One of our customers has a flower shop on the avenue. Forgot some stuff in the market."

"The FTD man," she says, rather unkindly.

"Not really," I explain. "We're wholesale. That was an exception."

"Going the extra mile," she says, like it's a commercial slogan. "Those guys must have had a field day when they saw you," she jabs.

"Those guys are even bigger pricks than I remember."

She smiles coyly and shrugs, trying to get me to think she's been with one of them or finds them attractive, which is pure horseshit. I keep my mouth shut, wondering how to get back to being civil, letting her wonder if she really wounded me.

"Do you want a share of the house?" she asks.

"No."

"Let me put it this way. Do you need a share of the house?"

"I've got a job."

"Come on, Paul..."

"Just sell the fucking thing." Too loud.

And several heads turn in our direction. Janet waits until they turn back, glaring at me the whole time, but still aware of when the coast is finally clear.

"Those conversation skills you mentioned over the phone," she says, low and intense. "I see what you mean. Nice job, Pryor. You're really opening up."

"What can I say, Janet? We're on such different paths..."

"Oh stop it," she snaps. "I've given you all your frigging space. Can you at least tell me, Paul," she's really having a hard time keeping her voice down. "Can you at least tell me why the hell you invited me out today?"

I stare at her, staring at me.

"Number 89," blares the loudspeaker. "Number 89."

That's us. I lift up the receipt.

"I don't suppose you're still craving this burger," I say.

"I'm craving an answer."

"Number 89," blares the loudspeaker.

"Hold on."

I get up and run inside to the counter, grab the burgers in their baskets and walk slowly back outside. She's still there. I place the baskets down and sit, gazing for a while at the jumble of fries with the half-wrapped burger turned sideways in the middle of it all, the bun looking like a pair of lips breaking the surface gasping for air. We came here after we moved into the house, I remember. Not a lot of furniture to move at that point in our lives, but domesticity of any kind always left us exhausted. We sat on this patio satisfied and content as if we'd just made love, as if any moment Janet would get up and go to the bathroom and I would get to watch her walk naked across the room, away from me. Nothing on, walking away from me...the most frequently recurring image I have of her these days.

"I'm sorry," is all I can say. The burger, the afternoon, our lives. "I'm really sorry."

"It's not your fault. It's not our fault." She again catches herself getting too loud. "You are not responsible for her death. Her husband killed her, not you."

Now that it's out in the open, I refuse to let her have the last word on the subject. This is one argument I will not lose.

"But I am responsible for the fact I slept with his wife. I am responsible for my actions," I say.

"Of course you are," Janet says, as if in response to a very stupid statement. "But you..."

"I'm not responsible for his actions," I finish her sentence. "That's what you were going to say, isn't it?"

She nods. I continue.

"Would've happened anyway, right? If not then, some other time, and then it wouldn't concern us and we could simply hear about it and ponder the horror of it all, for a moment over a latte on the way to work."

She says nothing. I get closer to her, a guarantee no one else will hear.

"Well it did happen then," I hiss. "And the only one who got out of the triangle alive is the least deserving."

She's working hard to let her anger keep the upper hand on her emotions, but she's starting to lose the battle. "Are we ever going to get past this point in the conversation?"

"Not today."

"Why did you call me?"

No loudspeaker this time to bail me out. Just a couple of burgers cooling off untouched and Janet refusing anything but the truth.

"I just wanted to see if you still cared."

She laughs and the anger is gone. But the laughter is just a release. It is not a part of anything she is feeling. Not cheerful, or full of relief, not even bitter. Just sad.

"The only reason I thought you and I could get away with what we were doing is because we were so in love," I tell her. "I honestly didn't think anything could come between us. But then I guess there's no such thing as the perfect crime."

She shakes her head, loosening a tear in each eye. She doesn't bother wiping them. I go over to her side of the table and try to comfort her, which I know is a futile act before I even reach her.

"I've got a date later on," she says, getting up and pushing off my chest, launching herself onto the sidewalk, into the street. She trots along with traffic for a few paces until she finds an opening to cross to the other side. I look around the patio, no longer the envy of anyone.

All that's missing is a drink in my face. Coke doesn't quite cut it as a weapon. Doesn't sting like alcohol. I hadn't planned on a long lunch, but I hadn't planned on ten minutes either. I leave the food behind. Leave the patio. Fights with a loved one will do that, I suppose: screw up your schedule.

"A loved one." Subconsciously starting to use legalese already, in preparation for the divorce which now seems inevitable.

So little to do, so much time. Dressed decently and well-groomed for the first time in months, state of mind understandably frazzled. No better time to visit my parents. Two birds with one stone. Two ravens, I imagine. I'll have accomplished quite a bit in one day. More than most on my calendar of late. And on a Saturday, undoubtedly not a trace of traffic heading in their direction. Everyone leaves, after all. There's not enough income circulating through the neighborhood I grew up in to characterize it as one of the more exclusive enclaves of Bay Area wealth, but there's enough to afford mediocre vacations every possible weekend. Or more appropriately, trips. Trips to man-made lakes and short-hill ski resorts. Not very beautiful or invigorating, as I remember our outings. Certainly exhausting. And for my parents, proof that they are, yes, they are in fact upper middle class. Their evidence for inclusion being that when asked what they did last weekend, they could honestly say something besides not much. My evidence being that our trips prevented us from talking to each other. We certainly did our part during the week. The dining room table was for holiday use only. All other dinners were wrapped in paper, came from a box, or had a note attached to them in the refrigerator.

"Neighborhood Watch Meeting Tonite—Be Home By 9:00!"

"Company Softball Practice—See You When We Get Home!"

Out of Palo Alto, south through San Jose, into the suburbs which were once lush farmland more recently than you'd think. A few acres remain. Some token growing, serving as a backdrop to a couple wooden fruit and vegetable stands complete with pony rides. Novelty items left over to retain some of the area's flavor, its history. As if only history was supplanted, not beauty. Barely a house standing more than thirty years old. Boats in the driveway, hand-crafted lettering scaling the front fences and stucco walls announcing the names of the families within, netless basketball hoops sagging over the garage. So close in lifestyle to the classes over which they profess superiority.

And so on our trips to the Sacramento River for water skiing with our neighbors (and their boat), I was taught to laugh at the Lodi rednecks using "ass" every other word.

"It's a hot-ass day today"

"Get your ass over here"

"I'm stayin' in the water a long-ass time"

And in the portable generator-powered campgrounds, I was encouraged to take a good listen to the cuss-ridden family spats and drunken wife beatings going on in the next camp site.

Them and us. Us and them.

But there we were, alongside them, apparently just to see how the other half lives. "The other half" simply because they didn't have as far to drive home. Just a quick trip to the sticks for "them." A long test of endurance back to civilization for "us."

I can tell already they're gone. The garage door is closed. No car in the driveway. But I knock. I ring. All is well. They are gone, silently driving along Highway 120 through the mountains. Wordless concentration necessary to set up camp, unpack supplies, search for wood. And there's little sense in trying to talk over the din of a motorboat or gas-powered generator.

I find a pen and some scratch paper in my glove compartment to leave a note, making sure to capitalize every word and end in an exclamation mark. The perfect conclusion to their weekend tomorrow night when they arrive home.

I've finally regained my appetite. Still suitably scrubbed and fresh-smelling, I decide to not only grab a bite to eat, but to see if I'm still a viable commodity in the singles market. Next time I see

Janet it might be nice to be able to say that I have a date, too. I pull off the freeway at the first trendy downtown area whose exit I can remember. Coffee houses, pool halls, cigar lounges, a micro brew pub. I scarf down an entire meal which has been shredded and wrapped inside of a green crepe, attempt a few sidelong glances at the underage help as a warm-up, and since I'm a lousy pool player, hate cigars, and would get the shakes from a cup of coffee right now, I hit a book store that has so far managed to survive the online assault.

The only aisle currently inhabited by an attractive woman is the "relationship" section. There are several women in the magazine section. But they're all reading gossipy type magazines, and I haven't seen any movies this year. Too bad none of them are reading Field and Stream.

My only hope is fiction. Old fiction, of course. Nothing on the best seller list. Small talk suddenly my Achilles heel. Not many ice breakers on the tip of a hermit's tongue. I pull a copy of One Hundred Years of Solitude by Marquez and stand there pretending to read it. I remember the book from a lit class I was required to take. Didn't understand it one bit, but remember some of the comments from those who did. I could even confess as much to any lovely creature who may take the bait. Let her talk about it all night, I'll nod intently at the right moments.

A few minutes standing with the book in an empty aisle, and I feel as ridiculous as I do perverse. Then I remember the routine Janet and I had in bookstores. We liked going to them after a movie or after dinner. A chance to go our separate ways for a while, collect our thoughts on the movie or the dinner conversation. I'd be glancing through a book and she'd come up behind me and hug me and whisper in my ear. She'd tell me about some erotica she just read, or which she actually made up herself, I'm sure, because no erotica I've read could compare to anything she ever whispered to me from behind in a bookstore. At least not from my perspective. She knew my taste in language and situations. One Hundred Years of Solitude starts to shake in my hand. I chalk it up to "not being ready," and walk back to my truck. Maybe there's hope for me and Janet yet. Maybe I should start getting out more.

I head back to the coast, taking Highway 17 back over the hill. The polar opposite of Highway 84, Highway 17 is the busiest route through the hills. Two lanes in each direction. Left lane if you want to be tailgated through the slopes and curves at sixty miles per hour, right lane if you would prefer being the tailgater, stuck behind a large vehicle of some sort. Usually referred to as "fucking" Highway 17, you don't reach the end of it...you emerge from it.

I listen to the radio, and during a "lover's only" request show several people call in and dedicate songs to their husbands and wives with promises to love them forever and always and so much. But the songs they dedicate are about love lost. Don't they listen to the words?

The coast is in the midst of a typical fall weekend invasion. The drive home will take twice the usual time. Every beach sprinkled heavily with people, the parking lots stuffed, cars poised at the exits, necks craned in the drivers' seats, heads swiveling, waiting for a break in the Highway One convoy of traffic. Accidents waiting to happen. I'm trapped behind a Winnebago carrying five mountain bikes. There's no way out. Each curve in the highway reveals a parade's worth of vehicles ahead, nothing to gain in passing but a single car length.

Breaking through the idling of the beach town onto the high speed loveliness northward on Highway One is an exhilarating reminder that one of the great things about the natural world is that you can often drive fast and unimpeded through it. Halfway home I notice a tractor tilling a forty acre patch on my left. The ground yet cultivated remains a dusty brown, while the freshly turned half is a rich muddy fudge. Hundreds of seagulls high-step behind the tractor, pecking at the goodies just uprooted in the darker half. They form a sea of white, the tractor looking like a boat leaving a foamy wake in its path. The gulls leapfrog each other in waves to keep up with the blades, having picked clean each new area within moments. The birds in back become the front birds become the middle birds, and then hit bottom again.

At long last gravel, popping like popcorn under my tires. No dog today. Must be inside. Leaving the eucalyptus tunnel, I see Dodge's van parked by my house. Turning into the yard, I see Dodge slumped on the stairs of the porch, hoisting a pint of something to his lips. Something whisky-colored. Whisky-smelling, too, as I approach with a wave.

"Yeah, I know," he says, looking at the bottle. "I'll have to re-set my 'days sober' count tomorrow. And I ain't even drunk."

"Should I even ask?"

"They're in Santa Cruz somewhere," he says. "We were at the Boardwalk and they said they were gonna buy some more tickets for the rides, and could they have some money, and thanks, and they'd meet me in front of the Big Dipper in fifteen minutes." He takes a drink and a deep breath. "That was..." he does the math. "11:30 this morning. Five hours ago."

"I'm sorry, Dodge."

"You ever been stood up by a woman?"

"Sure."

"This is...much worse."

He takes another swig and offers me some.

"No thanks," I tell him. "But I probably should. If it makes you feel any better, I tried a little reconciliation of my own today and failed miserably."

"Yeah?" he actually does brighten up a bit.

"Yeah. My wife."

"Your ex-wife."

"My wife. I'm still married."

Dodge breaks into a smile so wide his tongue fights through the gap in his teeth.

"Why, you sneaky son of a bitch, you," he points at me. "Married the whole time, huh?"

I nod. He throws his head back and laughs.

"Well, good," he says. "I hope you learned somethin' today."

"Learned something?"

"What's done is done," he slices a hand through the air. "And there's nothin' more done than a done marriage."

I lean against the banister. "Yeah, I guess I did learn that."

"And I hope you know you're better off without it. Without her."

"You don't even know her."

"Doesn't matter."

"What about your kids?" I ask, getting defensive. "With all due respect, they seem like a couple of total assholes."

"They are," he raises a toast with his pint. "But they're my assholes."

"And a wife doesn't mean that much?"

"Nope. A wife don't have your blood in her veins. A wife is a girlfriend gone too far, fucked one too many times."

I start for the door. "Now you're sounding like a drunk. You had me for a while."

"You gettin' a divorce?" he asks.

"Probably."

"I imagine she's a pretty smart woman."

"She is."

"She'll be just fine, huh?"

"Yes," the finality of divorce starts to sink in for me, right into my stomach. "I'm sure she will be. Just fine."

"Wish I could say the same for my boy and girl," he says as he gets up and places a hand on my shoulder, tentatively, as though trying to see how close he can lower his palm over the flame of a candle. "You didn't hurt anyone that bad," he says, his hand like wood, not a single nerve inside it seems. "People get over it."

I'm touched by the effort, but he's so wrong. In my case, at least. I look out across the meadow and almost feel like laughing, he's so uninformed. By no fault of his own, of course, and I consider telling him what happened when he takes his hand away and speaks up again.

"Look," he shifts and clears his throat. "You heard Roman a few days ago. They've got company soon and they wanna use the guest house. If it ain't askin' too much..."

"Sure," I tell him. "You can crash here if you want."

"Won't be for another week or so."

"Whenever. Hell, it's your old house."

"Thanks," Dodge sighs. "It beats livin' outta my van, I'll say that much."

He surveys the outside of the house, scanning the floorboards of the porch, up the columns and along the roof. "You know how many times I re-built this thing? Gretchen's father put it up. I'd say he built it, but that's givin' him too much credit. Helluva farmer, I guess, but he wasn't no carpenter. Put it up like a wood tent." He stops his eyes from wandering. "Franky figgered why spend money on a contractor when I got slave labor under my roof?"

I force a little air through my nose and smirk so that Dodge can call it what he will. He looks at me and does the same.

"I'm goin' back to the guest house," he says. "Make those little fuckers come to me for once."

"You want to give me that bottle?"

Dodge smiles. "No. But I will." He hands it over. "Just wanted to remind myself how it tastes."

"You okay to drive?" I ask as he walks to his van.

"It's only the dirt road, for chrissakes."

"You could go over the side."

"I said I ain't drunk. But still…" He turns around before getting in. "Don't throw that puppy away. I may need it later on."

He slams himself inside and speeds away in his usual cloud of dust. But instead of making the loop at the end of the meadow and heading up the road to Roman's like he said he was, he keeps going towards the highway. Even after he's gone, his vapor trail still hovers unsettled along the length of the road, all the way up to the mouth of the eucalyptus tunnel.

I decide to take a walk. Plenty of daylight left and in need of a reminder as to why I came here in the first place. A hike up to the ridge atop the hills behind the house, the perfect tonic I'm sure. I don't even bother changing clothes, just start walking with my date costume still on.

Walking soon isn't good enough. I jog. Shoes killing me, flat-soled and heavy. Too many clothes, long sleeves and pant legs. A wardrobe designed for sitting on your ass or striking a pose. The trail rises on a steady grade above the meadow. I almost step on a gopher snake sunning itself on the path. Maybe shedding, maybe digesting a rodent, it doesn't budge when I straddle it in stride for that split second, even with my gasp of horror included.

The trail switches back, climbing through a dense forest of Monterey pine and scrub oak. Surrounded by so much ground cover, I start thinking about those stories of joggers being ambushed by mountain lions, dragged by the throat and covered with leaves for something to munch on later. Something noble in it, perhaps. I could feed a cougar family better than any deer.

Near the top my body won't let me continue to run. I emerge from the tree line hunched over and panting. On the last switchback leading up to the crest, all I see is the chalk passing beneath my feet, the little broken pieces of beige clay marking the top of the mountain range. Tracks of those ahead of me: deer, coyote, bobcat, mountain lion. No pigs—the ground is too hard and unrootable for them—but a few mountain bike tracks. My breath is still vacuuming between my ears as I reach the prime viewing area.

Straightening up, looking over the land I live and work on from a thousand feet, I could be inhaling all of it. The shoreline's edge rough-hewn as if torn from a piece of old parchment, the surf from this height tracing a continuous white trim along the land's end. Like the live version of an ancient map, I half expect to see a four-pointed compass in the shape of the North Star painted on the ocean surface, complete with mermaids and sea monsters and Poseidon drawn around it for effect. The consistency of the ocean and the jaggedness of its meeting with the coast gives way to the geometry of the land. Half of the point which stretches out into the sea is farmland, parceled into near-perfect squares. Some of the squares hold rows of green, some rows of orange, and some hold the solid colors of vacancy—tan if it's arid, yellow if wild mustard has staked its claim, and green if a cover crop has been planted. White feather tails of water pirouette in some of the fields, sprinkling the crops. The square parcels are outlined by either dirt roads or tree lines. The longest-running line of trees separates Joe's ranch from the state reserve, the reserve growing wildly to the south of the line, a contrast in use.

Various reservoirs form random puddles of blue. Their source is a subtle stream of water trickling from one puddle to the next. The stream snakes underground for the most part, its path hardly traceable, visible above ground thanks only to a thin greenbelt of shrubbery which sprouts along its damp trail. The sinking sun's reflection occasionally shines through the water's bushy ground cover, as though there may be a ditch full of diamonds beneath the scrub.

Highway One passes by the reserve and the ranch, toy-sized cars carrying tiny passengers, and then re-connects with the ocean on each end of the point to skirt along the ocean once more. The stream flows through a culvert beneath the highway and works its way through the dense forests on this side of the road. Meadows stretch in front of the old new Demos houses, and in much of the space between them. But it's mostly trees. Hiding places for whatever needs hiding. And behind me, as I turn around, even more trees and less structure. Uninterrupted forest dipping in and out of the valleys and over the mountains towards Silicon Valley, still invisible from here, a green rolling calm before the storm.

So this is why I'm here. I'd almost forgotten.

Clothes soaked through, shoes scuffed beyond a shine.

But then forgetting only comes in waves, if it comes at all.

# SUNDAY 9/28

Joe has had season tickets for the Forty Niners since the days when they played their games at Kezar Stadium, the cement bowl downtown off of Golden Gate Park—now extinct but for the end zone entrances and some bleachers along the sides for high school games. He took me to a game last season at Candlestick when Lorraine was under the weather, and since then football has been an easy way for us to talk to each other. Whenever the team is on the road, as it is today, I have an open invitation to watch the game in the Mirabellis' ranch house.

I walk the two miles from my house to theirs. Their house is located by the main reservoir, where the ranch yard ends and the flower fields begin. They jokingly call it "the lake house," a reference which conjures up gauzy images of mint julip country living to the strains of Theme for a Summer Place. But the first thing you see when approaching the house is a huge satellite dish standing right by the driveway, as suitable for contacting alien life forms as it is for picking up football broadcasts, while the house itself looks like it should be part of a tract, surrounded by others that look just like it. But they do have the lake. Calling it a "reservoir" doesn't do it justice. Sand bars rising in its middle, cattails around its perimeter, it also hosts a constant presence of bird life—duck families, night herons, snowy egrets, and plenty of songbirds balancing on the surrounding reeds.

Lorraine is just as into the game as Joe is, while Aldo sits in the kitchen eating breakfast and reading agriculture magazines—California Farmer, Ag Report, Vegetable Grower News, Western Farm Press. The game is being played in Philadelphia.

"Hey, Stanford," Joe asks. "You ever been there, to Philadelphia?"

"Just once."

"Nice town?"

"Yeah, it's fine. People talk bad about it, but it's fun to visit if you like history."

Lorraine cuts in. "They sure have rowdy fans."

"Jesus, I'll say," Joe adds, hands in the air. "Crazy sons o' bitches."

"They definitely boo a lot," I say.

Joe continues. "You've probably been up and down the whole East Coast."

"I've been to a few places. Had some meetings in New York, of course. Can't be in finance without going there at some point. Went to Boston for a convention. The usual spots."

"Never made it out to the countryside back east?" Joe asks.

"No. No time. Strictly business."

"I hear it's beautiful. Some nice farms."

"Joe," Lorraine waves at him. "Save it for the commercial. They're inside the twenty-yard line, for god's sake."

"I know, I know," Joe waves back. "I'm trying not to get so worked up, remember? Bad for my heart."

"Well find a more quiet way of distracting yourself."

Joe looks at me and shrugs his shoulders in surrender.

"They've had their problems inside the twenty, haven't they?" I ask Lorraine.

She shakes her head, still looking at the screen. "It's been driving me crazy," she says. "Field goal after field goal."

A time out is called and a commercial blasts onto the screen. Joe reaches for the remote control and mutes the intrusion. "Working here, with us," he says. "It must be a helluva lot different than your old job, eh Stanford?"

Joe's never shown much interest in my life before Mirabelli Nurseries. There was the novelty of discovering it, which he pounced on, but then that was all. My nickname was given to me and there was work to be done. Tractor parts to be picked up in Salinas, rat poison waiting in a warehouse in Watsonville, plastic buckets on order in Gilroy.

"Very different," I say.

"Is that good or bad?" he asks.

"It's good," I assure him. "I needed a change for a while."

"For a while," he repeats the last thing I said. "In other words, temporary."

"Well," I stall. "I didn't even plan on working when I came out here. It was an added bonus." I smile.

"For us too. We really like having you around. And...well...we're certainly not getting any younger."

I know where he's going with this, of course. But before he can continue, the Forty Niners score and Lorraine jumps up and screams "Touchdown!" We all clap our approval, and then after they make the extra point Joe finally gets his chance to tell me how Aldo is a fine grower but has no interest in the business end of things—which Aldo confirms by shouting "that's right" from the kitchen—and how Manuel's language skills and familiarity with the routes enables him to take over my job when the time comes.

"And what time is that?" I ask.

"We've always kept it in the family," he says, now settling into a more confident place, talking about the way he conducts his life. "But the business is bigger than it used to be. Dad used to ride up to the city on a streetcar with a few flats of flowers and buy supplies on the way back with cash in hand from the market. Not anymore," He waves his hands as if he just made a silver dollar disappear. "You work with us in the market, you know about how much money we make there. Put that together with the grocery chain accounts and the stuff we ship through the wholesalers and the trucking companies and the airport once in a while, well...you do the math and you see how much product you've gotta move these days just to be considered a 'small' busniess. Millions of dollars, for chrissakes. And hey..." he puts up his hands as though I should brace myself. "If we're a small business then just think about what we're up against."

"I know," I say, simply to agree with him but instead I seem to have embarrassed him.

"Of course you do," he says. "What was I thinking?"

"It's a different kind of business," I assure him.

"That's right," Lorraine adds, trying to get Joe back on track. "Like the operating costs. Tell him about the operating costs." She turns to me. "Not many people realize what it takes to run just a few hundred acres."

"Ah, Jesus," Joe puts both hands on his head. "Don't ask me about the operating costs. I'll have a heart attack, for cryin' out loud."

I realize he's joking so I pitch in. "I make the runs," I tell him. "I see the bills. Equipment parts and maintenance, payroll account, seeds, chemicals, packaging, water rights, fuel—unleaded and diesel, inspection and upkeep of the underground tanks for that fuel, land leases..."

"Stop," Joe chuckles. "Stop. You see, honey?" he asks Lorraine. "The kid knows. Business is business."

"Yes," I'm quick to point out. "But I have no experience actually running one. I only know what they're worth on the market."

Joe doesn't waver. "But you're smart," he says. "We could train you easily. You're a Stanford boy."

"That's not necessarily saying much," I tell him. "I should introduce you to some of the people I went to school with."

"I don't care about them," he waves his arms. "I know you. And try as you might, you are not going to drive that truck and answer phones forever. You're a winner, a born one, and those are hard to come by."

I consider how subjective the term "winner" is.

"We're thinking we'll have to interview some people to fill Lorraine's job someday soon," Joe continues. "We don't expect you to keep the books, too, when the time comes. But as far as dealing with the clients and managing things...we figure we've already been handed the best candidate. Out of the blue, for chrissakes," he practically shouts. "Jogging through our fields, a big-shot businessman living next door. Talk about a blessing."

"What about Dodge?" I ask.

"Dodge?" says Joe, rubbing his chin for a moment. "Well, I'd like him to always have a job with us if he wants it and can keep it, but if you have a problem with him..."

"No, no," I say. "What about training him to run the place?"

Lorraine and Joe give me the same look at the same time, neither of them aware of the other. "You can't be serious," Joe says.

"Why not?" I ask. "He can do anything."

"I know he can," Joe agrees. "But he can't do it for very long."

I don't have a comeback on hand. Lorraine turns back to the game. Joe leans back and strikes a more fatherly tone before going on.

"I think it's great you're interested in helping him out as much as I am. Believe me, it makes me want to keep you around even more. But he's got a stack of second chances this high," he holds his palm flat above the floor. "And I don't take chances with my business."

I've never dealt with Joe on a business level, and to be quite honest it frightens me. I've never looked into the eyes of a business owner and seen this sort of passion. Working for something besides money. I've heard it's possible, I've heard it's the way to go. I've just never experienced it before.

Joe continues with his sales pitch as the game goes on, spinning more family history and flattery around me. I alternate my attention between him and the game, and by halftime the floor is mine. Lorraine goes into the kitchen.

"At this point," I tell him. "All I can give you is my standard response when confronted with a major business decision, and that is: I need time to think it over."

"Of course," Joe says. "Take all the time you need. Hell, I'm not leaving anytime soon. They'll have to drag me off this ranch, godammit. I love it too much. I just wanted to plant the seeds early, plan ahead."

"Like any good businessman," I say.

"Like any good farmer," he says, and slaps my knee. "Son of a bitch, great minds really do think alike, don't they?"

Lorraine comes back in the living room.

"Hey, hon...Stanford says he'll think it over," Joe tells her, as if it's the best possible answer they could expect.

"That's great," she says in kind.

And we watch the rest of the game as if the subject never came up. After we enjoy what Lorraine calls a "victory lunch" following the game, an Italian meal straight off a red-checkered tablecloth in North Beach, I tell them how much I appreciate the offer before I leave. We hug at the door, me and Lorraine, then me and Joe, and it feels like the only way we could possibly conclude our impromptu business meeting, unlike all the others I've had in my life which ended in arm-wrestling matches disguised as handshakes.

"See ya, Stanford," Aldo calls out from the kitchen.

"Yeah. See you tomorrow, Aldo."

And I walk very slowly through the ranch yard, looking around, retracing my steps to this point and realizing the impossibility of planning a life with any thoroughness.

Reaching the front gate I can hear Spanish radio and rapid fire conversation. A group of the men are lined up along the fence drinking beer and watching the Sunday traffic go by. Some sit on the top beam, some stand around an old Honda Civic parked with its doors open, stereo blasting, the source of the music. Sunday is the closest thing to a traditional day off on the farm. Joe gives the workers their choice of what days they want off, and most have chosen Sunday because they're used to going to church. A few of them still do, and then pick up the beer for everyone on the way home.

I walk by and say "hello" in English. "Buenas dias" always sounds half-assed to me unless I'm going to try and speak a lot more, and since these guys speak a dialect that's completely foreign to any American textbook author, this is not the time to try. Either putting a crimp in their day off or me being made fun of is no way for any of us to spend our free time.

A high-pitched whistle pierces the music, and I hope it's not intended for me. Again the whistle, as if the dog isn't responding.

"Hey, Stanford," says a female voice. I turn and see Veronica hanging over the fence surrounding the garden her mother keeps behind their house. Unlike the standardized quality shared by the row of houses lined up for the field hands, Javier's house has a classic, Midwestern white-picketness about it. It truly is "the foreman's house."

"Got you working a Sunday?" she asks as I approach.

"Nope. Just watching the Niner game with Joe and family." I lean on the fence like she does, so we have to turn our heads to talk. I can see over her shoulder that the men are looking at us and smiling.

"Did they win?" she asks.

"They did."

"Good. Makes for a nicer week around the ranch. Especially when it comes to Lorraine. Walking home?"

"I am."

"Rough neighborhood."

"That's what I hear. A real jungle."

"So what are you going to do if you make it home?"

"Hadn't thought about it."

"Then let's go to the reserve," she says, straightening herself up.

"Next door?"

"It's the closest one."

"I haven't been there since a field trip in the fifth grade," I say, trying to remember something from that trip other than the fact we took it. The two-hour bus ride, the "thank you" letter we composed as a class to the park ranger...but no memories of the ranger himself, or herself, no recollection of the seals, the area.

"Not even since you moved here?" she sounds genuinely surprised.

I shake my head. "Tried to jog through it once, but some lady ranger stopped me."

"Red hair, long braid down her back?" Veronica asks.

"That's the one. How did you know?"

"Remember, I worked as a docent in high school, giving tours. Figured it would look good on my college application."

"Oh yeah," I recall her telling me about how Roman used to circulate those petitions every time Joe had the helicopters come and spray. "Don't we need tickets?"

"Not now," she says. "It's off-season. The females and the alpha males don't start swimming by until December. Just a bunch of young males molting and practicing their moves out there this time of year."

"Am I dressed okay?" I ask.

"They'll lend you a coat and tie at the gate if you don't have one," she pokes my arm. "Come on, Stanford. Quit thinking up excuses and let's go."

I agree and she tells me to wait while she goes inside for a second. Even on the spur of the moment a woman needs to duck behind the curtain and back out again. I glance over at the guys down the fence a ways. Like a dozen fathers and brothers they are, staring at me, deciding whether or not I'm worthy of her. I smile weakly at them, like any nervous kid on an unfamiliar living room couch, and then Veronica appears. No keys jangling on her finger, no change in hairstyle or complexion or clothes; she may simply have stood behind the door and counted to ten. But somehow she does look even prettier than before.

"Let's go," she says, hopping the fence and walking ahead of me.

I catch up and we pass by the men. The comments start. Veronica has an answer for everything they throw our way, and they love it. Plenty of fake laughter and appreciative yelps follow us.

"What did they say?" I ask her.

"Not real quick on the draw yet, are you?"

"No. Estoy muy despacio."

"Nice accent, Mr. Gringo. And say despacito. You sound like the California Driver's Handbook."

"Despacito."

"Very good."

"So what did they say?"

"I'll give you three guesses."

I don't want to embarrass her, or myself for that matter, so I change the subject. "What about in general," I ask. "What do those guys talk about all day when they hang out on Sunday?"

"What any group of guys do," she says. "They talk real tough and crude about life and women, and then as the day goes on and they get a few beers in them, they start missing their wives more down in Mexico, or their girlfriends. Some of them have families. The talk gets pretty sad sometimes. They don't say as much, but I can hear it in their voices. They're lonely. Hangin' out with the guys just isn't enough after a while."

We turn into the driveway of the reserve, but cut onto a trail along the Mirabelli fence line instead of continuing towards the kiosk at the entrance to the parking lot.

"We're not going to get in trouble?" I ask.

"Damn, Stanford. Get out from over the hill already."

"That's just what they tell me on the other side. Maybe I should move on top of the hill."

"Your ex-wife think you're trying to keep your alimony payments low or something?"

"Jesus, Veronica…"

"I'm prying, yeah, but come on. Help me understand why you're letting a Stanford MBA go to waste."

"Are we going to go through this again?"

She smiles and walks a few paces before keeping it up. "My point is, as long as you're in the process of forgetting, and using work to help you do so, why not make some bucks at it?"

"You're breaking my heart, Veronica. Aren't you a little young to start thinking so much about money?"

She laughs. "You're never too young. Besides, this is my last year. Come spring, I'm out there with you, Wise Old Man. What are you, ten years older than me, maybe?"

"Maybe," I tell her.

"So coy. I wouldn't care if you asked me how much I weigh. I don't believe in etiquette. As long as something isn't mean-spirited, who cares?"

"I'll do you one better," I say. "How would you feel if I told you my wife made just as much per year, if not more than me, our whole marriage?"

She's thrilled. "Really? So alimony's not an issue?"

"No, it's not."

She punches me in the arm just below my shoulder. "Then why the hell are you letting that MBA go to waste, you dumb-ass?"

I rub my arm, pretending it hurts, but enjoying the light throb below the skin. I'd forgotten how exaggerated first contact can be. We settle into a quiet walk for a few moments.

"Have you ever heard of that study someone did on Yale and Harvard graduates and their lives after college?" I ask her.

"Should I have?"

"You tell me. They interviewed them ten years into their careers, and 73 percent said they were unhappy with what they were doing. 73 percent. Kids don't go to those kinds of schools because they know what they want to do with their lives."

"They go there because of the name," she completes my thought.

"The name," I emphasize. "That goddamn name."

I drift off for a moment, trying to be conscious only of the breeze passing through every hair on my body and a few selected images: the cypress trees to our right, the hawk circling the brush to our left, something rustling in the brush just off the trail. Bird? Snake?

"Stanford," Veronica says. I look at her and she's smiling. "Are you telling me you were lousy at what you did?"

"Quite the contrary," I say. "I decided that as long as I was in a job I hated, I'd become the best in my field, which I figured wouldn't be as hard as you'd think since so many others were miserable, too. 73 percent of them, at least. So I aimed for the top, by any means possible." I shiver at the memory. "Any means possible."

"And then bam," Veronica slams a fist into her palm. I jump slightly at her sound effect. "Instant burnout."

"More or less," I say, staring once more at the horizon.

"So what is it you want to do?" she asks.

"I don't know," I look at her. "I've only recently considered the question."

She regains her cocksure tone. "All that may be true," she says. "But I think there's more to you being out here than re-evaluating your life."

She is good. Those pouty lips are nothing but camouflage.

"Maybe I was forced out here," I tell her. "But maybe being the more reflective type suits me."

"Forced out here?" she says, intrigued by the phrase. "How?" And I'm going to snap at her about minding her own business when I see that she actually cares. Not a hint of morbid curiosity in her eyes. Compassion. Plain and simple. I look away and try to regain my balance.

"I thought you were going to show me some seals," I say, with some difficulty.

"Sure," she says, soft and sincere. "We can do that."

And she takes me by the hand and we walk through the dunes towards the ocean. More gentle than a punch in the arm, but far more powerful.

The dunes are sometimes over our heads, creating miniature valleys for us to walk through, ice plant and prairie grass peeking through the sand. The barking of the seals grows louder, the smell draws closer to that of a gigantic bird cage years past its last cleaning.

Something comes back to me about that fifth grade field trip. I remember some controversy, I tell Veronica. A situation right here in the dunes. One boy wanted to beat up another boy. He "called him down." That was the phrase. You wanted to fight, you would "call him down." The boy had asked Jillian Rifkin to "go" with him, and the other boy was already "going" with her. That was another phrase. You liked a girl, you wanted her to be your steady, you asked her to "go." Then if she said yes, you avoided each other until you didn't want to go anymore. The boy who got called down was terrified and walked near the teacher. He didn't tell her, of course. Then he'd be a wuss. Besides, the teacher was surrounded by the same group of kiss-assy little girls who all wanted to hold her hand. Jillian wasn't one of them, obviously. She was too popular. All of us boys inevitably had to side with the tormentor. If we had any empathy for the kid being tormented, we couldn't show it. The group taunting him was so big, too big to take on. We didn't pay any attention to the seals until the docent mentioned sharks. Great White Sharks swimming offshore, waiting to prey on the seals as they came and went. How big are the sharks? We asked. How many of them are out there? Have you ever seen a seal get attacked by one? Have you ever seen a person get attacked by one? Has a person ever been attacked out here? How close do they come to the beach? Have you ever seen one?

"What did Jillian Rifkin think about all this?" asks Veronica.

"Who knows?" I tell her. "Girls in one group, boys in another. As usual."

"No color-coded wristbands on that trip?"

"Nope. Free to choose on that one."

"Fascinated by violence and mystified by girls," she muses. "So it starts that early?"

"At least that early."

We reach the shore and hundreds of elephant seals recline across the beach in groups of six or seven. At least one seal in each group is either throwing its head back to bark or tossing sand on itself with its front flipper. Veronica tells me that scientists still aren't sure why they flip sand on themselves, to keep warm or to keep cool, as she launches into her old docent speech.

"Shall I keep going?"

"Definitely," I assure her. "Enlighten me."

So I learn about the elephant seal lifestyle and life cycle. They come here every year to perpetuate the species. Months alone at sea, solitary seals bulking up on the tiny organisms of very deep waters so they can land here in winter and stay beached for months without eating, losing several hundred pounds of body weight for the sake of the life cycle going on. Females having babies and reluctantly agreeing to mate with the persistent males. Males fighting for the alpha positions atop the harems of females, fighting and fucking such a vital part of their lives that they often crush infant seal pups in the process of doing either. Sometimes a male on the outskirts, not powerful enough to challenge for a harem, will try and mount a newly weaned pup. Dozens of flattened young carcasses are left over by the end of mating season, Veronica says.

"Do you find them ugly?" she asks.

I look at the males lolling around in preparation for the upcoming season. Snouts like trunks, elephant trunks cut off just beneath the lower lip. Dark bodies bigger than sofa beds, gashes and gray calluses marking their complexions.

"No," I say. "Ugly isn't the word. It isn't fair."

She seems pleased at my answer, which was the whole idea. "These aren't even the alpha male candidates," she says. "They're still out there somewhere, maybe the Bering Sea, getting ready to come ashore and show these guys who's boss. To impress Jillian Rifkin and ask her to go." She smiles.

"You said these guys don't even ask," I remind her. "Give us that much credit, at least."

We walk behind the seals along the ridge of the beach, where the dunes start to plane out towards the ocean. Every whitecap in the choppy waters reflects the sun, it seems. The island rises above the shiny surface, the fallen metal tower and the abandoned house having turned it into something of an eyesore. From here, just across the foamy channel, I can see how badly decayed the old house really is. Its exterior resembles the bottom of an old boat, the hollowness of the windows and front door seems deeper than the house itself.

I notice some movement in the door frame. It's a seal. Then I realize there are seals all around the house, and around the entire perimeter of the island. Veronica tells me they're harbor seals and sea lions, left to conquer the island since the elephant seals have claimed the shore. Every so often one of them dives into the water. I concentrate on one and try to locate its head breaking the surface, but the channel is filled with dark rocks breaking the surface in spots, easily confused for seals.

Several elephant seals are swimming between the rocks closer to shore, their home territory, while others fight one-on-one in the shallow waters. Chest to chest, backs curved U-shaped, clubbing each other with their heads as they try to dig their teeth into the other's neck. Several dozen people, mostly tourist types, point at each of the different spectacles in groups of their own, all of us prevented from reaching the beach by an occasional docent positioned along its perimeter.

"The females are very different," says Veronica.

"No kidding," I say.

She smiles. "Different-looking. They're more like what people think of when they think of a seal. Gentle faces, really round, with the puppy dog eyes and nose and whiskers. Oh shit."

"What?"

"Ranger Roman dead ahead."

A human wall coming up marks the end of where we're allowed to stroll. A huge herd of seals shifts and barks in the distance beyond the gawking people, and a talking sunburned head bobs above its captive audience, wearing a ranger's hat and a salesman's grin.

"Let's go," she says, grabbing my arm to spin me around. Too late.

"Oh my God," Roman's voice rises a couple decibels above his seal spiel. "Veronica!"

"Keep walking," she implores me in a whisper, squeezing my arm.

"Ladies and gentlemen," Roman announces to the crowd, now all turned in our direction I see as I look back over my shoulder. "We are in the presence of greatness. The best docent to ever walk the shores of our famed reserve—Veronica Suarez! Give it up for her, folks."

The crowd applauds. Veronica sighs.

"I wish it was in my nature to be as bitchy in public as I can be in private," she says before she turns and waves, a grin painfully spreading across her face. Roman beams victoriously at us and sure enough pours it on.

"And who's that with her, my friends, but the one and only Paul 'Stanford' Pryor, a dominating figure in the world of high finance turned colorful local. Living proof, ladies and gents, that you really can get away from it all."

The audience laughs in appreciation. One camera-toting man in a tennis hat tells Roman he missed his calling. "Shoulda gone into show business," he says.

"What do you think this is?" Roman answers, and the party continues. "If you'll excuse me for a moment, folks, I'd like a word with my friends. Look!" he points out at the ocean. "Sea otters."

And the crowd all turns toward the water and looks for sea otters which aren't really there.

"Well, well, well," says Roman as he reaches us. "I figured this would happen soon enough."

"It's not what you think," snaps Veronica.

"Does Stanford know that?" he grins, looking over at me.

"If you were worth taking seriously I'd slap your face," she says. Roman laughs.

"I love this girl," he says. "You're a lucky man, Stanford. She wasn't old enough to drink when I was giving the orders."

"As if booze is all it would take," Veronica rolls her eyes.

"Of course not," Roman nods in my direction. "It obviously takes money."

She shakes her head. "Let's go, Stanford."

"See why I need your advice?" Roman says to me as we turn to leave. "Dude, we have got to sit down and talk dollars and cents some day."

"You couldn't afford me either, Roman," I tell him.

"You may be surprised," he says, his smile growing into an even broader smirk.

The tourists, meanwhile, have convinced themselves that there are otters splashing around offshore, the sun's reflection and choppy waters disguising the fact they're only rocks peaking just above the surface. Roman returns to center stage and starts telling them about sea otters.

"Did he make a habit out of hitting on all the female docents?" I ask Veronica.

"Only the ones with inside information on Mirabelli Nurseries."

I actually find myself saying "Hmmmm" and pondering the implications of what Veronica just told me and what Roman said about his personal wealth. There may very well be connections to make between everybody's favorite ranger and everything else that's been going on. Gretchen told me that Franky left her all the money, and nothing but the house to Roman, which is much better than the one dollar bequeathed to Dodge, but certainly not the kind of inheritance that would allow him to play with much of his salary, which I assume is paltry.

Any connection leading to Roman would please Dodge, perhaps too much. I'd never be able to pry his jaws off the possibility. I'll wait on that one until proof presents itself: hard matter with no shreds of doubt.

I'd start making the connections now, but our conversation is turning small again, Veronica and I, and that's a lot more enjoyable. Good things in small packages, I believe is the saying. Anecdotes and more childhood flashbacks and more recent memories of college and what I like about the country and what I miss about the city and Veronica wants to live in a city so badly. Any city. Chances to think out loud in front of each other. Connecting. And there's that word again. But the kind of connecting Dodge wants will have to come later. I am quite frankly enjoying myself too much, and Dodge would understand. Friends clear out for one another if something looks this good. No problem. Unless it gets serious. Then you start to wonder if you're being replaced. Serious? This is the first time I've even spoken with Veronica anywhere outside the office, where the phone could ring at any time. But I suggest dinner and she responds "yes" so quickly. So I suggest Santa Cruz, then, on the wharf. As long as she's so enthusiastic. She even offers to drive.

Not a single pause the whole way there. The radio never reached for. She never met anyone on campus she looked twice at. She says personal hygiene was considered fascist by many at UCSC. The politics of the bathroom. The politics of you name it. Clothes like they were found on the side of the road, and who needs shoes? All very intriguing, but all very fashionable, according to Veronica. Identity-starved students just trying to fit in with the local community at best—as Santa Cruz seems to have incorporated homelessness into the fabric of its culture—and at worst just rich kids living out a four year beat poet fantasy. The bearded hitchhiking sage has bought into just as much bullshit as the briefcase-toting pair of khakis, it's just a different kind of bullshit. I thank her for the compliment and we laugh for the one hundredth time this evening. I try to recall if I was so opinionated and knew pretty much everything in college and then realize I'm still that way but just keep it to myself. So I laugh even longer. Every bubble in the beer feels charged going down and I can follow the trail of its coolness through my body. Every bite of salmon is life-affirming in its smoothness with just the right amount of bitterness from the lemon and I had forgotten how good it feels to feel so all over the place. But I can't help but feel like an elephant seal, a male one of course. I'm still married, after all. And then Veronica asks how my marriage ended.

"If I tell you about my marriage and how we conducted ourselves you'd ask for the check," I tell her.

"But you're paying," she says.

"Trust me," I say. "I need time to put together a presentation when and if I ever tell you about Janet and me. A slide show, handouts, bar graphs..."

"Her name is Janet?"

"Yes."

"Do you still love her?"

She takes a certain pride, it's clear, in creating a startled pause every so often. I weigh my answer and decide that avoiding the truth and telling a bold face lie are entirely different. And unlike my previous life, I am now only capable of the side-step, no longer able to look into someone's eyes and pretend to be sincere about something so huge.

"Yes," I tell her. "I love her very much."

Veronica smiles. "Are you going to tell me now that love just isn't enough sometimes?"

"It's plenty," I say. "More than enough. As long as you're careful with it and don't take it for granted. As long as you realize you're not the only ones, that there's lot of people in love out there." I take my last sip of beer. It's warm with no bubbles left. "As long as you don't flaunt it."

She's intrigued, but the evening is clearly over. If I needed a reminder to take it slow, I have it now. For a moment I firmly believe that openness is a bad idea and the world needs to get back to small talk and forget the never ending confessional. But there it is now, right where we can see it, and though it may only prevent us from getting together in the long run, the truth does save us from an uncomfortable pause in my driveway later on. No kiss. No internal debates about it. She may not know I'm still married, but she knows enough. She knows the most important thing of all: I love Janet.

"Good night," we say, one after the other, and she kisses me on the cheek.

"Can we do this again sometime?" I ask.

"We can do it as often as you want."

That goes over well with both of us since we both really know what it means. At least we think we know, and the uncertainty makes it even more exciting.

I stay on the porch to watch her drive away. I go inside and turn on the light. The house is of course empty, so I go back onto the porch and enjoy being there, to watch night fall on the meadow and the trees all around it and the hills that the trees climb up. I'm standing on a front porch after a date, and damn that feels good. I should really put up a swing on the porch, one of those suspended wooden love seats that Jimmy Stewart would swing on with Donna Reed after walking home from a dance. I'll invite Veronica to sit in it with me. Hold hands, watch the stars, get nervous.

It takes about a half an hour until darkness has settled in cold enough for the fog to flow over the hills, through the trees, across the meadow. A hollow thud on the front porch and I jump two feet in the air.

"Didn't mean to scare you," Dodge says, coming up the stairs. I can't see him, only hear him. He sounds like he's talking with his mouth full.

"You been there all this time?" I ask, as he draws closer to the faint light spilling across the porch from the front windows.

"I was asleep in back. Woke up and saw the lights."

"Did you find your...Jesus Christ!"

He reaches the light. His left eye is swollen shut and his upper lip flares out to where you can practically see it throbbing. Cuts line both his lips and more cuts fly across his face like war paint.

"It wasn't one of my kids," he coughs before going on. "Let me just say that right off."

"Who then?"

Dodge looks at me for a few moments, his breathing through his nose kind of bubbly sounding.

"County sheriff," he says, and blood starts to run from his nose onto his freshly grown lip. "Shit," he tastes it. "Took forever to stop that blood."

"Is it broken?"

He shakes his head, pulling a red-blotted wad of toilet paper from his back pocket and sticking it up his nostril. "Don't think so. But then I ain't feelin' much right now."

"Did that Deputy Bert guy do this?"

Dodge laughs. "Come on, now. You think I couldn't take him?"

"Well if he had a gun..."

"It was two a them young hotshots they been runnin' out here every few weeks."

"What for? Why did they do this?"

"I was up in Pescadero..."

"What were you doing up there?"

"Just shut up and I'll get there."

"Sorry."

But Dodge doesn't start right in. He keeps looking at me with his one good eye catching the light from inside the house, making sure I'm done before going on. "I went into town," he says. "Into Santa Cruz one more time to look for my kids. Couldn't resist. And I found 'em. Actually found 'em. Hangin' around downtown Santa Cruz with a bunch a those kids who look like runaways they got crawlin' all over the place down there. My kids see me and take off like I'm a probation officer or some fuckin' thing."

"Oh, man..."

"Yeah, I'm sorry too. So I was gonna go out and get wasted right there in Santa Cruz but figger I'd end up sleepin' in the park or somethin' since I don't know no one down there and I'm not plannin' on gettin' anything but as fucked up as I can get. If I'm gonna blow it, I'm gonna blow it big. Right?"

"I can see that."

"So I drive back up to Pescadero where I'm just a lot more comfortable. Hardly any buildings, hardly any people, and I figger I'm bound to know some sorry sack a shit at the bar at some point in the night—hell, it's a one bar town—and that's what happened. I was one of the guys again. They were all there, as usual. And the more I felt like one of the guys, I got real lonely and scared, like that was all there is, all I'm ever gonna be."

He pulls the toilet paper out of his nose and checks the flow of blood. Stopped for now, so he puts the wad back in his pocket. "We were leavin' the bar and there's this group a Mexicans across the street on the corner, where the road goin' out to the highway and Main Street cross. I thought it was the same group that's always there lookin' for work, but it was mostly a bunch a guys I never seen before. Just a couple familiar faces. And they're pushin'. Usually I'd give a fuck, but there's those deputy sheriffs parked right across the street from 'em. Right there where there's always a sheriff's car parked at the intersection, waitin' for somebody to roll that stop sign. But there ain't nobody comin' into town at that hour, and there they are, sittin' there plain as day with those guys dealin' right across the street"

"How did you know they were dealing?"

"How do you think I got my drugs all them years? Mail order catalogue?"

"But with the cops right there? That's ridiculous."

"That's what I said, especially since Deputy Bert ain't on the beat around here no more. The place cleaned up since they canned his ass. But there's those cops just sittin' there waitin' for a speeder who ain't comin'. Like Pescadero's known for its night life, for chrissakes. So I go over to ask the two young lions in the cop car what the fuck they're doin' and they tell me to get off it. Step away from the car, that kinda bullshit. No, godammit, I tell 'em. I'm a citizen, you tell me why you can't see what's goin' on in front of you."

Dodge has to stop before he goes on. He takes a deep breath through his blood-clogged nose. The taste, sound, and feel of his breathing seem to remind him of the incident.

"The deputies, they threw me in the car and took me out to a field. Tied me to an irrigation pipe and beat the crap outta me. They said I was free to go once I dragged the rope under that maze a pipes to someplace I could slide it through a break in the joints. Before they left they said to think twice about tellin' anyone." His breathing gets deeper and he grows more despondent, staring at the floor. "Couldn't even start tryin' to slide the rope to a gap in the pipe 'til I got some strength back around sunrise. Didn't take long, really. Just down to the end of the aisle and the pipe ended there. Took me an hour to get back to my van, and I been here waitin' ever since."

And I've been having a wonderful time with the Mirabellis and then Veronica ever since. To deflect my guilt I ask if he wants to stay here for the night.

He seems to appreciate the offer, but says "Nah. I'm goin' up to the city and wait for you guys at the market. Sleep in my van."

"You sure?"

"I wanna be alone, lick my wounds in private."

"Okay. But meanwhile shouldn't we tell someone?"

"Who you gonna trust, Stanford boy?" Dodge's voice floods the meadow. "Huh? Who you gonna trust? Tell me who we should talk to and we'll talk to 'em."

"I don't know, but if we asked..."

"You don't know. That's right. You don't know shit. This is my gig. I'm makin' the connections. Not Franky. Not Roman. This is mine." Dodge is pacing now, back and forth on the porch as if looking for a way out. "I learned a long time ago what a dead Mexican's worth to the old school, and you don't know shit. I got a dead mother to prove it." He lunges at the porch railing and shouts over the fog-covered meadow "Time's up, motherfuckers! Time's up! It's my turn!" And as his echo fades, he seems taunted by its insignificance against the trees and the hills and the sky so heavy with stars.

"I'll see ya later," he mumbles, and then hurries around to the backyard. His engine blasts, his tires squeal as he swerves from behind the house, and gravel spews like hale on the porch as he passes. The trees spotlighted by his headlights, the eucalyptus tunnel flooded with light, and in those series of flashes he is gone.

I look up and still can't find any constellations in all those stars. Not a single familiar pattern. So Dodge is that convinced his mother was murdered. Is he out for reconciliation or revenge? A coyote howls and its cry sounds nothing like in the movies or the way people imitate them. The cry is more drawn out, lilting, up and down the scale, off key, and full of pain.

# MONDAY 9/29

Dodge is not in the market. Not in the parking lot, or any of the streets surrounding the complex. Joe fumes all morning and all I can tell him is I haven't seen Dodge since Friday and on that day he gave me no indication as to where he might be going, which is at least half true—the part about not knowing where he went.

No wrapped bouquet waiting for Gino at Santo's. But then no Gino today, either. Could I have witnessed the big score Friday? Maybe Gino made so much money in the exchange that he finally got out of the flower business for good. No word in the market, though. Gino's retirement would create some buzz. Then again it's Monday. No buzz possible. Very slow.

Only one truck today, so I get to sleep in the passenger seat of the bobtail on the way home. I wake up dazed and unable to do anything but remember how to breathe and blink for a few moments. The road to Pescadero flares off inland to the left. The wood carved sign marking the entrance to town as "two miles away" and "established in 1856" pulls me finally into consciousness, hoping that Dodge didn't go back there for revenge or something almost as stupid.

In the ranch yard I tell Joe that I'll ask Veronica if she's seen Dodge. I jump out as soon as Joe stops the truck to back it up towards the walk-in refrigerator. Veronica is standing in the doorway of the office. She smiles as I jog towards her.

"How sweet," she says. "You just couldn't wait to see me again, could you?"

"That, too. But I need to know if Dodge showed up here this morning."

"He's not with you?"

I shake my head. Veronica looks worried. I can't be positive, but I'm pretty sure that every other woman I've known, considering our date last night, would be too pissed about my failure to indulge her in sweet talk about last night to bother looking worried about Dodge. I want to kiss her and tell her to take the rest of the day off and take her up to Half Moon Bay for fish and chips.

"Have you been to the house?" she asks.

"I'm on my way."

"Let me know if he's there." She looks even more concerned.

"I will." And I take a step forward and kiss her. Fish and chips will have to come later. She looks at me and grins, close-mouthed, no surprise, just a sense of it's-about-fucking-time.

As I turn to go I notice that Joe and Lorraine are still angling the rig backwards. He's concentrating and she's telling him what to do. I'm glad they didn't see us kiss. That's the sort of thing I'd rather keep private, the first kiss. I jog over and ask Joe if he wants me to help unload the leftover flowers into the fridge.

"No. Lorraine can handle it," he says.

Lorraine sighs in my direction and rolls her eyes. "He'd rather knock the refrigerator door off its hinges than be told he's about to do it."

"I'm going to see if Dodge is home," I say as I head back to my pickup.

"You find him, you bring him here," Joe calls through the window. "I don't want him starting his shit again." I turn and salute.

"And don't forget," he adds. "You're going to UFP for Aldo today."

Nodding and waving as I duck into the driver's seat, I swing by my house but don't stop. Seeing that he and his van aren't there, I circle the house and head back down the road, make the U-turn up the hill, and then at the top, turn right to Roman's house.

As I drive along the road below the stucco monstrosity, I see Roman in the driveway waxing his surfboard, which is suspended between two sawhorses. He grins and pretends to shoot me with his index fingers extended and thumbs raised. I wave and follow the curve in the road over the hill and into the miniature valley behind the main house. The small pre-fab guest house is definitely deserted. Driving past the main house once more, Roman salutes from halfway up the hill then pretends he's drinking a beer, pointing from himself to me, back and forth several times. I give him a thumb-up through the window.

I take a shower and the phone rings before I've finished drying, maybe the fifth time it's rung this year. One time I was late for work, and the other four times were wrong numbers.

"Hello?" I ask, truly curious as to who it could be.

"Stanford?" it's Veronica. "Dodge showed up right after you left. He's in bad shape."

"I'll be right there."

I pull over by the office and Veronica tells me he's in his van across from the Mirabelli's house. I continue down the center of the yard towards the house and see his van right where she said it was, parked next to an old plastic fertilizer drum twenty feet high, several stacks of wooden pallets even higher, and the old truck trailer—wheels removed, Mirabelli Nurseries' old logo painted across it fading and peeling. I knock on the van and the side door slides open, revealing Dodge sprawled out smoking a cigarette on a raft of dirty clothes, his wounds now scabbed and his shiner turned a darker blue. The smell of stale beer and whisky is even stronger than the usual dirty laundry smell coming from the back of his van.

"I never did get a chance to break my sober streak without some cops beatin' on me," he announces.

"What did you tell Joe?" I ask.

"Got drunk, got into a fight."

"And what did he say?"

"I've gotta stay here for a while. I can shower and keep food in their house."

"A grown man," I shake my head. "Grounded."

He massages his temples, cigarette in hand. "The good news is I feel like shit. Don't know how I ever did that every night, and this every morning."

"And what did you do last night, exactly?"

He runs a hand down his face and blinks a few times. "Got drunk by myself. In the woods. On the beach. I made up the fight to explain my face to Joe and Lorraine. Didn't wanna tell 'em about the cops."

"Oh, you mean those cops you could've run into again last night?" I scold him.

"Don't worry, Stanford. I wasn't out for revenge."

"You sure?"

"Well why the fuck do you think I couldn't make it past the liquor store last night, 'cause I was feelin' all manly and proud?" He stares at the ceiling of his van. Completely and utterly stares at it for several moments with no conclusion in sight. I feel as though I'm contemplating a portrait of someone completely alone. There's nothing I can tell him that he doesn't already know. He's heard enough speeches. But there may be something I can do that could take his mind off his next drink.

"I saw Roman out waxing his board while I was looking for you."

Dodge keeps staring at the ceiling, comatose.

"I thought maybe now would be a good time to have that beer with him, have that talk. Since I know he's home and all."

It works. Dodge swivels his head in my direction and the glaze over his eyes melts instantly. "You got a plan of attack?"

"Not yet," I say. "But you never want to go into a meeting without one. I'll hash it out on the road, on my way down to Watsonville. Aldo placed an order at UFP. Then I'll head up to the house this afternoon."

"Perfect," says Dodge. "Hey, I need a new hat. Pick one up for me?"

"A new hat? Where?"

"United Farm Products."

"They don't sell hats."

"I know. They give 'em away. There's always some chemical company dumpin' a box a baseball caps on their doorstep with their logo on 'em. Like how doctors have those drug company logo clocks on their walls."

The last time I was in a doctor's office, my old doctor, he made a point of telling me the new clock in his lobby was a priceless Cartier his wife found while antique shopping in Carmel.

All the way down to Watsonville, a 45 minute drive, I compose scripts on how my conversation with Roman may go. He'll be easy to pry for information, I'm sure. He'll want to show off whatever kind of money he has, he'll want to impress me. His means of acquiring it will be only slightly more difficult to find out. I need to know more, I'll insist, before I would dare to give my advice on anything financial. I may be on the bench right now, but I still have my reputation. That should reel him in. Any reluctance on his part and I'll make him feel naïve, give him the look that answers the question 'they shoot horses, don't they?' The last thing he'll want to come across as is foolish.

South through Santa Cruz, where all the 1969 VW Buses in the world come to die, and the mentally ill mill through the streets like mascots at Disneyland. South through the hidden upper classes of Soquel and Aptos, the kinds of real estate featuring power-walking elderly couples in canvas sweat suits, arms swinging high. South until the estate-sprinkled hills melt into the lush valley which hosts Watsonville.

The city is a very small part of the valley. The real action swirls around it in thousands of acres of farmland—strawberries, lettuce, raspberries, apple orchards—the source of the city's very existence. And while cement fortresses selling bulk products are starting to crop up around its edges—Cheez Whiz by the six-pack, toilet paper by the pound, tube socks by the barrel—at this time on a weekday it still seems as if everyone is in the fields and only the schools are inhabited. Everyone is working in the warehouses rising in between the city and the surrounding crops, and Main Street is practically deserted. Not a single window shopper or panhandler, nobody lounging on patio furniture in front of coffee houses or waiting in line for a matinee at the movie theater. There's too much work to be done and not much disposable income. Waiting at a red light with no cars passing in front of me, I have a feeling that much more of America used to be like this when it was young and hungry. Without the traffic lights, of course.

While Joe's truck is being loaded with drums and jugs and burlap sacks full of products with names I can't pronounce, I walk into the office and ask for a hat, any hat. The receptionist pulls a box out from under her desk and holds up a baseball cap for my approval.

"How's this?" she asks.

It's off-white with a green bill and the UFP logo in a circle on the front. She turns it around to show me the back. Stitched above the adjustable strap is the word "HORTALIFE" with a trademark indicator just above the "E."

"Came in yesterday," she says. "We've got others. Flo-Gro, Riddilex, Diaclear..."

"That'll do fine," I tell her. "Thanks."

On the way back north as I clear the Santa Cruz city limits, I get that similar feeling of breaking free as I always do once I pass the last stop light. But today it's a little different. Today I get the sensation of sprinting through a big sheet of paper like our high school football team did before a game. Go Stanford! Beat Roman!

I drive downhill, coasting towards a dip in the highway. A beach parking lot stands to the side of the road where the dip starts to rise again. A car waiting at the exit of the parking lot sees me coming and when I'm ten yards away decides that it would rather die than follow a truck. The car pulls out and I slam the brakes and turn the wheel at the same time, just the thing you know you're not supposed to do but still do in a panic. I slide with the tires screaming louder than I'm screaming, the truck slowly turning clockwise, the passenger in the car and I now facing each other through the side windows, eyes locked as we draw closer, looking deeper into each other's eyes but not seeing the whole face. I don't know if it's male or female, all I see is my life and the eyes and oh fuck you you stupid fuck is it so bad to follow a truck you stupid motherfucker—and I stop. The screaming stops. It's a woman. The passenger is a woman.

We stare at each other, catching our breath. She mouths through the closed window "are you okay?" I nod. She smiles and turns to the driver who I can't see and they talk for a few seconds. She turns back to me and pantomimes wiping her brow while making a face that says "woo-wee that was close" and they drive away. Mission accomplished. They are not behind a truck.

Glad you can be so cavalier about your near-death experience, folks, but when my life flashed before me I still didn't like what I saw. I need more time.

Closer to the ranch I reach a part of the highway where the surf splashes just below the shoulder of the road at the bottom of a half-mile stretch of dusty-colored cliffs. I see some brown pelicans flying in a long line skimming the water's surface, prehistoric-looking with their several-foot wingspan and pterodactyl-like beaks, as though they should be flying above a Tyrannosaurus Rex. Their tight formation, dozens of birds long, like a squadron of B-52s, their wings perfectly still. They gain altitude as I pass and start diving for fish one by one, free-falling from the sky as if shot down, cannon-balling into the ocean, then surfacing as if nothing ever happened, just duck-paddling along with a baggy beak full of food quickly swallowed.

I think of the old Peterson's Field Guide to Western Birds lying around the house I'm renting, which Gretchen either forgot or left on purpose as part of the furnishings. It says that pelicans eventually go blind from their kamikaze style of feeding themselves. They may have decided as a species long ago that this was the best way to fish, but the membranes which shield their eyes have not caught up, have not evolved enough to maintain their vision during their entire life expectancy—the span of which may increase if their eyes ever do evolve, because they die once they lose their sight.

As the highway rises higher above the waves and moves past the cliffs, I look in the side mirror and catch a few more of their splashes before the ocean disappears behind the trees now growing dense on each side of the road.

Dodge unloads the truck in his new hat. He throws his old one in the rusted oil drum serving as a garbage can in the center of the ranch yard. Joe calls me in the office and briefs me on tomorrow's agenda as Veronica sits in the chair behind him and tries to make me laugh by simply staring at me, straight-faced, like a cat looking out a window at the day it wants so badly to be a part of. It works, she gets me going, but fortunately I can disguise my laughter in response to Joe's diatribe about tomorrow's visit by the Wheelers. The land owners are coming on their semi-annual visit to be entertained by Joe and Lorraine at a barbecue by the "lake house." Free pumpkins for the kids, a ride around the fields in a tractor, "like a goddamn carnival," Joe complains, though he's the one who invites them every year. "Good policy," he maintains.

We're all excused for the day then, Joe tells us. It's surprisingly early in the afternoon for him to ignore the phone. "Those damn Wheelers have been staying at the camp for the last couple days," he says. "Probably come asking us to pull their Range Rover out of the creek any time now, so let's all hide."

Dodge is finished unloading the truck and is locking up the chemical storage shed a few doors down from the office.

"Guess I'll go for a jog," I tell him as I approach.

He turns around and grins. "There's a nice run by Roman's house." He notices something over my shoulder. "You need somethin' Ronny?"

I turn and see Veronica hanging around by the front of the office. "Just waiting for Stanford," she smiles.

I turn back and find Dodge raising his eyebrows at me. "Everybody wants to pick my brain," I say rather lamely.

Dodge sees right through me and laughs. "Don't be embarrassed, Stanford boy. There's born winners and born losers, and the only thing us losers hate more than a winner is a winner who pretends he ain't, like it's for our sake. For the sake of the losers."

Not the kind of response I expected, so I stand a bit dumbstruck. Veronica waits. Dodge launches into a rendition of "Stanford and Veronica sittin' in a tree..." which makes her laugh a lot more than it does me.

I'm thinking of some possible excuses as I walk her home about why I can't see her later on, something more convincing than "I'm tired" and less heavy than "let's take it slow" but then she saves me the trouble by telling me she has a presentation to prepare for school tomorrow as we arrive at her gate.

"So we'll stick to weekends then," I say.

"Good idea," she agrees. "We'll take it slow."

And as I kiss her I tell myself that she isn't a mind reader, despite evidence to the contrary. She's much better than that. She's understanding.

I go back and fetch my truck, driving home distracted, which concerns me just a little. But as I'm putting on my jogging shoes I remember how useful I'd always found it to mentally throw away my homework before a meeting, confident in the research and preparation I'd done, ready for war with my mind free and easy. There's still Veronica on the brain, of course, but the jog over to Roman's helps settle me down. And though I can't put her completely out of my mind, I realize all thoughts of her are pleasant ones, anyway, and it's not the CEO of any major conglomerate I'm meeting, after all, it's just...

"Roman," I shout in response to him flailing his arms from his front deck as I run by the house. He flags me down as if stranded on a desert island and I'm the first ship he's seen in weeks. "Would I still be taking you up on your invitation if I just had a glass of water?" I ask.

Absolutely, Roman says. Positively. Once inside the house with glass of water in hand, I wouldn't be surprised if he took my dinner order. He's bouncing around like a waiter who gets stuck serving the restaurant critic. Never mind that the house smells as if there's never been a meal cooked in its kitchen since its construction. I might as well be sitting in a great big new car.

"Where's your wife?" I ask.

"She teaches a class at the rec center down in Santa Cruz Monday evenings. She left early to meet some friends." He retreats to the kitchen to get himself a drink.

"Really?" I say, surprised that mousy Marcie could get up in front of a roomful of people and be audible. "What does she teach?"

Roman returns holding a can of Coors and sits down across from me with his eyebrows scrunched up. "Uh...she teaches dance, I think. Dance or yoga. Something where everyone ends up rolling on the floor."

"I see."

"Things start to run together when you've been married a while, Stanford," he explains himself. "But you wouldn't know, eh Slick?" He slaps me on the shoulder and sits across from me, winking and grinning. I smile right along with him. So all he assumes about me is that I made a lot of money and showed up on the coast by myself. Good.

"I guess I used to have a hard time putting my career second," I tell him. See Roman? See what a valuable resource I am?

"Dude," he says. "Priorities are personal things. If they're straight in your mind, they're straight."

"Words to live by," I tell him.

He lifts his can. "To the art of making money," he proposes.

I raise my glass in kind. "I've always considered it a craft. As in crafty."

Roman laughs much louder than my line deserves, rocking in his chair and trying to keep his mouthful of beer in check. "You're the man," he says, finally forcing it down his throat.

"There was a time, perhaps," I say, growing quite pensive. "But 'the man' doesn't work with guys like Dodge."

I've caught him off guard. That's right, Ranger. Your secrets are safe with me. This is all just temporary. Dodge, the Mirabellis...just wait until I get back into the game. I'll show 'em all.

"Don't sweat it, dude," he assures me. "You're hooked up. There's always a place for guys like you. I'm just glad I get a chance to hang with you before the other side of the hill pulls you back."

"And why is that?" I ask, jumping him to the point, keeping him back on his heels.

"Well," he stalls. "I've become something of a businessman myself over the years." He looks at me for approval.

"Nothing better than a self-made man," I tell him.

"I went to college, too," he protests.

"A double threat, then. Lethal combo," I appease him and get us back on track. " So what do you have cooking, Ranger Rockefeller?"

"It's complex," he says, leaning back in his chair as if he's about to light up a cigar. "You see, I've been dabbling in the stock market for years. Got a Schwab account to do my buying, but ever since my first year the input's been all mine. I make my own decisions."

"A rare quality," I compliment him.

"I've heard that, too," he says, his mogul impersonation temporarily reverting back to giddiness.

"But I'm afraid my ties to any insider trading are currently severed," I remind him.

"Well the truth is," Roman puffs up again. "I'm considering divesting from the market and putting my money into some more liquid assets."

"Is that so?"

He smiles wicked. "Oh yeah."

We then look at each other for a few moments, his smile in a holding pattern. I break the pause. "And...?"

"What do you mean?" he asks, very concerned. "You don't think that's a good idea?"

"That depends, Roman," I chuckle, condescending as hell. "What kind of liquidation are we talking about?"

"The most solid kind of liquid there is," he defends himself. "Real estate."

"Real estate?" I say, no need to fake my interest. "According to your mother it's been a long time since a Demos bought land instead of sold it."

"Well that's about to change," he snaps.

"Is it land on this side of the hill?"

"Kind of," he answers, backing down into sheepishness once more. "It's not exactly real estate, I guess. I mean...I wouldn't own the land, just a part of what's on it."

He's left himself wide open for a curveball. "Are we talking about the resort being built up the highway?" I ask him.

"We are," says Roman, as if confessing to a crime. I mirror his remorse. He starts to explain himself. "Hey, I know it looks bad, a ranger involved in something like this..."

"I don't care about that, Roman. What concerns me is the venture itself."

"Really?"

"The hospitality industry," I shake my head. "Honestly, Roman. I couldn't think of a more risky investment. Shall I quote you the statistics on the industry failure rate?"

"It's not going to fail," Roman says as if he's said it to himself a hundred times already.

"You got that in writing?"

"Not necessary. The developer's got a killer track record. Cicerelli and Munson."

I manage to simply nod and grunt while my brain shrieks holy shit, those crooks? Roman searches for a reaction from me so I tell him "Yeah, they're killers all right."

"So you know their reputation."

"Oh yes."

I came very close to handling Abner Munson's finances at one point, but even a snake like me couldn't get as low to the ground as that vicious piece of work.

"So then you can see why I'm so confident," says Roman.

"I can see why they need you," I tell him. "What do they know about the coast?"

He eats it up. "Just call me the troubleshooter. But I'll tell you one thing they know, that there's no other resorts between Half Moon Bay and Santa Cruz."

"And I'm sure the coastal commission wants to keep it that way," I cut his laughter short. "Resort-free."

His mouth drops open. "Dude, don't you see what's happening up there? The bulldozers, the lumber? It's a go. We've got permits."

"That specify you can only work after midnight, it seems. Have you seen any of the paperwork?" I ask him.

"Well...that's not my department."

"No such thing as a 'go' until it's open for business, Roman. There's always a way to jam a wrench into somebody's machinery if someone else wants to badly enough."

"No," he shakes his head emphatically. "No. Not while I'm around."

"Roman," I decide to corner him. "You don't even have water rights yet."

"How do you know?" he almost shouts.

"Because Joe's reservoir hasn't been sucked dry."

He recovers and does a bad acting job of being shocked. "Nobody wants to suck the Mirabelli's reservoir dry."

"Of course not. Just its source."

He stops acting. I figure he's about to ask me to leave. "You got what you want?" he asks.

"What do you mean?"

"You're here checking me out for Joe, aren't you?"

"No," I manage to answer very coolly. "I came here to help you, but you don't seem to want my help."

"Help me?"

"Do you know what you're getting into?" I turn up the heat. "Do you really know who you're dancing with in Cicerelli and Munson?" He tries to think of something to say but is working too hard to keep his balance. I keep the pressure on. "You really think those weasels want to do business with you? Let me tell you what's really going on, Mr. Demos. They're using you. They're using your connections to get this fucker built, and as soon as the environmentalists regroup and file suit, who do you think they're going to throw in front of the lawyers to take the bullet?"

He wants so badly to tell me I'm an asshole and I'm wrong and to get out of his house, but he's too confused. "They told me," he says meekly. "They said I'm in once it's built."

I sigh. "A human completion bond."

"What do you mean?"

"Roman..." I lean in as though talking to a child, telling him the Easter bunny is bullshit. "Nobody involved in a project in your capacity should have to pay to get a share of it. You ask for points."

"Points?"

"Percentage points. Of the gross profits. You're supposed to secure those before a shovel hits the dirt."

"They said this way was better," he fibs, like a kid caught with his hand in the proverbial cookie jar. I can't help but laugh.

Roman doesn't like that, and gets up out of his chair to make himself more imposing. "Don't think I can't pass the buck, too, Stanford," his voice raises an octave. "You think I'm stupid? The state can't afford to keep that land and they've been way easy to sway in whatever direction I want them to. California wants to let somebody else take the fall when the tree huggers come charging. I am the state in this project, so if anything hits the fan I can go ahead and point at the big bad developers with my employer's blessing. In other words, the governor's blessing, Stanford boy."

Roman glares at me as if he just dunked over me in a basketball game. I quickly dispatch his confidence. "The 'big bad developers' have a lot more pull with your employer than you do."

He starts to squirm again. "So how well do you know these guys?"

"They're only going to let an outsider in on so much," I say, and then rear back for a verbal kick in the balls. "But then, it's probably not a very big investment, anyway."

"It just so happens they're cutting me in big time." Roman actually puts his hands on his hips. I feel like we're in a playground at recess.

"Then you'd better be big time careful," I tell him. He deflates right before my eyes, so rapidly that it's hard not to take some pity. "Look, Roman," I say in my most soothing voice. "As ashamed as I am to admit it, I know how men like them think. I'm only trying to see things from their angle. It's for your own good. So please," I set him up. "Don't take offense to what I'm about to ask you."

He looks at me but I make him wait. Finally I ask "How can you afford to play the market that heavily?"

"Inheritance," he says, as though he wanted to follow it up with 'you asshole'. "Dad didn't disown all of us...just the losers."

I stare at him and think of how proud Dodge would be if I took a swing at him. But that's not my role in this, and digging for more information is what Dodge really needs me to do. I settle myself down and remember what Gretchen said about Franky's will, that Roman got the house but no money. Maybe there was some land involved as well that Roman could have sold. No sense in calling him a liar until I'm sure of it. I hold up my hands apologetically.

"Just playing devil's advocate, like I said. They're going to have to open up the books if things get hot."

"Nobody can touch me," he says.

I can't take anymore. I put down my glass and get up to leave. "I hope you're right," I say. "Because that's just the kind of attitude that can get you into trouble." I walk towards the door and thank him for the water.

"So what's your advice?" he calls after me. I stop in the doorway and turn around.

"You really want it?" I ask as if he doesn't really deserve it.

"Of course," he smiles, a game show host back after a commercial break.

"Points," I tell him. "Get them. Demand them."

And I'm out the door before he can ask me how. He walks out onto the deck after me but I'm already in stride. "Thanks for the water," I wave back as I jog in place for a moment. I continue on my way, yelling "remember what I told you" over my shoulder. If he approaches Cicerelli and Munson clumsily enough about a percentage he may just screw himself off the project, and kill it in the process. Two arrogant hotheads and a misinformed amateur. With a little nudge, there aren't enough bulldozers in the world to prevent that combination from collapsing.

I jog down to the ranch—I'm dressed for it, after all—and find Dodge outside his van. He's in the process of splitting the old plastic fertilizer drum in half with a chainsaw. He's got the tip of the saw jammed into the side as he circles it. He sees me and turns off the saw.

"What are you doing?" I ask.

"Makin' a hot tub. Got the idea and found the saw in Aldo's workshop. What'd you get outta Roman?"

I tell him everything and have to stand back a little more with each bit of information, he gets so wound up.

"We got him by the short hairs, buddy!" he screams. "Are you that good at pryin' information from people or is Roman just that stupid?"

"I don't know. A little of both, maybe?"

Something occurs to him. "Maybe that wacko really was Jesus Christ."

"The guy who ran up and took a swing at you last week?"

"Sure," Dodge can hardly contain himself. "He started this whole thing, and that's a goddamn blessing."

"Yeah," I agree, with some hesitation.

"What's your problem?" Dodge picks up on my tone. "You had that crooked son of a bitch eating outta your hand. We should be doin' a touchdown dance about now."

"It's great that we flushed him out on that resort deal," I explain myself. "Now we can try to stop him and keep Joe in running water. But how does this tie in to your ideas on Santo?"

"The money," Dodge pleads with me. "Where do you think he's gettin' the money to play with?"

"Assuming the part about the inheritance is a lie."

"Of course it's a lie," he says like he can't believe I said that. "You shoulda seen him when he found out he got the house and no money. You woulda thought he was the one who got one fuckin' dollar."

"Well, if he's on the take with the development company then I guess it's not much of a stretch to imagine him on the take with a drug outfit."

"Hell no it isn't" Dodge evangelizes. "They should put 'let's make a deal' on his tombstone."

"But..." I hold up my hand as if directing traffic. "We still don't know for sure that Santo's into anything like that."

Contrary to the reaction I expected from him, Dodge grins. "Not for long," he says.

"What do you mean?"

"I've got a plan of my own," he rubs his hands together. "Yours was so kick-ass I figured I better hold up my end of the bargain in case we had to take the next step."

"The next step?"

"We're gonna find out once and for all if we can put our two and two together. We're gonna sneak inside and take a look for ourselves."

I stare at him, hoping to read him for signs that he's just kidding. I finally have to ask. "You're serious?"

"Absolutely."

"What if they really are in the drug business?"

"Then we got what we need to put 'em outta business."

"Okay," I say. "But aren't they going to want to protect it?"

"What, you mean like with guns?"

"Yes. Like with guns. Maybe like with knives."

"Ah, Stanford…" he says as though I just missed a pop fly to blow a softball game. "Are you the same guy who tackled the loony bird yellin' about bein' Jesus Christ?"

Here we go. Preying on my urbanized insecurities about manhood. "A black eye is one thing," I holler. "A gun barrel pointed at your eye is another."

"I wouldn't put you in that situation," he assures me.

"You sound like you're trying to get me to go on some scary ride at an amusement park," I tell him. "This is reality, Dodge."

"You ain't even heard my plan."

"There's no point in me hearing your plan," I explain. "This is out of our hands. We go to the proper authorities and tell them what we suspect, and let them handle it. Let them plan what to do next. They've done it before. It's their job."

"And just what authorities are you talkin' about?"

"Yeah, I know. No one from around here, obviously," I say, trying to think of someone or something overriding the heads of the coast. "The DEA," it comes to me. "They must have an office around here somewhere. San Francisco, maybe."

"With what we got?" he says. "They'll laugh us outta the building."

"How do you know?" I ask.

"Plus," he ignores me. "Look at all the things that've been goin' on around here to bring attention their way, make 'em nervous. That fire, me catchin' those cops lettin' product move through Pescadero…"

"Yeah," I remind him. "Those cops who beat the snot out of you."

But Dodge won't hear any of it. "Santo's probably closin' up shop for a while right now as we speak. We gotta move and get some hard evidence before they start layin' low."

It's my turn, but I've had my say and all I can do is shake my head. The look on his face becomes more pleading. "I need you for my plan," he says with a bottom-line pitch in his voice. "Nobody knows you out here like they know me. I can't walk into Santo's yard and do what I need you to do. I'd be the one takin' the risk, believe me."

"Well then it's settled," I say. "We're not going in there."

He glares at me, his chin clenching and relaxing, clenching and relaxing. He could either be holding back tears or the impulse to slug me. He gestures for a moment, but isn't ready to speak just yet. He turns back towards the plastic fertilizer drum with its midsection sawed halfway across.

"Fine," he says, picking up the chainsaw. "But you don't get to use my hot tub when it's done."

And he fires up the saw and drowns out any further discussion. I'm unable to ask him if he's serious or joking about actually making a hot tub out of the plastic drum, about me not being allowed to use it, about the risk involved in taking a peak around Santo Farms. I walk through the dusty yard wondering about my stance on the matter, what could be holding me back from going as far as it takes to help Dodge. Using the term "gun shy" may explain.

I don't know who claimed her body, who identified the body of my victim. Technically she was her husband's victim, of course, but I gave him a head start. I was shown photographs at the police station once my name came up and I was brought in. They wanted to see how I would react. I vomited, which not only proved to the police that I didn't actually pull the trigger, but proved to myself that I did in fact feel something.

When I first heard about her, about them, I stared straight ahead. Just stared. It could have been for five minutes, it could have been for three days. Paralyzed, incapable of movement or speech. Even after I regained my motor skills I was not conscious of them. I walked because I knew how to walk, not because I knew where I was going. I spoke because I eventually had to answer the questions that were probably asked of me several times in a row before I'd finally answer.

Whoever claimed her must have wept openly and thrown their arms around her. They had to be led away and comforted, so positive of her identity they were. I'm sure of it. Her husband was perhaps a different story. Obviously someone claimed him, but the circumstances were such that someone probably had to volunteer. I'll identify the son of a bitch, someone finally said. The sheet was lifted and yeah, that's him.

I would be claimed, it's true, but would my memory pierce the smell of the morgue for whomever looked beneath the sheet? After turning away from the sight of me, will they remember much good about me, or notice instead the sterilized whiff of death hovering in the room and realize just how much the morgue smells like their high school science lab, a room full of frogs hovering in formaldehyde jars. Simply being claimed isn't enough. I want to be identified.

I jog behind the houses along the highway and through the tree line on the northern end of the ranch yard so I can make my way to the gravel road without having to run along the side of the highway. My stride hits a rhythm with my breath as I cross forty acres of Mirabelli pumpkins, each one glowing from within, it seems, thanks to the setting sun. The evening chill spreads, cooling my sweat and putting the air rushing through my nose on ice. I cut back towards the highway and stop at the mailboxes, stopping to check mine. A few catalogues marked "resident" and a flier asking me if I've seen the missing child on the front, with a coupon for a lube job on the back. I carry the stack with me to throw it away when I get home.

The dog lays next to the charred oil drum at Santo Farms and stares at me for a moment before resting his head back on his front paws. No interest in people on foot. The yard is empty, and some of the windows are lit up. Reaching the end of the eucalyptus tunnel, I'm surprised to see that my front windows are lit up, too. The crown of the meadow and the length of the grass obscures the front porch and the driveway, so I can't tell if anyone is there and can only assume for the moment that I inadvertently left the lights on. As the road swerves around the side of the meadow and draws closer to the house I see a car parked at its side. An unfamiliar luxury car.

I reach the gate, which has been left open. The cows have stormed the orchard and are eating the unripe fruit from the trees. Since there's only a dozen of them I herd the gang back out easily, which doesn't make me any less annoyed at whomever left the gate open. Swatting the rear cow in the hindquarters with my handful of catalogues, I close the gate behind them and turn to see someone on the porch watching me. The gray tint of dusk prevents me from seeing her very clearly, but I can at least tell it's a woman. Then she speaks and it's Janet.

"Aren't you supposed to say yee-ha or something like that?" She calls out to me.

"If a gate is closed when you enter," I ask her as I reach the bottom of the porch steps, "why would you think it's okay to leave it open once you pass through it?" She came here right after work, according to her suit—chocolate brown pants and blazer, the blazer buttoned up with no blouse underneath. Must have entertained a big client today.

"I couldn't figure out the latch," she shrugs. "No big deal. You handle those little doggies just fine, it seems to me. Isn't that what you cowboys call them? Little doggies?"

"Didn't recognize your car," I say, walking up to join her on the porch. She was planning on coming, I can tell now by her shoes.

They're flat, sensible, and somewhat scuffed. The heels she bought for the outfit she's wearing are probably sitting in the passenger seat. Her suit smells just a bit of new car, the rest of her a familiar blend of jasmine shampoo and apple-berry body wash from one of those organic lotion shops.

"The car's just off the lot," she says. "I'm leasing it."

"That's good business, driving up in the latest thing."

"Yes it is," she says, fading into a stare that makes it clear the small talk is over. "Can we go inside?"

"You've already been inside," I remind her. "You want permission now?"

"You didn't lock the door."

"We don't have to lock our doors around here."

"Nothing to steal," she says quickly, as though she was prepared to defend herself on the subject, figuring I'd say something like that. She's poised. There's no keeping up with her this evening. I head inside and gesture her to follow.

There really is nothing to steal inside. A couch and a chair with that second-hand look to them, the kind of furnishings people banish to their ski cabins or lake homes that they could afford to buy but not to furnish. The hardwood floors make the place seem even more sparse. I drop the catalogues on the TV tray which serves as an end table for the couch.

"Have any trouble finding the place?" I ask.

"Not really," she says, taking a seat in the chair. "I went back and forth a couple times before the mail boxes caught my eye, and I certainly didn't think you were living in that first dump along the dirt road."

"Santo Farms."

"That's a farm?"

"That's what they call it."

"I can't believe the wind hasn't blown it all over."

I laugh and ask her if the dog chased her.

"Yes," she smiles. "He does that a lot?"

"Every time."

"That's appropriate," she says. "Isn't that an ordinance for country living? Every driveway must have a dog biting at your tires?"

"Either biting them or pissing on them."

"I can see why you like it out here," she says, which surprises me. "It really is charming."

"And not that far from the city," I say, realizing only as the words leave my mouth how much it sounds like a sales job. So I ask her how her date went.

"What date?"

"The date you went on, you know, after the last time we saw each other."

"Oh...that date," she nods a few times, lips pursed. "I canceled it."

"Sorry."

She looks at me for a few moments. "Not your fault. I could have always rescheduled."

"But you're still seeing a few people, getting around?"

"There have been others," she answers.

She doesn't ask me likewise, so I have to tell her that I've started to date, too.

"Really?" she asks, truly surprised.

"Yes. Amazing, isn't it?"

"That's not what I meant."

"I know. I'm just saying it really is amazing."

Now she's intrigued. "So you've been getting over the hill more often?"

"Actually," I tell her. "It's someone around here."

She pauses. I've caught up to her at last. I seize the moment.

"What, you can date but I can't?"

"Oh, please," she waves me off. "Get over yourself. So you have someone to throw back at me this time."

I hate hearing Veronica referred to like that. "Maybe it's more than that, Janet."

"Well then," she says, sarcasm trying to camouflage the hurt. "Congratulations."

My sweat has dried enough so that I can sit down in comfort. I head for the couch thinking of a way to change the subject. I opt for the most logical, asking her once more "So what brings you out here?"

"What do you think?"

I land on the couch and cross my arms. "You got something for me to sign?"

"You think I'm going to let you off that easy?" her voice rises.

"Easy?" I ask her. "You said it yourself. I've got nothing to steal at this point."

She sighs and shakes her head. "Come on, Paul. You know I'm not talking about money."

"That's a refreshing change."

"Godammit!" now she's yelling. She gets up. "That's just what I mean."

"What?"

"You're always so fucking glib. You just waltz through life, or soft shoe, or whatever dance step metaphor pleases you..."

"Oh really?"

"Keeping everyone and everything at an arm's length..."

"Is that what you...?"

"Just observing, just looking. You want to sample anything sir? No thanks, just looking. Just looking and looking and tap dancing..."

"Give me a break..."

"Give you a break? Give you a break?"

"Okay, can you at least settle down?"

"That's all you get are breaks! That the story of your life, getting a break. Your life is one big break."

Now I get up. "Wrong!" I shout. "How dare you. You don't know what I'm feeling..."

"That's right!" she lunges at me. "That's exactly right! I don't know what you're feeling. I have no idea what you're feeling. Not a clue. And I'm not the only one, I'll bet."

"Oh, you think so?"

"Don't jump at the chance to change the subject," she downright orders me. "I'm only assuming that I'm not the only one who wonders what the hell is going on behind your smart-ass remarks, but I don't care because I'm your wife and I deserve some fucking answers!" She catches her breath at the height of her crescendo and glares at me. We're facing each other now like a couple of football players on opposite sides of the line waiting for the snap of the ball.

"Why can't I just sign the papers?" I haven't been screaming like she has but I still seem to have run out of voice.

She eases up. Her eyes grow sad and she crosses the line to hug me.

"I don't want to do anything until you talk to me," she whispers into my shoulder.

We face each other and I fully intend to start talking but instead have to kiss her. I have to because I want to and it's been so long since we've kissed and she wants me to. A full-body kiss, our mouths an opportunity for our whole bodies to do likewise, press and explore and remember every single inch, every contour, every little movement so familiar. She may groan first, or I may, but regardless we are soon speaking in groans, low moaning hums that make our lips vibrate and our tongues. Verbal visceral cues telling each other it's all right, we can keep going, you can keep kissing me, undressing me, because we always were so good together and my god, how could we have fucked this up? Such an essential human need, so well-rendered in our case. Out of our hands, I suppose. It was always somehow out of our hands, beyond our control.

"I stink," I tell her, becoming self-conscious as she pulls my shorts down. "I've been running."

"Then we'd better take a bath," she says, which is a great idea because the house has one of those old-fashioned tubs standing atop four brass lion paws bolted to the tile floor, the tub as long and wide as a rowboat but much deeper, up to our shoulders as we sit looking out the back windows at the hills catching the last batch of orange light from the sun barely keeping afloat above the horizon. We recline with knees raised just above the surface of the warm soapy water. She sits in front of me. I wash her hair, molding it into a variety of styles—a mohawk, a saggy beehive, a pompadour that melts before your eyes. I pull her hair back in a handful, twist it around my wrist, release it and push it forward to expose her neck which I kiss while rubbing her shoulders. It gets dark but the moon hangs in the window white and full, bright enough to keep the hills lit, every tree just visible in a bluish haze. Bright enough so that I can see Janet when she rises and stands in the tub, so that I can see what I'm doing as I slide my hands over her body.

She steps out of the tub and walks to the bedroom door without drying herself, the fresh moonlight picking up the drops of water on her skin making their way down her back, over her butt, down her legs and around her ankles. Walking away from me. Nothing on. She turns on the bedroom light and becomes a shadow beckoning me to join her. I get out of the tub and she watches me approach, the light streaking past her, illuminating my body. The physical labor of my new job, the lifting and pushing and leaner diet, has transformed my shoulders and torso into a shape more reminiscent of our early days together. I am only now aware of the sculpting, now that I'm standing naked in front of her. She lowers herself onto one knee and takes me into her mouth.

I close my eyes and feel everything from the base of my spine downward grow heavier and more rigid while my head starts to float, warmth giving way to a chill every time she pulls back to examine how far she's taken me. I remember to bend my knees as I arch my back slightly, not too far, thinking of the time in a Napa Valley bed & breakfast when I arched my back to its limit with my knees locked too long and blacked out, fell backwards, and woke up seconds later with Janet bent over me terrified but soon laughing hysterically once she realized I was okay—that same weekend I tried taking one of those mud baths but couldn't help imagining I was lying in a vat of dogshit. I consequently dry heaved for several seconds before making it to the shower in time to avoid losing my lunch and its complimentary tastings of Merlot and Pinot Noir.

I open my eyes and see the bedroom now, harshly lit with just a bed and an end table supporting a clock radio with the time flashing red. Just a bed against the wall—a stage, an altar. I reach across the door frame and turn off the light, letting in the moonlight, bringing back the romance. She stands up to kiss me and we walk the final leg of our journey to the bed.

I've been told that sex often reaches its most intense possibilities when a break-up is imminent. I've been told that, though it hasn't been my experience, seeing as I've never really broken up with a woman before. My relationships pre-Janet were all so brief, fading rather than ending, phone messages not returned or a lousy date sounding the death knell. And of course those relationships conducted while we were married, as part of our career strategy, were designed to end. They were practically scripted. I've always assumed then that the break-up equals great sex formula depends on a relationship being long-term. But I could never imagine sex getting any more intense than the most intense times spent with Janet.

Until now. Until tonight.

I actually feel as if I could pass right through her, emerging on the other side face down, gasping for breath to the point of tears. We never did make love after our plans destroyed another couple's life. We barely touched to say good-bye when I left to find a new place to live, pinning so much of my rehabilitation on geography. We never really broke up, so we never really tested the assertions of so many regarding sexual intensity and the inevitability of never sleeping with that person again.

I was afraid of intimacy at the time. A whiny claim, I know, but justifiable since the last person I slept with was killed because of it. She was still the last person I slept with until tonight with Janet. She was the last one, and I was always so sure I'd see her face on the body of anyone else I dared make love to. But I don't. Tonight it's only Janet on top of me, back arched, one hand pressed on my chest, the other hand reaching back between my legs. It's Janet beneath me, arms and legs wrapped around my back, mouth reaching up to mine for more kisses. It's Janet to the side of me, Janet in front of me, Janet behind me. She is all I can see, and all I can think is perhaps this is it.

Maybe we're finally breaking up.

With her astride me I look up at her face to search for clues as best I can, what with her hair falling forward and the moon's light intended for romance, not for research. But I can hear her. I can perhaps trace a sob in between her deep breaths. Yes, I can. And another. I reach up to touch her face, checking for tears. She leans further back, out of reach. I assume it's coincidence but have to know. I follow her path, sitting up and easing her onto her back, each of us then straightening our legs, feet now stretching to where our heads used to be. Hair spread out across the mattress, face exposed in full moonlight, damp with perspiration, shiny from exertion. If any tears were shed, they have blended in. Any evidence has been hidden. I'm left only with my suspicions.

Flat on our backs side-by-side, exhausted and satisfied. She always liked to get on the phone after sex, conducting business in the nude with a mischievous look on her face which was supposed to frighten me into thinking that any second she would blurt out "Guess what I just did?" to her client on the other end of the line. But that gag doesn't work at this hour. Our only distraction is the clock radio, whose tinny sound could actually be considered romantic in a honky-tonk sort of way if we could just get any stations that played off the effect, some Hank Williams or The Righteous Brothers. All we can get is a religious station. The evangelist standing in front of a microphone somewhere speaks in a monotone voice about all scripture being "God-breathed," and how the hand of man simply wrote it all down.

"Maybe a choir will start singing," says Janet, which makes me chuckle as she rolls onto her side and runs her fingers lightly over my stomach. She keeps her head down, an eye on what she's doing. The evangelist's voice cracks as he tries to alter his pitch to make a point and we're both laughing now. Janet leans up on her elbows and uses my chest as a podium.

"Have you prayed at all over the last several months?"

Not the kind of statement I'd ever expect from Janet.

"Why, have you?"

"No," she says thoughtfully, as if equally surprised that she brought it up, and is only now considering the question. "I wasn't raised that way and it seemed phony when I tried. I felt shallow for waiting until things turned to shit. Seemed so typical. What about you?"

I think about it for a moment and tell her that my salvation depends on there being no God, no heaven or hell. If there is any of it, I'm doomed.

She looks hurt, the red light from the clock radio reflecting in the whites of her eyes.

"Did you love her?" she asks.

"Did I love her?" I confirm. She nods gravely and I continue. "We make love for the first time in almost a year and you don't want to know if I love you?"

"I know you love me," she says.

"Oh really?" I answer, agitated but hoping that it sounds like a tease.

She lets out a sigh that seems to say "oh please," and I can't help but laugh a little at myself. We keep quiet for a while and it feels wonderful.

"It's not that far out here," I say, sounding as desperate as I feel. "And there's no traffic on Highway One. You can cover more miles in the same amount of time you take now, I'll bet."

"Why should I move and not you?" she asks.

"It's beautiful here," I say, such an obvious answer from my perspective. "And we can afford it. You need money to drop out of society these days."

"I've been raised in noise," she says. "Too much quiet is intimidating."

"You'd get used to it," I tell her, starting to feel like a real estate agent. "It took me awhile."

She sits up and crosses her legs. "And if I did," she looks me right in the eye. "Would you commute with me, or keep driving a truck?"

"Not good enough?" I ask with too much of an edge, so she snaps back.

"Don't pull your self-righteous bullshit on me," her head shakes in time with her hands. "You're just scared to get back in the race."

And she's right. Dead on. I have no comeback but to agree with her, silently, with a nod of my head.

"Why?" she asks in a manner more sympathetic, almost inaudible.

"I don't trust myself," I say to the ceiling before I look at her again. "I may find that I haven't learned a damn thing if I put myself in a competitive situation again. I could be just as grubby as ever given the chance, if success depended on it. I'd rather not be tempted."

Janet looks as though she just may agree to come and live out here, but when she finally speaks, she instead says "Say her name."

Her. She has overrun my thoughts but I've never spoken of her to anyone, other than to the police, and that was all business. I sure as hell wasn't going to open up to that goofy shrink who had written a book with a picture of herself on the cover. And Janet, well...I fled soon after it happened, and we were never much on opening up to each other on analytical terms about our relationship, anyway. We were always too busy having a good time.

"Is it that hard?" Janet says. "She has a name. Say it."

She has a name which I have not mentioned since she became such a big part of my life. And Janet knows it. She may not know what I feel but she knows me, knows my surface patterns. She asks me again to say it and so I say it very fast and loud, a retaliation to her insistence.

"Abby."

"Slower," Janet says. "First and last name, very slow."

I stare at her as if it's no big deal to say it just like she wants me to...

"Abigail Kern."

But when I do, I hear every syllable, every sound of every letter spends a moment in my mouth resonating before it leaves and becomes air. Visible air.

"Did you love her?" Janet asks me again.

"No," I say, finally answering her question. "Is that what's been bothering you about the whole thing? That maybe I loved her?"

"I was only wondering what has bothered you so much for so long."

"Feeling responsible isn't a reasonable enough explanation for you?"

"I just wanted to know if there was more to it."

"Besides our agreement, you mean? Other than our lifestyle?"

The radio evangelist drones on about the dangers of adding or subtracting even one word from the Bible and I leap up from the bed swiping at the power switch on top of the clock radio. The radio crashes to the floor but is still on. I yank the plug out from the wall, bending the metal prongs I'm sure. Janet is staring at me.

"Don't worry honey," I tell her. "I didn't break our agreement. I didn't fall in love with someone else in the course of fucking our way to the top." I take a deep breath, looking down at myself and remembering another time when we started arguing while we happened to be naked, how it loosened us up and made us realize how absurd our fight really was. But this time all I feel is exposed and ashamed, completely stripped. I look back at her and she seems to feel the same way, as though about to cry.

"I assure you," I collect my voice. "No genuine emotion was expressed until she was dead."

Janet stands up and approaches, embracing me on her mind, but caution in her step. "I'm sorry," she says very quietly, and hugs me just as softly.

Such a gentle action and yet I feel as if I've had the wind knocked out of me. I heave for breath having finally broken the surface. "I wish I did love her," I gasp. "I wish there was that much to it."

"I know you do," she says, rocking us gently back and forth. "I know you do, dearest."

"No romance in any of it," I say. "She didn't die for love."

"Maybe she thought so," she tries to reassure me.

I drop to my knees and press my temples to keep my skull from splitting open. The only other thing I can do is shake my head. Janet kneels down to join me.

"You never know," she says.

"I know," I manage to say. "I know."

"How?"

"Because I told her!" I scream, whipping my head up from its prone position between my hands. "She asked me if I loved her and I told her no…I didn't."

Janet can only stare at me before she tries to think of something to say. I save her the trouble by going on.

"And then she went home and was killed that very night."

She is now convinced that there is nothing she can possibly say. She leans forward and wraps her arms around my neck, pulling me towards her. "She died knowing there was no good reason for any of it," I say, worn out and growing comatose. "She died for my ambition. For our ambition. She died for us. She didn't die for love." I repeat it over and over again, she didn't die for love, as I slump onto my side, resting my head on Janet's lap and falling asleep to the sound of my own voice reciting that inescapable fact I'm sure will echo in my ears forever, no matter how far I put it behind me.

# TUESDAY 9/30

Sunlight flooding the bedroom, and my first thought as I squint into consciousness is that I must be late already. But according to the clock it's only six a.m., and when I relax I remember that Janet was here. We found our way back to the bed, apparently, or maybe she just put me here before she left, tucked me in and kissed me on the forehead. Put the clock back on the table, too.

"Good morning," she says, sending me into a convulsion before I realize it's just her, still here, standing in the doorway of the bedroom fully dressed with a glass of water. She laughs at me and says I could at least have some instant coffee on hand, for God's sake.

"But the tap water's just so tasty," I reach out for a sip and she holds the glass for me as I lean over and slurp. I thank her and she sits on the bed.

"I have to go home and put myself together before work," she says into the glass before drinking from it.

"Okay," I nod and just keep nodding. There's a morning-after sense of shame in the room which was never a problem for us, from our first night together several years ago to our nights apart in the arms of others. She notices it, too.

"So that's how couples stay together for so many years," she says. "They keep their mouths shut."

I stop nodding and grin. "Always worked for us."

We stare at each other for a little while and it becomes official. We're through. We had our chance and blew it, and staying together would only serve to remind us over and over again what happened. She looks down and takes a deep breath.

"So now we know," I say, and she laughs so that she won't start sobbing.

"Now we know," she says.

We kiss and then put our foreheads together. She tells me the divorce papers are in the kitchen. I manage to say that I'll be right down. She leaves me alone in the bedroom. I stare straight ahead, as I did when I found out about the murder of the woman I didn't love. I stare straight ahead, but this time I cover my face—even though there is nobody else in the room—and cry. Deep convulsing sobs, the cry of someone who has lost something very dear.

Once I stop, and once I catch my breath and my head stops pounding, I put on some jeans and walk downstairs into the kitchen to end my marriage. I go about the business in something of a daze, reminding myself to breathe every once in a while as three images distinguish themselves as those I will remember about this morning: my hand slowly drawing my signature and the date, Janet turning to smile bravely at me from the top of the porch steps just before descending, and her car fading into the trees at dawn to the roar of the gravel road, an occasional pebble striking the metal at a high pitch. I go back to bed and can't sleep for the two hours until I have to go to work.

Dodge has removed the top half of the fertilizer drum and is on his knees inside the lower half, his future hot tub, scrubbing the walls.

"Gotta clean it good," he tells me. "Clean it inside and out. I'm gonna use sections of the top half for seats, since it's the same shape as the bottom and the pieces will fit right in along the sides, nice and contoured. Then I just gotta run a pipe inside and scrounge up a pump and a water heater..."

"I'll do it," I interrupt. "I'll help."

"Somehow, Stanford, I can't imagine you'd dig a couple days fishin' through the junkyard."

"Your plan," I clarify. "I'll help you check out Santo Farms."

He gets up off his knees, looking at me skeptically the whole time. "Take pity on an ex-junkie, eh?"

"Maybe I'm feeling like I need to be a hero, too."

"I wouldn't think Veronica is that high maintenance," Dodge grins. "She's always been her own person, seems to me."

"That she is," I agree. "But she seems to like me more than I like myself. You know how that goes."

Dodge considers what I've said. "I'm with you on the not liking yourself part," he concludes. "It's the part about someone liking me that's a little sketchy. But who cares? You'll like this plot. We'll have some fun."

And he grins again while launching into the details of his plan. He'll wade up the creek to the back of Santo Farms while I create a diversion up front by asking about the dog, claiming that I ran over his foot while driving by earlier.

"But my Spanish is terrible," I remind him.

"Better than mine," he says.

"Your last name is Hidalgo, for chrissakes."

"My mother's name was Hidalgo and I never even knew her."

Mentioning his mother makes him pause. But he recovers in an instant and explains that my lousy Spanish will help drag on my conversation and thus extend the diversion, giving Dodge enough time to sneak around.

"There's about thirty guys creeping around behind those walls," I point out. "All of them are going to be fascinated enough by me to come out or peer through the windows?"

"You bet," he says. "Especially if you're willing to pay."

"Pay what?"

"Vet bills. You walk in, flash some cash, and act real bleedy-hearted. Show enough green while you're askin' about the dog and trust me, every damn ranch hand will be out there checkin' that dog for breaks and sprains and swearin' up and down that he's got one."

"Oh, come on Dodge."

"Just watch. You ain't ever had to live like them."

"No, but..."

"And that's just fine for what we're up to. An impressive-looking clean cut dude like yourself is gonna attract a lot more attention than me, even if I didn't have a fat lip and an eye that looks like a goddamn plum."

I'm about to protest without even knowing what I want to say exactly, but Dodge grabs me by the shoulders and says "Trust me."

The door slams to the Mirabellis' house across the way and Joe is standing there waving. "Stanford," he shouts. "The Wheelers oughta be here in an hour or so. Get going on the phones, will ya? Lorraine and I got a bunch of stuff to get ready."

I give him a slow nod.

"Dodge," Joe continues. "Give us a hand with the grill, huh? And we've got some tables and chairs need moving into the yard here."

Dodge waves that he'll be right there, and I ask him when he wants to carry out his investigation of Santo's.

"Anytime this afternoon," he says. "Tell Joe you're going on your lunch break and come get me."

"But Veronica's in school today so she can't cover for me."

"It won't take that long. Even if it does, Joe and Lorraine are gonna be so knee-deep in ass-kissin' they won't miss us. And when was the last time the phone rang after noon, anyway?"

I can't recall, so Dodge tells me to come and get him when things get really dead.

The morning passes with the usual orders called in and the arrival of the Wheelers: a caravan two Land Cruisers long, the children's faces illuminated by video screens projecting from the back of every seat and hanging from the ceiling. They pass by the office on their way back to the house and I stand in the doorway and wave. Nobody waves back. A middle-aged woman with bobbed hair gives me a tense grin before looking the other way, and the kids gawk.

Between tasks I compose some sentences in Spanish about how I ran over the dog's foot and how sorry I am, and figure I'd better leave it at that (bearing in mind Dodge's request for lengthiness). I don't have much cash in my pocket to flash, a twenty and some ones, but I can put the twenty on top and make the wad look like a hundred bucks or so, enough for the desired effect. I'm trying to figure out how to say "veterinarian" in Spanish—leaning towards "doctor of the animals" as my best choice—when Joe comes in muttering curses and grabbing the rolodex off the desktop.

"I told them to follow me, godammit."

"Something wrong?" I ask.

"Busted pipe. Ran right over it. I'm giving them a tour of the fields and next thing I know I look in the rear view mirror and there's the head man himself going his own way like some dumbshit teenager. He drives over the pipe and the fucking water comes up like Old Faithful." Joe smacks himself in the forehead as if that's what he'd like to do to Mr. Wheeler. "And then he blames his kids. 'They wanted to' he says. 'They said to go that way.' A grown man, pointing fingers like that. Those kids should be in school anyway. Shouldn't even be out here."

"Yeah," it occurs to me. "Why is that?"

"Home schooling," Joe says, eyes rolling. "They don't even trust the private schools with their little jewels. But what the hell, it gives the wife something to do."

"So do you need any help out there?" I ask.

"Aldo's on it with some of the men. But you can call the irrigation supply down in Salinas and let them know you'll be on your way tomorrow." He puts the rolodex back on the desk. "I'll call them later with the details on what we need. I gotta get back out there and do a circus routine and make sure Aldo doesn't come back and take a swing at the silly bastard."

I tell him "I'll take care of it" with a yes-sir sense of duty in my voice, and Joe returns to the barbecue after a deep breath. Once the call is made, I settle in for the standard afternoon period of inactivity. I check the progress of the swallows. Some of the nests are filled with little blue heads which instantly become screeching open beaks when a parent arrives with something slimy to drop into the frenzy. Only so many trips back and forth by the mom and pop swallow and I'm thinking once again about this morning. The idle mind wanders as usual.

Actually divorcing Janet, the act of signing the papers, was so simple I think for a moment that maybe I've been screwed. I never did read what I was signing. But Janet doesn't need to do that, and she wouldn't anyway, and so I feel ashamed for thinking that even for a moment. It just couldn't have been so simple, so anticlimactic. Some justification is in order. Months of avoidance and dread over that? Easy for me to say when she did all the work. All the work including the work I was supposedly doing myself. I just said good-bye to her this morning and I already miss her, miss her far more than during our year apart, which makes me wonder if time really will heal this particular wound, as the old adage says, or if in this case the exact opposite will occur and I will be forced to change bandage after bandage after bandage. Knowing that things can't possibly work only helps on the intellectual level, and intelligence is utterly useless in love.

An occasional squeal of childish delight or frustration from the Wheeler kids makes its way through the office window from the house hundreds of yards further into the ranch, which makes me wonder how loud they are if you're at the same table with them. An hour into the waiting game a light blue pickup mercifully enters through the front gate and herds my thoughts back into the present. The sides of the truck bear the familiar PG & E logo across its doors—Pacific Gas & Electric. It pulls up to the office and a hard-hatted man approaches with an unzipped orange vest framing his bulging gut. We exchange "good afternoons" and he tells me that he's got a work order to trim the branches of the trees crossing the telephone wires along the front of the ranch and he just wanted to check in to let us know what's up. I thank him and he drives out of sight in front of the workers' houses. After a few throttled attempts to start his chainsaw, he gets it going and the high pitch of the motor becomes constant. I lock up the office and walk back to fetch Dodge, stopping by the house first to tell Joe I'm taking lunch.

The Wheeler kids—all four of them, a perfect balance of boys to girls aged approximately four to twelve—are gazing at Joe as he indulges their father. They seem to be taking notes on how they expect to be treated once they become adults. A few pumpkins have been smashed on the Mirabellis' driveway, and several other pumpkins are being ignored at a picnic table with the mother Wheeler, who sits hunched with her arms folded next to Lorraine. Both women seem relieved that I have arrived, offering them a distraction from their strenuous attempts at communication. The kids also shift all of their slack-jawed attention towards me.

Joe introduces me to Mr. Wheeler. His name is Trent and he looks every bit of it. Thankfully, Joe fails to mention my background, which would force me into some sort of conversation with the man who is clearly miffed at any interruption of his ass being kissed. But when Trent Wheeler barely glances at me and refuses to either shake my hand or introduce me to his wife and kids I feel like reciting my résumé at full volume nose-to-nose. I note the look on Joe's face. He knows, he knows, but he's pleading with me not to get into it with the man, as much as he deserves it. I wink at Joe and tell Trent that it's been a real pleasure. On my way to Dodge's van I experience a few moments of mild depression concerning the cloning of the Wheeler kids into carbon copies of their father. Girls included.

Dodge is not at his van. I hear a "psssst...over here" and see him beckoning from behind the tree line of Monterey Pines protecting the daisy fields parallel to the ranch yard. I approach and find him dressed in faded army fatigues. I can't help myself. "Oh for God's sakes..."

"I should say the same about you," he snaps.

"What do you mean?"

"Look at the way you're dressed."

"So we'll stop by an army surplus store."

"I mean we've got our parts to play here. I'm the stealthy one, you're supposed to be the impressive one."

"You want me to wear a suit?"

"Never mind. You got some cash?"

I pull out the twenty wrapped around the singles and he sighs. "Here," he pulls out three more twenties and hands them to me. "They're desperate but they ain't stupid."

Adding the bills to the top of the wad makes all the difference, I must admit. We walk back towards the front of the ranch by way of the road alongside the daisy fields, cutting through the tree line across from the office to reach my truck.

"You got some kinda script worked out?" he asks as we pull onto the highway.

"Enough to get me started."

"Good. Pull over up here," he points to the side of the road where the creek intersects the highway through a culvert underneath.

"You're going to start wading from back here?" I ask.

"I can't risk bein' seen in your truck."

I pull onto the shoulder of the road. He gets out, leaving the door open as he glances up and down the highway. No cars. Then he slithers over the guard rail, disappearing for a moment with a splash before pulling himself up and resting his chin on the pavement to give me some last second instructions. "Wait for me where the creek runs under the gravel road before drivin' in. Shit this water's cold."

"What about after I'm done?"

"Right here, on the other side of the road," he says. "And take your time."

"Will do," I say. "And you remember what Joe said about that creek."

"What's that?"

"Look out for turds."

He tells me to fuck off and drops himself back into the water. I reach over and close the door. Within seconds I'm at the turn-off to the gravel road. I pull onto its rough surface and inch forward towards the twisted row of scrub oak bordering the creek. Pausing where he told me to, I look out the passenger side window and soon see Dodge trudging shin-deep through the muddy waters, arms raised in front of his face to keep the spindly lower branches and thorny leaves at bay. Just to have fun with him I feel like rolling down the window and telling him he could've gotten out right here after all. But as he crouches down to crawl through the culvert with a thumbs-up sign in my direction, it's clear that he's really enjoying himself. I raise my thumb back at him before he ducks into the metal tube. I drive on, chuckling a bit now that he's out of sight.

As the haunted-looking houses of Santo Farms grow bigger in the windshield, I start to tense up. My heart gets deeper in its beat and higher in my chest. There's a greater physical dimension to this sort of nervousness, unlike the kind before a big exam or presentation, knowing that part of the solution to the upcoming situation may be to turn and run like hell. Similar to going out on Halloween night with a can of shaving cream and a carton of eggs, I savor the opportunity to feel like I did before I had even kissed a girl, much less divorced a woman. Come to think of it, maybe there's another crapped-out ranch we can spy on after this one.

At the point where the gravel road rises towards the eucalyptus tunnel, I veer left and stay flat towards the wooden ruins. The dog, having heard my engine, is already running from the ranch to the road and is stunned to see me slowly rolling towards him. His ears go up, his head cocks inquisitively, and he starts backing up on pace with my progress. We push and pull each other past the outer rim of hopeless automobiles and farm equipment, drawing closer to the center lot. I stop and get out to walk the rest of the way. Now the dog starts barking and pacing back and forth in front of me, but still giving ground. His agility is going to make my fake concern for his foot even less credible. My chest and throat tighten even more.

The dog is the only sign of life in the place, though I have the feeling of being watched from inside the splintered buildings surrounding me. I should really have spurs around my ankles to complete the picture, jingling with every step I take. Of course the dog barks would swallow the effect. I stop and so does he. His blue eyes gain momentum from his black face now that he thinks he's prevented my trespassing, a job well done. The barking stops and he growls at a low pitch, mouth closed, lips trembling. The place seems even more deserted now with less noise bouncing off the paint-peeled walls.

His growling fades. He and I square off in silence, as if about to draw guns and fire at one another. I hear a snap and jerk my head to its source. The rusted oil drum has a fire dying inside of it, the flames only rising above the rim on occasion. It snaps again, some glowing embers popping up. I carefully scan the buildings, including the charred remains of the burned-down barn. Stock newsreel footage could be shot here depicting a village where a battle has been fought. The smells give away the presence of life. Food smells. The cafeteria-like blend of the same meals cooked over and over in the same pots and pans. Meat, rice, chicken, onions. A door creaks and the old man appears. The dog runs to his side. Great. No really...I'm sure that foot must be broken, sir. The old man waves and gives me his customary piano keyboard smile, limping my way as he does.

"Buenos dias," I say.

"Buenos dias," he says.

So far, so good. Your dog, I tell him (su pero), I think I drove on his foot with my tire (pienso que yo maneje en su pied con mi llanta).

"Si?" he asks.

"Si," I confirm, and then tell him I have money (tengo dinero). He asks me why, or what for, or for what, and I say for an animal doctor—un medico para los animales.

He looks puzzled at me, then at the dog, and then sprays me with rapid fire Spanish while gesturing towards the dog. I nod, smile, and pull out the cash from my pants pocket, repeating how sorry I am about the dog.

"Lo siento," I say. "Lo siento sobre su pero."

I hold the money up higher. He looks at it and smiles. "No," he says, waving his hands at the cash. "No lo necessito. El pero esta en salud perfecto. Mira..." he bends down with great effort to show me that all of the dogs' feet are fine. Or as he put it (once I manage to translate it for myself), that "the dog is in perfect health."

Dodge, you ought to be ashamed of yourself. I damn near put the money right under his nose and he didn't bite. The dog, meanwhile, loves his master's touch and attention. Panting, his blue eyes soften and his tongue curls out from what looks like a smile. See, Dodge? Even the dog is honest.

Another door creaks. All three of us—dog, master, and myself—look over to see a young man saunter over with an aggressive smile on his face. The young man briefly nods and winks in my direction and upon reaching him, asks the old man what the problem is.

After that I'm lost. They banter quickly and progressively louder, eventually coming across as two people standing beside a car wreck arguing over whose fault it was. A couple of other men materialize from the surrounding walls, and then a few more, and then several. They stand around the action, concentrating on the argument but occasionally taking their cue from certain key phrases to glance my way, almost all at once. I smile woodenly and ease the cash back into my pocket. The dog loses interest and lowers his belly to the ground, holding a sphinx-like pose for a moment before resting his head on his front paws. He looks at me and I'm convinced he would roll his eyes in disgust if he could.

"Señor," says the young man. "Señor," he repeats, and I realize he's addressing me.

"Yo?" I ask.

"Si...usted." He reverts back to his large grin and says something to me about the dog.

"Con permiso," I excuse myself. "Pero despacito, por favor," I ask him to please go slower, proud of myself for remembering what Veronica told me about saying "despacito" instead of "mas despacio." Then I conclude with my most familiar and well-rehearsed Spanish phrase: "Mi español es muy pobre" (My Spanish is very poor).

The young man nods politely as some of the men chuckle. He then repeats himself slowly enough to be both understandable and patronizing. "Cual...pied...esta?"

"Which foot is it?" I translate out loud before answering, a necessary stall tactic because I hadn't thought of that. "Uh..." I decide on a foot in English and gather my thoughts in Spanish.

"El frente," I tell him—the front, because I can't remember how to say the back.

"El frente a la derecha," I add—the front right, because "derecha" is easier to pronounce than "isquierda" (the left).

He nods and thanks me, getting down on one knee to inspect the dog, who growls then snaps at the young man's hand trying to reach for the front right paw. The crowd laughs. The young man glares up at the old man. The old man shrugs and plays innocent. The young man stands up and pushes the old man. The crowd pounces on the young man. He is thrown to the ground and they form a circle around him. He gets up and tries to escape and is pushed back and beaten. He tries again, getting up and heading for a different part of the circle, with the same results. Pushed back into the circle and beaten. And again. Pushed back and beaten. Again.

A gunshot fills the yard. Our reflexes force us into a crouch. We look around. No gun. Another shot shakes the weathered foundations. It is coming from behind the buildings along the creek. The men realize this all at once and run to the source, through front doors and between buildings, to the back by the creek.

The creek. Dodge. I don't know if I should run too and see what's going on. I'm paralyzed. Someone's just turned off the lights and I don't know my way around this room. And something's in the room with me. Something unknown. A gun shot, my God. If Dodge is right, these guys take no prisoners. I breathe, finally, and see that the old man is still there. The dog's ears are perked up, but the old man is steady. He smiles at me and says something. I can't translate. I can't think straight. But he gestures as if it's time to go. I nod. I turn and walk back to my truck and I have a difficult time walking. My knees won't bend. I have to think about walking, how to do it properly. I haven't breathed for several moments. I have to think about that. My eyes are so dry. Blink. Don't forget to blink.

I get in my truck but don't start it. This looks bad. I was there when they caught Dodge. I just happened to be in front offering to pay for some bogus dog injury when they found Dodge in back. Guilt by association. I should walk back and ask what's going on, play dumb, assert my innocence. But if they drag Dodge out to play us off each other, I don't want to face him and say I've never seen him before in my life. And I don't want to get shot at. You're right, old man. I'll be leaving now. Dodge is slippery, and those guys don't want any more trouble. A couple warning shots at best, and at worst Dodge was aimed at and missed. They had to fire twice, after all. Breathe. Blink. I start the engine and pop the clutch while trying to shift into reverse. Bend the knees. Now the elbows. Start the engine again. Breathe.

I wait for a couple of cars to go by on the highway before I turn left into the far lane and head south back to the ranch. I shift into second then third gear quickly, the car ahead of me still in view. A champagne Chrysler LeBaron with a rental car sticker on the rear bumper and some elderly passengers in the back seat, their pace is predictably slow and Jesus! Something lunges into my field of vision from the left side of the highway. I hit the brakes and it's Dodge, galloping towards me, hunchbacked as if imitating the wild animal I thought he was. He's soaking wet, head to toe, and covered in blood from the waist down. Blood. Gunshots. He leaps and rolls into the back of my truck. I open the back window and he yells for me to "just drive" back to the ranch, back to his van. I pick up speed, never having come to a complete stop, and stay on course to the ranch. He lies flat in back, not wanting to be seen, so I can't tell how badly he's hurt. I ask him, and he says just drive.

We pull through the front gate of Mirabelli Nurseries and he reminds me to stay on the other side of the windbreak, so I veer away from the central yard, towards the fields, and we stay out of sight behind the tree line. I cut the engine and roll the last several yards to his van so we won't be heard at the barbecue. I get out as soon as we stop, but Dodge keeps laying in back. He just seems tired, catching his breath, despite all the blood.

"It ain't blood. Don't worry," he says, keeping his voice down.

"But the gunshots," I blurt out. He sits up quickly and gestures for me to quiet down. "The gunshots," I try again. "Didn't they shoot at you?"

"Shot up in the air, I guess. Warning shots."

"So what's that stuff all over your legs?"

"Residue," he says with a smile. "The kinda residue left over from cookin' up a big batch of crystal meth."

He jumps out of the truck and walks over to his van while I let his information sink in. All those drugs I've seen in action and used on occasion myself, all the evidence which proves how large drugs loom in our culture, all information both personal and academic, anecdotal and imperial, all of it does not make Dodge's discovery any less surreal to me. There is a bag of pot, and there are boatloads with their unfathomable street values. I have always encountered drugs on the bag level, while the business level exists as an abstraction, as vague from my point of view as the lives of movie stars. I realize my curiosity about what goes on behind the propped-up walls of Santo Farms never really included the possibility of it actually being a meth lab. His announcement keeps bouncing off my forehead and fails to settle in.

"You're positive?" I ask him.

He opens the side door of his van to look for a change of clothes amongst the piles shoved into the corners. "Shots were fired. Remember?"

"You were trespassing."

"And what was I gonna steal, an old two-by-four? It's meth leftovers, believe me." He finds a suitable pair of jeans and black t-shirt, but can't find a match for the one dry tennis shoe he's unearthed.

"But how would you know? You said meth wasn't your thing, it got hot after your time..."

"I still got friends who use," he snaps. "And I also watched a clean up crew sweep a meth lab off Highway 84 in the hills a few years back." He gives up his search for the one shoe and begins taking off his wet fatigues, struggling to keep his voice down thanks to his frustration with my skepticism. "You shoulda seen it. An old livestock shelter. The dudes who had to clean it up were all dressed like astronauts damn near. Shiny suits, gas mask helmet things. They coulda walked through fire in those outfits. That's why I'm wet. I rolled around in the creek first chance I got to rinse that shit off."

"And you saw what the waste looked like as they were cleaning it up?"

"Hell no," he begins putting on his dry clothes. "They roped off a big huge area and put up all these warning signs. I asked one of the guys hangin' back in the truck what the big deal was and he told me about the leftovers. They once busted up a lab near an orchard and all the trees had died 'cause the red shit got in the irrigation ditches." He finishes dressing and takes a deep breath, safe at last from the wet pile of fatigues wadded up in the dust between us.

"He told you the leftover waste is red?"

"Said it usually is. And that it stinks." He scoops up the wet dusty ball of clothes and hoists it towards my nose to smell.

"That's okay," I decline. "I'm sure it smells horrible."

"It was even worse when it first got on me."

While the concept of rubbing elbows with genuine drug manufacturers still seems remote to me despite the fact I may have just done it, Dodge's arguments are sound. I figure then that I'd better remind him that this is all about gathering evidence. "Do you think there's still enough of it on your clothes for the DEA or someone to examine?" I ask him.

Unfortunately, but certainly not to my surprise, Dodge takes my hint as a slap in the face. "I saw where the shit was runnin' from, from which building it was comin' out of," he says. "Right down through a ditch someone dug from under the floorboards and into the creek."

"And then they shot at you."

"That's right," he nods emphatically. "So now the race is really on. If all the other things goin' on this past week didn't give 'em a reason to close up shop, then we just gave 'em the best reason of all. They know someone's on to 'em."

"So what?" I admonish him more than I ask him. "So what? Are you going to get a gun and start shooting back?"

"Don't have to," he says, simply making a point. "I know which building the shit's in." And he looks at me, allowing for what he considers to be a dramatic pause. I break it.

"So?"

"So we take out the building."

Now I pause, but in total disbelief.

"You said you felt like you needed to be a hero," he says. "And so I'm givin' you the chance."

"A suicide mission wasn't what I had in mind."

"What suicide mission? You haven't even heard my plan yet."

"If it involves taking a building down..."

"Ah, come on Stanford," he says. "You gotta do more than just move to this side of the hill if you're gonna change your life. A walk through the woods ain't gonna do it for ya. I been born and raised out here, and the ocean and everything next to it ain't done me a damn bit a good. You can stay out here all you want but you're still gonna end up with two chins and big glasses and hardly any hair on your head just like every guy on the other side who is twenty years older than you."

"Spare me the 'adrenalin rush' speeches," I tell him. "For someone who hates surfers so much you sure sound like one of them. I refuse to believe that the only way you can get the most out of life is to risk it. That's media slogan philosophy and it's horseshit. There's such a thing as peace of mind, you know."

"No, I don't know," he says. "I don't know what that is."

I'm about to say "neither do I" but hold back. Dodge knows I'm not at peace. He knows. Peace of mind may be easily confused with boredom to those who don't know any better, but restlessness leaves no doubt. It's in the eyes and the way our bodies can't stop moving even when we're standing still.

"I don't have much luck when I take matters into my own hands," I finally tell him. He makes a face like I just plucked out some of his mustache hairs. Whether it was intentional or not, his silent sense of disappointment forces me to reconsider on the spot. I don't want to let him down. But then Joe's voice carries through the trees. He's calling my name. I try to ignore it.

"Joe needs you," says Dodge.

"I hear him. Look…" I start to explain myself but need a few moments to figure out how.

"Don't worry about it," Dodge shrugs. "I can just as well do it alone."

Joe's voice interrupts me before I can even bother. "There you are," he says. We turn to see him coming around Dodge's hot tub project at the end of the tree line. "I was going to ask Dodge where the hell you were, and here you are."

"Here I am."

Joe reaches us and sighs. "The goddamn Wheelers are staying for dinner."

"You must be doin' a lotta listenin'," says Dodge.

"Haven't gotten a word in edgewise," Joe nods. "So I'm going to need more charcoal and some meat—chicken, I guess. We've already had burgers. Can you make a run into Santa Cruz for me, Stanford?"

"Sure," I answer, but he's already peeling some dollars off a roll from his pocket. I look over at Dodge, who smirks at me as if assuming I'm glad to be saved by the bell.

"Some kind of vegetable too," Joe continues. "Whatever looks fresh."

I nod and pocket the money, mixing it in with the cash we used for bait over at Santo's. Joe takes a deep breath and exhales slowly.

"I know land," he says. "Like a doctor knows the human body. And Aldo, hell, he can get a seed to sprout from a crack in the sidewalk. But we've never owned a single acre in our lives. Why the hell is that?" he looks at me.

I hesitate. "Are you really asking?"

"Why not?" he says. "I ask Trent Wheeler a question like that and I get a half hour speech."

"Well there's your answer," I tell him. "If you owned your land you wouldn't be able to have him over for a barbecue, and you'd miss out on all that valuable instruction."

Joe laughs, and I can tell Dodge would too if he wasn't angry at me right now.

"Okay then," Joe slaps his hands together. "We'll see you back here in an hour or so."

"Will do," I salute.

Joe seems to be gathering his strength while he looks at us as though he may never see us again. "Guess I'd better get back and grab my ankles some more."

"Just keep actin' like you enjoy it," Dodge reminds him.

Joe points at him as if to say you-got-it, and walks back around the tree line. He disappears and then Dodge and I are silent for a few moments. "Kinda fucked, ain't it?" he finally says. "Doesn't matter if you're right or wrong if you're from over the hill. You got all the toys so you got all the answers."

I was thinking pretty much the same thing. "Wait for me, will you?" I ask. He gives me a long look, so I add "Don't do anything until I get back."

"Relax Stanford," he says. "I ain't doin' anything anyway."

"You're not?"

"Nope," he says. "You're right. I was tryin' to say you're right with my little over-the-hill speech there, but I guess I'm just a little pissed about bein' wrong. We got enough to hit up the DEA or whoever. I'll sit tight and we'll head over there tomorrow after the market. Like you said, they must have an office in the city."

Now I'm the one giving him a long look. "Are you serious?" I ask.

"Hey," he holds up his hands. "They seen you face-to-face over there at Santo's place, and me...well, I ain't ever been shot at and I don't wanna be shot at ever again."

I want to believe him, but he came around so fast, too fast for someone as stubborn as he is. He senses my skepticism and continues. "We got our own shit to take care of, you and me. I was thinkin' about that while Joe was here all bent about havin' to answer to the Wheelers. That's just the way it works for most of us, I guess. Gotta answer to someone."

If he's bullshitting me, it's good bullshit. I couldn't blame myself for being taken in by it. I test him by asking him if he wants to come into town with me.

"Nah," he doesn't flinch. "Our little re-con mission wore me out. I'm gonna take a nap, get plenty of sleep for the market since we're gonna do our thing with the DEA afterwards."

"All right," I say, repeating to myself how convincing he is and how justified I am in believing him. "See you later."

"Don't wake me," he says.

I nod and get into my truck. In my rear-view mirror I see him standing his ground, watching me go from the same spot I left him in. I veer left at the end of the windbreak and the mirror fills with trees.

Twenty miles later in the grocery store parking lot, a man with a beard growing over everything but his eyes and nose drifts by, counting out loud. He is on the two hundreds—"Two hundred fifty two, two hundred fifty three, two hundred fifty four..." He turns my way and keeps on counting, but alters his inflection as though he's talking to me. Hello nice weather we're having comes out as "Two hundred fifty five, two hundred fifty six, two hundred fifty seven."

Santa Cruz. Such a lovely town, quintessentially by-the-sea, with plenty of places and activities to fill a day, but with a catch: there's always someone angry and untalented lurking nearby with a guitar he insists on playing, or a schizophrenic in a pith helmet and ski goggles who wants to tell you who really shot JFK when all you want to do is eat your sandwich and watch the sunset. The good life is paid for in requests for spare change.

A few laps around the aisles of the store and through the checkout stand, and I make it back to the parking lot in time for the man to tell me "Four hundred two, four hundred three, four hundred four..."

The clock is still ticking.

On the way back to the ranch with the requested supplies, I shift from justifying my belief in Dodge's assurances to justifying my passive stance in his vendetta by telling myself that my position is not really passive. It's active in a practical sense, a voice of reason to ground the vengeance and the need for redemption coursing through Dodge. A contrast. A counterweight. And plus I meant it when I told him that I need some of the same things out of this as he does. My way is just different. My way and his way balance each other.

I'm getting so good at excusing myself that maybe I can apply the same ballast to her death. Abby's death. Abigail Kern. There. I said it again. Her name. A crow wobbles through the air above the artichoke fields to my left. A flying shadow, every part of him pitch black, the big bird is hounded by several little song birds spiraling around him getting in their shots as they chase him from their nests. It's working. They've kept him away for now. Only for now. The shadow will be back whenever he feels like it, too big for the little birds to truly ever overcome.

The Wheelers are down by the reservoir spotting ducks and telling their kids not to throw rocks at them as the kids continue to throw rocks at them. Joe and Lorraine are stuck there, forced to watch them repeat the same act over and over. I drop the supplies off by the door to the house and walk away before anyone has a chance to see me. I glance towards Dodge's van as I drive off and consider checking on him, but remember his request: "don't wake me."

On the gravel road approaching Santo Farms I see a cloud of dust rising from behind the outer buildings. The dust gets thicker as the road rises towards the eucalyptus tunnel. Driving through the tunnel I can see between the trees to the arid field branching out from the central area of the ranch. A bunch of Santo's men are playing soccer again, kicking up the dust, eleven on each team. The rusted oil drum serves as one of the goal posts, a fire still burning inside it. Our visit earlier must have led to a lot of nervous energy which needed re-directing. Loser breaks the dog's foot, winner collects the money for it. Their voices hollering at each other to "pass" and to "shoot" make it above my engine noise and through the closed window.

With my perspective confined to the window and the trees passing in front of my point of view like black lines on a reel of film, it's as though I'm watching the game frame by frame. A flash of orange in the far left corner of the field catches my eye. The PG & E man, orange vest glowing, is now at work on the trees around Santo Farms, chain-sawing his way through the trunk of a big Monterey pine hovering over the last building into which the power lines run. Cutting down an entire tree seems odd. Usually their only concern is the branches. No gut pushing through his vest. It's a different guy. An incompetent guy, it turns out. I stop the truck and pay closer attention because I can't believe what I see. He's cutting the tree from the wrong angle, on the wrong side. That tree's going to drop right on the building beside it. The men are too involved in their game. They don't notice. I get out of the truck to shout a warning. Then I notice the hat. Off-white with a green bill, the same kind I picked up at UFP for Dodge. He stops sawing and turns around. He wears a brown bandanna over his nose and mouth and a pair of sunglasses over his eyes. Maybe it's not him. But it's not just the hat. It's the arms. It's the walk as he heads over to the building in jeopardy and knocks. It's definitely Dodge. While he waits for someone to answer the door he looks around, back at the game, up the hill, through the trees. He sees me and waves. I don't wave back. I can't. My arm won't move. He knocks again and still no one answers. He walks back to the tree and fires up the saw.

Seconds after he shoves the blade into the cut, the first loud crack rifles through the air. Then another. Dodge disappears behind the building and into the creek. Now the cracks blend into one long scream as the tree begins to topple. The men stop playing and freeze helplessly. They watch as the tree finally seems to lose consciousness and fall, fainting right onto the building, reaching its top speed just as it crashes through the roof and slices through the walls. The sound of the building collapsing, wood snapping and exploding, reaches me as the tree bounces on the ground a couple of times before taking its last breath. A moment of stunned silence holds everyone by the throat, then all the men charge the building at once, leaving the soccer ball by itself in the field.

I can't help but consider Dodge's plan pretty ingenious, and I laugh for a second in appreciation and utter disbelief. But just for a second. Then I realize why the men have rushed to the remains of the building. They frantically start pulling pieces of shattered wood and calling out a name I can't quite make out as they shout it all at once, constantly. Someone was in that building. Now my arm can move. I cover my mouth with my hand. Someone was in that building. Santo and his brother, the old man, come running along with a few others who weren't involved in the soccer game. Their voices cry the name of the one hidden inside. They swarm around the wreckage and pull whatever they can get their hands on and throw it aside. Some of the men tug at things they can't budge. Some wander off to the side and look at the impossibility of their task. I get in my truck and continue home. I have a hard time operating the pedals. My knees only bend when I concentrate on them. I pop the clutch, press down too hard on the gas, then too lightly. I only get the rhythm as I pull out of the tunnel and drive by the meadow towards my house.

I park in the driveway and get out, but can't walk directly to the house just yet. My whole body feels like it's asleep, as if my circulation has been cut off. I pace for a while, through the orchard, around the house a few times, up the steps onto the porch. When I feel like I have blood flowing through me once again, I lean against the house, bent at the waist, hands pressed onto my knees. A noise from the driveway. Footsteps on gravel. I look over and it's Dodge. A big smile, bandanna pulled down around his neck, chainsaw in hand, the lower half of his body wet from the creek.

"I ran upstream this time," he says, out of breath as he climbs the steps to the porch. "Figgered I'd meet you here." He reaches the last step and takes the porch as if it's a podium. "Can you fuckin' believe that?" he raises his chainsaw in triumph. "Just say no to drugs, motherfuckers!"

I can't talk yet. Otherwise I'd tell him right now, right away. But I can't talk.

"I wasn't even gonna do it, I swear," he continues. "I wasn't lyin' to you back there when I said you were right and we should just wait and report what we got. I mean, my original plan was a lot more complicated than this. I really needed you. I had this orange vest left over from when I had to pick up garbage along the freeway after a DUI a while back, but I needed you to get 'em all outta the house. Then I was on my way to Roman's to pick up some stuff from the guest house and I saw those guys playin' soccer and figgered my God, they're already outta the house. It's a sign. Time to seize the day, y'know? All I had to do was show up with my vest and my saw, wave at 'em and then point to the tree and the power lines. They just nodded and waved right back. Damn!" he says, unable to contain the grin on his face. "That was just too easy."

"You may have killed somebody, Dodge."

I can finally say it, but he doesn't get it. "Nah," he says. "You saw me knock. Wasn't a soul in that junk factory."

"No Dodge," my voice gets stronger. "I'm saying you really may have killed somebody. They all ran towards the scene afterwards calling out a name and clawing their way through the debris."

"Bullshit."

"I'm serious."

"I knocked."

"They could've been asleep."

"I knocked twice."

"I saw them."

"Show me."

His eyes have a glaze to them, as though he's looking at something far away. We get in the truck and drive by the meadow and towards the tunnel. He doesn't say anything, just stares straight ahead. He doesn't say a word until we drive past the trees watching over the disaster Dodge created. Santo's men are still desperately trying to burrow into the shattered wood. Then all Dodge says is "keep driving." So I drive down to the highway and ask him "where to?"

"I need a drink."

He props his elbow up on the inside door handle and holds his head in his hand, all the way down to the little town where we watched for the INS. The bar & grill seems pretty crowded.

"You sure?" I ask him.

"I'd smoke but my cigarettes got wet."

"I mean do you want to sit at a well-lit bar full of people right now?"

"I just want somethin' in a brown bag and a view of the ocean."

We pull into a space between the Playa Blanca Market and the post office. Vic is there, wandering back and forth, asking for employment or for spare change, depending on the passerby. The rest of Dodge's old buddies are absent, so Vic zeroes in on us as we get out.

"Not today, Vic," says Dodge.

"Oh, like we're still tight," Vic says. "Like we still hang out all the time..."

Dodge spins around and stops Vic in his tracks, giving him a look—bulging eyes like the mug shots on a post office bulletin board. "I said not today."

Vic wants to stare back but doesn't have as much motivation. "Fine," he concedes. "But just remember you're always a paycheck away from you and me being buds again, asshole."

Dodge rears back to punch Vic, who flinches and darts away. He makes a move to chase him down, but stops after his first step. He seems hypnotized by the ocean never ending in front of him. I come up behind him and ask if he still wants that drink. He snaps out of it. Vic paces nervously on the other side of the highway, in the dirt lot where a couple of cars have parked and the passengers are further away on the horizon standing near the edge of the cliffs. The tourists concentrate on the water as if they may just be able to see what's on the other side if they stand there long enough. Dodge looks for a moment at the same thing, but instead appears to see nothing on the other side. To him it's the edge, where you've come as far as you can go and can only pace, hoping some way of crossing presents itself.

"Yeah," says Dodge. "Let's get hammered."

But of course Playa Blanca has a meager selection. Nothing hard, much to Dodge's frustration. "We don't have a license for that," according to the owner/cashier. Just the standard selection of domestic beers by the dozen and some of those prefab fruity drinks in bottles: margaritas, fuzzy navels, piña coladas, banana daiquiris.

I go with a screwdriver and Dodge grabs a rum punch. I buy this round and ask for an extra brown bag so we each have our own.

We sit on the edge of the red brick planter box in front of the post office and Dodge has the shakes pretty bad. I pretend not to notice by staring at the ocean, but I can hear the brown bag crumpling as he tries to steady his grasp on the bottle. I want to tell him that I know how he feels, but realize how ludicrous that would sound at the moment. Unless I prove it. Unless I tell him.

"This may not help much right now," I say. "But maybe later..." I look over at him and he's still gazing across the highway at the blues, the indigo of the water and powder blue of the sky, each broken up with random whiteness—breakers below, clouds above.

"Dodge?"

"Hmm?"

He turns to me and I recognize his look. I didn't see myself of course when I found out what happened with Abby and her husband. But now I have. He's wondering if there is any way to recover. The victim's life, his own life. He's convinced forgiveness is something invented by those who haven't done anything so bad, or had anything done to them. He sees a life of reliving this day every day. No hope, and no punishment great enough, not even taking his own life.

"You're not the only one sitting here who's killed someone," I tell him. He stares back at me, no change in his expression. I continue, suddenly intent on spilling all of it, determined to tell the story I've never surrendered voluntarily. "As a matter of fact, I'm one up on you. I've killed two people."

He narrows his eyes as if to warm me against bullshitting him at a time like this. I tell him it's true. It's the God's honest truth and it's why I'm here.

I start from the beginning. The beginning of the end.

A friendly wave. Not the kind of gesture you would expect to signal the beginning of the end. A friendly wave in the aisle of a pharmacy. But then it's just a gesture. There is so much more leading up to it. The fact I have an EPT box in my hand. Early Pregnancy Test. And I'm not buying it for my wife. And I'm waving to a friend of my wife. That doesn't help. I only realize what I've been waving over my head after I reach the car. It's funny, actually. I laugh.

She will tell my wife, though, the friend will. Not out of malice. She doesn't know it's for someone else. Her friend will open her arms wide next time she sees my wife Janet and smile with every one of her teeth bared and say "Congratulations" very loudly. Janet will wonder what in the hell she's talking about. Not wanting to embarrass her friend, though, she will play along, her mind racing the entire time she is hugging her. Racing, trying to figure out what she could possibly mean.

"I didn't think you guys wanted kids," her friend says. "At least not for a while. That's what you always say."

Janet still doesn't quite understand. Why would I discuss kids with someone else? But at least she has something to go on. A lead. Now she can play along.

"So what was the result of the test?" her friend continues. "If you don't mind me asking."

This additional information only confuses Janet. There's more to this than she realized. What test? Janet thinks. But she has to play along. So instead she asks, how did you know about the test? And Janet's friend tells her about the day in the drug store, waving the EPT box. Her friend gets a laugh out of it, as I did in the car that day.

Janet doesn't laugh. She tries, but cannot. She invents an appointment she's late for. She confronts me that night.

The discussion between me and my wife may surprise you, I tell Dodge. We have an agreement, you see. We're both very self-confident, and very much in love with each other. Our sex life is the stuff of fantasies, fantasies most people are reluctant to admit they have. Nothing can come between us. Nothing. Which is why we agreed that an open marriage could be very beneficial to both of us.

Our careers, though lucrative, are moving too slow for our accustomed pace. We get what we want, both of us. Always have. That included each other. Each of us was used to being pursued. Objectified by interested parties. And there were many parties. And eventually it occurred to me. "Give 'em what they want." That's what I said. But more important: get what we want from them in return.

Against natural law? Depends. Is natural law mating for life? Or is it trying to successfully copulate with as many members of the species as possible? Are we birds or are we dogs?

Offending your sensibilities? I hope so. It offended ours, too. At first. We weren't brought up that way, of course. Who is? Nobody should be raised to think like this, to act this way. But we can handle it. We know we can. It's got mutual consent going for it. Both of us are completely self-aware. Nobody will get hurt. Everybody will get what they want. And that sounds like a lot of fun. Admit it.

But there are so many old adages about pride. Pride will do this, pride causes that. And eventually we find out there are good reasons why pride has been such an inspiration.

You broke the rules, Janet tells me.

What rules?

No strings attached. Love, commitment, pregnancy. Those are strings.

She wasn't pregnant. The test was negative.

But it was still careless. Stupid.

Careless. Stupid. All of it. We both begin to see that maybe this wasn't such a good idea. People do get hurt. I've had visions of her with the men I know she's been with. The visions make me shudder. The thought of her with another man, no matter how emotionally detached she may be, no matter how little they mean to her. I know how men think. I know how visual they are. What your wife was feeling at the moment doesn't matter. What matters to them is they saw her doing things to them. They saw her naked. Every part of her. And they will never forget. It is documented forever in their minds, spliced forever into their sex highlight reel.

I know how men think. And so in a way it doesn't surprise me what happens when the husband finds the empty EPT box in the garbage. The husband of the woman I've been screwing. The woman I've been screwing because she had seven digits in a savings account she didn't know what to do with, an inheritance she wasn't sure whom to trust with, and a husband who was lost when it came to anything beyond balancing a checking account. And I did give her some great advice. Her money was performing some breathtaking stunts, so she and her husband were starting to make plans thanks to me. Thanks to me.

And so in a way it doesn't surprise me when he murders her and then himself upon finding the EPT box in the garbage can. He was looking for aluminum cans to move to the recycling bin. He wasn't looking for any evidence of any adultery. He trusted his wife. They had been looking to adopt a child together. He was sterile. But they wanted to raise a child, raise a child well. Teach the child how people should conduct themselves. To be kind to others, to the earth. To recycle. But he was sterile. And he found an EPT box in the garbage can.

He loved her so much that he couldn't bear to face what he had done to her. So he killed himself, too. Turned the gun right around.

There is no way to anticipate the gravity of even a single friendly wave when you are plotting the perfect crime. Against nature or otherwise.

I take a big sip from my bottle and we are silent, Dodge and me. Just the roar of the ocean, the cars passing by on the highway, and the voices of the people on the cliffs occasionally fighting their way through the wind and into our ears. We each take a couple more swigs from our bottles.

"How do you know what happened that night he found the box?" Dodge asks.

"He called the police and told them what happened. They raced over to the house because they knew suicide was a possibility. But they were too late."

"At least you didn't pull the trigger."

"And what you did was not on purpose," I tell him. "My EPT box, your Monterey pine."

"You didn't pull the trigger," Dodge repeats himself, convinced our dilemmas do not run so parallel. Slightly miffed, I remind him that he did accomplish what he started, carried out the goal he had in mind.

"And I killed someone," he says, maintaining an inconsolable monotone.

"A few hours ago all you could talk about is how full of scumbags that ranch is," I say. "How we're making the world a better place by destroying their business. Now you're in mourning?"

"I never wanted to hurt anybody."

"At least your victim is a meth cooker. I killed two decent human beings."

Dodge throws his bagged-up bottle into the pavement and lets the explosion resonate before going on. "You wanna compare tragedies, huh? Is that the way you make a friend feel better? Pull out our skeletons and measure 'em like we're pullin' out our dicks?"

I've been put in my place, and I have nothing to say. Dodge puts his head in his hands and leans over the wet wound of brown paper and shards of glass. "I wish meth was around when I was doin' drugs heavy," he says. "It woulda killed me and spared everyone the time and effort of gettin' me back on my feet again."

I put a hand on his back. "Nobody's worked harder than you on that."

"Yeah," he says, sitting up straight, shrugging my hand off his back. "And maybe the guy I killed was gonna do the same thing pretty soon. Maybe he was just a desperate guy tryin' to feed his family back home, or start a family." He looks over at me. "In my world, Stanford boy, everyone's a decent human being compared to myself."

And because Dodge believes that and still feels so torn up about killing one of those decent human beings, because he refuses to lash back at a life he feels uninvited to, I now believe Dodge is the most honorable man I've ever met. I consider ways of telling him this that won't sound corny, that will manage to absolutely penetrate his grief, while at the same time a tremendous amount of my own grief starts to slide from my shoulders. The knots untie, the wads of tension are kneaded flat across every bound up landscape on my body—forehead, eyebrows, jaw, chest, back. The warm color that hackneyed psychiatrist suggested I imagine rolling down my body finally does. As always, the color is orange. Orange at last produces the necessary deep breaths as I look into someone else's pain that may just surpass my own. Not that I don't feel extremely guilty for experiencing this sensation while Dodge is standing at the crux of his troubled life...but the fact is there is something truly liberating about being in the presence of such deep distress. It was my hope that I could provide this very outlet, the same relief for Dodge, by way of my confession. But now that it's backfired I suppose it just goes to show that there is no way to manufacture healing. It's a purely organic process.

"Oh shit," says Dodge.

I look where he's looking and think the same thing. A dusty old pickup rolls onto the shoulder off the highway in front of us with Santo riding in the passenger seat, looking sharp and out of place in such a vehicle, with one of his men driving. My pulse jumps. Dodge's pulse launches him to his feet. Santo spots him and turns to his driver. The truck slows in our direction. Dodge turns to me, eyes deep in their sockets, trying not to pop out and give himself away.

"Stall him," he says, darting into the market before I can utter a sound. I look over at the truck, at Santo getting out, and act casual. And I do mean act. Santo arrives as I pretend to examine the brickwork of the planter box I'm sitting on.

"Dodge was here, no?" he asks, an easy smile on his face.

"Uh, yes," I tell him. "He went into the market for something."

"Another drink?" he asks, nodding towards the splattered ex-bottle on the pavement.

"Yeah," I jump at the ready-made excuse. "Can't hold his liquor."

At first I think Santo is wincing at my bad joke, but then realize he's concerned. "Dodge is drinking again?"

"Oh, no," I say. "Figure of speech." Then it occurs to me. "You know he had a problem?"

Santo nods and sits down, crossing his legs as if taking his place on a broadcast news panel. "You work with him, is that right?"

"Yes. For the Mirabellis."

Santo nods and contemplates things for a moment. "I like to keep track of him," he explains. "I knew his mother very well. I feel like I do her a favor to keep an eye on her son."

"You knew his mother?"

"Yes," he seems a little ashamed now of giving up that information. "Frank Demos is his father. You knew him?"

"I heard about him."

"So from who do you think he got his talents? Certainly not Frank."

I would laugh if I wasn't still reeling from his revelation. But I do smile. He does likewise and continues. "I need that talent. An idiot from PG & E cut a tree down onto a house of ours at the ranch."

I play overly dumb and say that certainly is a stupid thing to do, wondering aloud at the legal ramifications of such idiocy and waiting for him to mention the person inside the house, which he does not.

"Dodge is an excellent carpenter," he says instead. "He can build it in no time. That is more important to me than finding someone to sue."

I can't take it anymore. "Was anyone hurt?"

"Nobody, thank God."

Staring straight ahead to ponder how to stifle any reaction to this news, I decide that staring straight ahead will do just fine.

"What a relief," I steady my voice. "Somebody could have been inside."

"We are fortunate. But my brother is a little broken-hearted."

"Your brother?"

"Yes. His dog was in there."

"His dog?"

"He really loves that dog."

"The black and white dog with the blue eyes?"

"That's him."

"He chases the cars up and down the gravel road?"

"Yes," Santo chuckles. "He makes my old brother crazy with that. And now there he is at the ranch, on his knees next to the accident, praying that the men can find his dog under all that mess so that he can make him crazy some more."

I start to laugh too. All that anguish. All that "closure" and "healing" at Dodge's expense. And all of it over that damn dog. I'm already trying to remember the phone number of that therapist so I can tell her how effective her methods proved to be once a dog stepped in.

I'm starting to laugh a bit too hard, so I settle down abruptly and think of something to ask about his brother. Is he as old as he looks? Any chance his dog actually survived? But first I hear someone run across the pavement behind me. Santo's eyes follow the noise as he stands up. I turn in time to see Dodge cross the highway at a dead sprint. No traffic, a clear shot. He must have been waiting for the right moment. Vic is still over there and figures Dodge is coming after him, so he cowers behind one of the parked cars in the vacant lot.

But Dodge doesn't stop. He maintains his pace through the lot and between the wood stumps marking the boundary, past the signs warning people about standing too close to the edge of the cliffs. He keeps going straight ahead, refusing to veer left or right towards the trails that trickle down the sides of the rocky walls. He actually speeds up, as if gearing up to tackle one of the tourists staring at the sea, or to break through their ranks, as though one of them said "Red Rover, Red Rover, send Dodge right over." He doesn't slow down, and we both seem to realize at the same time, Santo and I do, that he isn't going to stop.

I run to the edge of the highway and have to hesitate as a car drives by honking its horn. Once I make it to the other side I start screaming, screaming his name. I don't know if Santo is behind me or not. I only see Dodge in full stride heading for land's end. The tourists hear him coming and turn around, clear the way, startled. I keep screaming and almost yell "it was just the dog" but realize that would give him away to Santo, and then realize it's not going to matter.

I stop and put all my energy into screaming his name as he hurdles into space, frozen it seems against the horizon for a moment, as though allowed to hover just long enough to have second thoughts which are too late. Then he disappears. I never see him fall. But when I reach the edge and get on my hands and knees to peer over the side, he's there at the bottom, across a flat rock on his back, arms and legs thrown about. He looks like a costume. A man suit. Discarded and deflated, I could pick him up and shake him out, let him dry and be "Dodge" for Halloween. Feet towards the ocean, head pointed inland, the same position everyone decides on when laying out in the sun. The tide swells over the rocks and rolls his body slightly back and forth, animating him, making him look alive as the tide recedes.

Somebody yells "call 911" because that's what you're supposed to yell in these types of situations, though Dodge is obviously dead. The cry for 911 comes again.

"What, once you say it you don't have to do it?" I holler at no one in particular, and turn to do it myself, as I remember this town has one of the few remaining phone booths, thanks in part to the lousy reception in the area that may be preventing anyone from getting through on their cell. After a wobbly first couple steps, I start to sprint as hard as I can towards the phone booth by the post office. I pass by Santo. He is kneeling in the meadow, completely despondent as he stares at the horizon where he last saw Dodge.

Touched by his concern, I turn to look at him again as soon as I'm inside the phone booth. I focus on his vigilant silhouette and almost forget to respond when the operator answers. I keep my eye on the horizon as well, for the duration of my phone conversation, and as I leave the booth.

A tug on my sleeve. Vic.

"Does this mean Joe's hiring?" he asks, and after I backhand the side of his head and he's rolling around in the fetal position moaning, I realize that life is, in fact, already going on. It was going on while Dodge was sprinting into mid-air. The world was rotating the entire time he fell. A breeze blows in from the ocean and something on the ground nearby skids along the pavement. Dodge's hat.

I walk a few steps to pick it up. Parked next to my truck, a man is standing beside his car, a new Mustang convertible, snapping pictures of the mayhem against the Pacific horizon. Walking towards him in an adrenalin surge, I fling Dodge's hat into my truck bed and swat the camera out of his hands, slap it down onto the pavement.

"Things don't happen here just so you can take pictures of it," I say, the tip of my nose practically up his nostril. "This is a place, not a postcard."

But he doesn't listen, just backpedals and stares at his broken camera, calls me a son of a bitch, and lunges at me. A dead friend outweighs a broken camera for motivation, and I've got him across the hood of his car a moment after he lays the first hand. On the other side of the Mustang, a dusty old blue Nova pulls off the highway. Veronica, on her way back from school. She peers through the windshield at me, shocked, demanding an explanation with her eyes as she gets out of the car. I stare back at her, trying to explain, loosening my grip on the camera man, who then launches a fist up my chin. A weak shot, not much leverage behind it, but square and unexpected enough to send me backwards into the side of my truck. He teeters after me but Veronica steps in between us.

"What's going on?" she finally has a chance to ask.

"It's Dodge," is all I can manage to say before collapsing into her arms. She holds me tight, breathing hard, joining me in a breakdown. With my chin resting on her shoulder, I see the camera man creep into his convertible, confusion and embarrassment hurrying his movements, leaving his broken camera behind.

"He jumped," I stroke the hair on the back of her head. "I couldn't stop him." And before I can say anymore I see that Santo is watching, completely sympathetic, hardly the sinister presence we had imagined. There is something wrong with Dodge's theory. Santo nods at me and heads back to his truck, the driver still inside, dutifully waiting despite all the commotion.

"Why did he do it?" she whispers in my ear.

"I don't know," I whisper back, which is the story I'll stick to for now, for Dodge's sake.

We sit on the brick ledge a few feet down from the remnants of his last drink impacted on the pavement. I pretend to speculate along with Veronica. The owner of the Playa Blanca market comes out and asks if I'm Stanford.

"Yes," I have to think for a moment in light of my surprise.

"Dodge said to give this to you," he holds out a folded piece of paper. "He wrote in on the butcher paper behind the deli before he slipped out the back door and ran. I haven't read it, I swear."

I take the paper, my hand shaking. Unwrapping it produces the same crumpling sounds as when it's around a sandwich. Written in thick black Magic Marker, as though it could easily read "no onions," are Dodge's last words:

I am sorry somebody had to die

I hope it was for a good reason

tell my kids about me

I turn to the owner of the market, hovering curiously to our side, and thank him, letting him read the note before asking him not to breathe a word of its existence to anyone.

"Whatever helps him rest in peace," he says, passing it back to me.

I thank him. He holds up his hand, letting me know it's not a problem, and walks back inside. Veronica leans over and reads it. She asks me what it means. I maintain my vow. I say "I wish I knew" while wondering if Dodge was perhaps including my past in his note as well, by mentioning how sorry he was that someone had to die.

Veronica looks at me, fully aware that I'm lying.

"I'll tell you later," I say, retracting my poorly-feigned ignorance, hoping that it really was for a good reason, sorry that someone had to die. That Dodge had to die.

"I'll explain everything."

# OCTOBER

October arrives with no sense of structure, no chronology; a drunken feeling that if you try and concentrate on more than a single thought or image at once, everything past and present would seem to happen at the same time. The blueprint through which Dodge pulled me during the last days of his life is gone and soon to be eulogized at a memorial service. I don't even have the San Francisco market to mark the days, or at least Mondays, Wednesdays, and Fridays. Instead I spend the early days of October driving slowly through the pumpkin fields, straddling the rows of orange behind the wheel of a flatbed truck. Manuel fills my position in the market as Joe needs me here to help harvest the pumpkins, the thousands of pumpkins uniformly orange, grown specifically for the larger grocery chains in the Bay Area.

The flatbed truck is lined with seven cardboard bins on each side, the kind of cardboard bins you see turned upside down with people living inside them along damp city alleyways. Four of Joe's men stand on the back of the truck, each one inside a bin up to their waist, two on each side. They catch the pumpkins thrown to them by a procession of several other men walking the fields behind the truck. The walkers choose in stride the closest things to perfection they can find, lift the mighty vegetables and throw chest passes up to the men standing in the bins, looking like a basketball team in a pre-game shoot-around, orange balls constantly flying at their target. A mobile assembly line, the people rolling by the product instead of the usual vice-versa.

The men waist-deep in the bins taunt the men walking below them. They gloat because they won the foot race to the truck and don't have to bend over and over again to pick up the acres of orange bowling balls which are an obvious strain on even the strongest back wearing the sturdiest back brace. They are the "king of the

241

hill." The walkers get their revenge when a pumpkin presents itself which is small enough to get some good velocity behind it, or when two pumpkins come flying at once towards the man in the box, a situation the walkers of course always maintain is sheer coincidence.

So I drive very slowly so all of this can take place. No radio playing in case the men have to tell me to stop for some reason. Just me and the rows of orange in front of me, the color's soothing effect now mute, no softer than the coldest gray or slate blue. As often as I assure myself there was no way I could have stopped him from reaching the edge that day, I can't help but feel as though there was much more I could have done to prevent it from reaching that point. I chose to be a voice of reason by simply writing off his ideas instead of seriously trying to refute them with ideas of my own, hard proof, a competing investigation. I hid myself in his obsession, rode on the trail he was carving towards redemption with the hope it would all just rub off on me, rescue me too, allow me to stare any ghost in the eye without having to contribute anything of my own.

A tap on the back window, right by my ear. The last bins, closest to the cab, are filled. One of the men in the cardboard boxes, Gerardo from El Salvador, powder blue University of North Carolina cap turned backwards on his head, lies on his stomach atop a pile of pumpkins rising above the rim of his bin as he reaches down to rap on the window. Back to the loading area.

All the men jump onto the flatbed and I pick up speed, winding through the dirt roads which split the fields, bouncing back towards a dried out parcel of land in the farthest corner of the ranch, ten acres of cracked dirt just on the other side of the tree line from the sand dunes, uncultivated and saved for the industrial leg of the harvest. A dozen aisles of filled bins stretching forty yards each are lined up on one side of the barren plot. Every other bin is stacked well above the brim with pumpkins, while the ones in between are covered with a lid. This is so the overflowing bins can be stacked on top of the lidded ones, so they can be loaded two at a time.

I pull up behind the other flatbed truck driven by Javier, which is currently being unloaded by forklift. Dodge had been one of the forklift operators in years past, so one of the other tractor drivers is learning how on the job this year. The men jump off and join the others from Javier's truck in teasing the lift driver about his inexperienced style of operation—lots of sudden braking and abrupt starts. The bins are added to the ends of the long orange aisles. At the opposite end, the other forklift takes from the aisles to feed the fifty-foot long trailers of the big rigs waiting in lines five or six deep at times. Veronica is there, squinting in the sun and the dust, supervising the loading with clipboard in one hand, bratwurst-sized piece of chalk in the other. She scrawls the store number across the bins being lifted into the long dark hallways of the trucks.

I get out to stretch my legs and she waves. I wave back and the men turn their teasing towards me. But I'm not as much fun to jeer since I can't shoot back, so my space is limited. We hold our ground, Veronica and I, thanks mostly to our duties. But I have been withholding the information I promised her about Dodge.

I withheld it from the police, too, within earshot of Veronica as they questioned me right outside Playa Blanca market. I just told them Dodge had gotten back into drugs lately. They nodded and seemed relieved at being supplied with a logical answer, a quick end to their investigation. I was a veteran of police inquiries, after all.

But unlike Veronica, I never promised the police anything. She has not been badgering or begging me. Of course not. Not her. But there is an expectant look in her eyes every time we talk. She's waiting, waiting for me to "explain everything." I just don't know if I can. I can tell her about his connections. The drug-addled lunatic attacking Dodge at the ranch plus the discovery of drugs in the drug-addled lunatic's car plus the eerie presence of Santo Farms with three dozen employees and nothing for them to do plus the fire Dodge presumed was ignited by the combustible ingredients cooking in the assumed meth lab plus the residue in the creek plus the sheriff's deputies plus Ranger Roman plus the resort and all the money tied into it. Equals? Equals? I can't do the work, add the levels. All I can think of is Santo. His face, during our conversation about Dodge and his mother, and after Dodge jumped. His face, wholly sympathetic and barely masking his own grief at the same time. His face convincing me that Dodge jumped for reasons far more misguided than the fact it was just a dog inside the building.

"I can't tell you anything until I figure some things out for myself," I finally tell her on our way to the memorial service.

"I could help you," she says.

"I can't accept anyone's help on this. I was supposed to be helping Dodge when he was alive. I need to follow through."

"This is hardly a case of better late than never. He's dead."

"If I need your help I'll ask for it."

Just the kind of clipped statement that sends couples to an event pissed at each other, not speaking the rest of the way, slamming their doors as they get out of the car, their own doors, no assistance offered one to another, no waiting for each other. Two parallel paths from the car to the church, a safe distance apart, we get close enough and smile sincerely enough at the entrance to avoid any inquiries as to "what's wrong?"

The church is one-quarter filled, if that. Plenty of space makes it easy to see individual faces. I see Dodge's kids turn to survey the attendance from their front row pew, and then their mother, Dodge's ex-wife, follows their lead. My first glimpse of her. She has a disheveled look, her sharpest feature a pair of leery eyes, reminiscent of those black-and-white photographs of aging movie queens who have hit rock bottom, alcoholic and several-times divorced, their bitterness the only sign of life behind those eyes heavy with mascara and hatred. She doesn't appear to be the least bit sad, as though sadness is something she put behind her a long time ago.

Nobody who knew Dodge personally gives the eulogy. The minister handles that duty with a standard lament, filling in the blanks with the name "Dodge." I hear just one consistent sniffle, coming from behind us. I turn and see Santo in the back row, looking up towards the ceiling, his tears pensive and under control, more a product of his thoughts than an outpouring of emotion. Facing front once more, I look for similar signs of sentimentality—shoulders or backs quivering, heads bowed extra low, hands reaching up to wipe eyes—but there are none. Just an audience that could be watching a serious movie or attending a lecture.

On our way out I see that Santo has disappeared, the back row empty. Veronica says she wants to see how her parents are doing. The procession up the aisle passes through the door. Javier and his wife emerge. Veronica hugs them and I shake their hands, a tradition of discomfort between parents and their daughter's suitor keeping us in its grip. Joe, Lorraine, and Aldo appear right behind them, granting us all a reprieve. Everyone stands and stares at each other for a moment, apparently in shock at seeing one another dressed up. We then exchange small-talk about the service, make sure that everyone has a ride to Roman's house, where the reception will be. Joe can't resist mentioning how hypocritical it is of Roman to host the reception. "Nothing but appearances," he flops both hands downward, a double-dismissive wave. "He could care less about his brother, but he cares enough about his image."

I keep an eye on the line filing out the door and figure it must be near the end, people in the first few rows bound to appear. I wonder if this would be a good time to tell his kids about what happened, like he asked me to in his note, to tell his wife. But I don't know what I'd say. I need time to prepare.

In the car Veronica notes how distracted and uncomfortable I seemed, and thinks it was because of her folks being present. I have to tell her that I'm just fine with her parents, and explain my indecision about Dodge's family and my fear of meeting them outside the church and causing a scene on sacred ground. She accuses me of using Dodge as an excuse to lay the groundwork for eventually bailing on her. In assuring her that my preoccupation with Dodge's death is pure, I am careful not to attribute anything to her own insecurities, the natural doubts anyone has while standing next to a new lover (potential love) in the presence of one's parents. Instead I just apologize repeatedly, and by the time we reach the top of the gravel road overlooking my rented house she at long last seems convinced.

As the road curves to the right and we straighten out into the home stretch heading for Roman's, I glance over at her during our post-war silence, the necessary breather for damage assessment. She is not gloating. No smug sense of victory, a chin-jutting smirk at having watched me grovel for the last ten miles. She almost seems a little ashamed, if not appreciative of my efforts.

Suddenly an understanding. My frustration with Veronica is a positive sign, an indicator of good things to come. Silent but now at peace, I sense we are learning quickly that being next to each other is about all there is most of the time, and is enough. Of course Janet and I never reached that point, so with no previous experience on the matter I suppose I can only hope we're learning that sunsets and fireworks are not sustainable. But as I get out of the car and walk around to hold the door for her, she smiles at me as she gets out. An apology. A thank you. All that, I swear, in one simple gesture. We walk to the reception having survived two hurdles of compatibility in one day—an argument and a solemn event—which is enough to convince me that we're on our way to reconciliation with the prospect of most days ahead being just another day.

Most days.

The first hard evidence presents itself almost immediately, the first clear indication besides the look on Santo's face that Dodge may have indeed been chasing his tail. We're standing on the front deck of Roman's house, the mid-afternoon winds kicking up off the ocean, threatening to blow the terra cotta flower pots clean off their perches along the overhang. Gretchen Demos is the first person we see and talk to, she having exercised the rights of her age and stature to leave the services a bit early and arrive at her son's house in time to hold court as people enter the house. I wonder as we approach what Dodge was to her, what he was to her in the familial sense, amongst the branches of the family tree, not in the symbolic terms I often speculated on regarding Dodge as a breathing reminder of her husband's unfaithfulness and abusive treatment of his employees. A stepson? But he arrived after they were married. A half son? Roman is a half-brother, after all—same father, different mother.

Different mother.

Not related to her at all, by blood. But she raised him. A bastard. The bastard son. It doesn't sound right. The word has taken on a new meaning. Bastard. It's pure slang now, the former definition as obsolete as those for words like gay and bitch. His father was the real bastard. Franky was the bastard. The word was badly defined from the beginning, putting everything on the shoulders of the child. Why not instead concoct a word for "absent father" or "father who turns his back on his child or children" or "man who fathers a child out of wedlock." Preferably something that resonates as effectively as bastard.

No renter-to-landlord conversations today. Before I'm finished hugging her, Gretchen asks what I think could have caused him to do such a thing, to take his own life like that.

"I wish I knew," I tell her, which sounds to me like the bullshit that it is. So I follow it up with "I wish I could have helped." Very true. A deep breath thanks to my sincere regrets.

"Was it money?" Gretchen asks. "Did he need money for anything?"

"I really don't think so."

"Oh God, I hope it wasn't over money. I wanted to help him any way I could, but by the time Frank died Dodge was so resentful. It was so hard to talk to him."

"He wasn't an easy man to know."

"I sent him some money once but he sent it back. So I figured I'd wait for him to ask, like Roman does..."

"Roman?"

Gretchen is startled at my interruption. I follow it up with a much softer tone of voice. "You gave Roman money?"

"Enough to send Frank spinning in his grave," she says, a moment of delight on a sad day.

"That much, huh?"

Veronica nudges me, but Gretchen doesn't seem to mind the questions. She continues.

"He always had a reason. Always had an excuse. 'I'm investing it, Mom' he'd say. 'Investing in something big. I'll double your money, share the wealth. Trust me.' That's what Roman would say after every request: 'Trust me.'"

"When?" I keep it up. "When did he ask you? Around what period of time?"

"All the time," she says. "He's always asked."

Dodge's theory starts to crack even louder, sounding in my ears like the tree he cut down, the snap it made just before it started to fall, sharp and loud, allowing everyone around it to speculate on just how hard it will land and in what direction. Roman's investments were subsidized by his mother. Why am I not surprised? No bribes from drug runners, no elaborate cover-ups.

I almost forget to thank Gretchen before ducking into the house to find Roman.

"Thank me for what?" she responds.

Good question. Thank you for what? "Thank you for caring. I don't know how many people did care, and Dodge wasn't really sure."

Gretchen bursts into a loud wail, bringing her hands up to her face, the familiar front-page image of a devastated woman witnessing a tragedy. The reception line behind us is several condolences long. Veronica and I stand awkwardly by, unsure if it's even appropriate to shift our weight. So we just stand. Veronica whispers in my ear that I should go get her a glass of water or something, so I ask Gretchen if she'd like anything and that's exactly what she asks for. A glass of water.

The guests fill the house more thoroughly than they did the vast interior of the church. But there is no din, no clash of competing conversations and rattle of ceramic and silverware. Just several small groups of people unfamiliar with each other and meeting under the wrong circumstances, the uncomfortable pauses outnumbering the guests, the small talk engulfed by the vaulted ceilings of Franky's legacy, this mission-style peach-colored monstrosity. As I run the tap in the kitchen, a voice hisses into my ear, "Thanks for the advice, asshole."

I turn to find Roman, teeth clenched tighter than a ventriloquist's.

"Do you know your mother's outside and she's very upset?" I ask him.

"Don't try to change the subject," he snaps. "I asked for points like you suggested, big shot. They barely stopped laughing long enough to fire me from the project."

I resist a similar impulse to laugh. The Roman angle established by Dodge having already collapsed before my eyes, I can at least enjoy the erosion of Roman's actual angle. He wags on.

"They may think they've gotten enough out of me to complete that fucker, but they've got a surprise coming their way."

"A surprise they're no doubt prepared for."

Roman says "Ha!" He really does. "You pricks from over the hill are all the same, making it your business to underestimate anyone who'd rather drink coffee instead of cappuccino. Not this time." He suspends a threatening finger in front of my face. He really does. "Cicerelli and Munson are gonna get bit, right in the ass."

He returns with a flourish back to his guests, leaving me grateful for the comic relief and still holding the glass of water for his mother. Making my way back to the deck, it seems as though people are growing more comfortable with each other. The bits of conversation I hear are shorter and run into others more often, as if I've been driving with the radio on searching for a station in a remote area and suddenly arrived in a major city with voices coming from every spot on the dial. A man I've never met before stops me and tells me he couldn't imagine being there on the cliffs that day, seeing what I've seen. His wife shakes her head sympathetically in my direction. A woman in the next group nods at me, whispers in my ear that she's also seen someone die. That she's seen a lot worse. Vic is there, dressed up in the way people do who are not used to it—necktie lying halfway up his stomach and tied with a knot better suited for mooring a boat. He sees me and takes a step back, eyes widening, relaxing as soon as I ignore him. Still no sign of Dodge's ex-family.

I return to the deck and complete my mission. Gretchen breathes deeply into the glass of water as she drinks it, finishing with a deep gasp of air as she puts it down, as though she has just broken through the surface of a pool after a long time underwater.

"Would you like another one?" I ask.

"No thank you, Paul."

Veronica and I each give her a hug and leave her alone to collect herself before the next offer of condolence comes walking up on her. Veronica is intrigued at finding out my real name.

"Paul?" she asks, as if disappointed with the prize she dug out from the bottom of the cereal box.

"Then forget you ever heard it."

"Sorry," she says. "I'm just used to Stanford."

"That name has a higher admission," I tease her. "It's going to cost you."

She acts intrigued, and under such flirty circumstances I figure is a good time to tell her that I'd like to collect my thoughts and think of something to say to Dodge's family when they arrive. She agrees, kissing me by the ear and wishing me luck.

But they never arrive. After an hour of pacing on the deck, I forget about my dread of facing them and try to will them there, mentally begging them to show up. It's his funeral, for God's sake. You can at least make an appearance. I stop wishing they were there and start cursing them. In my mind I scream at Dodge for wasting so much effort on such miserable jerks, and it comes across my mouth as groans and mumbles, across my body as fidgeting and stomping.

Everything eventually settles down in time with the wind. The evening light, as usual, is able to calm even the ocean's breath, sending it back out to sea, where it blows an endless fog bank steadily along in a north-south direction a few miles offshore. The wall of purple and orange fog travels fast enough to simulate movement, like a movie studio back-lot special effect designed to make stationary cars appear to be driving. Only in this case, it is the land which seems to be moving, the coast cruising by the ocean.

Veronica comes up behind me with a brilliant idea. Leave early and grab some dinner. I suggest anyplace more than an hour's drive so I can think. She decides on the city, downtown San Francisco, since we're clothed to the liking of any dress code a restaurant can throw at us. The city is ours. She respects my request for a thoughtful, quiet drive.

I decide to focus my efforts on unraveling the mystery Dodge had obsessed over, his last addiction. Just because Roman wasn't involved doesn't mean the case is closed. Maybe Dodge was right, not only about Santo Farms, but about his own family. It may take a splash that big to get them to come around, to honor his memory. Just because Santo seemed more upset than Dodge's family doesn't make him innocent. And if he really did like Dodge so much, well now is his chance to help him.

I get a rush from my newfound resolve to discover the truth, and revel silently at my good fortune of having Veronica with me during all this, at the benefits of companionship in times of doubt. I regret all the times I ever said "I want to be alone" to anyone who ever reached out to me under similar circumstances. I reach over for her thigh as the city comes into view.

"I'm glad you're here," I tell her.

She smiles, waiting until we've chosen a restaurant and are seated beneath a potted palm in a corner booth before asking "What was your wife like?"

Somehow I thought the intensification of our relationship would soften her need to alternate between throwing hot coals and cold water on our conversations.

"In other words," she replies, "you think intimacy should dull a personality. Is that your idea of romance?"

I see the waiter coming, a young and angry mercenary of the service industry just biding his time until the world discovers his genius. Not the type you want to let in on your conversation, so I hold off on a response, hoping Veronica will pause on the subject as well.

"Not a chance," she continues. "I made a vow a long time ago. Love me or leave me, that's my policy. Glass of merlot, please."

"Iced tea for me," I tell the waiter. "I'm driving."

"That's not what it looks like," he says, self-assured at his own cuteness. Veronica laughs as he times his exit to the bar for our drinks.

I lean back to size up my shot. "Janet is you," I say. "At least, twelve years ago she was. But then again, I was you too."

"Come on," she prods. "Details."

"Never call her at work..." I wait until I see her interest pique. "She has a bad habit of carrying on two conversations, one over the phone and one in the office, without changing her volume or covering the mouthpiece while she's addressing someone in the office. You end up answering questions you're not supposed to, wondering why she even asked such a bizarre thing before she returns her attention to you without hearing the confusion in your voice or even what you're saying. When you call her on it, she says 'I'm sorry' but keeps on doing it. Getting an apology out of her is an accomplishment in itself, though. She thinks that's part of what makes her such a great businesswoman, only because she bought into the bitchy stereotype thrust upon businesswomen. No apologies. For anything. Anything. Just a quiet period, an extended pause lasting anywhere from five minutes to a week, depending on the weight of the issue, and then a return to the way things were, all smiles and everything under the rug."

I notice a subtle look of disgust on Veronica's face, so I frame my memories with a more wistful tone and a smile. "Those were wonderful times."

Veronica's expression is now tempered with confusion, as I had hoped. Such are the recollections of ex-lovers, the protectiveness we feel for even the worst of them. Only we can criticize them, we who lived through the flaws first-hand. All others must simply listen to our complaints and not participate in the piling on. They weren't there. They haven't earned the right.

"So what happened?' she asks.

"We blew it."

"How?"

"We flaunted it."

Veronica is now more comfortable with the subject. She has withstood her first encounter with my past, a partial characterization of someone she can't help but consider a competitor. The competition may not be face-to-face, but there are always the rankings to consider, the lovers' polling data. "Well," she says. "As the saying goes, if you've got it, flaunt it."

"We didn't do the kind of flaunting you're probably thinking of," I start to explain. "I don't mean kissing in public, or making love with the lights on and the shades up or dancing on top of one another at clubs. I mean we did turn each other on a great deal and preyed on the jealousies of others, but in a much more cruel way than anything resembling voyeurism. I'm talking about letting those others in, allowing them to climb up the drainpipe to the open window and then slamming it on their fingers so to speak, luring them into the pool with us and then holding their head under water. I'm referring to our utter disregard for people's desires. Their idealism and the frailty that comes with getting that close to a fantasy only to have it ripped out from under them. The hole that kind of rejection leaves. The emptiness."

The waiter returns with our drinks to find Veronica a much less receptive audience. She merely orders and lets a couple more of his smart-ass remarks hang in mid-air until he understands the situation and simply does his job.

She doesn't ask me for specifics, to elaborate. For the remainder of our meal we talk about work, about her classes, about Dodge. Later we have a drink in a bar at the top of a tall building overlooking the city and talk about nothing but how beautiful the view is. We keep the radio on all the way home, a solid hour of good songs playing thanks to this late hour when the stations can put away their hit lists and break into the archives. We kiss good night for a very long time, the kind of kiss that offers insight into how good it will be when the time comes to make love, a time not far off.

The fog has settled in thickly by the time I drive home. My headlights are rendered useless, two straight beams unable to cast a glow beyond their path. Two, no...three cat-sized figures appear in the mist ahead, barely discernible from a distance but growing darker as I draw near, establishing their place in the smokiness, no longer blending in. Bushy black and white-ringed tails, fat bodies, short legs, pointed noses with eyes shining orange from their masks of Zorro. Raccoons. They are surrounding the dead body of one of their own, struck down by a passing car. I slow to a crawl, they fidget and pace, reluctant to leave their fallen comrade but eventually deciding to avoid the same fate. I steer clear of the corpse and am touched for a moment by their vigil. Then it occurs to me that they may be eating him.

"I keep hearing they're smart," says the truck driver the next morning. "But I see more raccoons dead on the side of the road than anything else, except for maybe possums."

"Smart but slow," I answer, staring ahead at the forklift kicking up dust on its way towards us. "They're too busy thinking about things and BAM, reality hits."

The lift stops, two bins of pumpkins stacked on top of each other teetering on the front fork. I write the store number on each one with the lime green chalk thick enough to fill my whole fist. The numbers curl and loop by my hand, a diagram of a barn swallow's flight path, and I finish with a flourish, the bird finally landing. The driver chuckles, understanding the need to amuse one's self during particularly dull work. Veronica's at school today and the harvest is light, so Javier drives one of the flatbeds through the fields while

I take Veronica's job. I slap the side of the cardboard bins, letting the operator know it's safe to load them into the truck. I add two more slash marks to the list on my clipboard as I backpedal next to the trucker again. We watch the bins rise and slide into the back of his rig. The stack then disappears and rolls loudly towards the back, apparently under its own power, actually pulled by two of Joe's men waiting in the trailer with a pallet jack.

"You know what I like to do at the end of this shift?" I ask the trucker.

"What's that?"

"Blow my nose and see how dark my snot is from the dust."

The trucker laughs, rotund belly quivering as though trying to jimmy loose his belt buckle and make a break for it. "What do you normally do around here when it ain't pumpkin season?"

"Drive."

"No shit."

"Nothing as big as your rig."

"Count your blessings," he says. "Instead of the logo of the supermarket on the side of this thing, they should put a bull's eye, a target."

"Oh yeah?"

"Yeah. That's what I am. A target for the cops. Just got pulled over on the way in here, wanted to check my log book and weigh me with that portable scale the CHP has."

He keeps talking but I keep repeating the word cops inside my head. He's talking about the CHP, but I'm thinking about the sheriff's department, in particular the two deputies who beat the crap out of Dodge.

Sorry, Dodge. I'm on it. Dirty cops may not be as satisfying a connection for you as Roman would have been, but their dirt could still lead us to the truth.

Joe has me drive up to Half Moon Bay on my lunch break to pick up the weight tickets at the truck scales. Pumpkins are priced by the pound, so we need the laden figures to get paid. I follow one of the trucks I just loaded into town. While I'm waiting for it to get weighed, I make an anonymous phone call to the sheriff's office on a pay phone behind the gas station adjacent to the scales. My voice lowers instinctively, my eyes narrow into a cold stare that just feels right. Dodge and I should have done this first thing after those knuckleheads attacked him. Not just because it may have kept him alive, but because it's so damn much fun. It's easy to imagine him in the door of the phone booth loving every minute of it. For good measure I close my conversation with the sheriff's secretary on a threatening note: "I suggest you investigate this matter immediately or I'll make the same call to the papers in twenty-four hours. Your men are there to protect law-abiding citizens, not drug dealers."

My grin is so wide I fear I may pull a cheek muscle. While I'm paying for the weight tickets I start to giggle and cramp up trying to prevent full blown laughter, barely making it out of the office before succumbing. Unable to stop completely, I buy a sandwich and head out onto the wharf up at Princeton Harbor to eat in solitude, to avoid the stares of those who associate private laughter with the lunatic fringe. A few seagulls land nearby and stare at me, waiting for a handout. But my quivering and snorting bothers even them, so they back off and eventually fly away. I bend over to catch my breath as I start to settle down, staring directly into the water below.

A cormorant slithers along the surface, skinny neck poised above the boat wake like a black snake ready to strike while its body follows along half-submerged. An unremarkable bird at a glance, not worth much attention. Until it dives. Tipping over and plunging towards a fish at a point just shallow enough so that I can still seen him, the cormorant seems to become a harbor seal, possessing the same torpedo-like stroke and the ability to change direction without slowing down, to swim even better than the fish he chases, if only for a few moments. His relentlessness pays off. The bird rises to the surface well-fed, back to its mild-mannered persona as the Clark Kent of shorebirds.

I adopt my anonymous phone call voice again. "I could use a bird like you," I tell it.

The bird reacts to the noise, tilting his head sideways to cast a yellow eye up in my direction. "Shhhhh," I gesture. "Don't blow my cover."

The cormorant has forgotten me already. He turns his attention to the fish which are hidden from the daylight, but which he somehow knows are there, diving deeper this time, out of sight. Several seconds later, I spot him breaking the surface thirty yards further out to sea, scooting much smaller across my perspective in front of some boats moored in the harbor.


Early mornings in Santa Cruz, the homeless stir along the banks of the San Lorenzo River, rising from the fog like the undead, up and over into town to offer their services to the boutique owners jiggling their keys in front of their glass doors or to stake out the prime curbside staging areas for bongo drum performances or a straightforward plea for change. I suspect that it's too soon for the papers to have any news of the investigation I hopefully launched with my throaty phone tip, and my suspicions are correct. But there is an article about the plans being downscaled on the coast side resort under Roman's jurisdiction. No more Plaza-by-the-sea, just wood frame tents surrounding a central bathroom and shower facility with an adjoining RV park. The spokesman for Abner and Cicerelli puts a plastic spin on the situation, being quoted as saying the money men are "delighted" to be involved in this "more eco-friendly" development now that certain "environmental concerns" have come to their attention. Roman of course did not see the light so much as he saw a lot of dollars sifting through his fingers and down the toilet. But with ends so victorious, there's no use quibbling over the means.

Less water needed for them means more left over for Joe. He'll be happy to see this, and I'll be happy to show it to him because he'll forget that I'm late for the first flatbed drive through the pumpkin fields this morning. Web access and newspaper delivery are things I haven't missed much until this morning. Aside from wanting to see if any recent events resonated, I can't help but wonder if checking the news indicates an interest in re-entering society, if that's the proper term for what I used to be a part of.

During a pit stop into the dust bowl as I wait for the flatbed to be unloaded, Veronica mentions a concert this weekend in San Jose she thinks would be fun, or at least a distraction, featuring a lineup four-deep of what she refers to (with a little help from the radio, I'm sure) as "today's hottest Latin groups."

"Hot" proves to be a good word for it. People don't just watch the bands, they dance to them. And although reluctant to join in (thanks to my lack of ability), it soon becomes clear that to not dance would be an affront to everyone there and grounds for ejection from the premises. The most macho-looking of men contort into their own interpretations of the beat, or at least shake a fist in time to the chorus while hopping on both feet accordingly. I stick to the Presbyterian two-step: step to the left, feet together; step to the right, feet together; again, again, again. I'm tempted to branch out into something which fills up the music more thoroughly but can't keep my eyes off Veronica long enough to concentrate.

She's exhilarating. A spontaneous series of game-winning home runs and touchdown catches strung together. She makes a dozen small moves for every one of mine, a barely perceptible bushel of pelvic gyrations, hip twists, head turns, and shoulder rolls throbbing in between each of my step-togethers.

"How are we doing?" she asks between sets, confident but concerned about the desired effect of the night out, her warm hands cupping my moist cheeks.

"We're somewhere in paradise," I tell her.

We never make it back over the hill. We stop at the first motel whose vacancy sign can't be attributed to a lack of cleanliness or safety: a boxy Best Western with drapes the color of slightly burnt toast squatting on the side of a six-lane well-lighted boulevard.

"Paradise?" she asks playfully.

"A change of scenery," I say. "We live in such a beautiful place that this is what we resort to in order to get away from it all."

The romance of the sordid, hotel/motel erotica, the intensity of clandestine meetings, so much passion, so little time, the legacy of otherwise nondescript bedrooms with numbers on the door helps us through whatever first-time jitters we may have. We become part of the roadside tradition the moment we shut the door behind us, utilizing the walls and floor of the room as much as the bed, easy chair, and bath—falling just short of the ceiling of doing a pornographic two-person imitation of Fred Astaire's rotating room dance in Royal Wedding. At one point we even jump on the bed like mischievous little kids, laughing at the sight of our bodies bouncing in places neither of us have seen on each other until now. We try and hold a kiss as we continue to trampoline, keeping our mouths together as the rest of our torsos and limbs brush lightly. My jaw bumps her lip. She says ouch but keeps on laughing. I apologize and kiss her lip. Our jumping slows, we come to a stop. I kiss her all over. We make love again and recline afterwards in a relaxed embrace as if celebrating our thirty-fifth anniversary. An entire life cycle, infancy to the autumn years, in a single night, $49.95 plus tax, in-room coffee machine included.

And then morning. The curse of the reasonably-priced motel. A look outside and the pavement looks as gray as possible in the dawn's light, while the interior of the room seems to have been decorated by accountants. The background noise is purely automotive. Horns honking, brakes squeaking, motors idling. I hear the newspapers arrive with a thud, the truck pulling away. I put on my exterior clothing, no socks or underwear, and go down to see if I've made a difference.

The newspaper says the deputies are in custody. The dealers have been arrested. And that's all. "An isolated incident," says the county sheriff. In the article the dealers are dubbed "drifters" and the cops are called "rogues." No mention of Santo Farms or of a steady stream of product flowing to the dirty deputies. "An isolated incident."

Dodge insisted he saw the dealers around the barn fire that evening, so either he supplied the identities in order to fit a round theory into a square hole, or the sheriff's department is hiding a potentially disastrous and embarrassing situation from the public. But of course the latter depends on Santo Farms living up to Dodge's vision of it. I bring the paper back with me to the room and spread it across my side of the bed. Veronica sleeps on her stomach, her breathing almost heavy enough to be a snore, her feet exposed bottoms-up from under the sheet. That's one spot I missed last night. I kiss them, one at a time, and then re-shed my clothes. She stirs for a moment before her deep breathing resumes its pace. Oh well. Back to work.

Meditating on the newsprint in front of me, I stare at the article and focus on key words—sheriff, drugs, crystal meth, deputies, intersection, migrant, isolated, Mexican—and ask the words what my next move is, look for answers in their ink, wait for them to trigger a response, a memory, a connection.

"I can help," says a voice, and I answer "I know you can" before I realize the words on the page aren't really talking to me. It's Veronica, on her knees behind me, her head coming to rest on my shoulder.

"With what?" I say, ridiculously trying to disregard my previous response. She sits back, bare butt to bare calves, forcing me to turn around and look at her. I notice the lift in her left eyebrow once I catch my breath at the sight of her.

"The Dodge project," she says.

It's my turn to raise an eyebrow. Both of them. She's apologetic but unfazed.

"I knew him longer than you," she reminds me.

"Time is nothing," I tell her. "I've known my parents thirty-three years and they're ceramic figures to me."

"I knew him."

"You knew his reputation."

"Everyone on the coast did."

"That's right," I agree a bit too loudly. "And that's all they knew. I'm convinced."

She gets up and harvests her clothes from the floor. I catch up to her and run a hand through her hair, over her ear.

"Don't" I plead.

"Why, because you want to talk or you want to see me naked some more?"

"Both." I wrap her up, hugging her close. "I'm very sorry. I just feel like he and I got to know each other so well in such a short time for that very reason, because he didn't know me before I moved and I didn't know him and neither of us could care less anyway. I'm not going to abandon him now like some friend from the fifth grade you stop hanging around once you're in high school. I'm sticking with him. I'm giving him credit." I release her and collapse backwards onto the bed, feet still touching the floor. "Am I making any sense?"

"A little." She too lands on the bed and swings a leg over my chest to straddle me. "But we've crossed the border here, Stanford..." she interrupts herself and smiles. "Paul."

I wince and she pins back my elbows with her knees before she continues. "I don't do this with just anybody."

"I figured as much."

"Good answer. As far as I'm concerned there's nothing more risky than this. We've exposed our bodies and our technique to each other and if that's not enough to make you feel totally vulnerable then you're a pervert."

"Oh I'm completely vulnerable."

"Then cut the crap and be honest with me."

I clear my throat and glance up at each of her knees on my elbows and then down at her pelvis across my chest. She smiles and gets off me, then moves to the easy chair.

"Thanks." I get up and walk to the window for dramatic effect while I think of where to start. But the window stretches below crotch level and I'm forced to duck for cover behind the air conditioner when my appearance catches the eye of several stalled and stunned motorists. I say "Jesus" and of course Veronica laughs. I remain sitting on the carpeted floor, in the lotus position. I figure such a stance may help me feel more wise as I commence with the honesty.

"Somebody else I knew died for no reason last year. Was killed. I'm trying to make sure Dodge had a reason."

"I got the impression he must have already had one."

"He did. But it was wrong."

"Is that really your decision to make?"

"It's the truth. I just want to find out if everything leading up to it was wrong, too."

And so I tell Veronica about Dodge's quest, his attempts to find a pattern and make connections in a world where it was growing more impossible for him to find any, how he was trying to chase down something substantial and fulfilling but may have once again devoted his life to something empty and dangerous shrouded in the illusion of fulfillment to keep its victim in pursuit. Drugs and heroism...prestige and ivy-covered homes in Palo Alto. What's the difference, really?

Not a word is spoken for a short while as Veronica considers all the pieces. Those of the puzzle itself—the attack on Dodge at the ranch, the car strip-searched on the side of the highway, the bouquet I chased around San Francisco into the arms of a tan man in a white Lexus, the barn fire, all those men fleeing into the woods, all those men with so little to do, the deputies, the dealers, the dead dog, Dodge's last words, red residue, Santo—and the motivations framing the puzzle.

"There's your answer," she finally says, something she obviously meant to say to herself that slipped out of her mouth. "Motivation," she explains.

"Whose?"

"Dodge's. Also yours to a degree."

I ask her with my eyes to go on.

"No matter what you find out," she says, leaning forward in the chair. "Dodge believed he was doing something worthwhile. He was trying to make things right. And the guilt he felt in thinking he killed someone is admirable really, as misinformed as it was. From his perspective he was on his way to redemption, and the only thing he did wrong he punished himself for."

"Do you know how many times I've told myself that?"

"Well it's true," she snaps, her pride in her theory jilted. "The man is resting in peace. Why can't you live in peace?"

"Because I was supposed to be helping him."

"You were."

"Yeah, with a big smirk on my face. A one-man Greek chorus who didn't really give a shit and never sounded a legitimate warning like he's supposed to. Just had a few laughs at the subject's expense."

"But he didn't know that."

"I know it," I yell. "And that's all that matters. Dodge had his conscience, and I have mine. That's where the real battles are fought. Inside. Right? That's what you've been trying to tell me all morning."

"Then get to the bottom of it," she yells back. "Talk to people. Stop making anonymous phone calls and eavesdropping around crowded rooms. Talk to the guy who jumped Dodge, talk to the sheriff, talk to Santo. If you want the truth then stop acting so scared of it."

I don't know whether to hug her or throw an article of clothing at her and tell her to get the hell out and catch a bus home. But she's so right. I choose the hug and tell her how right she is, ask her to bear with me and give me a chance to show her how remarkable I think she is. We kiss. We take a shower together. We realize we have to force ourselves back into the same laundry-bound clothes we wore yesterday.

While tying my shoes I consider telling her more about Abby, how her death so heavily influences my sense of responsibility for Dodge, what a vital statistic she remains in all of this. But I'm starting to believe that secrets are a necessary evil in being human, a novelty item of individuality. They are something to hold onto besides dreams, and in some cases more permanent. Someday Veronica may remember what I said earlier about that "somebody else" I knew who died, about Abby, and ask why I think she was killed for no reason. And I'll have to tell her everything. Then I'll have to come up with some other secret—maybe masturbate in the shower some morning and not tell her. I chuckle to myself. What a great day that will be when such is the extent of my secrets. She asks what I'm laughing about.

"Nothing."

A light day, only five trucks scheduled. Veronica has classes today, so Joe and I keep track of the loads. We have the last one on the road well before lunch, and while the rig pulls out I ask Joe if he ever got the name of the guy who jumped Dodge and trashed the employee houses.

Joe looks like somebody just shined a flashlight in his eyes as he struggles for the name. "Harken," he finally says. "Something Harken...Ken! That's it. Ken Harken. Fucker."

"Are they holding him or what?"

"That's what Bert said. Holding him in the county jail until his trial, whenever the hell that is. Of course that was a couple weeks ago when we last saw Bert, so who knows? Some goddamn lawyer might have gotten him off on some technical thing or other. If you were a lawyer, Stanford, I might not have hired you." He slaps his hands together and laughs. I do too, but I'm laughing at how much Joe enjoys his own jokes.

On our way back to the ranch yard, as we bounce along a dusty two-track through the pumpkin fields, I come up with an excuse to get over the hill for a while after Joe has me pick up the weight tickets in Half Moon Bay. I run it by Joe once we reach the office, and he buys it.

"I've been promised some chump change by my old associates," I tell him. "I've just got to stop by and soothe some old clients' fears and egos, assure them all what a capable bunch of people they've still got in their corner at the firm."

"Not as good as you, though, eh?" says Joe.

I shrug, full of mock modesty. "No. But anything for a buck."

Joe swipes his hands together and laughs from the gut. "Godammit, are you asking for a raise?"

"Just an extra hour for lunch today."

"As long as you bring me back a burrito from the joint in Half Moon Bay, you can take the whole damn day off if you want. We've got no food in the house. Been too damn busy with these orange bastards, those pumpkins."

I salute him and thank my good fortune for having him as a boss.

The last time I was at the county offices was to file a report against an old neighbor of ours in Palo Alto—a fad-sensitive systems analyst trying Buddhism on for size—who sneaked into our backyard and hacked off several branches of Janet's favorite tree, a long and lean sycamore that he claimed was disturbing the serenity of the Zen garden he had designed in his yard, complete with stone Buddha and lightweight gravel lawn he could rake into different patterns. Thus the disturbance. Falling leaves interrupted the energy flow, he would claim over and over again during all those conversations I couldn't believe I was having. Between Janet's tirade at seeing her beloved sycamore amputated and my pent-up aggression at having to endure weekly arguments with our neighbor the pacifist vandal, I had stormed into the county headquarters and practically shouted at the information desk "Where do I report a crime?"

And while this time around I have a much more grave project at hand, my demeanor is much more calm. "Where can I find the county jail?"

At the jail I announce myself to the guard on duty as a friend of Ken Harken's. I wait for him in the visiting room, which reminds me of the cafeteria in my old elementary school—long metal picnic tables and the smell of bologna sandwiches.

"Who the hell are you?" Harken asks as he sits down across from me. He's even more wiry and gaunt than I remember, a jail diet and wardrobe no doubt enhancing those features.

"A little conversation has to be better than staring at the wall," I say.

"I'm writing a memoir," he snaps, chin up.

"Isn't everyone?"

"I've got friends in publishing."

"Then I'll be brief," I say, which is part of my plan anyway. "We both know how much you were busted for carrying. What I want to know is how much you actually had in the car."

"I'm sorry," he smirks. "I still didn't catch your name."

"All you need to know is I'm a businessman whose interests are severely compromised by the presence of your leftovers in my territory, and that I have lots of friends who room with you right here in the county clink."

Not what he was expecting. As I had hoped, he's too confused to know what to think or to sort his thoughts into any legitimate questions or concerns about my identity. A verbal punch to the nose, blinding him temporarily.

"What makes you think there was more than what they nailed me with?" is the best he can come up with. Perfect. Just keep the focus on yourself, Ken. Never mind the bullshitter in front of you. I smile at how well this is going.

"Because it was obvious your car was searched before the cops got to it," I say. "And in the meantime several of my employees have become private contractors thanks to a surplus in product that I can't account for." I put on my hardest stare, but he's already shifting in his chair and looking down at the table top.

"I just want to go home," he quivers. "I live in an artist's colony way the hell up north. I don't care how low the rent is and how many goddamn leather key chains you sell, an artist can't make it if the big pieces just sit on the shelf being ogled. I'm an artist, not the curator of a frigging museum."

"So who were you running for?" I guide him back on track.

Harken nods. "Some guy, he works out of a body shop in Redding. He knows how tough it is to be an artist. He's always paying us a visit. Relentless son of a bitch. I'll bet he came down looking for his shit once he heard I didn't show up in Paso. Probably re-traced the route."

I try to maintain my act as the disappointment of discovering another false lead begins to sink in. Wrong again, Dodge. There were drugs in the car, but they weren't from Santo Farms. I use the drug lord from Redding as a point of focus.

"For his sake he'd better stay put up there," I snarl, trying not to wince at how fake it sounds. Fortunately, Harken is still too twitchy to notice.

"Godammit," he whimpers. "Why did I stop? It was such a nice day, a nice breeze bending the artichokes back and forth. Hey! Nice day to trip! Yeah! Ha..." he admonishes himself. "And I call myself an artist. A real artist wouldn't need drugs to appreciate the scenery. Asshole."

I figure now would be a good time to leave, while Harken continues to talk to himself. So I give him one last verbal jab—"If this ends up in your memoir, you'll never live to see it hit the best seller list"—and then exit with the arrogant gait of all great fictional tough guys, not knowing how an authentic one would act. I turn to stare him down one last time, and he quickly looks away, so I guess it worked.

Despite the fact that Dodge has been foiled again, it occurs to me as I head home along Highway One that all is not lost. Santo may yet be the real-life version of the character I just played in the county jail. Who's to say he's not seething over this fresh batch of stuff from Redding making a dent in his local profits? It was a long shot that the drugs in Harken's car were from Santo's anyway. Nobody's stupid enough to sample the product just a few minutes from where they picked up the drugs to be run. Not even Harken. My enthusiasm returns. I take in the surroundings. Sunset-lit clouds are spread across the sky like fish scales, salmon-colored and shining, swirling around a fiery center resembling Jupiter's Great Red Spot. The artichoke fields standing between me and the lighthouse seem to offer encouragement, as every artichoke which rises on its stalk from the bushy green base looks like a green fist pumped in the air; a thousand fists raised in defiance, in triumph. I happen to be looking their way when the waves break against the rocks beneath the lighthouse and rise in a white fan of foam, as though the lighthouse has sprouted tail feathers, if only for a moment. The Dodge project lives.

Of course I still have to plan my next move. I speculate on the whereabouts of the missing meth taken from Ken Harken's car. Maybe the two deputies that beat up Dodge found it and floated the profits towards a slush fund, a little gravy for the effort of protecting and serving the public. Then there's the guy with the body shop up in Redding with the starving artists doing his dirty work. Harken mentioned how relentless he was. But the roadside search took place way too soon for him to be considered a suspect. He wouldn't even know that his meth didn't make it to its appointed drop until the next day at the earliest, and by then the stuff was already gone.

Frustration builds once more. The surplus could not only have been stolen by just about anyone, but could have ended up just about anywhere. A fog bank hovers several miles out to sea, looking more like a mountain range than low clouds. I can see it so well from here, from where the highway skirts the tops of the cliffs. The sun will set earlier tonight. Behind the clouds, not the horizon. The fog will hide the truth.

As the highway sinks from the cliffs down to the marshlands outside of Pescadero, the sign marking the road into the little town grows larger in my bug-splattered perspective through the dirty windshield. The dealers on the corner. The sheriff's pets. Sure. They nailed the ones caught red-handed, but there's got to be some other guys still loitering who know something. If the stolen meth did stay in the area, those hombres are the only way to find out. Just ask.

Which reminds me that my most immediate move should be to thank Veronica again for the advice. Just ask. Genius.

Naturally, asking for information and actually getting it do not necessarily form a cause and effect relationship. I'm not so awash in film lore and my own revisionist history of the county jail episode to believe that I can coerce anything out of the gathering in Pescadero, via intimidation or cleverness, no matter how hard-boiled I make my voice. And my lousy Spanish is only a minor reason why.

With a diccionario de español within reach on the coffee table in my minimalist living room, I compose a letter to Manuel asking him to help me question the guys on the corner, the men I know are there primarily to look for work, but some of whom at odd times apparently have been "salesmen of drugs"—the best translation I can come up with since there is no word for "drug dealer" in my dictionary, not to mention any other appropriate slang which would help any dialogue with the men in question. I note this ideological discrepancy in my letter to Manny as one of the many reasons I need his help, and go so far as to outline a plan for how the street-corner meeting should go: assure them that we're not police, that we know the guilty ones were already arrested, that we'll never tell anyone anything they tell us, that this is to honor the memory of a dead friend, that this is a chance to clear his name (or to clean his name, as I translate). In all fairness to Manny, I also mention the incident between Dodge and the deputies. My little crank call may have busted the ones in question, but they may not be the only ones involved. I warn Manny that there may still be danger surrounding that corner.

I work on the letter all night, turning over as many stones as possible in writing in order to avoid any discussion on the topic which may exceed my range of verbal expression. I'd ask Veronica. This is essentially her idea. But an old-fashioned, maybe even chauvinistic, protective instinct does not allow for it. I know how men think in any language, and I won't use her as a weapon.

Manuel has a hard time reading my letter, in all its long-winded and illiterate glory. Plus he's just back from pulling an all-nighter at the flower market and I'm due in the fields this morning. So I tell him to hang onto it and read it after a nap, that I'll stop by his house this evening for a response.

Veronica notices my grin and swagger as we kiss good morning in the shade of an idling big rig, dust blowing, forklifts revving. She asks what's-with-me, and I thank her for the cattle prod to the flank about confronting people and asking questions. She says it's more a matter of me being an idiot than her being a genius, so I kiss her again.

"Are you falling in love or what?" she asks me. I must have a ridiculous look on my face.

"Only if it doesn't scare you."

"Not in the slightest."

"Okay then," I say, leaving it at that.

"Okay what?"

"I'll tell you later."

She attacks me with her big green chalk, trying to graffiti my forehead. I defend myself and say "Patience, my love. Patience."

The word love stops her, muscles slack, chalk hand dropping to one side, clipboard to the other. "Did I hear you right?" she asks. Those eyes, as if somebody just added cream to their coffee.

"That's right. I said patience."

No attack this time. A kiss instead. A forklift shifts into reverse and its warning series of beeps reminds us to get back to work. My flatbed is finished being unloaded, a fresh slate of cardboard bins lined up and ready for filling.

I walk towards the truck, through the men waiting for me, and they don't say anything. No teasing, no catcalls, really no indication that they were even paying attention to Veronica and me. The best sign yet, perhaps. Proof of our compatibility has made the move from interior to exterior. We blend into the landscape. No longer a spectacle, we're simply a couple, a sight people expect to see.

The men jump on the back as I start the engine. We drive for a few minutes over the bumpy road splitting some fields we've already harvested. The mustard weeds springing up between the two dirt tracks brush the bottom of the truck. We reach an untapped sea of orange and I let the color in, from the top of my head slowly down to the bottoms of my feet. The cab of the truck is already hot and stuffy, but the warm of the orange is different. It is relaxing, loosening each muscle it passes over, like that psychiatrist said it would. Doctor's orders...so easy under the right circumstances. So easy in love.

Each U-turn into a fresh row awash in orange brings me further into the future, the inevitable speculation on what a life together may look like. I glance into the side mirrors of the truck, filled with pumpkins flying through the air like bingo balls bouncing in a hamper that would seem to represent the element of chance regarding what lies ahead—'round and 'round she goes, where she stops, nobody knows—but it's the ideal vision, naturally, that occupies my thoughts. From the features of our children to the trim of our house. The vision stored under glass in our subconscious labeled "in case of emergency." By the end of the run, bins brimming with pumpkins, I have the future completely manipulated and firmly in place next to a healthy supply of hammers and replacement panes of glass, what with the real future being so fragile.

So when Manuel agrees to the request in my letter, I remind him he has a family.

"We are only going to talk to some guys," he says. "Maybe bad guys. But I want Daniel to know I am a good guy. I want to look at him and not look away."

Sounds familiar. If only Dodge figured it out when his kids were the same age as Daniel.

With a few hours of daylight still remaining, I suggest it might be safer to go into town now and see who's on the corner before its hours of operation kick in. Manny agrees.

"That way I will be home in time for dinner," he says.

Geographically, the town of Pescadero makes a lot of sense. Rather than insisting on shorefront development, its founders—whether by feasibility or a genuine appreciation for nature—realized it would be wiser to build the town inland a few miles and leave the craggy coast to the shorebirds. "Just because we fish from it, doesn't mean we have to live on it" seemed to be their motto, as the town lies in a fertile valley sunken amongst some of the softer hills along the coast, a hamlet which on most days rests beyond the fog bank which clings to the churning shoreline well after the morning sun is supposed to have burned it off. Within a mile of driving on Pescadero Road off of Highway One, the cool spray of the mist and white water splashing over the monumental rocks rising from the ocean is quickly replaced by the calm skies and warmer vistas of the kind of farm town so often called "sleepy," as though you've driven from a November in Northern Maine to a June in Western Kansas. The drive also seems to represent a transition in the town's history, as the farmlands appear prosperous enough to have made its early settlers wonder "why fish?"

Marshlands to the left side of the road heading into town function as something of a blender in which a mixture of land and water forms before one topography finally surrenders to the other. As Manny and I drive by the swamp, a couple of great white egrets poke around the damp meadows of the marsh, their feathers so bright that the birds are hard to put into sharp focus, appearing somewhat blurry against the murkier shades of the wetlands. Closer to town, as the marsh filters into a creek, the pampas grass grows thicker on the hills sloping above the shoulders of the road, their dandelion-textured tops as long as horsetails, flapping slowly up and down in the breeze like fans held by eunuchs ordered to keep their majesty cool. I imagine Manny and I riding into town on the backs of elephants, then quickly remind myself of my place in the world, to not get cocky, to remain alert to the task at hand. Too many questions still unanswered. So much to solve, so little sense of time.

The usual gang is there milling around the usual spot, a collection of flannel shirts and white straw cowboy hats gathered at the intersection where Pescadero Road intersects the main street of the downtown area...all one dozen buildings of it, no more than two stories each. But the usual sheriff's presence is not there, the car inevitably parked at the intersection apparently waiting for someone to run the stop sign visible from a mile away as we approach.

"Looks like we caught a break," I say.

Manny nods but with the same vacant expression I must get when I have no idea what someone said but don't want to ask them to repeat it or translate it.

"No police," I say. "That's good."

Manny smiles and nods.

Our conversation with the men on the corner is about what I expected. Tell them this...What did he say?...Tell them this...What did he say? Along those lines, only slower and even more frustrating because as good as Manny's English is getting, he's still not exactly ready to work for the U.N.

We come to an impasse when the subject turns to where they got the drugs. They look at each other and laugh, sort of, passing a few puffs of air through their noses.

"Tell them we know they are not guilty, Manny."

He tells them. One answers.

"What did he say?"

"He says they are also not stupid."

"That's what I thought he said. Tell them the police who are guilty have been arrested."

He tells them. Another one answers.

"What did he say?"

"He says only the police who watched were arrested."

"The police who watched? Does that mean a different one supplied the drugs?"

Manny asks them. Silence. They don't even have to look a each other this time. Just straight ahead, at us, a complete stonewall.

"Tell them we come in peace."

"We come in peace?"

"You're right. Tell them we mean them no harm. No...that sounds worse. Tell them no harm will come to them."

"How do we know?"

He's got me there. "We don't."

I take a deep breath and scan their faces—sullen and unflinching, as though carved in wood around the doorway of an old cathedral. But at the sound of an approaching car, they turn almost in unison.

A sheriff patrol car rolls through the intersection and swerves around onto the gravel shoulder across from us, assuming the traditional position alongside Main Street, looking out at the road which feeds into Highway One. A glare reflecting off the passenger side window prevents me from seeing who's inside, but I can see that there's only one deputy.

I look back at the men to see if I can mine their expressions for more clues as to whether this is the one who supplied them with the stolen meth. But they're already dispersing—a couple of them trot across the street towards the "downtown" area, a couple more retreat through the parking lot behind them towards the post office, and a few others simply mill about, acting as though they don't even notice me and Manny. All of which suffices more than if they had stuck around and shot me knowing glances.

"I think we have found him," says Manny, and as I look back at the patrol car, the window rolls down with an electronic hum. I realize that it's Bert a second before actually making out his features. He stares straight ahead at the vacant intersection in front of him.

"I'll be right back, Manny."

I cross the street and Bert looks my way once he hears my footsteps crunch onto the gravel lining the side of the pavement. "Good evening, Deputy Bert," I greet him as I come around to his side and lean towards the window.

"Can I help you?" he says, clearly unsure of who I am. His uniform looks even more tattered than the last time I saw him, and his sunglasses are so full of scratches that I can't help but wonder if he can even see me.

"Ever really caught anyone rolling this stop sign?" I ask.

"I know you," he remembers. "You work for Joe Mirabelli."

"That's right. Congratulations on getting your job back."

I say it with enough of an edge to make him pause. He re-enters the conversation on a more defensive note. "I never lost it," he says.

"Your old beat, I mean. Your home neighborhood. Reunited at last."

"Well you saw what happened when they put someone who didn't know the area on patrol," he says. "It just didn't work."

"Nope," I agree. "Too much meth on the streets."

"That's right," he relaxes.

"All of a sudden," I look him square in the scratched-up sunglasses. "Too much meth. Out of nowhere. Like magic."

And though I can't see his eyes, I can tell that he knows what I'm getting at. He faces front again and smiles. "Yup," he says. "And the new kids out here didn't represent the force real well, did they?"

"No they didn't," I goad him on. "Just like you expected."

He sighs deeply, keeping his gaze straight ahead. "You're not getting a thing out of me, Sherlock."

"They can put you behind a desk, but they can't turn off your radio, can they Bert?" I jab, the way in which he found out about the attack and the abandoned car suddenly occurring to me.

Bert turns towards me again, his smile melted into a begrudging smirk. "You can't beat experience," he says. "You just can't beat experience."

And the window rises up in front of my face, its electric whine ending in a light thud as it locks into place. I stare at my reflection for a moment before telling it "congratulations."

Manny and I leave town by way of the back roads heading south out of town. As night falls, we pass by a row of greenhouses lined up one after the other for a half mile from the road to the woods. The windows glow from the phosphorescent lights warming the seedlings inside. The whole complex looks as though it has just landed in the pasture from outer space. We come in peace. We mean you no harm. It seems to come from another world. We pick up the highway a few miles further to the south and I thank Manny for his help when I drop him off at the ranch.

I don't sleep so much as nap for a few minutes at a time. The night lasts longer than junior high school, it seems. Is the job that great, Bert? Worth filling the town full of drugs and bribes, just to make your colleagues look bad? And I can't do a thing about it. There's no way to catch him red-handed, like the young bucks he lured into his trap. Nobody saw him take the junk from the car, and the department is already reeling from the investigation of the deputies he sucker-punched. And, of course, none of it relates to the expectations Dodge had for Santo Farms.

For the first time since I moved here I crave some noise other than crickets. The hoots of the horned owls aren't loud enough, and screeches of the barn owls aren't consistent enough. The coyotes aren't calling each other. They're already in a pack tonight, surrounding a deer or an especially large raccoon, circling it, working themselves up into a rapture of yipping and howling and wailing as if they're the ones about to die, not their prey. Hardly a soothing sound, it rattles the senses like the kind of chorus a feeding frenzy of sharks or piranhas might make if they could howl underwater. I wonder if the coyotes' victims die of fright before the hounds can even sink a tooth into them.

All is quiet again. I try to imagine the sound of a garbage truck making its early morning rounds or an ambulance or a steady flow of traffic.

Dawn rises and quiets the crickets. I manage to tune in the surf and the seals beyond the daisy fields, beyond the dunes. The roar and the barking are faint. But the longer I listen, the louder it gets.

Veronica begs for and tries to trick me out of some answers the next day, each time we meet in the loading area. But my frustration is too great, so I stall her as playfully as I can. My standard reply is "What!? I can't hear you! The forklifts are too loud!"

"A Lexus in a pumpkin patch?" she replies, after about the sixth time I've repeated my battle cry.

I laugh and play along. "No. I said I can't hear you. The forklifts..."

But she wasn't saying it to me. She's narrating what she sees over my shoulder: a Lexus driving through the pumpkin fields beyond the edge of the loading area, driving towards us. A white Lexus with gold trim. A white Lexus with gold trim driven by a man with dark wavy hair and a deep tan. "Oh yeah. Him."

"You know this guy?" Veronica asks.

"Not exactly. He was the last leg on the mystery bouquet relay team—from Santo to Gino to Gino's stand on the wharf to George Hamilton here."

The Lexus pulls out of the fields and into the dry acreage of the loading area. He veers into a wide turn as part of his approach, a complete circle practically, as if participating in a car show, a Lexus rodeo. He pulls up next to us, the front end already pointed in the right direction for his departure.

"I don't know," Veronica ponders aloud. "This guy just might fit Dodge's drug cartel fantasies. There might be something to it after all."

The passenger window rolls down with an electronic hum. Dodge's last hope leans across the empty passenger seat and speaks up.

"Can you tell me how to reach Santo Farms from here?"

A heavy Latin accent. Are you listening to this, Dodge? Veronica certainly is. She's as riveted as I am. He fills in our dumb-struck gap.

"I saw the dust from the highway, and the trucks. Santo gave me such bad directions. You know him?"

"He's on the other side of the highway," I gesture towards the hills. "About a quarter mile south. The gravel road across from the mail boxes."

"Thank you," he says, leaning back into his seat. I desperately try to think of a way to get more information from him since I've got him here. Veronica's thinking the same thing. She's prodding me with a wide pair of eyes. I blank. She bails me out.

"Santo doesn't have much product," she bends towards the open window. "Is there anything we can help you with?"

"I know he doesn't," the man chuckles. "Santo wouldn't have any flowers to sell if it weren't for me. I'm an import representative. I give him a good price. Too good, and he knows it. But I like the guy and the only other thing he's got are those dried wreaths he charges too much for. Eighty bucks for a bunch of dead shrubs dipped in red dye."

Red dye. Red dye equals red residue, running down the creek, soaking Dodge's pants, placing another piece of the puzzle into the frame that unfortunately depicts a much different picture than the one on the box, the picture Dodge was expecting when he bought it. The man with the tan continues.

"Santo gave me a nice bouquet to thank me a while back. A nice bouquet full of my own flowers." He says it as though it's a punch line, supplying his own laugh track. "I came down to give that old goat a hard time."

The bouquet I trailed, I imagine. He doesn't strike me as someone who would show up anywhere before ten a.m., especially a place like the wholesale flower market, which is why Santo would have to deliver his gift by way of Gino's stand.

"Well, I have to go," he says. "Another minute in this dust and I'm going to need a new air filter for my car. Those are nice-looking pumpkins," he nods to the bins lined up behind us in the distance. "If they weren't so heavy I'd have our boys down south fill a whole airplane full. You're lucky."

He snickers, jokingly, but we all know it's the truth. The window rolls up and the car slithers away, trying not to kick up too much dust, trying to stay clean. Veronica and I stand up straight and watch it go.

I sigh as the car disappears behind the tree line. "Is there anything on Dodge's path to redemption that hasn't been pissed on?"

"There's still Santo," Veronica reminds me.

"What's so mysterious? He makes dried wreaths and sells imported flowers, like the man says."

"But so many guys."

I look over and there's a gleam in her eye. "Okay, okay," I tell her. "I'll go over and talk to him later."

"Now there's an idea."

She kisses me on the cheek and walks back towards the big rig with the refrigerator engine running and the forklift waiting behind it loaded with a stack of bins in need of Veronica's handwriting, of the store numbers in light green chalk. The hint of moistness she leaves behind on my cheek starts to lap over my body in small waves which crest one after another. Time regroups. Events start to fall in line. All the things which seemed to happen all at once since Dodge died all take their place in a chronological order. I actually start to sway back and forth, a slight bit, alone on my patch of flat earth which for the moment feels like a magic carpet that has just landed after taking me for a ride. I step off and notice a flattened cardboard bin on the ground nearby that had its chance to transport some pumpkins but apparently collapsed under the weight and was discarded. I grab a hunk of chalk from Veronica's supply and get down on the ground, on the cardboard, and start drawing on it like a kid on a sidewalk. I construct a crude storyboard, as I used to when I would rough draft a Power Point presentation for a potential client. Each slide contains the item in question, what Dodge thought it was, and what it really was:

Item: Drug-pumped perpetrator (a.k.a. Ken Harken, Jesus Christ)

What Dodge Thought: an indication of drugs being sold on the coast

What It Was: an indication of how challenging the art scene is in Redding

Item: His vandalized car

What Dodge Thought: was searched for drugs from a local source

What It Was: was robbed of drugs from Redding (close)

Item: Mystery bouquet

What Dodge Thought: a transport to deliver drugs from wholesaler to retailer

What It Was: a thank you gift to an import rep who looks like a drug dealer

Item: Barn fire

What Dodge Thought: accident caused by drug purification paraphernalia

What It Was: a barn fire

I run out of room on that side of the bin and flip it over to continue on the other side.

Item: Bad cops

What Dodge Thought: evidence

What It Was: guinea pigs in Bert's plot to get his job back

Item: Roman's real estate investments

What Dodge Thought: made possible by bribes

What It Was: made possible by his mother

Item: Roman's involvement

What Dodge Thought: ensured security for drug production and movement

What It Was: see: real estate investments

Item: Red substance from Santo Farms

What Dodge Thought: residue from crystal methamphetamine cooking

What It Was: dye for dried wreaths

Item: Santo

I stop there and stare at the name. I finally scribble a series of question marks under it and stand up. Muscles creaking, I spread my arms and stretch out my back as far as I can without falling backwards. A flock of turkey vultures drifts into my field of vision, half a dozen of them gliding in circles, their wings spread upward into a "V" shape. As they float closer, the bright red color of their heads becomes more apparent, a convenient color for sticking their heads into dead things. If there is something dead or dying nearby I should be able to see it, struggling across the cleared-out field. But the ground is as empty as it is flat. The vultures veer north, to my left, flying silently over the tree line, the wind carrying them. Just looking, I guess.

The final drive through the fields is the last run of the season. Tomorrow many of the men will take the two-day drive deep into Mexico, to their home towns, to spend the winter there with family and friends. They count out loud every pumpkin they launch onto the truck, as though counting down to the New Year. The wind picks up a bit as the sun falls closer to the trees, airing out the cab of the truck which has been so hot and stuffy all day, illuminating the hills across the highway.

We reach the far corner of the last field, the last row of orange, the end of the line. They cheer as the last pumpkin is tossed up to Gerardo and he slam-dunks it into the bin. Everyone piles onto the back of the flatbed, and as we drive through the picked fields the men all wave to the leftover pumpkins unsuitable for picking, wave to the withering vines, to the other truck across the field which is still a few pumpkins short of completion. They wave as though they are riding on a float in a parade, down Colorado Avenue in Pasadena, down Main Street in Disneyland. I start to wave too. I wave to the vultures, still gliding in the distance to the north. They maintain their multi-layered circle as they get smaller and keep on circling. And circling. And circling.

Much in the same way I do as I reach Santo Farms: circling the back-broken buildings that seem to be made out of doors. So many doors, none of which offers much hope for life on the other side. No more than there is on this side, the outside.

The property is once again quiet, abandoned of everything but dust and the breeze that stirs it. Maybe they packed up and left. Maybe this is proof of Dodge's ideas after all. The heat forced them to close shop, jump ship.

I walk around to the back, by the creek, under one of the windows Dodge must have tried to peek through before the warning shots. A radio plays faintly, a crackling transistor picking up a Spanish station. The DJ zips through the news and weather before playing a ballad heavy with accordion and tuba. I get on tip-toes and peer in. Through the layer of dust I can see bunk beds, concave as hammocks, the top bunks nearly touching the lower. My eyes adjust and I can see men inside the beds, their heads and feet mostly, as though each is laying in a soup bowl. The radio sits on the floor beneath one of the bottom bunks, its occupant on his side, away from the window, facing the wall. Wood walls—rotting wood walls—a splintered wood floor, the bunk beds, the radio, and that's all. And the men. The men separated from me by glass, dust, and circumstances.

I lower my heels to the ground, stare straight ahead at the wall, inches from my face. If I raise myself up for another look, they may not be there this time. They're apparitions. That's what it seems like. I hear the traffic pick up for a few moments on the highway, several cars probably passing a mobile home now that they have the chance. Then all is quiet. I keep my heels on the ground and walk along the creek behind the rest of the buildings and their doors. They could be houses, barns, dorms, anything. Chicken coops, kennels, tool sheds, anything. There seems to be no apparent purpose in their construction. They're all just places.

I come around the corner of the row, back to the front. Santo is standing in front of the middle door of the middle building, as though he's been waiting for me.

All he does is nod. All I do is stare, my heartbeat rising into my ears from guilt and embarrassment at being caught snooping around. I finally think of a response to his silent greeting. "Did the import rep in the Lexus find you?"

Santo chuckles. "Yes," he says. "But he could not stay long. He is the kind of man who can never stay long. Anywhere."

"And he thanked you for the bouquet?"

"He did."

"The one you sent him through Gino's stand?"

"How do you know that?"

Where do I start? My mind has a million ideas that I simply cannot process into words right now.

"This is about Dodge?" he says, sensing my paralysis.

I nod before saying yes.

"Come in," he gestures. "Come in and sit down."

The inside of the house is immaculate, and contrary to its cryptic facade, it truly is a house. Cozy, comfortable, congenial—all the "c" words. Even "quaint." A mishmash of furnishings classified somewhere in between antique and old are strewn about the room, closer to the former thanks to a lack of dust on anything. The wood shines, the velvet is fluffy, and you can see yourself in a variety of mirrors which peak out from behind the shelves of an oak sideboard filled with china, from the front doors of an armoire, from the wall on each side of a plush couch. The reason for such a shine is obvious, as two men dressed for field work, yet holding squirt bottles of cleanser and dish towels, prowl around the room looking for imperfections. Another one dressed similarly in greasy jeans and a used pinstripe dress shirt enters holding a tray stacked with cookies, tea cups, and a pot of coffee.

"Please sit down," says Santo, as he points to a high-backed wicker chair on one end of a teardrop-shaped coffee table. The man with the tray leaves it on the table and exits. Santo tells the two others wrapped up in their dusting to take a break, and they also leave.

"If I can start the conversation off with a question..." he says as he lowers himself into a leather throne across the table from me. "Why did it take you so long?"

"I guess it's just easier to creep around the outside and speculate."

"And more fun, certainly," he joins in, gesturing to the tray of cookies and coffee.

"No thanks," I say. "I'm jittery enough already. The last thing I need is sugar and coffee."

Santo chuckles and lets his laughter fade into a sigh. "But that was Dodge, no? Life is not exciting unless it is difficult, unless it is dangerous."

I agree with him as he leans in for a cookie. "We never really introduced ourselves," he says. "But then you know who I am."

"My name's Stanford."

"Ah, the college boy." He bites the cookie in half.

"Word travels fast."

"It does around here, yes. But only certain words. Only the small talk."

His statement makes me feel a bit ashamed, as though I'm about to get a lesson on the nature of truth as it travels within small circles and amongst them. Sure enough, he continues.

"So tell me...why did he jump?"

My silence is met by his anticipation, he leaning forward in his chair, me leaning back. I consider whether to give him my standard "I don't know" line as he eases up on his intensity, realizing that a more gentle look from him may come across as more encouraging to me. But I go ahead and tell him that I don't know, without much confidence behind it, and the intensity in his eyes rekindles.

"That answer only works for those people who do not care. For those who are merely curious. I care, Stanford. I care very much."

"Why?" I'm genuinely curious. "Why do you care so much?"

And suddenly Santo is on the defensive. I have him now, thanks to nothing but an honest question. No strategy, no manipulating the conversation. I only want to know why a man to whom Dodge rarely spoke should care so much that he died. It seems Santo can't help but wonder the same thing. He looks in my direction but may as well be looking into space. Then, gathering himself, he searches for some way to tell me, sifting through a variety of approaches which I try to narrow down for him with a more pointed comment.

"I saw you at the funeral," I say. "I remember your face the day he jumped, when you were kneeling in the meadow. How sad you were compared to all the horrified faces around you."

"Then you may remember that I told you I knew his mother," he says after a deep breath.

I can already tell how much he loved her. He stares at the floor and I wait patiently. A quick glance to the heavens and he continues.

"That was when I worked for the Mirabellis, for Joe. Soledad worked for Franky Demos. That was her name. Dodge's mother. But sometimes Franky needed more men for harvest time, he had so much crop, so goddamn many brussel sprouts. Joe hated him, like everyone else, and was also as afraid of him, like everyone else. So he let Franky borrow some of his men, and as foreman I was in charge of bringing them over and making sure Franky gave them breaks and treated them with decency. That's how I met Soledad. She did the cleaning and some gardening around the old Demos house, the house you're living in now. Franky would invite me in sometimes and talk to me about what a great farmer he was, about how much money he made, but all I would do is look at Soledad whenever she was around..." Santo smiles at the memory. "And she would look at me."

His smile proves to be doomed, as smiles often are when recalling the past. It fades and he distracts himself by asking me if I'm sure I don't want any coffee or cookies. He takes a cookie for himself and realizes as soon as he bites into it that his mouth is too dry for it to taste very good. He pours himself a cup of coffee, hand shaking, the spout of the pot rattling against the rim of the cup. Holding the cup with both hands, he takes a sip and continues.

"We could never talk in front of Franky. He was the kind of man who you keep all of your personal business hidden from. So I wrote her a note and saved it for weeks, waiting for the next time I could go over there and have a chance to give it to her. I would stare at that note and find something to change in it every time, every time I imagined her reading it. I wanted it to be perfect. I carried it with me everywhere I went in case I saw her in town, at the market, or at a dance. But I never did. I had plenty of chances to write it over and over. Finally Joe told me I had to bring some men over for Franky. He wondered why in the hell I was so happy. Usually I hated going over to the Demos ranch. I told Joe why it was my pleasure, and he wanted to give me some flowers to bring to her. Joe and I were good friends back then. Good friends. But I told him how scared I was of Franky knowing anything about how I felt about Soledad, or about how she, hopefully, felt about me. I couldn't bring a bouquet of flowers. So instead we pressed some flowers into the folds of the note. It was early winter, I remember, so they were cala lillies. They love the rain. We still had some pink and lavender stock left, too, from the fall. The last of the crop that year. Stock is the only flower Joe grows that has a scent, a scent as strong as perfume, so I put some of its petals in with the lillies since that note had spent so much time in my jacket pocket, which smells so horrible. Then I decided to add some daisy petals and some yellow yarrow, too, while I was at it. What the hell? That's what Joe said. Like a little pressed bouquet, it looked like. A flat bouquet. I could barely get it back in my pocket, and I wrapped it extra tight with some ribbon to make sure nothing fell out."

Santo's face tells me more about how the letter looked and smelled than do his words. He is as wrapped up in his memory as the pressed flowers were so many years ago, inside that letter which is right in front of him now, within his reach.

"That day Franky did not invite me over to the house. He barely greeted me and started cursing about how there were not enough men, that I would have to grab a machete and help the men hack the leaves off the sprouts, too. You have to hack those big fat leaves off to get at the sprouts stuck on the stalk. It'll keep you honest, he said. Keep you from getting cocky. And so I hacked away at those goddamned sprouts with all the energy I had saved up from waiting for this day, for the day I could finally contact Soledad. I swung at the leaves like they were Franky's arms and legs. It was a foggy day and the ground was unable to dry, everything you touched was wet, my clothes were cold and damp and stuck to me. Finally I slipped in the mud as I swung my machete and almost cut off my toes. I was in such a rage that I stayed down and cursed as loud as I could, screamed to the tops of the mountains nearby. Some of the men thought I really had hurt myself and they came running, which gave me an idea. Yes, I told them, my ankle...I can't walk on it. Get the patrón. Get Franky."

He starts to laugh now, the thought of pulling one over on Frank Demos still a source of pride.

"I knew things were looking good when Soledad offered to wrap my ankle. Not only did I have my chance, but she wanted to give me that chance. Franky left very angry, mumbling about how I had become a lazy Mexican since Joe gave me some responsibility, and Gretchen was over the hill Christmas shopping with her precious little Roman. We were alone. Neither of us said anything for a while. She started to massage my foot and wrap my ankle and ask me where it hurt, and it was such a wonderful feeling I didn't tell her that there was really nothing wrong. I just watched her and answered her questions. It hurts right here, I told her, and pointed to my heart, which is also where my jacket pocket is."

Santo gives me a sheepish look and I play along. "Oh, man," I tell him. "Two cornball moves in a single bound."

"Very true," he says. "But it was the second one that did it. She, too, was giggling when I pointed to my heart. But when I took that note from my pocket...the look on her face...it will be the last thing I still remember when I start to lose my memory. I am sure of it."

And judging by Santo's eyes, I believe it.

"The note had gotten wet from the dampness in the fields," he continues. "So once I was able to recover from staring at her face, at her expression, I remember looking down and being crushed. The ink was running through the paper, and I just knew the flowers were turning to mulch. But this touched her even more deeply, when I told her that I had not expected to be in the fields that day, and that my ankle was fine. We kissed passionately for the first time, and we agreed to meet every evening in the same place, a place I will always keep a secret. But I will tell you that it was in an oak grove, the most beautiful kinds of big old oak trees, the types that twist their way into the sky and drip moss from their branches and they let just the right amount of sunlight through their leaves. We talked freely about marriage from the first day, when and how we could go about it. We drove each other crazy with passion, careful not to go too far, careful to save ourselves. Which was funny, because each of us was not old-fashioned that way, but with each other it seemed natural. We were so in love that we just knew we would always be together. It's part of what made our meetings so fun, to see if we had the strength to keep waiting. And we did. We waited, and we never did make love."

He acts as though that's the end of the story, and reaches for another sip of coffee.

"Never?" I ask.

He puts the coffee down and looks at me, obviously wishing that I hadn't asked, but aware that it was to be expected.

"Never," he confirms. "Franky made sure of it."

The sentimental portion of his recollection having passed, I hesitate to urge him on. We are entering the darker ages of his history. His eyes stare deep into it, and I try to think of a way to look at it along with him.

"Dodge was convinced Franky had her killed," I say in my best doctor-to-patient voice. "Do you agree?"

He can only nod—first as a response, then as a way to stall for time before plotting his explanation.

"Soledad only did it to save her job. She refused Franky's demands for some time, much longer than most would have because of how much power Franky had. She knew how much fire she was playing with, and she only agreed when he said to her out loud how much she would lose. She told me she always would keep her eyes closed and imagine that she was in some other place, that she was with me in the oak grove, or on a warm beach. Manzanilla Beach was her favorite, in Colima. She told me all about it right away, long before she was pregnant. She said keeping the truth from me or waiting to tell me was not only going to make it worse, but that it was not necessary..." Santo purses his lips, bites them, and continues. "It was not necessary because she knew that I love her so much, that nothing could stop us, that I would understand."

Now he has to take a deep breath, a quivering deep breath, while I take a good look at my own past. The parallels between their union and mine with Janet are as disgusting as they are ironic. We, too, figured we could survive sex outside our marriage. Only we were the aggressors, not the victims. And while our arrogance was always apparent to me, at varying levels of acknowledgement, it was never as nauseating as it is now, not even compared to the night we heard about the murder. That was a physical reaction, an emotional knee-jerk. This is an analytical one, and yet the necessary distance between myself and the event still fails to keep emotion out of it.

Real love pursued with real dignity makes those of us who had real love and took it for granted look that much worse. Santo may be fighting back tears, but I'm the one excusing myself.

"May I use your bathroom?" I ask.

He seems relieved to get a break. "Through that door," he points. "It's in the corner of the kitchen."

I'm actually flattered to find that the kitchen is a mess. Given the presentational flair of the living room, this section of the house is obviously not intended for public viewing. I'm allowed to look behind the scenes, and that seems to surprise even the two men working on cleaning it up—one having put down his dusting rag from the living room in favor of a clean one to dry the dishes he is washing, while the other has traded his liquid cleanser for powder and is cleaning the tiles. I answer their startled looks with an apologetic grin and a gesture to the bathroom door. "Necessito el baño," I tell them, which seems to only add to their astonishment. "I need the bathroom" is a phrase I'm quite adept at, so I know their reaction had nothing to do with language. I have clearly entered confidential territory.

The bathroom is the kind considered to be a "half" in the real estate listings: a toilet and a sink with a mirrored medicine cabinet hanging on the wall above it. I practice the old splash-water-on-your-face-and-stare-at-yourself-in-the-mirror routine, but I don't see myself. I see a man I never met, Franky Demos; a woman I never loved, Abigail Kern; and the man who did love her, her husband—so much that the thought of her with another man drove him insane. But then, and most of all, I see Santo. I see a man who was forced to confront something even more awful about the woman he loved, but loved her even more and tried to think of a way they could move past it.

"We may never earn our forgiveness," I say to Janet, wherever she is...in the city, in a meeting, fully aware that the man across from her is staring at the top button of her blouse every chance he gets. The button strains and hovers just above her cleavage, the outline of her bra visible through the white silk held together by that single button, that thread, the same flimsy thread that separates a man from the stampede of wild pigs inside of him. I return to my place across from Santo and wonder how he managed to domesticate all those internal pigs.

"The baby was finally more than she could stand," Santo continues. "Soledad was not going to pretend for Franky's sake that it was ours. She wanted Gretchen to know what little respect her husband had for love and marriage—our love, their marriage. She wanted to confront him so bad, but I begged her and convinced her to wait, to give me a chance to think of something, a plan to get us out of that nightmare. So when she started to show, she told Gretchen the baby was ours. I went to Joe for help. I asked him if he had room to hire Soledad, if he had a place for her at the ranch. He was going to agree to that, I think, but wanted to know more about the situation. And that's when he got scared and said no."

Anger tightens his face as he goes on. "Mirabelli Nurseries was in trouble at that time. A lot of debt, a long time coming to pay it off. 'And I don't wanna add Frank Demos to my list of troubles,' Joe told me. 'He might really love that gal,' he said. And that hurt the most. From that point I got more scared, too. Maybe Franky did love her, if the man was able to love anyone, and even if he did not, he certainly would not let her ruin him. It was obvious then just how desperate things had become. I worked out a plan to set her up in Mexico, in a small town where I have many friends and contacts and I knew she would be safe. She was grateful but wanted to wait until she had the baby so that it could have citizenship in the United States."

He stops and fidgets into a more defensive look, as though about to launch into some sort of justification. "I agreed," he says. "It was a good idea. I thought it would make our life more easy. American citizenship would be a good thing to have if things got tough in Mexico. So when Dodge was born we were all ready to follow our plan…" He catches himself and repeats "When Dodge was born," and then lapses into silence.

Refusing to let me in on what is accompanying the quiet, I ask him if he was there for the birth. He nods.

"She delivered him at my place," he says. "The foreman's house at Joe's ranch, where Javier now lives with his family. And it was my turn to pretend. Just as Soledad had to pretend at her job, telling Gretchen that the baby was ours, now I had to watch her struggle and scream in pain and whisper in her ear how much I love her, how everything will be all right…I had to squeeze her hand so tight and wipe her forehead with a towel and stroke her hair, knowing it was not ours, that it was not made from love. I had to try to forget that and be a good husband…" He seems to remind himself that he wasn't really her husband, and corrects himself. "I had to be there for her." He reaches for a cookie from the tray, but puts it down as something occurs to him. "Some people, like Dodge, they have more to overcome from the day they are born than some of us will ever have to in our whole lives. I told you that me and Soledad were not old-fashioned, did not have superstitions, but we could not help to wonder if Dodge was going to be cursed because of the way he was created."

"What was his real name?" I ask.

"We never gave him one." He looks at me, examining my reaction. But there is none, as I am not really surprised. It seems all too appropriate.

"Do you know why?" he asks, perhaps intent on getting at least a raised eyebrow out of me.

"She must have disappeared soon after."

"There were problems," he doesn't miss a beat. "Complications. Joe and Lorraine were in San Francisco at a board meeting for the

Flower Growers' Association, and there was no time to get to a hospital. There was too much blood and it would not stop. I had no choice but to go to the Demos house and ask for help. Gretchen was still thinking it was our baby at that time, and I was afraid Soledad would say something. Her rage was growing more every day she was pregnant. But if I did not get help, she would never say anything to anybody ever again. She would die. I went to the house and Gretchen was very concerned and very happy to help. She always liked Soledad. Franky looked at me with devil eyes for putting him in such a situation, and as Gretchen went to get some things from the bathroom, Frank pulls me to the side and says that it may be difficult for him to do anything to me since I was Joe's foreman, but that he could crush Soledad without anyone noticing or caring and that he would have no problem doing so if she says anything to Gretchen."

He stops abruptly, his voice snatched right from his throat, it seems.

"And Soledad said something," I complete the thought for him.

"I have no idea what she said, exactly," he starts to regain his voice. "As soon as she was out of danger, when the bleeding finally stopped and she had a chance to get her breath and hold the baby, she pulled Gretchen close and whispered in her ear. Gretchen then looked at the baby, stared at the baby Dodge forever, it seemed, with no expression on her face. Then she stood up and looked right in Franky's eyes like she was a cat, no blinking. Frank would look away and try to look back at her, but she would still be staring at him, not making a move. He did that many times, look away and then back, until she decided it was time to stop. 'You can go now,' she told him. 'Santo can drive me home later.' And as he left, Franky gave me a look that cut my legs off at the knees. The same look the grim reaper must have under that hood of his if you could shine a light on his face. And he was smiling, letting me know how much he was going to enjoy whatever he was planning to do."

Santo reaches for the coffee. It's cold now, and he puts the rattling cup down immediately after feeling its chill on his lips.

"I tried to act on our plan, to get her down to Mexico. She was still weak. Joe gave me the time off. I made him feel guilty about not having a job for Soledad. But honestly, it was clear now that Franky never would have let her go, and trying to take her away would have been as risky as Joe said it was. Anyway, by then it was too late for anything to matter. For any regret or solution to make a difference. Franky was out for revenge, and all the evil he was capable of was on display. Any friend you think you had was for sale. Frank would let them name their price if they help him. A blank check to make your mind blank, to bury your compassion and feelings of guilt. So it's hard to know who told him what. And it was so dark that night..."

A deep breath. Santo turns his gaze from speculation to what his five senses remember from that night so many years ago, the night that seemed to seal Dodge's fate in life.

"I wanted to keep the baby and Soledad separate. She was upset about that, but I told her it was best, that to make it easy for Franky to hunt us down all at once was foolish. We would meet in King City, two hours to the south, and drive together the rest of the way to Mexico. I sent Soledad away first, with one of the men from Mirabelli Nurseries that I trust. Still I told her not to tell him the destination until right before it was time to exit the highway. Then we kissed for a long time, and they drove away. She was gone. Nobody followed them. The highway was quiet. Five minutes...ten minutes. Finally a cement truck drives by. Not the kind of truck anyone uses to trail another car, so I decide it's safe to go. I drive with the baby, with Dodge, to King City as fast as I can. The longest two hours of my life. But they are not there. Soledad, the driver...nowhere. I drive all over the town, walk the streets all morning. I ask people going to work if they saw anything or heard anything. I go to the police and tell them what is happening with

Dodge in my arms. We are far enough away from Franky's territory, I think, to talk to the police. It should be safe there. Maybe not. But maybe because I'm acting like a crazy man, they take Dodge away from me and put me in their jail. I call Joe, and he has to come down and get me. On the way home, he says he talked to Gretchen, and that she is going to take care of Dodge and guarantee Frank will not bother me."

He starts to get angry, lips curled, teeth bared.

"And I say so what? Franky Demos got what he wants. He ruined my life already. He took it from me. I blame Joe again and tell him I have no reason to live now, and so no reason to work for the man who helped kill my life blood. Joe tries to stay calm and tells me to think about the baby, how it's a part of Soledad. But I say 'fuck the baby'..."

His anger crashes down around him, collapses into a gasp for breath. He stares into his own personal void, then back at me.

"I said 'fuck the baby,'" he repeats, punishing himself with the sound of it, flogging himself with the memory of saying it in the first place. He recovers and continues.

"I tell Joe the baby is also part of Franky, and that I can never forget it. I can never forgive, and it is the Demos family who need to always remember Franky's crime, Gretchen who needs to stare at the baby born from the greed and hate of her husband. I said all that, Stanford."

Hearing my name comes as a surprise, what with the memories taunting him so mercilessly. I was beginning to wonder if he even remembered I was in the room.

"And I acted as bad as my words," he confesses. "I did all the things Joe probably told you about. I used my contacts in Mexico to bring men up here for money like a slave trader. Joe fired me when he found out. But I was not doing my job well for him anyway, not for a long time, just like I warned him the day he drove me from King

City with Dodge in my arms. But I no longer cared about making an honest living. I wanted to be as big as Franky. To scare him. I moved in on the drug business he ruled for so long."

I lean forward in my chair; pure reflex.

"Drugs? Really?"

"Oh, yes. I stopped asking for money from the men and told my contacts in Mexico that the fee was now drugs, that each man should be a pack mule. I stole some seed from Joe and leased this ranch, planting flowers as a disguise."

My heartbeat pounds up into my ear drums. Dodge was right. Dodge was right. A posthumous reprieve, a stay of execution, the governor calling moments after the switch is thrown on the electric chair. Midnight? The governor says. My watch says quarter to twelve.

"Were you into production?" I blurt out. Santo looks a bit confused, perhaps wondering why I'm so interested in this phase of the conversation. I ease up. "Did you start making the drugs here?"

"Yes," he answers.

Now it's my turn to stare ahead at a spiteful self-portrait that only I can see, mentally drawing my hands up to my face, so Dodge can't see me.

"But that was long ago," he adds.

Those imaginary hands slide down my cheeks. "How long?"

"Twenty–five years, maybe." I sink slowly and don't bother looking for something to grab onto. "It was quite an operation back then," he continues. "All natural ingredients shipped to us up here, and then we cut it down with things you can buy at the grocery store, and then bag it. Not like now, when all you need is one man who knows how to cook the stuff, the right chemicals, and some fire. No, we were like a factory. We could make anything—cars, vacuum cleaners, whatever you want. We happened to make drugs. And it was when I was doing my best, when I was making the most money, that Soledad came to visit."

He gives me a wry smile.

"But you're still going to tell me you aren't superstitious," I say.

"I'm not," he holds up his hands. "But love, true love, breaks all kinds of rules in your life. She came to me when I was sleeping one night, but I never called it a dream. It was much more real. We walked down to the sand dunes together, along the beach, and she tells me how disappointed she is in me. I tell her how much I miss her, how I am always running from her memory and looking for ways to forget what happened to us. But she shows no sympathy. She tells me I am a different person, a man she could never love if she were alive. I swear to her that I will change my ways, over and over, on my knees, like I am praying to her, head down, hands together. And when I look up, she is gone. Now, if it was a dream, I wake up then, no? But I only wake up after I walk back through the dunes, through the fields, back to the ranch. I go back to bed, and only then do I wake up. I wake up determined to change my life."

I give him the same kind of devious smile he gave me regarding the ghost of Soledad. "So what do all the men do here now?" I ask.

He beams, full of pride. "Changing their lives, too," he says. "I know it looks nothing like that. It's dirty and bare. But we have so little money coming in, I have to keep our costs low. All this," he gestures around the room. "The furniture, it comes from alleys and the sides of roads all over the state. We use it as an example to the men, something to aim for, and we pay them to keep it up and clean it. See, I started a new program with my partners in Mexico," he settles back in his chair. "Land for labor. For a very small price, these men will buy pieces of land in a part of Mexico we are trying to develop, my friends and me. But a farming community, not the kind of place you think of in California when you hear the word develop. A farming community that supplies some large companies with some of their more precious materials—wool, goose feathers, goat's milk, grains and vegetables and fruits that are more rare and get a good price wholesale. We make sure our community is not a bunch of regular farms, so they do not compete with large farms owned by companies. No, ours are very different, with men who work hard and have pride in their land, because it actually belongs to them. They own it. So now the shipments go in the other direction—the men come up here with nothing, only a reputation for working hard, and it is only when they leave that they carry something. Money, some new types of seeds and methods for farming from here in the states, all to make sure our community holds the attention of our customers in Mexico."

I stare at him for a while before I realize he's finished. I've never been so entranced by a public service announcement. Not only thanks to its noble cause, but how much grief would have been spared by an earlier introduction to it.

"Why do you keep it a secret?" I ask.

"Size," he says. "You know what happens when even the best idea grows too big. We do not want every worker on the coast to start knocking on our door. We only want to add people we know, from the same area in Mexico where the people can see what we are doing, and what we expect. The money may not be a big investment, but the time is very big. That is why some of the inspectors have been kind enough to take it a little easy on us. And fortunately they too have been good about keeping things quiet."

"But the locals," I insist. "Why can't the locals around here know? You'd get your reputation back, people would know you're a good man..."

"Impossible," he snaps. "Reputations are trapped in stone in this place. Like fossils. Maybe if I did something easier to forgive, but I did not. I put myself as deep in the stone as Franky, almost. After what I did, if people now learned about my new life, they would still believe what they want about it. They would be sure of some hidden badness, they would think that there is much more in it for me. That is the problem with living in a close community. The ghosts are as thick as the fog."

"Times change, Santo."

"Very true," he nods. "The bay is now much closer to the ocean than it used to be. Look at Roman. So much like his father, Franky. But to conquer the coast these days, you must compete with those from over the hill, and you must work with them. Roman is not capable of that. He makes the same mistakes Franky was starting to make at the end of his life when things started to change. A farmer can no longer be a bully. The bullies of the coast do not live on it any longer. They live over the hill. Maybe if we were farther away from the city, from all those companies stretching between San Francisco and San Jose. But we are too close...farmers surrounded by computer makers. We amuse them. We provide pretty pictures for them to take, and a place for them to take deep breaths and wonder where all the places like this have gone."

I let him take his dramatic pause, take an invisible bow. But there's one more thing he hasn't answered to.

"What about Dodge?" I ask, and as the words come out of my mouth, they feel more like a baseball bat in my hands, swung right into his gut.

"What about Dodge?" he says back, trying to deflect the blow.

"Why couldn't you tell him about what you do here? Tell him about his mother?"

"I tried before. Many times."

"Once. Maybe twice."

He glares at me. "Okay, then. If you knew him so well, you look me in the eye and tell me it was never too late. Tell me there was a chance to cut through his anger."

And I do. I look him right in the eye. "There was."

"I don't agree," he brushes me off.

"You know why he jumped?" I ask.

Santo doesn't fire back. He just stares at me.

"You asked me earlier why he jumped," I remind him. "And now I'd like to tell you."

He shrugs, like a child trying to conceal his curiosity.

A pause. Perhaps to decide how to tell him the news, but more likely for effect. A long pause, and I tell him all about Dodge's opinion of him, about what he thought Santo was up to here on his ranch—the meth production, the exploitation of his men, the bribes, the cover-ups—all those things Santo thought he had left behind, that he had left in the settling dust of his past.

Then, as he sinks inside to his lowest point of regret, and only then, do I tell him exactly why Dodge jumped. I hit him with the misinterpreted event concerning the fallen tree, the man who wasn't there, the dog that was, the misunderstood climax to the misguided quest that Dodge never would have been on, never should have been on, had he known the truth—the truth about the event, and everything leading up to it.

And I enjoy telling him. A guilty thrill gets my heart beating faster and pushes my nerve endings through the surface of my skin. I feel as if I'm sweating pure adrenalin. I stand up—maybe because I truly blame him for Dodge's death, but more likely because the blame he is putting on himself deflects my own sense of responsibility—and I hover over him, slumped there in his chair.

"That's why he killed himself, Santo." I jackhammer my index finger down at him, as though I've just tackled him in a football game. "That's why he killed himself."

He puts his head in his hands, his fingers gripping his skull so tightly that it appears he may try and pull his face off. The palms of his hands muffle a series of wails and moans that, were they set free, would surely shake the walls. He takes heavy gulps of breath in between sobs, and the guilt starts to seep in at top speed....but it is my guilt, not his.

I share every false move he made, just as I did with Dodge when he was alive. We are joined by the blatant introspection and self-pity that prevents us from noticing others while over-analyzing ourselves. It was a team effort, where the members didn't even know they were all on the same side. We didn't know because we never asked. We were too busy fulfilling our destinies—born to win, born to lose, whatever Fate supposedly dealt us. And so we simply waited for every opportunity to "share our pain."

I remember the note Dodge wrote, in which he hoped it was all "for a good cause". We weren't after drugs, after all, or chasing money and power. But it was yet another empty pursuit. So I'm as sorry as ever, Dodge. I'm sorry, too, that "someone had to die". All because we enjoyed immersing ourselves in our own ideas without making an honest effort to challenge them.

"Look," I sort of whisper to Santo. "I wish there was some way we could all go back and make things right, but...if you need anything—help with your program, an extra hand, a cup of sugar, whatever—just let me know. We're neighbors."

He looks at me, eyes moist, and manages to say "I will."

I pat him on the shoulder a few times. "You're doing good things here," I tell him. "If there's such a thing as redemption, you're well on your way."

And if you get there, I think as I walk out the door, be sure and send me directions.


My thoughts are still on Santo as I stand on the porch of his old house, the foreman's house at Mirabelli Nurseries where Dodge was born, long since overtaken by Javier and made a home by his family. It occurs to me that this is the first time Veronica and I have been on a good old fashioned date, the kind where I stand on the porch and wait for her father to open the door and exchange knowing looks with Veronica as I talk to her father. Come to think of it, this may be the first time in my entire life that I've done this. I briefly scan my past and find nothing but "Meet me here" and "Meet me there" and but a single "Meet my parents," the day before Janet and I got married, at the bridal dinner.

I hear Javier's booted footsteps coming towards the closed door, and worry for a moment what he thinks about me with his daughter. But I remind myself that all I can do is face whatever the facts may be, savor every mushy look Veronica gives me over his shoulder, and promise to have her back safe and sound.

"For God's sake," she sighs as we walk down the porch steps to the car. "I'm twenty-three years old."

"Your father loves you," I say. "He can fret and bristle all he wants."

I get the kind of look from her I'd expect to get from someone who is already aware of the "wisdom" you just imparted, but I kiss her anyway.

Dinner and a movie, keeping with the traditional theme of the evening, and on the way home it's dark—just a sliver of the moon and the sky thus free to stage every star in the hemisphere. In the bay stretching beneath the point and the island, several dozen fishing boats gently bob in place, leashed to their anchors for the night until morning. But from the highway they are just lights, a light on each boat to mark their spot in the darkness. As we approach, it looks as though a city has risen up from the water, the lost city of Atlantis, complete with electricity.

We cross the southbound lane and pull over onto the shoulder which stands just above the tide. And the tide, the to and fro of the waves lapping at the breakwater beneath us, is all we hear as we get out and survey the temporary skyline. The boats offer no hint of their existence, no creaking or grinding, no conversations. They are simply lights on the water far enough out of reach to cloak the truth. Now and then a car passes by and breaks the rhythm, but other than that it remains me and Veronica, the tide, its salty smell, the steady cool breeze, and Veronica's warm hand—the soft inside of her forearm crossed over mine, our fingers locked.

"It's just the right distance," she says.

"The boats?" I ask.

"Any closer and we could see them," she continues. "Their rusty old selves. It's like the distance that makes a stray cat so cute."

"And then you get closer," I say.

She nods. "And then you get closer."

I kiss her for about the one-hundredth time that night. We take a breath and look out to sea again. My focus slightly blurred, the salt in the air now dashed on my lips, the lights seem to grow larger, seem to sprout petals.

"If you told me those were boats," I say. "I wouldn't believe you."

"I'm sorry Dodge was so wrong about Santo," she replies.

"That's not what I meant. I really was just talking about the lights."

"I know," she turns to me. "But when you told me over dinner about your talk with him, there was something I kept thinking but couldn't really say since you were so disappointed."

"What's there to be disappointed about? Santo's a saint. Just like his name says."

"I'm talking about Dodge," she says. "Have you forgotten what this is all about?"

"Of course not. But he was wrong, and so was I. Story of our lives, so why dwell on it?"

"His kids," she reminds me. "This whole thing started over his kids. You want to honor his memory? Then do what he asked you to do. Tell his kids about him."

I look out at the lights again, bobbing in the night air. "How come I've got ten years on you, but you're always right?" I ask her.

She doesn't answer, just eases herself into the crook of my arm beneath my shoulder. "No need to rush," she says. "Do it when you're ready or when the opportunity presents itself. But for your own sake and for Dodge's sake, talk to them."

I kiss her on the forehead to assure her that I will, and figure if we stay here just a few more hours we would see what those boats really look like.


The pumpkins still left in the fields benefit from the same deceptive distance. It may look as though thousands of them, perfectly formed, went un-picked during the harvest, but a closer look reveals the deformities, the rot, the rat damage, and the bugs.

I ride on the back of a forklift through the leftover orange on my way to the loading area, sitting behind the driver on the metal chassis just above the engine which is getting hotter as we push the lift to its speed limit of fifteen miles per hour. Two men ride on the raised fork in front, one on each of the flat metal arms, with the pallet jack straddling the gap between them. As loud as a car driving on the freeway in second gear, we bounce in a cloud of dust towards the big rig looming above the remaining rows of bins spilling over with pumpkins. The bins are the last load of the season, carried over the hill by this last truck now idling, its pumpkins coming to a front porch or store window near you.

Pausing well behind the truck, on the opposite side of the bins, I jump off and the driver hands me the clipboard before he taxis to the rear doors of the rig. I walk the corridor between the line of pumpkins and the truck trailer. I'm taking Veronica's job today, supervising the load while she's at school.

Just before I reach the tractor, a little head pops through the window and shouts "hi" down at me. I shout "hi" back and hear a hoarse female voice telling "Jared" to "get back before he falls out."

If I hadn't heard the name, I wouldn't have been able to guess the child's gender. The door swings open and a short-legged man jumps out who is clearly the boy's father. An awning of dirty brown bangs zigzag along his eyebrows as wispy vines of hair creep down his back. He's wearing a sleeveless shirt and an adolescent-looking face with features so beady he could be a ghost for Halloween without having to cut up an old bed sheet.

"What's up?" he asks.

"Not much."

"Mind if my wife and kid look through your fields?"

"Not at all. It's been picked out, so they can keep whatever they find."

"Thanks," he says, and then turns to the open door and tells them to go ahead. "We got a little farm over in Turlock and grow pumpkins, all different kinds."

"You got them white punkins nearby, I saw on the way in," the wife says, who looks pretty much like him, only taller.

"Sure do."

"We need some of them seeds. Them and some of them bright red ones that look all bumpy."

"They're right next to the white ones," I say.

"Hi," the kid shouts again.

"Hi," I say again.

The forklift wheezes as the two men and the pallet jack levitate on its metal arms towards the open mouth of the trailer. "Should be about a half hour to load," I tell the truck family.

"We better hurry, then, Jared," says the wife, the tone in her voice urging the little boy to start sprinting towards the fields. She trots after him. The husband watches them go as if watching a sunset.

"Your family always drive with you?"

"On the short hauls. I go cross country most times."

"Must be rough."

"It's paradise. I got hunting and fishing licenses in forty-two states. Got a freezer in back and feed my family better than any sportsman's lodge." He glances over at me and seems about ready to tell me a secret. "I'm the luckiest man in the world," he says.

In a matter of moments he's gone from redneck to globetrotter. I pry as much information out of him as I can, trying not to lose count of the bins sliding into the trailer as he regales me with the stark differences between summer and winter in the Thousand Islands off Lake Ontario in upstate New York, the fishing along the emerald coast of Georgia, the cow elk that he happened to watch give birth while chukar hunting in the woods of northern Idaho, the team he was a member of which was commissioned by some Colorado ranchers to trap a family of black bears in Tennessee and release them in their home state to control the cougar population, and the Utah rancher who simply wanted him to shoot the cougars, "the bastard...no cougar could catch that many sheep and she sure as hell wouldn't let the carcasses lie there and rot after just a few bites. It was a pack of wild dogs, like I guessed, and I'll be damned if it wasn't led by an old hound that son of a bitch had kicked out of a litter for turning out useless as a bird dog. Wouldn't listen to me, though. Just wanted a goddamn trophy. So I told him I was a hunter and not a barbarian and he could run his own big cat slaughter."

But most of all, he talks about his family, about how none of his prizes or stories would be worth a damn if he didn't have somebody to share it all with when he got home. The wife and child arrive with an armful of pumpkins, and my story time is over. He is too enthralled by the sight.

"I've had a lotta guys I met on the road give me that tired-ass old slogan about being a rolling stone, free bird, king of the road, whatever bullshit," he tells me. "But I see it in their eyes, usually. They're just plain lonely, most of them, and need to feel better about it. And even if they're not, they will be eventually. That's what happened to me."

His family arrives and he squats down to greet his son and hear the results of the pumpkin hunt.

"Five," screams the little boy. "Five."

Though it's really a half dozen. The trucker looks over his shoulder at me and smiles. "Everything's five," he says. "I guess 'cause it sounds like hi. His favorite word."

And sounds like 'bye,' which is what the kid yells my way as he climbs up the side of the tractor and through the door, the mother standing behind his ascent as a precaution. She follows him inside with a wave and a thank you aimed at me, and the father shakes my hand and looks around breathing deeply.

"I do love coming out here," he says. "You got the right mix of loneliness and civilization. Mountains and plains, trees and ocean. You're a lucky man, too." He slaps my arm and joins his family above.

As the men and the pallet jack are lowered to the ground, the forklift driver gestures to me.

"Quiero a caminar," I tell him. I want to walk.

I let the truck pull away, then the forklift, and then wait until the dust settles before heading back to the ranch. But first I stand there and enjoy the isolation, the feeling of being alone which terrified me so when I first moved here. The loneliness made cozy by understanding how to find the remarkable in the ordinary, to sit still long enough so that a sound you may never have noticed reaches your ear, to discuss the phone bill with your mate and appreciate the time together, by refusing to be bored.

A few bins remain, the sagging, frayed bins unsuitable for shipment. Dozens of pumpkins are strewn across the desolate ten acres—some smashed, some whole. A stack of unused pallets stands near the tree line in the distance, as well as a stack of unused bins still flat and folded. The props and set pieces waiting to be struck after the final performance, the next crop of the season waiting in the wings.

My footsteps and I are about halfway through the plucked fields when Joe pulls up in one of the dusty pickups from the ranch fleet. I walk over to the driver's side as he rolls the window down.

"Christ, I thought we had another derelict taking drugs in the fields," he says. "Didn't Humberto offer you a ride back on the lift?"

"Sure he did. I just felt like walking."

"Did the last load go okay? I wanted to come out and make sure, but didn't get back from the market until just now."

"It went fine."

"Super," he says. "Hop in. I know it's a nice day for walking, but I want some company, godammit."

"Well it is a long drive," I deadpan, and walk around to the passenger side.

"So what did you think of pumpkin season this year?" he asks as I sit down. A thin cloud of dust billows up from the seat and I slam the door shut...twice, as it doesn't catch the first time.

"I thought it went well," I assure him.

He slaps the dashboard, leaving a handprint in the dust. "You bet it did," he roars. "Those choke and sprout growers are gonna be ringing our phone off the hook and snooping around the ranch once they're done crying in their beer."

Still feeling a bit whimsical from walking, I return his laughter briefly and let some silence fall as we work our way through the withering fields, allowing Joe to work his way up to the question I have a feeling he wants to ask. He finally clears his throat as we reach the gate leading through the tree line separating the pumpkin fields from the main ranch. "So," he says. "Have you thought about what we discussed during that Forty-Niner game a few weeks ago?"

"There's been a lot of things going on," I tell him.

"Oh, of course. I understand," he tries to hide his embarrassment by concentrating more than necessary on guiding the truck through the narrow gate. It's hard not to feel guilty when you knock someone as energetic as Joe off his stride, if only for a moment. But the whimsy has me feeling impulsive, and the subject of Dodge has been broached, so what the hell...

"Did Gretchen give Dodge a name after she took him in?" I blurt out.

He still has the gate to focus on.

"Joe?"

"I'm thinking," he says. We pull through the opening and roll down a slight grade towards a fallow couple of acres overrun with wild mustard. "She must have," he continues, his voice more hushed than I've ever heard it. "But I can't recall what it was. It was Dodge as long as I can remember. He found out early on what happened with his father and his real mother and refused to be called whatever Gretchen named him. There was one nickname after another, none of them stuck, and finally it was Dodge."

"I'll bet that never made any of the local history books Gretchen's been interviewed for."

"Probably not," Joe nods, my sarcasm going unnoticed.

We skirt the edge of the field and veer down a path which takes us along the shore of the reservoir. I let Joe change the subject to the water level, and how we're going to need some rain soon to get the surface up to a point where he feels more comfortable. He seems to be begging me to leave it at that, and I oblige because it's unfair to think that someone like Joe, even with all his good humor and energy, shouldn't be entitled to some secrets of his own, some baggage, however small. For this reason I decide not to tell him what really happened with Santo after Dodge was born. Not now, maybe never. I would rather have him hear it from Santo himself, arrange some sort of accidental meeting, and let them discover on their own how satisfying the truth can be, how painfully satisfying.

I look across the reservoir at their house, the "lake house." Joe may have waited until Dodge was fully grown and Franky was on his death bed before trying to ease his own sense of guilt over what happened, but he tried. He gave Dodge a job and insisted he get cleaned up, and I refuse to question his motives. I've always suspected there is no such thing as a truly unselfish act. I shift in the seat and start to amend our conversation.

"I know this much is true," I tell him. "The more I'm out here, the more I like it."

And just like that, Joe is back. "Who wouldn't, for chrissakes?" he takes his hands off the wheel for a second in order to gesture at the landscape. "It's God's country."

"Gorgeous," I catch up with his energy.

"I want to check on the daisies real quick," he says, and takes a sharp turn up from the reservoir. We roll over a crest in the landscape as if we're in a boat taking a wave head-on, and plane out in full view of a daisy field half a mile long and a couple acres wide, the rows flaring out ahead of us like rays from a green sun. "I mean, just look at that," he says, obviously utilizing the sight to help his cause, and not to actually check on anything.

I think of another adjective. "Stunning."

"And there's only two kinds of people who can live out here," he says, aiming the truck down the center aisle. "Those who work at home, and those with a shitload of money. And you know what working at home means."

"Farming," I play along.

"That's right," he taps the horn and laughs. "And even though we may miss a few sunsets and nature walks, it feels better to earn your right to be out here, don't you think?"

"It certainly does."

"By God, we'll make a farmer out of you yet," he wags a finger and laughs some more. I realize there is no way to keep up with him, and simply contribute to his laughter. "But take your time," he suddenly settles down, apparently reminding himself of something Lorraine must have told him about pressuring me. "This is your decision."

Not that he relents, necessarily. He lets the daisies speak for themselves, driving slowly through them, their petals so bright against the thick green bushes that they seem to be staring at us, strengthening Joe's argument without him having to say a word. We turn left at the end of the aisle, the rows of daisies rolling by in long strides, and then pass through a break in the line of cypress trees to the crop of daisies in the next field over. Several of the men who are staying for the winter are picking from it, the daisy bushes chest-high. Javier's truck is parked along the side of the dirt road waiting for the results, and he's in the fields picking along with them. We pull over and Javier comes over, a bouquet of daisies in one hand. Joe asks him how close they are to filling today's orders, in Spanish. Javier answers him in English.

"The market orders we got real close and we a maybe two hours away from a the grocery truck orders all done."

"That's what I like to hear," says Joe, slapping the steering wheel.

"How you doing, Stanford?" Javier asks.

"Fine, thanks, Javier."

"Veronica says she have a real nice time the other night."

Not what I expected. "Oh," I fail to hide my surprise. "Good. She seemed to. Yes."

"Yah, she never seem so happy before after she have a date."

Joe joins in. "You see there, Stanford?" he grins at me while pointing his thumb back at Javier. "This from a man who guards his daughter like a goddamn Marine."

Javier laughs. I try to.

"Well," I say. "She was raised well. She's quite a person."

Her father beams. "Yes, she is," he nods. "Yes she is."

"That's only because I was taking care of her half the time," Joe clamors as he starts to release the clutch and roll forward.

Javier smiles. "Yah, you got two fathers you answer to now, Stanford," he says, much to Joe's delight.

"We'll see you back in the yard," he says to Javier.

I chime in with my good-bye and sit back as we continue along the bottom of the field to the center aisle, where we turn and make our way back up through even more daisies. A breeze picks up from the ocean and the flowers sway in the same direction we're driving, as though we're sailing through the fields, through a sea of flowers.

Back at the yard, we drop the truck off amongst all the other reclamation projects behind the tractor implements, and walk by the packing shed. Manuel is in the process of boxing up and labeling the most recent batch of daisies brought to him from Javier's truck. Behind him stands a wall of boxes all ready to go. They all share the same product code and date, but the destinations differ. One-third say Seattle, one-third say Spokane, and the rest say Portland.

"Did the truck for Phoenix already come?" Joe asks him.

Manny nods and tells him it came about an hour ago. Joe nods and takes a deep breath, appearing quite satisfied as he gazes at the boxes yet to leave for the Northwest; the Southwest having already been taken care of.

"Makes you wonder," he says to me. "How many people must have had our flowers in their house or in their businesses. And in how many different places. Some of those wholesalers in the market send our stuff all over the world. To who knows where. We may have seen some of our flowers on TV and not even realized it. Our delphinium could be in the White House, for chrissakes."

He laughs, always his own best audience, and suggests I take an early lunch so that he can go back to the house and take a nap. "It was slow at the market," he explains. "But it was still three in the goddamn morning."

So I jump in my truck and head out, trying to keep the dust down on my way through the yard. But even at a snail's pace, I see in the rear view mirror that it's impossible not to leave a trail. A miniature twister swirls behind me as I wait for my chance to enter the highway.

There's only one car on the road, approaching from the north. It slows down and veers onto the shoulder, as if preparing to take a right turn into the ranch. No blinker flashing, though, so I decide to wait and make sure. It's an old green Pontiac Firebird, the kind of car one of the workers or his buddies would drive, only there's a big shock of blonde hair behind the wheel, along with somebody in the passenger seat. Now I remember that car. Dodge's kids.

They make their turn into the ranch. As they do, I can see their mother in the back seat, flicking the ashes of her cigarette out the window, her pink eyes still surrounded by those heavy rings of mascara I recall from the funeral service.

I sit there after they pass. The highway is empty, it's my turn. But my mind is badgered by Dodge's suicide note and Veronica's request to follow through on it. I wonder if I'm up for this right now. But if I don't do it now, I'm giving myself a host of ready-made excuses about not knowing where they live, not having the time to visit them, and so on. Traffic fills the highway again as a battered old school bus slowly drives by with a man who looks like Jesus behind the wheel. A couple of orange cats are stretched out on the dashboard of the bus, and their bearded chauffeur waves to me as he drifts by...followed by a parade of pissed-off motorists waiting for a chance to pass him by. It may not be a sign, but it's enough of a coincidence to convince me it's now or never. I back up into the yard and turn towards the house.

The three Hidalgos are rummaging through the piles of clothes in Dodge's van, which is still parked next to the plastic fertilizer drum he split in two. I can't imagine what they hope to find, but don't dare ask.

"He was going to make this into a hot tub," I announce my presence and tap the fertilizer drum as I approach. "Hook up a motor, a hot-water heater, the works. Pretty ingenious."

They stop and stare at me, lined up in front of the van like a row of suspects behind a two-way mirror. "Pretty fucking stupid, if you ask me," says the daughter, her voice already starting to deepen from nicotine.

"Who the hell are you?" asks the mother.

This is going to be harder than I thought. "I worked with Dodge quite a bit this past year on the ranch. Got a chance to know him pretty good."

"Gee, what's he like?" sneers the son, which gets a laugh from his sister. The mother, meanwhile, takes a few steps in my direction.

"Save your breath, sport," she says. "You ain't the first junkie to try and tell me what a great guy Dodge was. Our whole marriage, I had losers like you crawlin' outta your holes to tell me that shit. Totally fuckin' typical. And why not? Shit. Hangin' out with the guys was all he did. That's all that mattered to him. Maybe if we had a line of coke leadin' up to the dinner table he'd of shown up once in a while."

"I'm not like those other guys, Ms. Hidalgo," I get defensive. "I'd tell you why I'm not, but this is about Dodge. I saw what he was trying to do all year, the way he was trying to make it up to you all. Your kids, especially."

"Big fuckin' deal," the son barks. "The guy finally starts doin' shit parents are supposed to do, and we're supposed to kiss his fuckin' feet or somethin'?"

"Yeah," the daughter chimes in. "A little late, Dad."

I'm speechless. I had no idea how deep their hatred ran. The wife picks up on my expression, and seems to have something of a sympathetic moment. If not for Dodge, then for me. She pulls me aside. "Keep looking, kids," she tells them. "If you find anything you like, it's yours."

Once they oblige, she turns back to me. "You do seem to be a little different than the usual crackhead he had stickin' up for him," she tells me. "So let me ask you...you ever seen a kid sittin' alone at their sixth birthday party, surrounded by empty chairs and a cake that ain't ever gonna be cut?"

I shake my head.

"Of course not. But that's what happens when you got a Dad like Dodge. People talk, and then it don't matter how many invitations you send out. No parent wants their kid to set foot in the house." She laughs to keep herself from getting emotional. "Hell, if they only knew he was never there. Then maybe they'd let their kids come, and we wouldn't be stuck with all that cake." She can't help it anymore. Her eyes moisten and she has to clear her throat.

"I'm sorry," I say, wondering whether I should put a hand on her shoulder.

"It was a Winnie the Pooh cake," she says. "That damn bear smiling at us the whole time, even as we were puttin' the garbage can lid over him. The whole cake. And that wasn't the only time that kinda shit happened, you know."

"I don't imagine it was. It must have been difficult."

"Ha," she releases a fake laugh and puts her head in her hand. The kids stop to check that everything's all right. I nod and wave them off, which doesn't go over well with them.

"What the fuck is that?" the daughter yells at me. Fortunately, the mother helps me out.

"I'm all right," she says to them over her shoulder. "We're just talkin' about some stuff."

Only after a few more moments of staring me down do the kids hunch back into the van. I seem to have earned her approval, as flimsy as it may be. I give her a chance to gather herself.

"You must have loved him at some point," I finally say.

She takes a deep breath. "Well you don't marry someone like Dodge for any other reason now, do you?" she says. "Sure, he had access to some Demos money back then, but you wouldn't know it to look at him, to know him. I figured he'd already been cut off from it by the time I met him, the way he'd talk about the family. When he officially got cut off, it was news to me."

I believe her, and by bringing up the past, something occurs to me.

"What was his real name?" I ask. "Nobody seems to know. Not even Dodge."

She smiles. "He knew. He just didn't wanna tell you."

Now I can't help but smile. "Was it that bad?"

"No," she says. "It was actually real ordinary. But it was given to him by a family he never felt like he was a part of, so he made up his own name. He said he felt like he was on his own from the day he was born. So he told people to call him anything but Paul, and finally he heard a nickname that he liked."

"Paul?" I ask, not sure whether I'm saying it out loud or inside my head.

"Yeah," she answers. "Big deal, huh?"

"Actually..." I start to tell her that it's my name, too, but decide to keep it to myself. "I'm not that surprised," I say instead.

"Well, he was great at making mountains outta mole hills," she says. "I'm sure you picked up on that. But he sure as hell didn't know what to do with the things that already were mountains. Except run away from 'em. Anything big, anything that took some effort...pffft."

She sweeps the air with one hand, as if wearing a Dodge puppet, showing me how he would run at the first sign of real trouble. She may be able to look upon the more distant past with something of a smile on her face, but she clearly isn't ready to smile at the recent past. As much as I want to try again to tell her how much his kids meant to him, I look for something else to stall, to keep her trust. I look back at the kids sifting through the mess inside the van.

"Do you really expect them to find anything in there?" I ask her, and she actually laughs.

"No," she admits. "But when there ain't no will, and nothin' to put in a will anyway, you take what you can get."

"There was a note," I blurt out.

She stares at me, checking to make sure I'm serious. "What did it say?" she finally asks.

"Not much," I say, wishing I hadn't brought it up, realizing neither of us was ready for this. I imagine the disastrous scene which would follow if I should reveal to her that his note asked me to tell her kids about him, to act as more of an authority on Dodge than she is. So I lie.

"It just said he was sorry for everything," I tell her. "That he tried his best, but it just wasn't good enough."

But my fib goes over even worse than the truth. Her eyeballs inflate and she stamps around in a circle before raising her voice at me. "So he blames his kids for that jump he took?" she spits. "It's their fault he was such a fucking loser? Goddamn...that's just perfect. That's just completely fucking typical of that son of a bitch. Kids..." she calls over to them. "Fuck this. Just take the van. If you wanna drive it home, I'll take the Firebird. Or I'll drive the van. Whatever."

The kids aren't sure what to make of her tirade.

"Are you okay, Mom?" the son asks, and then asks me "What did you say to her, asshole?"

"Yeah, motherfucker," the daughter starts walking towards me as if she's going to take a swing at me. "What did you say to her?"

"I lied to her," I say, which stops them in their tracks. "I lied to her about what was in your father's suicide note."

Now they're not only stopped, they're frozen. I continue before I can think of a reason not to. "I told her that he wrote how sorry he was that his best wasn't good enough for you, but that isn't what it said at all. No. He was completely torn up inside because he thought he had killed a man by accident, so the note really said how sorry he was that someone had to die. And he said he hoped it was for a good cause, because the accident was part of this idea he had, this plan he had to be a hero so that maybe he'd win back your respect, since working hard and trying to make it up to you clearly weren't enough."

"Are you givin' us a lecture on our own father, motherfucker?" the daughter says.

"Oh shut up," I hear myself say. "And watch your language. It's people like you that take all the fun out of swearing." I resist wagging a finger and instead turn towards the mother. "And why don't you do something about it," I tell her. "All I've heard out of you is what a shitty father Dodge was, and here you are raising a couple of foul-mouthed little pricks who have nothing to offer the world but attitude. Goddamn..." I take a deep breath and continue. "When Dodge was at his lowest point in trying to reach out to you, he was never angry that it kept blowing up in his face. Never. He was sad, he was depressed. He tried to think of new ways to get you back. But you're all such a bunch of bitter creeps that the only way he could think of to get your attention was through this outrageous plan he concocted about this local farm really being a meth lab and that by taking it out he would be a big shot and you might give him a second chance. And I know that sounds ridiculous, but it's true, and the most ridiculous part is that it was even necessary, that for you to forgive him he had to be some action hero. Is that really what it takes to get through to you people?"

They're either too angry or too stunned, but either way they have no comeback. The floor is still mine.

"I'm sorry but I guess it takes a stranger to be this honest. Dodge was too afraid to say anything because he didn't want to lose you forever. That's why he let you walk all over him and why he had to watch helplessly while you made all the same mistakes he did at your age. While you developed into the same brand of loser he was. Only who knows if you'll ever pull out of it, like he did. Personally, I'd be shocked if you did because it was hard for him. It was hard. You have no idea how strong he was. The last line of the note asked me to tell you about him. 'I'm sorry someone had to die. I hope it was for a good cause. Tell my kids about me.' That's what it said, verbatim. So I'm telling you...he loved you very much. I don't know why. I guess only a father could know. But then you're all he had, in case you hadn't noticed while you were rummaging through his stuff in the van. You and that cockamamie plan of his, that was it."

I still can't read them. There is no way of knowing if I'm getting through, or if they're planning to jump me. "So there," I announce. "I've done what he asked. Now you can go out and keep being angry and screw up your lives some more. I couldn't care less. And take the van while you're at it. Why not? Jerks."

My head aches and I'm out of breath. I turn and walk back to my truck, listening for footsteps behind me. But none come. I get in and start the engine, glancing their way. All of them are in the same spots, watching me go like a group of alley cats. As I start to drive away, the mother snaps out of it and hails me as though I was driving a cab. I stop and roll down the window as she trots over to my side of the truck.

"So he didn't jump because of my kids?" she wants confirmation.

Not quite the reaction I expected, but then I surprised even myself with my outburst. "No," I assure her. "He jumped because of somebody he had never even met before in his life."

"That's a relief," she sighs.

I wait for her to say something else, but she doesn't. We share a lengthy few seconds in uncomfortable silence. "Well," I say. "Good bye and good luck."

"Yeah, you too."

And I drive off, trying as usual to keep the dust from swirling.

I actually do manage to keep it down this time, since I've never driven slower. I try to remember if I ever told Dodge that my name was Paul, too, or if he had overheard it at some point. I guess not. He would have said something.

And I try to keep myself from being too disappointed at his family's reaction to my explanation of why he jumped, and from admonishing myself over the way I told them. But that may have been the only way they could understand, and planning it out beforehand or writing a letter wouldn't change the fact that there's no such thing as closure. Once something is under your skin, it's all a matter of size. It's bigger some days and smaller others, but it's always there, for better or for worse.

All the same, I hope this helps you rest in peace, Dodge. Maybe they'll think about what I said just enough to honor you in some small way within themselves at some point, someday. At least I know the truth. Me and Veronica, Joe and Lorraine, Santo and Soledad. Your mother Soledad. We know.

Once on the highway, Veronica's house glides by on the left as I shift into fourth gear. Whitewashed fence, her mother's garden bursting on all sides, a weathervane with a wrought iron rooster perched atop the shake roof, the screen door full of creaks and slams. She'll be interested to hear about today, and I'll be interested to get her reaction about today. I start to get that orange feeling I've become familiar with lately thanks to her.

I suppose she'll have to jump into the shark tank over the hill before I could ever convince her to stay. She'll have to work with the likes of me, dare I say "the old me", before I could ever in good conscience try and keep her down on the farm, as the old saying goes. But I have this vision of us, of she and I running the ranch and outsmarting Roman and making Joe and Lorraine so proud that they'll relax and enjoy their retirement; so much so that they'll take month-long vacations and buy a house next to a real lake, which may not necessarily be any more beautiful than their current faux lake house, but it would be theirs, and if Joe stayed around here, he would not be able to resist working. Veronica and I would make smart business decisions based on research and analysis and she would see, like I finally saw, that the hills don't separate the coast from the valley as much as she may think.

Approaching the entrance to the gravel road, I see yet another amateur photographer has pulled over and is snapping pictures of Santo Farms, of the dried out sunflower stalks and the decrepit sheds in the background, the eerie setting that I'm sure the cameraman figures has a haunting quality and perhaps represents some sort of thesis.

As I turn off the highway and the gravel starts to pelt the bottom of my truck, a couple of quail sprint ahead of me, running for several yards in a frenzy until they remember that they know how to fly. They take off in their unwieldy style, undulating up and down in the air like a carnival ride for toddlers, and I return to thoughts of me and Veronica. I see us taking walks through the fields to the reservoir, spotting herons and egrets and counting how many ducklings the mallard couple had that year. I see us being ambitious, but honest and hard-working, setting a fine example for the kids that maybe, just maybe, we'll raise.

I drive by Santo's and honk, a friendly tap to say hello, the kind of familial tap I will give to Walter the UPS driver, to the gray whale research scientist with an old-fashioned TV antennae strapped to the roof of his second-hand Suburban, to the mailman who wears a red flannel shirt and jeans in lieu of a uniform and makes his rounds in a rusted yellow pickup truck, and to anyone else whose face I tend to see on a regular basis.

And then I hear the dog.

Barking stride for stride, his ears bounce in my side mirror for a second, but quickly fall back to reveal his head, his body, his legs. Then he gives up. He stops in the middle of the road behind me. I stop, too, and get out. So they managed to find him under all that debris, all that wreckage. They found him in spite of everything.

He walks towards me, dangling his right hind leg, struggling along on the remaining three. Again he starts to bark as he limps forward, insisting on doing what he feels he has to do, even if he is the only one who understands why. He thinks he's doing something important, and that's all that matters. He barks steadily and doesn't back away as we meet.

"You're still here," I say.

His barking echoes through the eucalyptus tunnel between my house and Santo Farms.

"You're still here."

# Also by Sean Boling

**The Current Mr. Orr**
Devin's Best Afterlife
Once in Two Lifetimes
Revenge and Wellness in the Sweet Hereafter

**Standalone**
Cut Flowers
Abraham the Anchor Baby Terrorist
The Summer of Our Foreclosure
Satellite Campus
A Charter to That Other Place
The Latest Version of My Love Story
Show Them What They Won
The Name Field
Should
Moral Adjacent
Over Here We Have
The Current Mr. Orr

# About the Author

Sean lives with his family in Templeton, California. He teaches English at Cuesta College.